IMMORTAL JOURNEY:

DEATH OF INNOCENCE

VOLUME ONE

Ruth A. Souther

This version of Death of Innocence differs in that the story has been divided into two parts, as the original book was very long. The second half has been renamed Surrender of Ego, Volume Two.

Reprinted with permission by Crystal Heart Imprints
Immortal Journey: The Death of Innocence:
Copyright © 2004 by Ruth A. Souther

Cover Design by Chad Adelhardt
Cover Photo by Sabrina Trowbridge
Edited by Michaeleen McDonald

ISBN 978-0-9721003-2-8

Second Edition
First Printing, 2004
Second Printing 2014

DEDICATION

I dedicate this book to my husband, Latham Souther.

He stoically suffered at the hands of a madwoman while I completed this work. He patiently listened to my ravings, stayed calm during my tantrums, dried my tears, hugged away my despair, and always lent himself to research. He never wavered in his loyalty, always believed in me and continued to encourage me in spite of my abject fear of both failure and success. He knew I could, even when I did not. He is my heart and soul. Thank you, Latham, for being there. I love you.

ACKNOWLEDGMENTS

I respectfully thank my family and friends who supported me in both the original writing and the conversion of this story into a new format. I could not have done it without them. A special thanks to both my writing groups who kept me focused and encouraged, my editor, Michaeleen McDonald, who has the patience of a saint, Chad Adelhardt for his cover designs and Sabrina Trowbridge for her beautiful photographs.

By popular demand, there is a listing of characters and locations in the back of this book, and no, I did not offer pronunciations of the names - this you must figure out for yourself.

DEATH
OF
INNOCENCE

VOLUME ONE
OF THE
IMMORTAL JOURNEY
SERIES

RUTH A. SOUTHER

Prologue

"THERE ARE THOSE WHO WALK AMONG US, UNSEEN BY MORTAL EYE - THEY ARE THE GODS - THOSE WHO NAME OUR DEEPEST MYSTERIES. THEY ARE THE REFLECTION OF THE MORTAL WORLD, CREATED BY MORTAL HANDS. THEY ARE QUICKENED BY OUR DESIRES AND THEY REMAIN WITH US FOR ETERNITY. THEY ARE BOTH THE BIRTH AND DEATH OF OUR INNOCENCE, FOR THAT IS THE WAY OF ALL IMMORTAL JOURNEYS."

I am Niala Aaminah - Najahmara is my home. The village lies in a valley, nestled between two rivers that create a great lake hidden from prying eyes. From these waters, life springs eternal as we honor the great goddess, Gaea, with song, dance and ritual. I have protected Najahmara from a twisted and forsaken world for over three hundred years, though this is a well-kept secret.

My journey to this beautiful valley was fraught with many perils but once here, I felt safe. I was concealed from those powers that would search the world over for me, powers that were not of the mortal caste.

Who would understand such things? Certainly not the folk who live a simple life in Najahmara. They would not understand how my path crossed that of a god known as War, or how Ares the Destroyer believes I belong to him and only him. They would not believe that I ran away from him, that I escaped such a powerful being.

They would not grasp the fear that has hounded me for the past few moon cycles, knowing he draws near. It is just a matter of time before Ares the Destroyer finds me.

I pray my beloved Najahmara will survive his rage.

ONE

Niala Aaminah knelt on the ground in front of five tall stones that reached into the dusky blue sky of early evening. The stones were bleached white, battered by the wind and worn smooth by the rains, ever proudly outlined against the horizon. In darkness, when moonlight poured over them like shimmering cloth, their shadows crossed the valley as silent sentinels.

Etched upon the face of each towering rock was a name, barely discernible after the many generations of standing guard over Najahmara. Gently, Niala traced the inscription on one stone. It was the name of a woman, written in the ancient language of Earth.

The monoliths identified the resting place of four of those courageous souls: **Seyyal. Mahin. Edibe. Layla.** The fifth was reserved for Niala.

Five women who traveled to the ends of the known world to escape the wrath of a god. Sighing, Niala let her hand drop to her lap. How long had it taken them to find Najahmara? Forever, it seemed. She felt the weight of those years even now, though it seemed no more than a blink of the eye since *her* arrival.

She remembered how she huddled on the busy docks of Athos, frightened and alone. How, out of a crowd of rough men, a smiling woman appeared and gave her sanctuary. How Layla offered an oasis of warmth and friendship in the middle of hostile surroundings. How Niala met the other women who also hid her from a fate worse than death.

How, of the five who began the journey, Niala was the only one left. Sadness washed over her like waves rising and falling with the tide. It receded quickly, but the emptiness lingered. She rubbed a hand across her forehead as if to wipe away the old grief and tried to focus once again on the present.

The past still called, reminding her of the search for this valley. Five women and a poor tribe of people who did not know their destination but trusted the land would speak when found.

And it had, for when they opened their eyes upon the dawn that first morning in the valley, they were astonished. Weary and nearly drowned by a deluge the night before, they emerged from their wet bedding and bedraggled tents to see a meadow alive with sparkling drops of water nestled in a carpet of delicate purple flowers. The blooms rolled away from them in a blissful corridor that led right up to the sandy shores of twin rivers

The Bayuk streamed down from the north and the Maendre pin-wheeled in from the east to meet at the west side of the valley. They created a glistening lake before continuing on their way across the land to spill into the sea. A deep forest grew at the far end of the valley and to each side rose gentle cliffs, white, like the five standing stones. As the cliffs marched toward them, they formed a deep bowl, declining outward to meet the great meadow where they camped.

One river, yes, but two? They had followed the Bayuk for over six months, never suspecting that it joined with its sister in a land of promise, the sacred land of the earth goddess herself. They felt Gaea's strength drawing them into the very heart where she made her home. There they settled and carved out a tiny village that was now a thriving town filled with the sounds of happiness.

Najahmara, lying below the ridge in contented unsuspecting grace, unprepared for the descent of pain and fear.

Just as the warmth of the day gave way to the coolness of the evening, Niala's sense of peace gave way to disquiet. For two moon cycles, uneasiness had crept over her in a slow migration throughout her body until it finally burst over her in a dread she could not shake. All around her, from the trees to the fields, upon the winds and in the waters, there was a constant warning that something in their land had changed.

In the past few days the fear had increased and Niala felt the restlessness beneath her feet. The winds pulled at Niala's hair and whispered in the grasses of things to come. The waters gurgled of caution and even the skies grew clouded, hiding the sun far more than usual.

There was no reflection of this in the faces of her people. They went about their lives as they always did at this time of the season. It was with diligence they looked forward to the harvest. Fields of grains to reap, fruits to dry, herbs to gather, and medicines to prepare. They behaved as if they must survive a brutal winter instead of the mild cooling of their lands.

It was good to be prepared for no one knew when there would be a flood, or famine, or worse. Niala thought of those things that could be worse. Although there were no outward signs of disturbance, Niala knew danger was there. It waited in the shadows as a treacherous creature stalking the unwary.

There was a darkness settling over the land and the fear in her heart was choking. She came to the windswept plateau to sit in front of the stones, as she did each evening, trying to grasp the cause.

Forcing herself to an inward quiet, Niala settled back, eyes closed; she sought calm. She relaxed into silence with the chill of the air seeping into her skin and waited. The only response was a shivering of the earth. Niala smoothed one hand down the long, thick braid hanging over her shoulder and let her mind empty into the vast open space of darkness without moon or stars that filled her inner landscape. Bringing her breath into a rhythm, slow in, slow out, she felt her body grow heavy.

A hushed sigh swirled around her and rustled through the dry grasses as if a caressing hand trailed across the plateau. The wind stroked her arms and face, down her back and along her legs in an eager greeting as Gaea merged with her.

For that was the way of Earth, to become a part of life and see the world about her through human eyes. If she spoke, it was with Niala's own lips and if she walked, it was with Niala's feet. It was a gift Niala gave willingly and with joy.

Gaea revealed what she would through visions, fragmented, diluted and at many times difficult to understand. Niala waited with patience, for it was not Gaea's way to rush. Immediately, she felt Gaea's disappointment and sadness.

When the vision rose before Niala, it seemed as real to her as the stones themselves, as real as the birds darting about in the sky.

Day turned to night and a figure stood at the edge of the plateau looking out across the valley. He was tall and imposing, chest as thick as an ox. His shoulders were wide and strong with a straight, unforgiving back. He was built ruggedly with a face as beautiful as the heavens and eyes black like the deepest night - as depthless as the seas and without mercy.

Niala knew him well.

He was War.

She had deceived War and fled his embrace, hiding herself from him for countless generations. Trembling, she watched as he held his head cocked to one side, listening. She clamped her lips together to keep from crying out, and tucked herself in as if to become invisible. He did not advance toward her. Instead, he turned toward the valley and fixed his gaze upon Najahmara.

Niala crawled on hands and knees to the edge. Huddling on the brink, perilously near to falling over the side, Niala looked up at him. Silvery moonlight kissed his face, the broad sweep of forehead, the high arch of black brow, the straight, bold nose and full lips. Black curls fell along his neck, covering his ears, blending into the darkness of his clothing; his bearded chin lifted; his countenance impassive.

War was exactly as she remembered him.

He did not look at her. His gaze remained on the valley, and so it was that her eyes were drawn downward. There she foresaw a swarm of men blanket Najahmara, an army of warriors sweeping down upon the quiet town in unyielding waves. With stealth, the men invaded. Shrieks of pain and terror burst over her beloved home.

The shadowy men struck down her people with wicked blades that glinted in the moonlight until the streets ran thick with blood. Though distant and dark, she knew there was not one in Najahmara who had sufficient weapons to fight back.

No one could stand against War.

Then, and only then, did War turn and look at her.

War said nothing, but a cold and mirthless smile touched his lips. Niala shuddered and wept into her hands. When next she looked, the apparition disappeared. Across the valley she saw no more than a serene town washed in the glow of sunset. Gaea lingered for a moment before she, too, receded like the winds. Niala was left all alone.

Stunned, Niala stared out over Najahmara unable to move. She sat until darkness fell and the people slept, until her legs were cramped and her mind was numb.

Then, and only then, could she stagger to her feet. With one last glance at the five stones, she made her stumbling way down the path to the valley. Walking through the gardens behind the temple, she prayed no one would be awake, for she could not even begin to speak of her vision.

Sleep would not come to her that night, no matter how she tried. Lying in a woven hammock hung from a wooden frame, Niala stared into the murky corners of her quarters. The night outside her window was equally as indistinct with the moon no more than a sliver, waning past its fullness into a black disk. The gloom only added to her distress, for every rustle outside her window caused her to start, ever expecting Ares the Destroyer to appear.

Sweating, Niala threw back the light cover and sat up. The room was silent except for muffled sounds beyond the building, in the gardens that lay outside her window. She listened to the night animals snuffling about and to the predator birds as they swooped on fast wing searching for food. She hoped there would be no sudden squeal of a snared creature, for she could not bear it.

Her mind was too filled with the images of Najahmara's destruction to hear the death of an innocent, even if it was the earth's way. She rose from her bed and went to stand by the window. With a gentle breeze coming through, she was grateful to have the sweat dried on her face. It brought the fragrant scent of late flowering bushes to fill her room.

When would War bring this savage army to cut down her people?

"How can I stop him?" Niala half-pled, half-wondered, yet already knew in her heart there was only one answer. Restless, Niala climbed through the window frame and slid to the ground.

The grass was damp beneath her bare feet and she breathed in the cool air with a small sense of relief. As she moved toward the paths leading into the center of the gardens, it seemed all nightlife froze except for the constant buzz of insects. She swatted at one, then remembered to let her energy seep outward, pushing away any that would sting or bite. The whirring of their wings faded away and she was left alone.

Niala went to one of the low benches near the pond and sat in the darkness with a canopy of stars spread across the sky to keep her company. The water was a long oval mirror for the stars and crescent moon, and looked as if a piece of the heavens had fallen to earth. It seemed as though she could wade into the sky and disappear into that brilliantly studded archway where Ares would never find her. So tempted was she, that she rose to her feet and went to the edge of the water.

As her toes grew wet, she shook her head, amused at herself. Niala turned back toward the temple, gazing at its discordant shape with affection. Over the years, a single room had grown into a sprawling, half-circle building connected by hidden passages, breezeways and narrow corridors.

It was not a thing of beauty, but it held her fondest memories and the people she loved most. The building was draped in shadows. Not a single glimmer of candlelight seeped out, not even in the section that held a second story sleeping room for the younger girls. They should be the first to sleep, as hard as they were pushed throughout the day. Yet they were often the last to put out their lights. This, Niala understood, for she knew the excitement of being in the early stages of learning, though her trials had been in a distant land.

The land of Ares the Destroyer.

His visage once again swam before her eyes and with it came the memories of her time with him. She prayed never to see him again, but she knew she would.

"But not at the sacrifice of Najahmara," she whispered. The tortured screams in her vision filled her ears once more and the bittersweet scent of blood rose from the earth.

Niala shuddered as cold fingers gripped her shoulder. The hand of doom was upon them and there was naught she could do.

"Niala?"

She was shaken from her reverie, not by the hand of doom, but by Seire's bony fingers. Still trembling, Niala felt for the bench and gratefully sank down.

"Niala, what is wrong?" Seire touched Niala's face, feeling tears.

Looking at her, Niala could not help but chortle, for she should have known Seire would wait for this exact moment to seek her out. Seire's slight form was nearly indistinct in the darkness, blending with the tall bushes behind her. She did not need a lantern to find her way, for she was blinded with age, and though she was bent and gnarled, using a staff to walk, her grip was firm.

"You are a sly one." Niala wiped her face with her skirt and made room on the bench for Seire to sit. "How did you know I was out here?"

"I heard you talking to yourself. You do far too much of that these days."

"I have a great deal on my mind."

"You should learn to pass duties to others, rather than do everything yourself."

"You are right, but I find peace in work. You witness yourself what happens when I ponder too long. Besides, there is not a one of us that slacks."

Seire sighed and leaned a bit on Niala. "It is true. More and more I find I cannot keep up. Soon, another need take my place."

They had talked of this before and each time Niala rejected the thought. As she put her arm around Seire, she noticed again how frail she was, how age was stealing away her health.

"We have already lost one. I cannot bear to lose another." Unbidden, the gentle face of Basimah came before Niala.

"How long has it been?" Niala murmured. "An entire turning of the seasons, or more, since Basimah passed?"

"More," grunted Seire. "And I did not say I would lie down and die. I merely said soon I would be of no use."

Niala made a rude sound. "You may be blind and crippled, but of no use? Not until your bones are without flesh."

They both laughed and then fell silent for a moment.

"Niala," began Seire. "Something is wrong. I feel it. You have been very quiet of late. Now, I find you out here. Though it is your habit to wander at night, I know it is not our daily life that causes this grief." She paused before adding, "I, too, have felt something amiss. We all have."

"I should have known you would feel it. All of you."

A twinge of guilt leapt up as Niala thought about the little lines of worry on Jahmed's forehead as they shared their evening meal. The way Inni threw out hints to speak of it. Even Pallin, the youngest of the five, eyed her with a concern that Niala ignored.

"I have had a vision." With a deep breath, Niala told the old priestess of all she saw and when she was done, she felt panic rise up all over again. "I fear he comes for me, Seire."

"But why? Who is this being and why have I not heard of him before?" Though the old woman spoke forcefully, her body trembled.

"It happened a very long time ago, when I was little more than a child." Niala swallowed hard and stared across the shining waters of the pond. "I do not like to speak of it."

"Perhaps now is the time for you to tell, if he threatens our safety."

"Yes, you are right, but how I loathe to speak his name. It is as if I will invoke him if I so much as whisper it. Ares…" Niala passed a hand across her face and paused. "Ares the Destroyer. The only ones who knew of him are long dead. They were the ones who helped me escape him."

"I have heard the tale of your arrival here. Of course, I notice you leave out your own name now and your role in this valley's discovery."

"It must be so, Seire, for it is too hard to explain how I was there and I am still here."

"They would understand."

"How can they?"

"They would try," Seire said with patience. "You do not give them the opportunity."

"Yes, but who would believe you are my daughter? A gift from Gaea but now appearing so much older. I do not want it known, do you?"

"Uhhh…"

"What?" Turning, Niala added, "What do you mean, old one? I know that tone."

"People talk and just because we are priestesses does not mean we are above such gossip. I have not told them all about it, yet there is much speculation."

"So I am indeed subject to discussion amongst the women?"

"More likely, everyone in Najahmara, but they are too polite to ask."

"Well, even if they did, I would not answer."

"And they do not need one, Niala, for it is you that sustains us. You give us strength and hope. You keep us well and in health. Why would anyone question that?"

"Do not be silly, old woman. It is Gaea who does all that. I am no more than her servant."

"Perhaps that is why Gaea wants you to here."

Niala shrugged. "And does Gaea want Ares the Destroyer to find me?"

"She warns you of him, does that sound like she wants him here?"

"Or does she advise he comes, no matter what I do? The merciless slaughter of my family, my entire tribe, was ferocious. The invaders took me, the sole survivor, and gave me to him as a gift for sacrifice. I ran away from him." Niala shook her head. "He will stop at nothing to claim me once more."

"Mercy," whispered Seire.

"I came here for sanctuary. We have allowed no such terror to touch our world. We have not made a place for bloodshed and I have prayed this one would never cross my path again. I did not believe he would find me, although the fear has always lain in my heart of hearts." Niala paused with a deep inhale. "But I should start from the beginning."

"Yes, yes, you should."

"I should have told you before." Niala lifted her shoulders in defense. "I thought I had escaped him, after all this time."

With loving tenderness, Seire touched Niala's cheek. "Tell me, then, and do not be afraid. Whatever happens, it is not your fault."

"The story is lengthy."

"I scarce sleep anymore and why would I? I have no time to waste." She poked Niala in the side. "Tell me."

Niala nodded and squeezed Seire's fingers. As soon as the first words left her mouth, she was a child again reliving the tale as if it were now.

"My parents had only me and each night they thanked the heavens for their good fortune. They said I was a gift from the goddess." Niala smiled. "My mother knew what happened to females, no matter what their ages, for we lived the life of herders. Women were taken very young and most did not survive to any great age. My mother was determined that would not be my fate.

"They claimed I was a male child, kept me covered and sheared my hair in the manner of the other boys. As I got older, they wrapped my head in cloth and, instead of doing work common to the women, I walked along side my father and did as he did. I had the strength of a boy and knowledge of the herds. Though I was very young, I was tall for my age and broader of shoulder than most girls. It was easy for me to fool even the closest of my father's family."

The smile faded from Niala's lips and a sad, faraway expression took its place. "I was an obedient child and did as my parents bid. As I grew, I spent more time with the herds and less time with them. It was my tenth year." She stopped and cleared her throat.

"We were high up in the hills where our goats liked to wander when the first snow hit us. Seire, you have never seen a time when rain becomes hardened into white flakes, when it falls from the sky so thickly you cannot see your hand before your face.

"It comes down from the heavens in a perfect drape, like feathers or clouds, if they could fall to earth. Everything becomes quiet, as if you plugged your ears with your fingers. If the wind is not blowing, even the cold is not bothersome.

"Snow can freeze man and animal in their tracks. Sometimes, though, it is this drifting soft blanket of pure white that touches your face like the wings of a bird in flight. You can catch one flake on your tongue and feel the coldness melt into the freshest water."

"We would roll in it and play in it." Niala stared out at the warm night that held Najahmara. "It was that kind of beauty falling from the sky."

"But this time was not about children throwing snow at each other. As we lay looking at it from our blankets, we could hear a strange pounding, snorting sound that made me think of animals when they are frightened. Slowly, around the edges of these odd noises, we could hear shouting and then screams. Then crackling, like the tiny fire we made to keep the air dry, although it had gone out while we slept.

"All this was in the distance. The darkness was distorted by light from burning tents. It was like a dream. What we heard did not fit in with what we saw. My eyes were open and all around me was beauty, but instead, it was a nightmare come alive."

Shivering, Niala rose to her feet and began to pace back and forth along the pathway. She had pushed this tale away for so many years, refused even to think of it and yet, with a few words, it sprang forth with all the horror of the moment.

Seire hesitated and then said, "If you do not want to finish, I understand."

"No, no, I will tell you. I must, for I have never spoken of this to anyone here. There seemed no need." With a deep breath, Niala went on. "There was no chance for my tribe to escape. These savages attacked while my folk slept, attacked those who were harmless, those whose only defense was to run away. But they were not even given the chance to run. Emerging from their tents, they were killed. There were bodies everywhere and more blood than I had ever seen.

"We should have stayed where we were, but the boys with me were older and filled with such anger that they raced down the hillside with the intent to murder. Of course, they were cut down before they had a chance to fight."

Niala's breath quivered and she closed her eyes.

"I followed the boys down but slipped around the edges to find my parent's tent. It was gone. Burned up. They were not. They lay in the snow with their blood spread out in an evil blackness I will never forget.

"They were dead, staring up at me. I knew they would want me to run, to live. Instead I knelt in the snow, weeping and praying that I, too, would be struck down. I hoped it would be quick and merciful so I would again be with my mother and father."

"Oh, my sweet child," Seire whispered. "All these years you have said nothing."

"No, and it shall not be repeated. This is for your ears, that you may understand. My story has not ended, but has only reached the point of another beginning.

"My parent's blood stained my hands, my face, my clothes but I did not care. I wanted to die with them. I could no longer hear the noise around me. I did not know if the strangers still brought terror to the rest of my people. Then it happened. I felt the sting of an arrow pierce my shoulder and I fell over in a swoon on top of my parent's bodies.

"I do not know how long I lay there but it was dawn when my eyes again opened. I staggered to my feet, half-frozen and stood blinking into the rising sun. I did not know the men were still there, that they had stripped our poor tribe of anything useful and gathered our herds to take as their own.

"I knew only that the sun rose and I believed myself to be dead. All I could do was stand and cry out in my anguish, for there at my feet were the poor, frozen bodies of my mother and father.

"Then I saw a few who had attacked us and I wanted to kill them. I could scarce move for the pain and grief, but I tried, Seire. I tried and would have killed them all, if I could.

"They first took me for a ghost. When I rose from a pile of frozen bodies, they were filled with dread. It appeared to them that I had come back from the dead for I was covered in blood and snow, a walking specter. The savages who killed without mercy were afraid of me.

"I had an arrow sticking from my body, yet I screamed at them, cursed at them. Instead of striking me down again, they believed I was not human. They took me with them, believing I was a talisman, a charm that would keep them safe from their enemy's weapons.

"I would have far rather been slain as I stood than to be taken prisoner by my tribe's executioners, I swear to you, Seire." Niala's voice was filled with old pain.

"But I went because there was nothing else to do. I was a child and had not the strength, nor the cunning, to free myself. And even though I fought them, it did no good. I could not speak to them and what would I have said? They spoke a tongue I did not know and, in turn, their words meant nothing to me.

"I was with them a long, long time and never spoke to them, not once. But always listening, I learned some of what they said. This took many, many moons to understand even a few words, as their language was very different from my own.

"The sounds they made were awkward for me to hear let alone try to make with my mouth. I did everything to stay separate from them. I did not want to know their filthy ways. Even then, I could not afford to let them see me cry, nor show any weakness. They believed me to be a male child and to that end I had to stay true.

"They were a cruel lot and I saw much more killing before it was over. I wondered what my people had done to be slaughtered, what we could have had that was so valuable? In time I learned there was nothing. No reason for the killing. It happened because my tribe crossed their path. They stole life for sheer pleasure and punished any survivors with torture until they also went to their deaths.

"Women and children were raped. Any that were not slaughtered became slaves, until they were destroyed or left behind when they became too weak to travel. I was spared for two reasons. I was thought to be a boy and a boy who was not like anyone else. That made me valuable to them. I was a talisman that warded off evil."

With a harsh laugh, Niala continued. "Imagine that, the sole survivor of a murderous rampage and I was to keep them safe. Oh, that I had the power to wipe them all out. I would have, Seire. There are some that do not deserve this life. I do not set myself up to judge, but by their own hands they create the cycle with which they die.

"If I could have been the tool that ended the cycle, I would have gladly, even now. Even now," Niala repeated, and knew this to be true.

"I have stood as protector of our tribe, of our people and I will continue until I live no more. But now, this moment, I forgo my vow of peace. I swear here, on my mother's blood, if I must destroy others who would destroy us, I will."

"I cannot believe this would happen here, to us." Seire gripped her staff between both hands and pressed it into the soft ground. "It is clear to me your vision was of the past, not of the future."

"But it was Najahmara I saw, for my family's tribe had no buildings, only poor tents."

"It was not Najahmara," Seire repeated. "What you knew then and what you know now has blurred. It is often so during such moments, you have said so yourself many times. And besides, Gaea does not discern between here and there, past and future. To her, it is all the same. She warns you of this demon, that is what this is about."

"I hope you are right," Niala voice was faint. "But you have not yet heard all of it."

Seire grew silent for a moment before answering. "Then you had best finish your tale for I do not understand how you would come to know such a creature as this."

Niala eased back onto the bench, her gaze faraway, reliving the sheer terror of the moment when she first laid eyes upon Ares the Destroyer.

"He is no simple creature, Seire. He is a god."

TWO

Niala sat with her fingers clasped together in her lap, eyes closed. "He is an immortal being who can step into our world at will. He is unlike anything I have ever known."

She shivered, as if those depthless black eyes were still upon her.

"Gaea is everywhere. She radiates all around, in everything. But he - he breathes. He has body and form." Holding up a hand, Niala sighed. "I get ahead of myself. Where was I? Oh, yes.

"I did not know the full reason they kept me alive when so many others died. I understood I was their talisman, yet I did not know I was destined to be a gift to their god. What better thing than a ward to offer the god who has so blessed you with successful ventures? They returned to their home wealthy with their stolen gains and wished to offer their most prized possession to their god in sacrifice.

"There was no way for me to know where we were going. I had no understanding of a god who had a home. We have a temple for our use and we call it Gaea's in honor of her, but truly, she does not live among us. We cannot go to her as I can go to you in your room. Our goddess lives in all things.

"Where we would find her dwelling? We would not, would we? And would not Gaea laugh if we asked her directions to her house? Yes. Yes, so it is with Gaea. But these other gods, they have a place to reside if they wish. They walk with their feet in two worlds.

"As I have said, this was over a great length of time and I began to change. I lay in terror at night wondering when one of the men would notice and I did my best to keep from them during the day. I knew they would see my breasts as they began to rise, so I bound them with strips of cloth."

Niala paused and held her hands to her chest. "Seire, I cannot tell you the pain that came from the binding. Sometimes I could not draw in air and I would have to bite my tongue to keep from crying out. When my first blood came, I thought surely my disguise was over. I was certain they would smell it, or see it stain my clothing. I knew what would happen should anyone discover the truth."

"What did you do?" Seire asked, her own heart beating hard.

"It sickens me to say." Niala stared at her hands. "Even though I cared for my tribe's herds, I never ate their flesh and never helped with their slaughter. But that is what I did: I covered myself in the fresh blood of their meat at every opportunity to keep myself from discovery.

"We arrived at our destination long after my capture. Many died in the wake of our path and there were others who had been collected to serve the same purpose as myself. The home of this god was high on a mountaintop.

"The trek up was difficult and very slow. There were times when my sides ached and I could not move, but was forced on. We all were. The closer we came to this fortress, the more excited theses savages became. When we reached the gates, they all fell to their knees and begged entrance, though it was not allowed.

"We sat outside in the cold for several days before we were bid enter into a long stone hall that stank of blood and roasting meat. I was surprised to see how many were there before us, all besotted from the wine in barrels that lined the walls.

"Treasures of all sorts lay heaped in corners and many animals waited in pens for their turn to be offered up to this strange and vengeful god. The sounds were deafening, the smells revolting. I was not allowed food or drink and was made to stand tied together with the other boys.

"Finally, we were taken to a huge hall, a horrible place. There was an altar so dreadful, I do not even want to tell you what it was like. I knew then I was to be killed and I thought I would swoon with fear. I would have slit my own throat just then without regret.

"The chamber was dark and cold and echoed with their talk. The savages ignored us, for all they could think about was that finally, finally, their god would give them audience.

"Behind the altar was a giant throne chiseled from the same gray rock as the rest of the castle. Everything was gray, like storm clouds as they roll in. Everything was shadowed, dark, bleak, frigid." Niala closed her eyes and let the words roll off her tongue, envisioning the temple as if she stood there once again.

"I had never seen anything so big or so grand. There were great arches sweeping upward to peak in a high ceiling. I could hear the faint sounds of birds that had found their way in to roost on the ledges.

"Slabs of the gray stone made up the floor, unevenly laid and clear of any coverings, as if waiting to catch the unwary whose errant toe would strike an edge and send him sprawling. Around the altar was a thick, black pool of dried blood. I knew it was blood from what was on the altar. And the smell."

Niala stopped to catch her breath, for the fear lived again inside her.

"I do not know how long we waited. My feet and legs were numb and my back ached from standing. We had grown quiet and huddled together in a miserable clump. The men prayed to their god to grace them with his presence, telling him of their long journey and of the treasures they brought for him. Still, he did not come. I began to think them all fools and that this god did not exist.

"Then, just as I thought I must surely fall over, one of the boys was snatched from the group, his throat slit and his body thrown onto the altar. It happened quickly, horribly and the rest of the boys set up a howling, clinging to each other.

"I thought I would vomit and that my bowels would spill upon the floor. I could not tear my gaze from the child lying there, dead and knowing that, too, would be my fate. All I could hear was the sputtering of candles from the spray of blood."

Again Niala stopped and pressed a hand to her mouth. Seire patted her back but did not speak. After a moment, Niala went on.

"I do not know where he came from. He was simply there. This giant filled the stone seat from top to bottom. He was broad of shoulder, sitting squarely in the center, arms thick as small trees resting on the sides.

"My chest cramped so that spots danced before my eyes. I stared at his hands as they gripped the carved ends of the throne. His hands were big with long fingers. Hard, cruel fingers that could snap my neck with one move. I dared not make a sound, not even a whimper.

"When he spoke it was deep, a vibration like the drums of this village calling us to gather and my eyes were drawn up to look at his face." Niala paused, the memory returning with such force that her breath was once again pulled from her.

"When I looked at him for the first time, I saw fierce eyes, but his face...his face, Seire...as perfect as the sunrise...as painfully beautiful as the morning light across the water. He should have been grotesque, a monster."

Niala stared at the temple pond. "But he was not. He was fair of face and body and the ugliness I saw was in my own mind. I wanted to turn away from him, but I could not. His eyes were as black and endless as the winter night and every bit as cold. I shuddered and prayed I would die quickly, for although beauty reigned outside, there was no flicker of it within his heart.

"He saw through me. I knew it at once. Of course he would, he was a god, was he not? I was more afraid at that moment than in all the time I traveled with the ones who slew my parents.

"When he finally turned away from me and spoke to the men, I fell to my knees. I could not help it, Seire. I did not want anyone to see my cowardliness, but I could not stand any longer. I knew not what they said, for they spoke in words I did not understand. I was then released from my bonds, dragged forward and made to stand before him, I knew I would soon die.

"They could not make me look at him. They tried, but I would not lift my head again. Even so, with my eyes downcast, I knew he watched me. I could feel his gaze upon me but I would not raise my head. I prayed to the goddess to take me into her arms at once and spare me the disgrace. The roaring of my own heart sent me into deafness and I could hear nothing else.

"But then something, something, made me lift my head to meet his gaze, to show even though I feared him, I would not bow to him. He looked straight into my eyes and I was caught, pinned like an animal.

"He seemed to know my thoughts and I could not believe what I saw. The smallest movement of his mouth, a quirk, as if he laughed at me. And then he spoke again. His voice echoed in the great hall, a thunderous, angry voice. All around me, the men went silent. What next befell me defied belief.

"A sword to my neck or a dagger in my heart, yes, but no. My tunic was ripped from my shoulders, baring me to my waist. Warsus, that was the chieftain's name, stood over me, gaping at the bindings around my breasts.

"Aaiee." Seire covered her face.

"Warsus went mindless with rage, for women were not allowed in the temple of this god. It was the worst kind of insult. He stared at me with hatred, forgetting where he was. He pulled from his belt a knife and raised his hand to kill me on the spot. I was no longer afraid and faced him, waiting for the moment I knew would come.

"Just as the knife was to plunge into my heart, Warsus gagged. His skin became as purple as ripened grapes and he fell over at my feet. The war god had not moved, yet I knew it was by his hand that Warsus was now dead. In another instant, the rest of the warriors choked, gasped and also fell down dead.

"I begged for the boys, pleading for him to spare them. I cried and pleaded until the war god stood up and came to stand in front of us. He ignored the bodies and the filth, for he had eyes only for me. He was still tall and broad, but not so much as he had seemed while he sat in the throne. When I looked up into his eyes, it seemed again that he laughed at me.

"And then he answered me in my own language, *And what would you trade for their lives?*

I could not believe my ears. I was struck dumb and could not speak.

You are bold to enter my temple, girl, and now you refuse to speak? What would you trade for them? Tell me now or you all are doomed.

"I finally found my voice and said, I have nothing to give but myself and that you already have. His reply was unexpected."

Boldly spoken. And so, because you ask it, the boys are free.

"The ropes fell from their hands and necks and he bid them to go back to the warriors' quarters. I could not help but ask what would happen to them. His response was callous.

I care not what befalls them. I have let them go and that is all I will do.

"And what of me? I asked, but he did not speak again. Instead, he beckoned me to follow him into the depths of his fortress. The passages were narrow and dark, no candles or torches to light our way. There were many rooms off to the sides but he did not hesitate at any doorway, he continued through this monstrous dwelling until we reached a staircase.

"There we climbed up and up and up. The stairwell was as dark, if not darker than the passages, and I could scarce see him in front of me. There seemed to be no one else there at all. Our steps echoed, but no one called out to us as we journeyed upward.

"We arrived in a chamber lit by a large fireplace, its warmth, and even more so, the bright glow welcoming me. He left me standing by the fire while he went through yet another doorway across the chamber.

"I stared in wonder, for though the room was made from the same rough-hewn blocks of gray stone, set in the center of the floor were shiny slabs of black laid out in a spiral. Looped inside the spiral were slabs of red, going the opposite way. It shone just like the water, Seire."

Niala blinked, a slow descent of her eyelids. "To this day, I am unsure of what it was made. But, no matter. My eye was caught by a giant sword hanging above the mantle and I gasped. I could not help myself, for the blade shimmered in the light, a glowing, living thing so beautiful it hurt to look at it. The wicked blade was broad and longer than I was tall, pointing straight down as if to pierce the top of my head if I stood too close.

"My gaze rose to the hilt and found it to be plain, wrapped in unadorned leather, fit for a large hand. Of course, I knew who it belonged to. I felt a chill of renewed fear and turned away lest it leap from its place and cut out my heart.

"The rest of the room was sparse. Two chairs covered in red and black cloth near the hearth, low couches here and there against the walls, a few towering, unlit candle stands and, on the other side of the room, a table with six wooden chairs. That was all.

"There were other doors, great arches leading into darkness. I did not want to know what lay beyond that one room. I swear I did not want to know. I could scarce take in what I was seeing.

"It was a strange place. A temple, a place of worship, a slaughterhouse, a home. I shook my head, confused by it all. Gaea does not live in a dwelling. She dwells in life. Everything stems from her, into and out of her; she is everywhere, in all living things. She is nowhere and yet she is everywhere. I did not understand what manner of being he was."

Niala grew quiet, unwilling to go on.

"What happened next?" Seire's voice was quiet. The old one's face was turned up toward Niala even though she could not see.

"You know what happened - I need not tell you." Niala stood up and took Seire's elbow. "It is late, old one, and we should try to find what sleep we can."

"Did a child come of the union?"

"A child?" Startled, Niala stared down at Seire. "No, there was not a child. Why?"

"A child would be a very good reason for him to seek you out, even after all this time."

"There was no child."

"It would seem a creature such as War would insist you bear a child."

"Yes, it would seem so, but it was not."

Seire heard a hint of satisfaction in Niala's voice as they walked along the path toward the doorway nearest Seire's quarters, but she asked no more about it.

Niala remained quiet until they reached the entrance to Seire's room. "There is much more to the story, but we both need sleep. Dawn will be here soon."

"I suppose," Seire answered, her body further hunched from weariness. "But I want to know what happened. How did you escape him? Why does he seek you now after all this time?"

With a pat on Seire's back and a gentle kiss to the old woman's cheek, Niala said with a heartiness she did not feel, "It was only a vision and all Gaea's visions do not come to pass. They are warnings of possibilities. She plucks images from my memories to tell her stories and sometimes one has nothing to do with the other."

"But this being - what could he want with you now?"

"Perhaps nothing. Perhaps everything. Tomorrow, we shall talk more of it with the others."

"Yes." Wheezing in relief, Seire entered her quarters. "Yes, we will talk with the others."

As Niala made her way along the dark corridor to her own room, she shuddered, though she was not cold. The air around her was damp with heat, yet it was as if she waited once again for him, terrified, but fascinated. In her youthfulness, she had believed all he could take from her was what was left of her innocence.

She could not stop thinking of him and the events of long ago.

Niala stood shivering, in spite of the blazing fire. Numb with fear and resigned to her fate, she could think of nothing but the way the fire leapt about within its stone prison. The flames licked the sides of the rough-hewn blocks, looking for an escape only to fall back into the bottom. There was nowhere to go. Its source was contained within the walls. It could not climb, or fly, or even creep out of its prison. It had no choice, but to stay until it was extinguished.

Tears pressed against Niala's eyelids but she would not free them. They, too, must stay in their place for she would not be further shamed. She blinked them back and sighed, only then noticing the war god had returned and stood beside her. She had not heard his step ring against the cold floor.

"You must bathe, eat and then rest." His voice was far less harsh than when he sat upon his throne.

Hugging herself, Niala shook her head and refused to look at him.

"You misunderstand me. I do not pose a question, but tell you what you must do. In the adjoining room, there is a bathing pool filled with hot water. You have been long in your travels and stink of the animals you have kept."

Niala hunched her shoulders and did not answer him.

"And you have not had food for days. I know the ways of my warriors. Even as a gift to their god, there is no need to waste good provisions on one who is doomed. I see that gaunt, hungry look on your face. Here there is no need to starve. You will bathe first, because I cannot stand the stench, and then you will eat."

He waited a moment and still she did not speak. "It will do you no good to ignore me. I will put you back among the men, if you wish. I am certain a female would be heartily welcomed as there are no others here. There is not a one of them would concern himself with the scent of goat dung."

"How is it you speak my tongue?" Niala stuttered. It was almost as if she were drunk on wine; the words would scarce form on her lips.

He made a noise that might be called a laugh, but was more a snort. "I speak all tongues and why would I not? I am War. Everyone knows my name."

"I...I do not..."

"Your people do not know me? Do you tell me there is no violence? No fighting, no killing or beatings go on in your tribe? No one is envious or greedy or even stupid? Do you tell me all is always well?" The word twisted with scorn. "And Love is forever present?"

From the corner of her eye, Niala saw him pace a few steps away and then return to stand before the fire. "If you tell me that, then you lie. What other force would bring you here?"

"I do not tell you anything except I do not know your name."

He watched her, weighing her sincerity. Finally, he spoke again. "And I do not know yours."

"Niala." She spoke in a faint voice, then a bit louder with pride. "Niala Aaminah. It means golden gift."

"Niala Aaminah, you are indeed a gift."

Again, he sounded as if he laughed at her. Niala flushed and shrank further into herself.

"It is a pretty name. Niala. Here I am known as Ares the Destroyer. In other places, I am known as Enyalius, or Teshub, or a legion of other names. I have been called the Storm god and the War god, and sometimes...." His voice dropped, "I am known just as God."

He fell silent so long Niala could not help turning to look for him. He was right behind her, a grave expression set on his face. "But it matters not what I am called, only that I am." He gestured toward the table across the next room.

The empty table was now filled to the edges with all kinds of food. Where it came from, she did not know, nor who brought it while she stared into the fire. She felt the hollowness in her belly, but did not want to eat in front of him. She stayed her feet from rushing to the table but eagerness lit her face. She looked back to the fire, not wanting him to see her need. When next she raised her head, he was gone.

With no more thought, she began to stuff her mouth with fruit and bread, drinking great gulps of clear, cool water until her belly threatened to give it back. Once filled and still alone, she grew curious. She did not know where he went and, though she told herself she did not want to find him, she could not stop the childish urge to open a set of arched, double doors behind the table. They were heavy, but once started, they glided inward and revealed luxury beyond her wildest imaginings.

It was a pond enclosed in blocks of stone. A sweetly scented fog rose above a rippling pool of hot water. At the far end, in a hearth that went nearly from one wall to another, a huge fire crackled. Along one length were small doors cut with a corresponding arch and the same heavy, ornate handles as the big double doors.

Niala crept into one to see what treasures a god might have hidden away. Instead of precious gems, she found a seat with a round hole cut out. Under it was a pot. She stared at it for long moments before understanding what it was for. Laughing aloud she said, "At best, I have used naught but a hole in the ground to relieve myself, this is truly set for a queen!"

Backing out, she looked again at the steaming water. Near it was a table that held drying cloths, perfumed oils, and a handful of mint twigs to clean her teeth. A beaten silver jug shaped like a horned animal held more of the cold, sweet water, another comfort of which she was not accustomed.

All she was offered during her years traveling with the savage men had been stale water from stinking skins or a sour mash that made her stomach heave.

Chewing on a twig, Niala undressed and for the first time in many months, unwound the cloth holding her breasts tight to her ribs. As they were released, she felt the rush of instant pain and cried out. Once she sank into the hot water, there was yet another thing she never imagined, the pain eased and she began to enjoy the scented water.

She stayed there as long as she could, floating on the surface, staring up at the rooftop. She was instantly entranced by the high dome and the moldings that danced across the ceiling, all the way down the four corners to the floor.

Gleeful, laughing people. Horned ones, half beast half man. Winged ones with pointed ears. Naked, lustful, wallowing together, erect and waiting, abundant breasts and heavy thighs parted.

With slow dawning, Niala realized they were happily and willfully making love in such complicated positions she could not sort out who did what to whom. She stared in fascination and attempted to trace a hand, or a leg, or even a mouth, back to its owner only to be surprised at which being it was. When she found her own fingers slipping along her wet skin, she flushed.

The ceiling was bewitched. It moved and changed just as the water did, seeming to mock her and her befuddled innocence. Yet, she could scarce pull her gaze from it. Her breath came rapidly and her heart pounded, for she realized it was this exact reason he kept her.

Frightened beyond words, Niala climbed from the pool and drew on a thick, straight gown that was much too large. She stood at the closed door for long moments while her knees shook and her gut clenched. He would have her and it mattered not whether she was willing.

For one fleeting moment, she considered rushing back to the pool and drowning herself. Would it not be better to die than to submit? With one hand gripping the metal pull, she turned back to look at the water. Did she suppose it called to her? Did it beckon her back by name to save her from him?

But no. It was Ares the Destroyer who waited for her. He called to her again. There was no choice other than death, and she was not willing to sacrifice that which was most sacred. He would have to take that from her as well, for she would not willingly give either.

Ares sat beside the hearth, leaning back, eyes closed, arms folded over his middle, his legs stretched out and crossed at the ankles. He seemed asleep. Niala stopped, uncertain now who had spoken to her just a moment before. Hesitating, she half turned away when he opened his eyes. Fear made her stumble and the tears she had held at bay slid down her cheeks.

"You are frightened of me."

"And who would not be, my Lord?" she whispered.

"Come here, Niala Aaminah. Do not be afraid."

With great reluctance, Niala went to stand in front of the fire, but not close enough for him to touch her. Too long she fought to survive, too long she kept her wits and strength about her, avoiding the men who made her prisoner. She would not simply go to him.

She held herself rigid and silent until she felt his hand upon her hair. He was behind her; she could hear him as he breathed. She trembled beneath his fingers. He did not laugh at her, but stroked her short locks and then her bared neck.

"How did you deceive them? They could not tell you were female? Even with shorn locks you cannot hide your beauty." He touched her cheek and felt the tears wetting her skin. His hand smelled of sandalwood and warmth and made her heart jump.

"It will not be unpleasant, I promise. I will not hurt you."

The gown slid to the floor with the smallest nudge and he put his arms around her. He was much taller than she and bent forward, the curve of his body held her in its embrace. She could feel the softness of his cloth tunic upon her back and the hardness of his erection pressing against her. Her trembling grew and the tears would not stop.

"Shhh." Ares brought one hand up to caress her cheek. He followed the line of her chin to her neck where he paused over the frantic beating of her pulse in the hollow of her throat.

"Please, do not," she whispered.

He did not answer, but touched the triangular scar on her shoulder. He lingered there for a moment before his fingers glided downward to her small breasts. First one, then the other in a slow, feather-light drift and then to slide across her ribs as if counting each one before reaching below her navel. His palm was hot and rested in the center of her belly, fingers splayed against her flesh.

Niala twitched as if to move away, but he held her there until the heat spread to her back and opened like a fist along her spine. Her knees grew weak and she shuddered; sweat broke out and she gasped, arching her back. A great, aching need filled her body. It began between her legs, traveled down and rushed up through her chest to her face.

She cried out and sagged in his arms. He turned her to face him and his mouth came down on hers. She felt his teeth grind against her lips. With a jerk, she strained to break away, her mind clouded with a sudden terror that overlaid longing, but Ares would not release her.

"Niala, I bade you not be afraid of me."

Niala could not speak, for hers was a shadowy fear, undefined, but built of inexperience and the knowledge he was not human. "Will you stop?"

"No." He drew her close again. "For this is meant to be. I see more than you and there is more to us. We are linked, you and I."

Here he paused and looked at her. Tears had begun again

and, although she tried to hide her face against his chest, he tipped her head back with ease. "Despite your bravery and cleverness, you are so very young. I know I should leave you alone, take you back amongst your people, anything but what I want."

He breathed her name next to her ear so sweetly it wrapped around her as soft as any fur. "Niala, I should leave you and your innocence for another time."

On his inhale, he took her breath. "But I cannot." When his lips touched hers again, she did not fight him.

THREE

Heart pounding, Niala started from a troubled sleep and gasped to see full daylight through the window. Pallin bent over her, face split by a huge grin, her dark braid tickling Niala's nose.

"Long have I awaited this day, Zahava! To find you still abed with the sun fully up and everyone looking for you. It is lovely."

She brushed the end of her braid across Niala's upper lip and giggled at the look of irritation that crossed Niala's face. Never did a bad-tempered word come from that tender mouth, or such a flare rise in those autumn eyes as in that moment. Pallin could not contain her glee. She danced about as Niala tried to pull herself from the hammock only to rock back and forth and finally dump onto the woven rug on the hard-packed dirt floor.

Disheveled and flushed, Niala squinted at the window, "It is well into the morn, why did you wait so long to wake me?"

"Seire said to leave you alone, you were tired."

"Then why are you here?" Niala retorted, climbing to her feet.

"Because, Seire now says that you have laid abed too long."

Pallin bowed her head, put her hands behind her back and balanced on her toes like a child would do when in trouble. Her tilted, brown eyes held a sparkle of mischief that could not be disguised as she peered up at Niala through black lashes. She was much smaller than Niala, with a fragile build that belied her strength, but lent credence to her show of submission. Still, her cheeks were tinged pink with the effort to show proper respect.

Niala frowned for a moment, then smoothed the front of her

nightshift. The skirt was rumpled and damp with sweat and clinging to her in a most uncomfortable way. The dreams of invasion coupled with Ares the Destroyer seemed to cling to her in the same way. As she watched Pallin, Niala could not help smiling to herself. Pallin had only just taken initiation during the spring gathering and her exuberance was often annoying.

"You are far past the age where such a stance will win me over and, as far as that old woman is concerned, I will have a word with her." Niala's voice was stern.

Looking up at Niala, Pallin's laughter faded. "Truly, Niala, we were worried. I heard you and Seire return to your beds close to dawn, but Seire would tell me nothing of why you were up. This morning, she said you needed to rest. She said...."

Pallin stopped, biting her lip.

"Said what?"

"Said you were not well." With a light, quick touch, Pallin reached up to feel Niala's forehead. "Indeed, you look as if you have a fever." She withdrew at Niala's impatient wave, but not before she felt the clamminess of her skin. "I am sorry I woke you, Zahava."

"You do not have to call me teacher any longer," Niala said, softening. "You are one of us."

"There are times I believe I should not be here, Zahava, for I do not think I deserve it."

"You have earned your place, dear one, or Gaea would not have approved."

Pallin nodded, the deep black of her hair catching glints of sunlight. Across her back was the image of the Delphinus, the great spirit fish as it leapt up into the air from the sea. It had been beaten into her skin during initiation, a symbol of her role as priestess and her connection to the element of water.

"I know, but I still wonder at my worth." Folding the bedcovers, Pallin straightened the tiny room while they talked.

Niala remembered how overwhelmed she felt when the Corvidae, the winged one who connected earth with sky, was placed on her back, and again when the image of Kulika, the Blue Serpent, was etched onto her leg. The memory of smoke laden with herbs to lessen her pain filled Niala's senses, as did the sharp stinging of the tiny stone needles used to place the dye.

It was a quick sensation, here and then gone. Niala recalled all too well how she was bidden by Gaea to carry the image of her mate, her protector, and how that changed Niala's life.

The upcoming girls were given many years to decide if becoming a priestess was worth committing their entire lives to Gaea, for once accepted, there was no release until death. Niala could see in Pallin's face the right choice was made and Pallin need have no fear that she belonged.

With this thought, Niala patted Pallin's cheek. "Do not worry, you have not offended me. I should not be lying here like a lazy ox."

"But if you could not sleep." Pallin's voice was hopeful to hear more.

"And I could not." Ignoring her interest, Niala added, "I must bathe, dress and then join you for what, midday meal? Mercy, I cannot believe I did not wake up with the dawn. What of the girls and their lessons?"

"Jahmed took them over, though the children hoped to be let out of their studies when you were not there. And see here, I have brought you water to wash, and some fruit to eat in case you did not feel like going about."

"That was good of you, Pallin. Please tell Jahmed I will be there soon."

Dipping her head, Pallin withdrew and left Niala to ready herself for what was left of the day.

Niala poised at the entrance to the long, low-ceilinged room where everyone took their meals. Like many other additions or extensions in the temple, the room was added as they grew in numbers. The room was open and breezy, with three doorways, one on each end. Another larger, double-door entrance at the center of the outside wall opened onto an expanse of grass belonging to the gardens.

Above the great room were sleeping quarters for the younger girls, all of whom were now gathered together to eat. But, instead, of concentrating on their meal, the girls were chattering away like so many birds at dawn.

Watching them brought a surge of affection that lifted her heart. Niala smiled at their earnest faces, as she knew the giggling, girlish talk reflected the most valuable lessons. The girls earned the respect and love of their sisters by listening. They learned humility by telling about themselves. They earned forgiveness and compassion from each other. There was no instruction that could come close to the gift they gave each other every day they spent together.

'I will defend my people to the death,' Niala thought with fierceness. *'Whatever I must do, I will.'*

At that moment, Niala decided she would not share her vision with the others.

After all, what could they do?

Nothing.

Niala straightened her shoulders and walked through the benches filled with laughing girls. Nodding and smiling at each, calling out names, patting a few on their heads as she passed. The girls clamored for her attention; always, but more so on this day since she had been absent from their studies. They were happy to see her well, and they became louder in their quest to tell her.

Raising one hand, palm outward, Niala gave the signal all were familiar with. It meant to finish quickly and get back to work. Though each girl bent her head over her meal, the room was still far from silent. Niala smiled to herself and went to her own seat next to Seire.

With her dark skin and many braids, Jahmed looked up at Niala with honey brown eyes and a flash of well-kept teeth. Her gaze carried an unusual and disturbing shyness. Niala wondered once again what Seire had told them.

Jahmed sat beside Inni, who was as pale as Jahmed was dark. Tiny freckles marched across Inni's nose and her hair was yellow like sunflowers, tied back in a single narrow braid that fell down between protruding shoulder blades. Inni did not smile. Her slender lips were pressed together as if she was angry, but her blue eyes held anxiety.

"Are you quite rested now?" asked Inni. "Staying up all night is for the young ones, Niala."

"Yes, please, I know." Niala held up a finger to stop her. "I am sorry to have caused alarm, but we can blame it on this old one, here, who could have told the truth and woke me up."

"What truth?" Seire lifted her head and gave a toothless grin. "That you could not sleep for dreams of an old lover come back to haunt you?"

"Indeed," Niala murmured, hoping the rest of her vision had not been revealed.

"I have not known you to take a lover, at least since I can remember." Jahmed concentrated on her plate but a slight smile played about her lips. "I have wondered why, for there is no lack of those who want to share your bed. Now I find you have one hidden from us."

"Yes, and how is that?" Inni lifted her eyebrows. "How do you hide a lover from us?"

"I do not, good sisters." Niala cast an evil look at Seire, though Seire could not see it. "The old one tells tales of long ago, before I came here."

"So why do you dream of one from the past? Perhaps he is saying it is time for you to choose another." Pallin offered with a timid glance.

"Or is he saying he will have you back?" Inni spoke with harsh surprise. "Is that what is to happen, Niala? Is he going to steal you from us? What will happen to all of us if he does?"

Inni did not say it, but the meaning hung before them as if she had. A tiny flare of fear ran through them. It was clear to Niala that Seire had told the rest of the vision. Niala sighed inwardly and worked to keep from showing her own concern.

Jahmed put her hand over Inni's and squeezed, lacing her fingers through Inni's. Inni paused to exchange a glance with Jahmed, her own fingers tightening. No words were spoken, but eventually Inni shrugged her thin shoulders and let a smile tug at the corners of her mouth. Jahmed smiled back and, for a moment, they were lost in each other. When Inni spoke next, it was with a softer tone.

"Who is this being that threatens us?"

"I am not certain that it is important right now." Niala glance around the now-quiet great room.

"Oh, but it is," cackled Seire. "It is clear this one is angry and seeks his revenge. How else can he tear you from us unless he destroys everything?"

"Have you taken leave of your senses?" Niala scolded Seire, who had the grace to show contriteness, even if it was only a small amount. Niala spoke again to the other women. "I do not wish to frighten you."

"Who is he?" Jahmed would not take her gaze from Niala's face. She felt something was terribly wrong deep in her gut.

Niala stared at her simple fare of cheese, flat bread, honey, and a handful of grapes as if an answer would appear within the food. "He is War."

"What?" They all spoke at once. Pallin jumped to her feet, unable to sit still. "What do you mean?"

"What are you speaking of?"

"He is an immortal being who brings destruction and death as his companions."

"Impossible," cried Inni.

"I do not believe such a creature exists," gasped Pallin.

"Niala, perhaps I am simple-minded, but a god? A being named War who invokes violence? The only violence I have known has been at the hands of men." Inni clucked her tongue and shook her head.

Seire continued to laugh as the room full of girls turned in unison to stare at their table.

Jahmed stood up, clapping her hands. In a ringing tone, she addressed the long tables of wide-eyed young women. "The meal is ended. Hurry now, clear away the dishes and food and go to your next lesson. If you await one of us, then study, for there will be consequences for those who do not know today's work."

The girls scurried about in their rush to do as Jahmed instructed. Niala concealed a smile as she watched the solemn expressions on the youngest of the children, while the older ones cast curious glances back at the five women as they completed the cleaning of tables. The room was emptied within a matter of moments.

Niala felt the swell of pride as she watched the last to leave, a young woman called Ajah who herded the rest of the girls from the room. The little ones tugged at her sleeve, asking questions in shrill voices. Ajah gave gentle pushes to the girls while murmuring answers. The last they saw of her was a quick smile thrown back their way.

"Ajah is ready." Seire raised a palm to the ceiling.

"Ajah is ready for what?" Pallin leaned toward Seire.

"To be initiated."

"What does that mean?" Pallin's mouth fell open. "Are you planning to die?"

"Does it have to be death that leaves the door open? I have already told Niala."

"You have picked your replacement?" Inni frowned. "That is

not up to you to decide whether Ajah is truly ready."

"Stop, all of you." Jahmed snapped her fingers with impatience. "No one is dying and, for now, no other is to be initiated." She exchanged a glance with Niala, who continued to smile. "Let us return our focus to this vision Niala has had."

"Ah, yes, the one who comes down from the sky to bed you," snorted Inni. "The one you do not tell us about until he threatens us."

"There are many things that go unseen." Niala was undisturbed. "Here, we know only Gaea's grace and goodwill, but in other places there are beings that fulfill the worst nightmares of the mortal world."

Jahmed turned to Niala. "Though I have been with you for more years than I care to recall, I was not born here. I know there are other ways outside ours. I just do not see how he connects to us."

"You bedded this one?" Pallin nearly choked. "I can scarce believe it."

"It was a long time ago." Niala rubbed at a spot on the table. "A very long time ago."

"But now he seeks you out?" Twirling one braid, Jahmed stared at Niala with half-closed eyes. "I fear if he is angry, he will punish us."

"I do not know if he is angry. It is his nature to go where there is violence. Indeed, I cannot say if he brings violence or if it merely draws him. In my vision Najahmara was under attack." Niala twisted a small piece of bread between her fingers. "He watched just as I watched. He did nothing and I did nothing."

The terror relived itself and Niala shuddered as it flashed before her eyes.

"Tell us," Jahmed commanded.

"I cannot."

"Yes, Niala. Let us all hear of this fearful thing. Perhaps we can understand better what it is about."

With hesitation, Niala related the vision to them. Her voice was low, nearly inaudible as she told them in detail of the destruction. When she finished, Niala exhaled and added, "It seemed as though Najahmara was attacked, though I cannot be certain. I do not know what was meant by it all."

"It is a warning, to be certain," said Inni.

Jahmed pursed her lips. "A warning, yes, I agree. However, I wonder if it is not meant to say we have unrest within our own city. Niala, you know I speak the truth. We have had much disagreement of late."

"Yes." Inni nodded. "We have had many quarrels over land since those who came by sea joined us. We should not have let them stay."

"How could we not?" said Pallin. "We do not turn away those who would live amongst us. It would be against Gaea's will."

"Her will is that we live well and in peace." Inni's tone held a sharpness that brought a startled look to Pallin's face. "Those who have come to us of late do not understand that. Just yesterday I had to stop a fight over a basket of fish. Fish! There is more fish than any could ever eat and these two fought over a handful. I am sorry to say, it seems there is more of that every day."

"There." Pallin held up placating hands. "He is drawn to the quarrels in our city. We must stop the petty arguing and he will leave us in peace."

"Oh, indeed, let us stop fighting over fish and that will keep this god from our midst," snapped Inni. "I am certain that is all he wants of us."

"Shush." Jahmed thumped her fist on the table. "It may be Gaea warns us of some storm that is to come and all she can pluck from your thoughts is this being."

"Were you thinking of him?" Pallin bit her lip in concern.

"No." Niala was slow to answer. "Yes. I do not know, but a day does not go by that I do not think of him. Perhaps I invoked him myself."

"Perhaps." Seire spoke in strong voice. "Perhaps you call him here, perhaps you have need of him."

"No. No I do not."

All the women fell silent at the pointed tone of Niala's words.

"What does this do to our celebration?" Pallin hovered near Niala's shoulder.

"It does nothing to our gathering." Inni began to gather the dishes into a stack. "Why would it?"

"I just wondered."

It would be Pallin's first time to stand before the people as right hand to the goddess during ritual. She would hold space for Gaea while Niala called her into their midst. Pallin would act as her handmaiden while Gaea was with them. She was both frightened of her role and excited, wanting it more than anything else.

Pallin had seen it done many times over and she knew she was capable. Yet, she could not help her worry. What if she did not do it right? Would Gaea be angered? Would she be asked to leave the sisterhood?

Pallin rubbed her hands on her skirt and glanced at Niala. Niala smiled and said, "You will do fine, Pallin. You will make us all proud. The harvest celebration will go on as planned, for we have such abundance this year and we must thank Gaea for her generosity."

Standing, Niala addressed them all. "As for this vision, it will be clear soon enough. I can think no more of it, now, for there is much work to be done. I hear the drummers have already begun this afternoon's practice and that can only mean we need also to begin preparations."

Each woman nodded once and rose to help clear the table. As Seire hobbled past Niala, she whispered, "Do not be angry with me, Niala. I knew you would change your mind about telling them and they needed to know of this evil."

"Old woman, you overstepped your place."

"We must fight this together. You, alone, must not shoulder this burden."

"It is mine to bear. I do not want others harmed because of it."

"No one needs to be harmed. We will find a way to stop it."

"We do not yet know what comes our way, Seire."

"Whatever it is, we will stand together as we always have. And my hope is more will be revealed during the harvest offerings, if not before."

"Perhaps," Niala mused. "Perhaps Gaea will give us answers."

Inwardly, Niala was not so certain Gaea had an answer.

FOUR

"There she is. The rising up of the River Maendre, a sight glorious enough for even a god to feel humbled!" King Hattusilis leaned forward on his mount, the reins held tight between his hands. "She is magnificent, is she not?"

His gaze was riveted on a giant fountain of water shooting from deep inside the red cliffs before them. Midway up, it burst from the rocks with a roar, as if attempting to proclaim its greatness by imprisoning all other sounds within its own voice. Hattusilis shouted to be heard, glancing briefly at his companions before his gaze was drawn back to the thundering waterfall.

Telio, son of Hattusilis' sister, said, "Truly, Uncle, it is exactly as you said it would be. I have never seen anything that rivals the beauty of this place. Our own lands pale in comparison."

"She is the most beautiful thing I have ever seen. See how she arches with the grace of a bird in flight, leaving behind a mist as sweet as any fruit I have ever tasted." King Hattusilis followed the curve of water with his fingers, caressing the air as if he had dipped into the river itself.

Breathing deeply, he felt the kiss of light rain on his cheeks and the full flavor of the water on his tongue. "The Maendre, she is everything I have been told. Since a mere babe, I have heard stories of this very place, where water meets sky, where rain is created from rock and all the colors of the earth bow before the great river in greeting. I confess I did not think the Maendre truly existed, yet we stand at her birthplace and witness her entrance into the world."

"Uncle, I never doubted you would be able to find this place."

The other two men who rode with King Hattusilis shared a glance, for they both knew the game Telio played. He was young and filled with his own importance, chosen for this campaign only because of the blood ties he had with their king.

From the beginning, neither man carried respect for Telio and, thus far, their thoughts remained the same. When Hattusilis placed Telio second in command, they both shook their heads and went about the true art of war without him.

Telio nudged the taller of his companions with his boot and said, "You say nothing, Deimos. What do you think now of our king's quest? Are these not the most magnificent falls you have ever seen?"

Deimos shrugged and fought the temptation to knock Telio from his mount right into the blue-green pool at the base of the Maendre. Instead, Deimos concentrated on the indescribable uneasiness he had felt since their arrival in these lands. Watching the tower of water as it spewed from the crevice in the ridge, he again felt the shivering of the land beneath his feet.

Dismounting, Deimos stood very close to the edge. Nodding, he deliberately ignored Telio and answered Hattusilis, "Yes, Hattu, the Maendre is indeed a thing of beauty."

The fourth of their party was a grizzled man who had seen more campaigns than the king, having served Hattusilis' father before him. Zan's dislike of Telio went beyond compare, but as the king commanded, Zan obeyed. He merely grunted his response, knowing Telio cared nothing for his comments.

Zan had remained silent from the moment the four of them split from the army to trek up the side of the mountain for a view of the river they could only hear from the valley. The site of the great river was stunning, but Zan did not wish to encourage his King's ramblings. Already Hattu sounded like a boy at his first mating instead of the great warrior he was.

Hattusilis grinned with idiot pride. "I feel this land beckons me, it waits for my embrace - I shall spread the wings of my kingdom over her."

"All her riches will be ours." Telio's greed shone in his eyes. "And you shall be the most powerful king this land has ever seen."

Zan's snort rivaled the horses, but he covered it with a cough.

Deimos fell silent as a shudder crawled down his spine. Hattusilis was oblivious to their restraint, yet neither man was surprised.

Coming from the barren plains of the Steppelands, where only a few sheep and low scrub trees were to be seen, the Maendre river was nothing short of a miracle. Shades of green covered the descending walls of stone as vegetation flourished with the abundance of moisture, growing into a lush basin at the bottom.

The water spilled into a churning pool, eventually expelling into the riverbanks that wound away into the distance. From their perch on a rocky ledge midway up the waterfall, they could see coils of the river shining through the canopy of trees here and there like a giant serpent gliding across the countryside.

It was named Maendre for a reason. If they followed the path of the river as they planned, it would be a tiresome road, crisscrossing their own steps to keep with the waterway. As enamored of the Maendre as King Hattusilis was, Deimos knew it would be difficult to convince him to take a more direct route to their destination.

Shifting with restlessness born of a long journey, Deimos turned to Hattusilis. Deimos intended to point out the folly of Hattu's plan, only to realize Hattu had never stopped talking. He was droning on about the Maendre as if it were his lover, his eyes alight with adoration.

"I have heard this country described as a land of smiling waters, more favored by the skies than anywhere else in the world. Is that not what we see before us? Exactly that and more." Hattusilis dragged his gaze from the causeway to scan the descending valley.

"Already I hear the Maendre's laughter and see the flourishing of plant-life from just this small view. There is an entire land yet to be explored with an abundance of game to feed our men and clean water to drink. We should be comfortable in our travels and soon we will find Najahmara."

The beauty of the River Maendre could not be denied, but Deimos' thoughts were more of the wilderness they were about to enter. A vast area by all accounts, the region was divided by two mighty rivers, the Maendre and the Bayuk. For all the pretty pictures Hattusilis painted, in reality, the land was more treacherous than the high plains.

There might be fertile farmland and rich cities beyond the

woodland, but they first had to battle hillsides so thick with underbrush a man could be entangled and become food for the foraging beasts. Then there were the deep gorges cutting swaths across the valley. Once in their depths, there was no way out. A far cry from the magical land described by Hattusilis.

Deimos shrugged. Hattusilis knew of these things as well as he did, for the stories of traders who traveled from one sea to the other were filled with the perils of this land. It was Benor, a traveling trader who caught Hattu's attention. Benor's detailed descriptions of a city he called Najahmara had brought the grieving and withdrawn king into action.

After the death of Hattusilis' wife and child, he was frozen with sorrow. When a spark returned with new stories of Najahmara, he wished to take a campaign south. Not surprisingly, Hattusilis was supported by his tribune.

Yet the tribune had not witnessed the full extent of Hattu's obsession, Deimos thought, an obsession that grew on a daily basis. "Yes, Hattu, I must speak to you about Najahmara."

"….their Queen…." Hattusilis scarce paused for a breath, "…is said to be more radiant than the sun and her beauty rivals the finest jewels. Even the moon hides in shame in the face of this Queen." Hattusilis lowered his voice.

His next words were nearly lost in the rushing waters, "It is said she is not human at all, but a goddess in disguise. Perhaps even the mother goddess herself."

Deimos stared at him, a sudden chill raising the hairs on the back of his neck. Perhaps there was some truth to the trader Benor's foolish rambling, bespoken in the glowing voice of the king. Deimos had felt the disquiet from the moment he dismounted and now could put a name to the feeling: intrusion.

He should have known who called from the edges of his mind. The power of the earth goddess radiated all around them, beneath his feet, in the air he breathed and in the mist of the Maendre. This was her land they entered and they had not given her due respect.

He was surprised he did not recognize the power of the most ancient goddess of all, the one called Gaea. Listening closely, he waited for her voice to speak and heard nothing. Shaking his head, Deimos wondered if he was mistaken. Did he truly feel her power? Yet there, another tremor, as slight as a touch to a spider's web, unlike any other he had ever experienced.

"Hattu, there is more here than meets the eye. We must tread with care, for I feel Najahmara may not be what you think it is."

"What do you speak of, Deimos?"

"This is a dangerous land and much is hidden from us. Do not be so proud as to think it will fall into your hands."

"You have doubt of my skills as a leader?" Eyes narrowing, Hattusilis turned to Telio. "Is this true? Does he question me?"

"It appears so, Uncle." Telio smirked at Deimos. "He says he does not think we should invade these precious lands for fear of our lives."

Deimos cast his gaze to the ground and took a deep, steadying breath. Though he could not help the flare of temper that leapt up, he kept quiet. Telio was not a good influence, but he was the king's blood and Deimos dared not throttle him, though he wished for the thousandth time to do exactly that. He felt Zan shudder next to him and knew Zan picked up on his anger.

"We must go with caution into this land." Zan's voice was measured even though he did not know why he spoke thusly.

"You are afraid?" Telio mocked Zan as well, which brought a hidden smile to Deimos' lips. Zan would not hesitate to find Telio alone and beat him senseless.

"No," growled Zan. "I am not stupid. I beg your forgiveness, my king, although we have shared many campaigns together, I must agree with Deimos."

The scowl he cast toward Deimos made it clear he did not like it one bit. "Something is afoot in this land and we must be vigilant."

Hattusilis sat in silence for long moments watching the rainbow of colors from the spray of water as it descended into the river. "We will proceed with caution, but make no mistake, my word is final."

With this, he met each man's gaze and received a nod from each. "Good. Then let us make camp at the foot of the falls."

"There, my lord?" Deimos blinked, listening to the thundering of the waterfalls. They shouted now at each other to be heard; sleep would be next to impossible.

"Yes, there. We will have the splendor of the Maendre to sing to us."

"You mean we will have the noise to keep us awake." Deimos ignored the new flash of irritation that crossed Hattusilis' face.

Instead Deimos' gaze swept the skies. "There are several hours of daylight left, let us move further down the riverbank to a quieter, more level area." He paused to wipe the spray from his face. "And less damp place to pitch camp."

"Your King has spoken. Go set up camp," Telio sneered.

Hattusilis said nothing. He turned his mount and began the trek to the bottom of the ridge, shoulders tight and squared. His army waited there for his signal, restless and weary from riding since dawn.

Knowing they were close, Hattusilis pushed hard to arrive at the falls and knew, as a good commander, he should release the troops from their pain and allow a bit of play. Speaking for himself, he could not wait to shed hot leathers and sink into the waters of the Maendre, to wash away the stink from his body along with the haze of travel.

Hattusilis' former good mood did not return even though no one offered further challenge. Zan and Telio went about arranging the campsite, much to the relief of the men. Deimos spoke not at all, choosing instead to withdraw from the preparations.

After bathing, then eating the evening meal of flat bread, dried meat, and a handful of figs, Hattu lay in his tent alone with thoughts of Deimos running through his mind.

Though Telio was young, he was family. Hattusilis knew he gave Telio rank and privilege beyond his experience, but could not yet trust Telio in battle. He was happy the boy turned out to be a favorable captain, for he did whatever Hattu bid, and he was confident Telio would grow into his role.

But of late, each time Telio caught Hattu alone, he complained bitterly about Deimos. Hattusilis was disturbed by these comments. Telio said the men did not like Deimos nor did they trust him.

He said Deimos gave rise to their anxiety because he walked as if on air and made no sounds, appearing and disappearing so quietly even the beasts became agitated. Telio said the men were afraid of Deimos. During battle, his gaze seemed to cut through flesh causing terror and instant retreat without bloodying his weapon.

Hattusilis had not noticed such things in a skirmish. He saw only a great warrior who fought well and gave allegiance to his king. Still, Hattusilis could not help but wonder if his confidence in Deimos was misplaced.

Though Deimos was an outstanding commander, he was a strange one. And, after all, what did Hattusilis really know of Deimos? Without explanation, he had shown up beside Hattusilis during the bloody quelling of the cursed sand-dwellers, fighting boldly, but appearing more foreign than those they fought against.

Deimos went without a beard when it was unthinkable for any man to do so, and wore his black hair short, letting it lie in curls across his forehead and around his ears. He had deep-set brown eyes that were always guarded, often distant, as if his thoughts were roaming elsewhere. His nose was long and narrow, his lips thinner, his chin prominent. His skin was fairer than those of the Steppelands, but darker than the sand dwellers, and he towered far above the legions of men he fought beside.

Deimos talked neither of his homeland nor of any family and never indulged in drink or pointless conversation. If it was not about battle plans, he withdrew from the ranks to be alone. He played none of the idle games and took no interest in any of the women who followed the troops.

Hattusilis could not readily blame Deimos for that, however, for those women were a filthy lot, coarse and loud-mouthed, spreading their legs for any who would pay. Hattusilis stayed clear of them although he knew Telio sought them out on a regular basis. Hattu attempted to curb this behavior, for the women caused more than a few to die from jealous rages, yet Telio persisted and Hattusilis finally looked the other way.

He knew Deimos held nothing but scorn for Telio in return and, perhaps, that was the root of Telio's complaints. But there was some truth to it all. As with this night, Hattusilis had no doubt Deimos would wander off and not be seen again until they were ready to take up their journey. And where did he go? He would never say.

With an irritated snort, Hattusilis turned on his side. He did not care what Deimos did or did not do. It was time Telio learned to keep his thoughts to himself. They had arrived at the Maendre and, soon, they would find Najahmara and the queen he wanted so desperately to take as his own.

For that, Hattusilis decided, he would be willing to ride with a band of demons. Closing his eyes, he sought the refuge of sleep, though it did not easily come in the proximity of the incessant thundering of the falls.

Deimos did not wait for the vast legions of men to settle into their encampment before he slipped away. Though he was commanded to oversee a part of the army, he had no interest in it and left them to take care of their own comfort. His only thought was on the presence of the earth goddess he felt as soon as his feet touched the ground at the head of the Maendre Falls.

Gaea was long thought to be dormant, her energies lying at the root of all life, but uninvolved in the cycles of her children. This is what he was told and this is what he believed until now. Was it Gaea he felt? Deimos did not know for certain, only that the surge of energy at the falls was not caused by any being he had ever encountered before.

He escaped into the night, away from the stirrings of two thousand soldiers and the slaves who fed them, to better hear the sighing of the earth. Restive energy crawled up his spine as he sat at the pinnacle of the falls. Staring out over the basin, he watched the wandering lights from torches and the stationary fires marking the camps of the army below.

With no more than the shimmering starlight to keep him company, Deimos waited. He wanted Gaea to speak to him. Directly. With words or images. Appear to him, show herself to him. He called out to her, asking that she give him some proof of her wakefulness. Was it Gaea or the rumblings of another immortal who held the lands of Najahmara within her grasp?

'Why this land?' Deimos thought, as he idly tossed pebbles at the water. What was it about this land that brought Gaea into his awareness?

Before they reached the Maendre, the earth was as always, a respected solidness beneath his feet, but no more than that. He gave no thought to the spirit that dwelled within, for she was only a legend amongst his kind. An ancient being, who gave them life and then withdrew from it after her duty was fulfilled.

Those like his father and grandfather took for granted Gaea no longer was interested in the lives of either mortals or immortals. She birthed the races and then receded like the tides. Or so everyone thought. When Deimos felt the force beneath him, he knew it was Gaea, though she remained silent.

Power radiated out like fingers, dancing along his arms and legs, touching his face, tweaking his hair. He shivered as tiny bumps rose on his flesh, though he wore the heavy riding leathers and long sleeved shirt of the northern lands. He sat up straight and jerked his head from side to side, once turning to look over his shoulder. He saw no one, smelled no one.

As he turned back to stare over the encampment, he saw the small flames suddenly grow into rivers of fire flowing from the center as if an elemental spirit blew outward, sending its breath of flames rolling across the men. He heard shrieks of agony, heard the sizzle of flesh and smelled the charred remains of humans burned beyond recognition. With a shout, he leaped to his feet only to sway and nearly tumble into the Maendre.

Scuttling backwards, Deimos tripped over a root. He rolled and came to his feet again, gasping. As he swung back to look over the encampment, he saw the roaring flames were no longer there. All was quiet.

There was no shouting, no screaming, just the usual barks of laughter and bits of talk echoing up through the darkness. He squeezed his eyes shut and rubbed hard across his face before looking out once more.

The sprawling jumble of an army and its followers was spread out through the foliage near the banks of the River Maendre. The torches and campfires were once again flickering lights dotting the shores. As he stood balanced on the edge, eyes blinking rapidly. *Why? Why would I see such a thing?*

Was this Gaea's message?

"She sends a vision of terror." Deimos skin prickled with alarm, for he had no doubt she knew who he was. And why he was there.

But why did Gaea care?

Just as quickly, he knew the answer. Najahmara.

Of course.

There was something in Najahmara she protected.

As soon as this thought occurred to him, there was a calming sensation, as if the earth exhaled in relief.

"Gaea, I can offer you no help. I belong to War and carry out his will. I walk this land with a purpose."

An angry wind blew through the tops of the trees, whirling down to catch him unaware. It tore at his hair and clothing, howled in his ears and swooped down the side of the falls to cause flames to flare and then die.

Darkness fell all along the riverbanks as men clung to their bedrolls. Slaves struggled to calm the mounts, tents were overturned, and everywhere there was shouting. The wind came and went with unexplained rapidness. When it was gone, Deimos held up his hands, palms out.

"Peace, great mother." Deimos asked for an affirmation and he received it. He was now compelled to seek out Najahmara, out of courtesy to Gaea. To at least see what it was she kept there and what it was she did not want Hattusilis to destroy.

There was a fleeting moment when Deimos thought perhaps he should inform Ares of this discovery, of a place called Najahmara where Gaea's energy was strong. Clearly, there was more here than meets the eye.

In the end, he did not. Ares did not approve of Deimos' quest to understand human life. Deimos, himself, could not explain. The less spoken of his adventures in the mortal arena, the better.

And though Deimos was curious and not a little unsettled by Gaea's message, he kept it to himself. After all, she spoke to him, not to any of the Ages. She ignored them to the point they believed her dormant. Why should he tell them her secrets?

As if in agreement, the earth shimmied.

"I will do what I can, Gaea, this I swear to you."

Deimos began to search for Najahmara that night and discovered it was no easy task. From his stance above the Maendre, Deimos reached out for the peculiar pattern of contraction and expansion that happened when a human breathed. With each inhale, the energy was disturbed and with each exhale there was a mingling of mortal essence with the immortal world around them.

Najahmara was not the only existence in the lands they crossed. Each time Deimos found another isolated pocket of mortals, he grew excited, only to find they were no more than scattered tribal bands on the furthest edges.

People who made their homes wherever they stopped for the night. He would go and stand near their camps, scanning across the tattered tents and meager possessions until he assured himself they were not what he sought. Then he would reach out again until he found the next group.

Deimos moved from place to place with little effort. If he were asked how, he would say it was a matter of concentration. He could not do these things as a child. He walked where he wanted to go and dressed himself like any mortal. When he was young, he did not have the extra sense of energy that now allowed him to travel quickly, to be present in the mortal world or keep himself invisible to their eyes.

It was the same ability that let him bring forth something from nothing or, by the same token, make something go away. He realized early in his life that if he did not have this ability, he would never have choice.

Those immortals who did not become skilled in commanding their own desires never left their niches, whether that be forests, waterways, or the netherlands that could not be seen by mortal eyes. Deimos refused to be trapped. Therefore, he learned and he learned well.

His father called it arbitri, at one's will and pleasure.

"Have what you shall have, be where you shall be, but know it is by your own will and pleasure. No other can do it for you." Ares' words rang in his ears as surely as if he stood next to him.

Deimos twitched, glancing over his shoulder just in case that resonating voice was not his imagination. If Ares called, then Deimos must obey and return home to Athos, but he did not want to leave just yet.

There was much left for Deimos to discover about the world and his interest in Gaea and Najahmara had no bounds. Yes, he should advise Ares of Gaea. He should tell the Council of Ages she was active. He should. He knew he should. But he would not, for he wanted the moment to himself.

When at last Deimos found Najahmara, the sky hinted of daylight. He was on a dusty trail blazed along the top of a ridge with scrub bushes clustered on the very rim and thick grass growing down the rounded backside of the mount. Toward the city, it was steep and rocky, with small trees and thick brush speckled between boulders.

Deimos could see the path continue, angling downward until it reached the valley and the edge of a placid river. He knew it had to be the Bayuk, for the twisting Maendre emerged from the forest and wound through the valley until it reached the lake, pouring into it just as the same body of water swallowed the Bayuk.

On the other end, the path went on across the back of the ridge and wound down into the depths of a thick forest where it was lost from his sight. The forest was ominously dark and convex, with the boughs of the trees creating a thick canopy.

Across from him, but somewhat lower, was a long, wide plateau with five tall white stones arranged in a half-moon. He could feel the vibrations emanating from it from across the valley and knew he had indeed arrived at Najahmara. A large burned out area was in the center, a fire circle, but otherwise the plateau was clear.

It, too, gently sloped until it reached the shoreline of the lake. Three bridges crossed the Maendre, which narrowed considerably from the headwaters. One was near the forest, one led directly through the center of town to a sprawling building and the third was on the outskirts of the valley. Huts dotted the land, interspersed by patches of yellowing grains and dark green rows of trees. As living quarters spiraled inward toward the central building, huts became bigger, and closer together with squared corners. The rooftops were flat instead of made in the manner of the rude hay thatches.

Deimos guessed the odd-shaped building was a temple of sorts, neither pretty, nor grand. It was not decorated in any manner that would let him know who was honored, yet, he knew without being told, Gaea was resident.

He could see the first signs of life in curling wisps of smoke rising from cook fires along with a few people moving about as they prepared the morning meal.

He knew he should return to the encampment and at least pretend to have slept, but he was not yet ready to leave Najahmara. As the sun's rays began to seep over the top of the wooded area and lay across the blue-green waters of rivers and lake, it was as if the valley was encased in liquid light. Dew glittered like jewels on the grass, and the thick leaves of trees he could now see were loaded with either fruit or nuts.

The grain, nearly ready for harvest, took on a glowing red-gold appearance, like fire straight from the heart of the earth. The squat buildings, nondescript in the dark, were made of clay bricks interspersed with the same white stone that laced the side of the ridge that descended to the edge of the valley.

The center building, constructed in a rough semi-circle, continued to expand outward in layers of different materials. The combination gave it a somewhat scraggly appearance, haphazard, as if slapped together here and there whenever someone felt the need to grow. It was amusing and he found himself drawn to it. From this core place of Najahmara, he felt strong waves of energy flowing outward.

A thrill of excitement filled him. What if Gaea was embodied and resided there? No such thing had ever been suspected, or even taken as a serious thought. Gaea was the Earth. She did not take physical form as did all the others. Or she never had, to anyone's knowledge. Would not his father and all the Council of Ages be amazed at his discovery? Perhaps not pleased, Deimos thought, but still quite amazed.

Donning invisibility and with his gaze riveted upon the rounded building, Deimos took himself down into the city of Najahmara and straight to the entrance, but did not dare go inside. There were no doors, only an arched entrance that led into the dim depths of the building. No statues, no carvings, not even an urn decorated the front.

The entry was a simple open-arched doorway that jutted out from the rest of the building like an alcove. There were no stairs and was perhaps the width of two men lying end to end. The deep angles contained neat rows of plants, some flowering, some cut back to short stalks.

There were no windows or openings cut out other than that of the main entrance. Deimos could not see inside, though he longed to know what lie hidden within. Sorely tempted, Deimos started toward the doorway and then drew back into the shadows when he heard voices.

Two women emerged, one old and bent, drab with age and leaning on a staff; the other, tall and straight with bronzed skin and auburn hair in a long thick braid. The old one's eyes were blinded and she turned her head from side to side as she moved out onto the dirt path.

Deimos stared at the tall woman. In her, he glimpsed the energy that had drawn him to the doorway. Her aura was subtle, easing around her in a serpentine fashion, seen here, felt there, in an elusive sort of way. She did not project the immortal strength that others of his kind did, but it lay within her just the same.

Deimos could not decide what she was. He wanted to touch her, to see if by laying his fingertips on her skin, he could tell what energy lie veiled within her, yet he dared not show himself. Instead, he watched her with keen interest.

Her face was oval, with high cheekbones and slender brows over slightly tilted amber eyes. Her lips quirked upward and her chin was raised as if in defiance, which made Deimos smile. She appeared strong with squared shoulders. Though she wore an ankle length gown, the material could not disguise full breasts and rounded hips.

Her sure movements and graceful steps instantly captivated Deimos as she helped the elder one along the street. When she inclined her head down to speak to her companion, her voice was music to his ears. It lilted up and down with an amused undertone that made him quiver.

Deimos could not help himself. Following along behind them, he skirted the edges of the low buildings taking care he did not bump into those who emerged from their doorways to greet the two women.

Out of their conversation, Deimos learned their names. The old one was Seire Neval Zahava and the other, Niala Aaminah Zahava. Both were greeted with reverence and, in some cases, a bowing of heads. Both women responded with smiles, waves, and the occasional moment of exchange that happens between mortals: how are you, how are your children, your beasts, your possessions. Whatever was on their minds came out of their mouths.

To this, Deimos shrugged. He did not care how they fared. He listened only because it afforded him opportunity to hear Niala's voice again and again. He was left yearning to speak with her, to know who she was, or even what she was. Was she aware of the spark that resided in her?

Perhaps not. She seemed overly comfortable living as she did, within this mortal community, and he could not imagine such a life.

Deimos lived among the warriors, but when he felt stifled, he roamed about at night, entering the lives of other beings for entertainment. He was compelled by the desire to be close to humans, to understand the frailties that drove their behavior. He knew Ares did not understand this preoccupation with the mortal realm, yet Deimos could not turn away from humans.

Not yet.

Lost in thought, Deimos strayed in front of the two women, as they paused to speak with three tousled children gazing up at them with adoring eyes. He stood staring at them in a sudden fit of gloom and was startled to see Niala raise her head and smile at him. Turning, Deimos looked for the one who her smile was meant for.

There was no other. Deimos was alone on the path. Niala met his gaze, still smiling, though her eyes held a question. Deimos gave a quick nod in response and then ducked his head. With his heart pounding, he made a hasty retreat.

Niala Aaminah had seen him.

She should not have been able to see him, cloaked as he was from the human eye. As soon as he rounded a corner, he left Najahmara and returned to the encampment, but his mind was not on that of moving an army.

Deimos did not respond to the words of Zan or Telio and scarce answered Hattusilis. He could not stop thinking of Najahmara and the secrets within the heart of their priestess.

FIVE

"What is it, Niala?" Seire felt Niala's hand tighten on her arm. Seire felt Niala lean forward, her attention drawn away from the little ones hovering at her skirt.

The parents of the children continued with their exchange of pleasantries, unaware of Niala's distraction. Niala glanced at their calm and smiling faces and knew that no one except herself had seen the stranger on the roadway. Seire gave a polite nod to the folks and kept her confusion hidden behind a bland expression.

"It is nothing." Niala began to draw Seire away from the family with cheery, yet firm, goodbyes to all.

"If it is nothing, why are we consumed with haste?"

"There is someone I need to speak with."

The two women moved away as the family watched. Seire noticed the children did not follow along beside them, as children often did, but remained with their parents. No offense was taken, but there was a definite feeling of puzzlement behind them as Niala and Seire picked up their pace along the path.

Hobbling as fast as she could, Seire finally huffed, "If it is nothing, why then must we race as fast as we can to the bridge?"

With a chuckle, Niala stopped. Her stride was long and, next to Seire's wizened frame, she seemed to be running. Niala could have left Seire with the family and alone pursued the man, but did not think of it. Now Niala realized she fair dragged the old woman, who was gasping and holding her staff in a death grip.

"I beg your forgiveness, Seire. There was someone I did not

recognize and I wished to catch up with him to find out his name."

"Of late, there seems to be many new people in Najahmara," Seire complained. "I am told they make their way along the Bayuk from the sea, though I wish they did not."

"Yes, there are new ones, but this one." Niala paused, her gaze wandering over the few men who stood outside their homes along with the handful of women and children beginning the routine of meal preparation.

Najahmara was rising with the sun still hidden behind the ridge to the east. All that could be seen were streaks of pink and purple as the sky brightened. Very soon, the sun would be above the rim of the valley and the day would be in full force.

"Had it been lighter, I might have known who it was, but as it is, there were too many shadows."

"Why do you worry so about one man? He will show himself again, I have no doubt."

"Perhaps," Niala murmured, certain now she had lost him. "But there was something different about this one."

"Not him?" Seire lifted her face toward Niala, concern creasing her forehead. "Not that beast?"

"No." Though Niala used a soothing tone, her chest constricted, for that was exactly it. The man she saw reminded her of Ares the Destroyer. It was not he, could not be, for Ares would not have turned heel and strode away.

"No, though for a moment his eyes were familiar." Niala shook her head. "It was the early morning light playing tricks. This man was slimmer built, tall enough but his hair was short. He had no beard."

"But did you not say this Ares is a god? Must he always appear the same? What if he disguised himself?"

"I had not considered such a thing, for he never changed during my time with him."

Seire reached for Niala's hand. She found Niala's fingers lax and cold though the heat of the morning was growing.

They had not spoken of Ares since the night of the vision, though Niala knew each woman waited with undisguised eagerness for her to say more. She knew they hoped to find out what happened to her and why this god would seek her out, even after so many years were past.

Niala rebuffed their hints, convinced there was naught they

could do about it. If there was to be war, they had no way to protect themselves. If War came for her, then discussion would serve no purpose. Seire was the only one who pressed her on the subject. It did not escape Niala's notice that at every opportunity, Seire threw out a hook, hoping to catch Niala unaware.

Wicked old woman, Niala thought. *I should tell her nothing.* But the words fought to spill out, as if Ares demanded her consideration, in thought, in action, even in her dreams. It was just a matter of time before he found her.

A small voice in her head said, *His feet are already set upon the path to your door.*

All Niala could hope for now was that Ares' retribution would be swift and directed only at her, and Najahmara would be safe. She shrugged away the thought, refusing to linger on what might be.

"What sort of things do the gods talk about?" Seire prodded. "As a mere mortal, I am curious. What would they have to say? Do they converse with each other? They do not speak to us."

With a long-suffering sigh, Niala nodded. "There were times when Ares' talk seemed endless. Other times, he did not speak for days."

She grew still as she recalled how his black eyes would bore into her while he waited for a response, how he would not look away until she spoke. "As to each other, I could not say, for there were no other immortals at his fortress. There was only one visitor."

With a sudden exhale Niala recalled the night a young man entered Ares' chambers with an abruptness that bespoke of familiarity.

The hair rose on Niala's neck the moment the youth stalked into the sleeping quarters, such was the power of his presence. He scarce gave her a glance before he addressed Ares in an angry undertone.

The young man looked very much like Ares, with the same fierce eyes and dark brows, the same long, straight nose and curl to his lip. His stance mocked Ares, though it did not appear deliberate. It was the same coiled energy that held him square and rigid, with his jaw thrust out and his gaze locked on that of Ares.

With no more than a silent exchange, the two retired to the sitting room. The thick double doors closed behind them and only muffled tones were audible. Niala huddled beneath the blankets, quaking, until she fell into sleep.

Ares never told her the young man's name. She assumed he was mortal, a warrior, perhaps a servant, though he did not behave as such. The youth entered through the doorway, unlike Ares who merely appeared within the chamber.

And yet, there was too much arrogance displayed by the bold entry to be a mere servant and, even in the unspoken exchange, there was a distinct challenge that would have earned death for a mortal.

Niala had seen the young one no more and eventually forgot about him, having more pressing thoughts to concern her.

That was it. This was the same one, the one who stood before her today. He was clean-shaven now, his hair cropped short, but yes, even in the dull light of early morning, she was certain he was the one.

"He was not mortal," Niala murmured. "Of course he was not mortal - how was I to know? All I saw were filthy warriors in the lower regions. But he was none of that. Not coarse nor crude, but handsome, terrifying, just like...."

"What do you babble about?" Seire clung to Niala's arm, chastising her. "People will wonder if you have lost your sense."

"What?" Niala blinked and looked down at Seire. "Why?"

"You talk too much to yourself and I feel the breeze from your hands flapping in the air."

"They will think I am speaking to you."

"Will they? And if I wandered away while you carry on? You would not notice."

To this, Niala could not disagree. "Come, Seire, let us go home. I must think about this."

"What does this mean?"

"The man I saw belongs to Ares the Destroyer."

"The man just now?" The old woman's voice rose to a shrill note. "The one who stared at you?"

"That one, yes. He belongs to Ares' realm. I have seen him before, there in the fortress."

"How do you mean, he belongs to Ares?"

Smoothing her braid, Niala watched the roadway, looking for

another glimpse of the young man. "I do not know for certain, but he appears very much like Ares and I have seen him before."

Niala stopped, mouth slightly open as she thought she caught sight of him again, slipping around the corner between dwellings. It was no more than her imagination and a hound that cast a long shadow.

Startled, Niala drew in a quick breath. Hounds. She had forgotten about the hounds. Every night, she heard their vicious snapping as they snarled and growled and fought over prey. They always sounded as if they were right outside the doors, yet they could not have been in the upper reaches. She never laid eyes upon them, but they were always there with their demented howling.

Ares said they were his beasts, these hounds, and not of the mundane world. They were creatures of darkness and did only his bidding.

Do not leave these walls, he told her, for they will tear you to shreds if they find you. Furthermore, I cannot stop them once they have tasted your blood.

Niala shrieked as a dog bounded up to them, its tongue lolling from its mouth. It sniffed once, gave a friendly lick, then ran off leaving Niala to cover her mouth with a trembling hand.

"Niala, what has come over you? Surely you are not afraid of that idiot hound?"

"No, no, not that one." As she glanced behind them she saw only the back end of the dog with its waving tail. With a sigh, she chuckled at her own silliness. Had she ever seen Ares' beasts? No. For all she knew, they did not exist and had been a trick to hold her within the austere walls of Athos.

"This man, do you see him still?" Seire tugged on Niala's sleeve.

They had taken the next turn to circle back towards the temple and were greeted more often as people emerged from their homes. Niala allowed only a cursory greeting as they kept moving but tried not to rush Seire so much that the old one would become winded, or worse, fall and cause herself injury.

"No, I have not seen him again. He disappeared with the wind. Perhaps he was not there at all."

"Do you think it was a vision?" Seire wheezed. Much to her relief, they approached the temple where she could feel the change in the energy of the ground beneath her feet. The temple sat on a slight rise and the closer they drew to the doorway, the more the dirt path became imbedded with flat rock.

"A vision?" Niala stopped dead in her tracks, jerking Seire backwards. The old one tottered and would have tumbled over if Niala had not caught her and stood her on her feet, all the while recalling the moment she had first seen the young man.

Indignant, Seire slapped Niala's hands away. "I have said I am fading and perhaps another should take my place. I have not said I am ready to die."

"What?" Niala blinked and studied Seire's careworn, brown face. "Forgive me, dearest. I did not intend to cause you harm."

"Well, you have not yet, but if you keep this up, you will no doubt drop me off a cliff and forget that you ever had me with you!"

Clasping Seire in a fierce hug, Niala said, "Never. I will not lose you. What would I do without you?"

"Ahh, I see how it is, without me, you are nothing," Seire laughed. "And, so, if I am indeed your guide, tell me about this man. How did you know who he was? And if he is a vision, what does it mean?"

"You are not far from the truth, you wretched old woman." Niala released her and they both headed into the temple. "I do not know his name, for I only saw him once."

"You did not ask his name?"

"There were many things I did not ask," Niala said. "And as to this being a vision? No, I think not. A vision does not behave with surprise when noticed."

"I suppose not," Seire mused. "Though I have never been blessed with this sight you have."

"It is far from a blessing and, in truth, this one was vastly different from any other. Though I have been up to the plateau every night since I saw the vision, I have yet to have another."

They made their way through the narrow maze of corridors into the main temple room. It was simply furnished with mats and a few cushions scattered before a center altar. Anyone could enter and sit before the image of Gaea and Kulika, her consort, and ponder the ways of the world. There were no restrictions, for it had been built to honor their goddess and all were welcome, however, Niala was happy to see they were alone.

The room held an air of serenity, of goodwill and great

compassion. There was none that entered who did not feel cleansed when they left. Through her stone eyes, Gaea witnessed countless confessions and floods of remorse, she saw the resolution of conflicts and pain. By the same token, her tranquil face smiled down upon the joy of new loves and new life, always blessing the bounty and fulfillment of their days.

Kulika, the Blue Serpent, wound around Gaea's feet with head lifted and gaze unwavering. He was the image of protective vigilance, always watching out for the good folk of Najahmara and for his beloved Earth.

"Niala, I do not know if it is wise for you to sit up on the plateau for so many hours into the night like you have. Do not think you move about in secret, for we all know when you return from the ridge."

"I hoped I did not disturb you," Niala murmured. They both settled onto cushions for a moment's rest, though only for a moment, for soon they would be called to the morning meal.

They could hear the faint sounds of kitchen work being done as they gave a silent thank you to those who fed them.

"I also hoped Gaea would tell me more, but alas, she has not. She comes as she always does, eager to be with me, but it is a communion of spirit. She says no more of him and behaves as if she has no more concerns. It is a very odd thing, Seire. I am most puzzled by Gaea's behavior."

"Can we hope this danger has passed? If Gaea says no more?"

"She seems pleased with herself," Niala went on as if Seire had not spoken. "She comes to me with a light heart and truly, the hours pass and I am not even aware of it."

"But this man, you are certain it is not Ares?"

"There is no mistaking Ares, when once you have…." Niala flushed. "…when you have known him. He is like no other."

"Why does he want you, Niala? It is a simple question that deserves a simple answer. If he threatens our well-being, and you are that to us, then I must know why."

Niala knew Seire spoke the truth. "I could say that what Ares has once possessed, remains his forever, but it is a much more complicated matter than mere control."

Staring up at Gaea's image, Niala's voice softened. "Seire, do you believe we live again and again?"

"What do you mean?"

"That we have many lives and this is just one of those many lives."

"Hmm." The old woman stroked her chin. "I would say yes. Is that not Earth's way? Everything dies and everything grows again. The leaves fall, the grasses retreat, the plants curl up - even the insects and animals have their time here and then are gone. Eat a grape and throw out its seed, and more grapes appear. It is so with everything. Why not us?"

"But a leaf, a plant, a grape, they know they are grapes, they remember they are grapes. We know only what we learn as we grow, we do not remember what we were before, what shape or size or color. We know only now. If we lived before, should we not recall what we were?"

"We evidently know what we are, for we do not suddenly become a fish or a goat or a grape." Seire smiled. "But why do you ask this?"

"Because it is why Ares seeks me." Shifting with a sudden restlessness, Niala cursed. "He believes I am another."

Seire jerked her head towards Niala, mouth open with surprise. "Another? What other?"

"Another being. It is difficult to explain for I was very young and could not grasp the meaning of his stories. In truth, I thought he made them up to scare me, but then he would become angry when I denied his words."

"Why did he believe this? Surely, he could point to something that led him to this door?"

"He said it was because I found my way to him. Impossibly so. I should have been dead a thousand times over, but was not. The Fates brought me to him."

"Impossible as it was, you survived the journey. I would call it more of a miracle than a gift from the Fates."

Niala plucked at the loose edge on one cushion, her gaze wandering about the room. She found comfort in the familiarity of it all, in the common aspect of her daily life, in the routines that took up her time and created the fabric of her existence. It was through this reflection she knew herself and not through the eyes of a god.

"He said he could see into my spirit - see the spark of this other one hidden inside me. He called her name so often, I began to wonder if I was, indeed, this Ilya. He wanted me to remember her, but he refused to tell me why it was so important."

Niala heard the rumble of Ares' rich voice, strained with lovemaking, cracking under the burden of an unwanted emotion, when even War was vulnerable. She heard him say 'Ilya, why do you torment me so? Have I not paid enough even yet?"

Only then did his arrogance fall away and the mantel of War slide down to expose the anguish. He would lie beside her in the great bed in an aching silence that reached into her very depths. She would curl up at his side, as close to him as she could get, to share in that brief moment of humanness. She remembered his scent, the smoothness of his skin, and the heat of his body pressed against hers.

She would have given anything to be able to answer him as Ilya, to soothe his heart wounds, to say whatever he had done was forgiven. But she could not, for she did not understand.

With a slight wave of her hand, Niala made as if to wipe away the image, for she, too, had become vulnerable under this spell. She fell in love with him. Under this aspect, she could have remained there with him for the rest of her life.

But all too soon, he would rise from their bed and assume the mask that set him apart from the rest of the world. His fury would erupt and he would shout that she knew the truth. He would accuse her of denying him out of spite. And then, he would storm from the fortress, leaving her all alone. It was his punishment for not remembering. Cruel, hateful punishment.

"Niala?" Seire squeezed Niala's fingers.

Shaking her head, Niala grunted. "What? What was I saying?"

"That he called to her often."

"Yes, yes, he called her name and I could not answer the way he wanted. It made him angry and that was his undoing."

Straightening her shoulders, Niala pulled her hand free from Seire to jab at the air in front of them.

"He would go away for lengthy periods and leave me alone in his fortress. As you know, I am not one to languish. I could not sit quietly within those walls.

"I spent a great deal of time in a courtyard that opened from the sleeping chamber. It overlooked cliffs that fell straight down, and, in truth, I thought often of throwing myself over the side onto the sharp rocks. Instead, I would stare for hours at the sea.

"I was entranced, for I had never seen so much water. It went so far, it met the sky. If I watched long enough, I was sure to see sailing ships creep over the horizon and sail into the port at the foot of the mountain. They looked like giant birds flying low across the water, these ships.

"Soon enough, I began to explore the fortress and, eventually, I found a door that led outside without going through the warriors' chambers."

Niala paused and chewed at a fingernail as she thought of both the fear and excitement of once again stepping out of the shadow of that dismal, gray castle.

"I wish you had known me then, for I was very bold. I thought Ares would surely kill me if he caught me, but I no longer cared. I stole a warrior's beast and rode down the mount. Though it was a long ride, it went quickly. Those I passed paid no attention to me, for their eyes were set upon their goal at the top of the mountain and I was of no consequence to them.

"I do not think I intended to return. Indeed, I had not thought of it. I made my way to the wharves and slept there in any wretched corner until I was too hungry and cold to think straight. Then I became terrified Ares would do worse than kill me, that his punishment would be greater than I could bear."

"So you went back."

"Yes. But he never guessed what I had done. The next time he left, I went again to the bottom, into the town and sat on the wharves, dreaming of my escape. It was there I met the woman who would steal me away from Ares."

"Ahhh," sighed Seire. "It could be no other than companion."

"Layla." Niala spoke her name with longing. "A woman so filled with courage she would risk herself to take me from a god. His revenge would have been merciless had he ever found us and Layla knew it, but she did not care. We were together many years and I was happy with her."

Niala touched her fingertips to her forehead. "I have lost so many I loved, Seire, and still I breathe."

"By the grace of Gaea you are still with us."

"Yes, but I have come to realize over these many years that Ares was right. I have lived before and have accepted that this Ilya Ares spoke of is, indeed, part of me.

"During my years of training to be a priestess, I spent much time in deep meditation and received visions from Gaea. I asked to understand the deeper meaning of Ilya. Who is she? Why does Ares seek her? What has she done to invoke such passion?

"The answer came to me quite a long time ago and it was simple: she is my core essence, the piece of me that moves between lives. Ilya was my name during my first existence.

"We all have such a spirit, Seire, though most do not recognize it. To this day, I do not understand what transpired between Ilya and Ares - and he says he did not go by that name then - but I fear he is also right when he says I belong to his world instead of this one."

"Never," said Seire. "You belong to us, to Gaea. And if he comes, we will fight him."

Laughing, Niala hugged Seire. "Yes, we shall fight him. Listen, there is the bell calling us to our morning meal. Let us put aside these morbid thoughts and join the others."

SIX

"This worthless piece of flea-bitten filth!" Telio kicked the curled edge of a dried piece of hide with his booted toe. Small crude marks were burned into the leather indicating the flow of the Maendre and at the point where it entered the village. "When I return to Ankira, I will have Benor beheaded for this bag of lies."

"No, you will not." Hattusilis spoke in flat dismissal, without even a glance at his nephew. He crouched over the map, carefully smoothing the corner where it flopped over.

"We are close to the Najahmara Valley, I know it. See here." His finger traced the winding path of the river and then stabbed at one stained spot. "We passed this mark days ago. Did you not notice that flat rise to the east?"

"I saw nothing but more trees, more brush, more vines, more cursed flying things." Telio ran his fingers over the ugly welts and specks of dried blood on his face. The back of his hand was splotched with blisters and drying scabs.

"Then you pay no attention. You would have us hopelessly lost, were you in charge." Hattusilis scratched at a fresh insect bite.

"And we are not?"

"You may be lost. I am not." Irritation coated his words.

Deimos sat on his heels as he watched an ugly flush spread across Telio's face. Their gazes met and Telio's resentment roiled out towards him in a nearly visible wave. Ignoring him, Deimos stared down at the bit of map.

"I believe we are near this point." Deimos traced a forefinger along the river, considerably past where Hattusilis had shown the flat-topped ridge.

"Perhaps we have miscalculated our path." Zan frowned at the map. "We may even have passed by Najahmara and not realized it."

"The Maendre still flows by our side. We have not yet come to the Bayuk," Hattusilis answered with stubborn resolve.

"The story of this valley may be fallacy, my king. We have traveled long and hard and have yet to see any sign of it." Zan shaded his eyes as he stared off at the rough landscape.

"It is out there, I know it is!" Rising to his feet, Hattusilis began to pace. "In all accounts of the city, the Bayuk and the Maendre come together. We have not yet found the Bayuk, therefore, we have not yet passed Najahmara. She is out there waiting."

"We may well reach the sea before we find this place," Zan replied.

"And if we do, then we will backtrack," answered Hattusilis.

"I tell you, we are lost." Telio slapped his palm against his leg. "Benor has lied to us."

"No, we are not lost." Deimos spoke with quiet confidence. "Najahmara cannot be more than a fortnight away."

"How do you know that?" Telio stared at Deimos. The younger man sweated profusely in the heavy wool and riding leathers of the Steppelands, but refused to remove even the outside vest because of the thick swarms of stinging, biting insects. Now he yanked at the collar of his shirt and swore, as yet another insect lit upon his hand. With great show, he crushed it between his fingers.

"Here is the distance between this ridge and the valley." Deimos held thumb and forefinger together. "It is this far. We have already traveled from here...." He pointed at the Maendre Falls. "...to here. See for yourself. Unless we run into hostile tribes that ambush us, we should arrive there in far less time than it took to get here."

Hattusilis rubbed his bearded chin. "Yes, I believe you are right. In that case, we are very close, though I wonder why none of the scouts have yet returned."

"Most likely because they have been swallowed up by this cursed land," snarled Telio.

"Connal will return." Zan had not the slightest flicker of concern. "Connal could find his way back from the fires of the underworld if given the chance."

"You would say that, he is your brother. Yet I believe he is either dead or he has joined the ranks of this Najahmara so he does not have to crawl through this land again."

"Connal is loyal to our king; he will return." Zan's weathered face closed and only the squint of his eyes showed the malice he held for the king's nephew. His big, square hands flexed at Telio's cocked brow. Zan unfolded his legs and prepared to stand up.

"Enough." Hattusilis held up his palm. "I will have no quarrelling. Connal will return. He has never failed me. Then we shall know exactly where we are and how far Najahmara is from us. We shall know the level of protection on Najahmara and what we need do to capture her."

Deimos remained silent during their exchange, but now he spoke with care. "I am given to understand that Najahmara is a farming community. They have no real protection."

"All the better," began Hattusilis.

"How would you know that?" Telio interrupted. "We cannot even find this place, let alone understand what defenses they have. It sounds as though you have a better knowledge of this city than you should."

"Yes, how would you know that?" Zan stared at Deimos, for though he disliked Telio, he bore a deeper distrust of Deimos.

Deimos looked at each man, at the sudden wariness reflected in degrees upon their faces. How best to say what he knew?

He could not tell them that each evening he went to Najahmara and spent countless hours watching those who lived in the city. That he walked their streets while they slept and stayed until well after dawn to see them begin their day. He could not say he had already seen the land surrounding the valley and he knew the best method for invasion. And he would not tell them where Connal was, though he knew that as well.

With a bland expression, Deimos waved one hand. "Benor told me."

"The trader?" Zan blinked.

"Of course," Hattusilis shrugged. "He said as much to me. However, he did not say there was no army, only that they were a rich community with an abundance of goods to bargain. I would find it difficult to believe such a place would not have an army to protect their queen."

"Benor did not indicate to me there was such a queen," Deimos avoided looking at the men for fear the truth would be reflected in his eyes.

"Then you did not listen well enough, for he told me a tale of a beautiful woman with immense powers. Indeed, he was frightened of her, for he said she could look right through him and know his intentions. He meant to cheat them, but thought again and dealt fairly."

It was, of course, Niala Aaminah of which Benor spoke, Deimos thought. She was the reason he returned to Najahmara night after night in the hopes of seeing her again. And he did, for he often found her before the five white stones, sitting in silent meditation well into the late hours.

He watched her until she stirred, looking over her shoulder, sensing he was there. Then he was even more careful to keep his presence shielded so she could not see him. He desperately wanted to speak to her, to have her acknowledge him, yet it was his own nature that thwarted him.

Being the God of Terror was a double-edged blade: to be truly seen, his darkest side would be revealed. Unveiled, Terror could drive a mortal to madness and death. Fully clothed in his power, destruction was inevitable.

He could not bear to have Niala Aaminah flee from him.

"And he called this woman a queen?" Deimos asked.

"To me, he described a simple priestess."

"How could that be?" snorted Telio. "A dirty, ragged priestess brought fear to a grown man's heart? As I have already said, Benor is a liar. Uncle, I would not trust this information."

Hattusilis crossed his arms over his chest and glared at them all. "Queen or Priestess, she is the key. Once taken, the city will fall. As soon as Connal returns, gather up my captains, for it will be time to begin planning."

Without a backward glance, Hattusilis took his leave. After a moment of uncomfortable silence, Telio rolled up the map and stuffed it in his belt. His parting comment to Zan and Deimos was, "Be ready."

That night, Deimos slipped away to Najahmara with the words, 'Be ready,' still uppermost in his thoughts. As he stood on the ridge watching the activity below, he wondered if Najahmara would be ready for invasion.

How could they not know it hovered on their horizon like a brewing storm, a black maw ready to swallow them whole? Unlike others, Najahmara seemed oblivious to the possibility. Even the most remote tribes, the most primitive peoples, kept watch for predators. Yet, Najahmara went about unconcerned.

Deimos could not warn them, for he was a minion of War, dedicated to the awful throne that held power through devastation. Though he had regret for these gentle folk, his loyalty lay in the realm of his father.

"There are worse things than Hattusilis," Deimos said to the darkening moon, as if she chided his callousness. "Hattu is a fair man. There will be little death at his hand if they refrain from fighting back."

But mortals were unpredictable. That was why he could not resist their world. Just when Deimos thought there could be nothing further to learn, a mortal would surprise him by striking back. Each moment in a human life seemed fraught with the ever-changing desire of what it was they truly wanted. Deimos was mystified by the actions that came from these same desires, regardless of consequence.

He wanted to feel what they felt. He wanted to know the utter joy of living and the pain of death. He wanted to be one of them. But he was not.

He was Terror.

He held forth the torch of blood and bone to let humans see the true face of their every fear in his light.

He was what he was and could not change that, but the bitter longing in his heart was acknowledged by his very presence on the ridge. He was obsessed with a village that would soon be dismantled, if not destroyed. What, then, of the people? What would they do when Hattusilis rode in?

By the light of the crescent moon suspended just above the tree line, Deimos could barely see out across the valley, past the glittering waters of the lake and the shining ribbons of the Maendre and the Bayuk. The harvesting had begun.

With swift labor, many fields were already shorn of their bounty, left only with stubble marking where the tall stalks had been. Fruits and vegetables had been gathered, and clearly all who were able worked late into the night to prepare and store the food.

Najahmara was a beehive of activity which Deimos watched with even greater curiosity. There seemed to be a constant flow of people along a lane on the opposite side of the valley. An evenly spaced row of small oil lamps gave clear view of the narrow path that, from a distance, looked like the scales of a giant serpent wending his way up to the dark hole of his lair.

Deimos squinted, for the wavering light of the lamps distorted his view. He had not noticed such an opening before. Surely, there it was, the entrance to a cave midway up the ridge. People carried large baskets of vegetables and grain into its depths then emerged with empty containers. A constant stream of people brought more baskets filled with the next cache.

He could not resist the temptation to see the cave more closely. As his feet touched the earth before the opening, he felt the pull of the earth goddess. What were mere rumblings in his head erupted into roaring. Gaea slammed into his consciousness without words. She came into him with a swirling arc of color that brought him to his knees. Hooking into his energy, Gaea hoisted herself onto his back, buzzing into his ears, boring into his eyes, and burrowing into his soul.

He saw for the first time the creation of the earth - the heaving ground that spit forth the mountains, the raging waters that carved oceans and rivers, the fecund greenery and arid deserts. He witnessed the birth of his own race, the stewardship given to them in a time when no other would accept it.

He saw mortals come and go, flesh ripe and round like the harvested fruits, decline, then lie dead and decayed, melting back into the soil. He saw the cycle of life repeated over and over, saw it as if he were Gaea.

It flashed over him within a split second, sparking upward until he gasped, and then it fell away. Deimos staggered to his feet, breathing hard. As he lifted his head, he saw the priestess Niala Aaminah moving toward him, a basket in her arms. Willing himself back into the shadow of a tree, he grew as still as the wood itself and watched her enter the cave.

She emerged a few minutes later free of her burden, swinging the basket. She stopped for a moment, glancing around and behind her, toward the mouth of the cave, scanning the area with a perplexed expression on her face.

With a small shrug, she set the basket down and began to climb higher on the uneven path until she reached the summit of the plateau. Deimos followed, taking care that she did not hear his step.

The five stones glowed as if with an inner light, their shadows casting long fingers across the ground. Niala strode across the grassy circle to gaze at them. She did not sit cross-legged on the ground, but remained upright, her head tilted back. Deimos lingered near the fire circle, watching her.

She stood thusly for a very long time and then spoke without turning. "What is your name?"

Startled, Deimos thought to flee but instead answered, "Deimos."

"Why do you stand behind me and gawk? Do you not realize how ill-mannered that is?"

"I am sorry, my lady, forgive me."

"Do not stay in the shadows." Niala Aaminah beckoned to him, still without turning. "Come here, where I can see you."

"I should leave you to your peace, instead, my lady."

"I prefer that you join me rather than follow me in silence."

What compelled him to walk forward, Deimos did not know, but he could not refuse her. When he stood by her side, she turned toward him, her gaze traveling from head to toe and back to linger on his face. "Deimos?"

"Yes." His heart beat faster.

"Why are you here?" Niala's voice held no fear.

"I am curious."

"Of me or a larger mystery?"

"Both." Deimos shifted. "How is it you can see me?"

"How can I not? You loom large and your energy is bright. I have always seen you."

"And you said nothing until now?"

"I waited for you to speak." Niala Aaminah smiled. "Or perhaps, I waited for you to strike me down or carry me away."

"That is not my purpose, though...."

He bit back the rest of his words. He would not tell her of Hattusilis and his army. What was to happen was already woven into the fabric of life by the Fates. He could not change the outcome. "Tell me, priestess, are you a goddess in disguise or a mortal with extraordinary power? I did not wish to show myself to you, yet you can see beyond my mask."

Niala Aaminah turned away from him to stare at the five white stones. When she spoke it was with a measured voice. "I am neither, Deimos. Neither this world nor that."

"Sometimes it is so for me as well." Deimos reached out as if to touch her, but let his hand fall back to his side.

Niala turned to face him, half in shadow, half exposed. Her expression was fierce. "But I choose this world."

"And I have no choice." Deimos spoke with deep regret. "I am not human and the differences between our races widen the understanding between us. My home is beyond mortal sight, but Earth connects us. We are linked one way or the other, Niala Aaminah, but there is a spark in you I do not see in others."

"It is my priestess work and my connection to Gaea that lends me my strength. Without it, I would have no more light than the others."

"I do not believe you."

With an impatient wave, Niala retreated, going further into the shadows. "Why do you come here? Do you bring some terrible injustice down upon our heads?"

"Injustice?" Deimos pondered that word for a moment. Was it an injustice for Hattusilis to want Najahmara for his own? Deimos did not think so.

"Do you bring War?" Niala Aaminah's voice quivered.

"War?" Did she mean the invasion or did she speak of his father?

"Do not mock me. You have followed in my footsteps, you have watched and said nothing." She stepped before him, out of obscurity. "Why are you here? Do you bring War to me?"

Terror flared between them. Deimos felt her draw it out of him, capturing it in those few words. He heard the anguish of exile and deep longing for a lover. He heard loneliness and despair, hidden passions and self-hatred. He heard both pleading and denial. He heard himself.

He knew Niala Aaminah did not speak of the armies camped within a few days from her city. Niala Aaminah spoke of Ares.

"Do you want me to bring him to you?"

Her lips parted and he could hear her soft inhalation, dark desire trembling on the tip of her tongue. When she spoke, it was with a breathlessness that hinted of secrets.

"No."

Denial had won. She licked her lips and rubbed her forehead with her hand. "Yet you are of his house and you will do his bidding."

"If he inquires, I must reveal all to him."

Niala Aaminah inclined her head in acknowledgement and they fell silent for a moment.

"Tell me, priestess, what do your people do within the cave?"

Pulled from some timeless reverie, Niala Aaminah blinked. "They store food deep in the recesses where it is cool and dry. They prepare for our harvest celebration. A ritual to honor Gaea and the bounty of her body."

"Gaea. Yes, I have felt her presence. We thought she slept."

"Then you did not listen, for she is awake and with us."

"I have discovered as much."

Another long silence and Niala Aaminah spoke again. "She requests you attend her ritual."

"What?" Deimos looked up at the five stones. "She speaks to you?"

"In her own way. She speaks to me and she speaks through me. She wants you to come and honor her."

Nameless fear tightened his gut and he did not know where it came from. Gaea, the most ancient one, mother of them all, requested his presence. "And if I cannot?"

"It is your choice. When the harvest is complete, we will celebrate. You will know when. All you have to do is join us."

Deimos shrugged, an outward signal that he heard, but inwardly, he could not help but wonder why Gaea would want Terror at her honoring. He needed time to think before he gave Niala Aaminah, or Gaea, an answer.

"I will go now, leaving you and your goddess in peace." He fled back to his army then, and left her staring out into the darkness, her back to the five stones.

******

The slow, torturous journey continued for another six days before Connal stumbled into Hattusilis' camp. Glad cries rose up at his appearance and word of his arrival spread along the lines. He brought with him a lifting of otherwise downtrodden spirits and a heightened sense of purpose to the legions of once proud warriors.

Undefeated, they had ridden away from Ankira for over an entire year with the intent to follow their king into a land of wealth.

Rather than riches, they found unbearable wet heat and a sickening of over half the army. Those who did not die were weak, and those whose stalwart bodies kept them going were doubly plagued by boils and insect bites.

This dripping dense land was far different from the desert that lay to the distant east. There many of the same warriors had fought with courage and conviction beside their king, pushing back the savages who would encroach into the northern reaches of Hattusilis' domain.

They had shed blood upon the ever-shifting sands that held heat like the ovens of their homeland. They suffered blinding windstorms, near-suffocation and felt the wrath of foreign gods as they gained back what was theirs. A successful campaign that led to arrogance.

In spite of the setbacks, Hattusilis believed what could be taken there, could also be taken here. The men of King Hattusilis' army held that victory close, expecting another. But, so far, the land of Najahmara was winning out over them.

With the advent of Connal, a man thought lost to the fierce terrain, hope swelled in their collective hearts. Word spread that they were closer to Najahmara than previously thought, within a two-day ride. Hattusilis was overjoyed. His first inclination was to press forward, to ride day and night to reach the edges of Najahmara. So anxious was he to see this fabled city, he would risk detection by the posted sentries who would surely see his massive army wending its way up to the city gates.

"There are no gates, my lord." Connal chewed with distaste on a dried strip of meat. "There are no sentries. These people take no care to watch for strangers."

"Connal, has it taken this long for you to find your way back to us? How long before you discovered the whereabouts of this city?"

With the grace to look embarrassed, Connal ducked his head. "Truly, my lord, it took a great deal of time to find Najahmara. They lie in a protected valley that could easily be missed if not for the Maendre running through it. The end from which we should approach is covered by a thick growth of forest which will hide us most effectively until we are ready to strike."

"That is all well and good, but you seem...."

"Fat," snapped Telio. "While we toiled throughout this wretched black hole of earth, you rested in this fabled land. Could this be considered an act of treason, Connal?"

When Hattusilis paused to truly look over his man, Connal did not seem wasted. His small, thin frame carried more bulk than before he left. "You do appear well cared for."

"The kindness of the Najahmaran folk was evident the moment we rode into the village. They thought first to feed us, for they believed we were starving."

The many captains gathered to hear Connal's story murmured amongst themselves with growing discontent. Only Deimos held his tongue and stood with arms crossed, listening to Connal.

Zan rose to his feet, anger stirring in his voice. "What is it you accuse my brother of, mongrel?"

With a hand resting on the dagger at his belt, Telio turned on Zan. "I say no more than the truth about which we all have wondered. And what has happened to the other four men sent out with Connal?"

"To that, I cannot answer." Connal dropped the bit of meat into the fire. "Once we reached Najahmara we split up and I have not seen any of them since. I will tell you that I was welcomed within the bounds of Najahmara and its land with open arms.

"I followed the Maendre to a forest and backtracked around it. On two sides plateaus rise, stone walls that keep the town hidden. On the fourth side, the valley opens up and is fed water from both the Maendre and the Bayuk."

"I knew it," Hattusilis chortled. "As was foretold, it is where the two meet that we shall find Najahmara."

"Yes, my lord, though it is on the far edge of the valley. Najahmara lies in the heart between the plateaus. It is not the city we expected, but rather a modest town surrounded by farmlands. While at the peak of the ridge, I was noticed by a youth, a boy nearing manhood."

Connal dipped his head with shame and added, "Somehow this child managed to creep up on me while I hid amongst the scrub bush and rocks watching the town. I thought to kill him before he set off an alarm, but instead of running away, he offered to share his food."

Waving his hand through the air, Connal went on. "And he

spoke to me using the common language of traders. I was quite taken by surprise, for I did not expect this from a child in such a remote place."

"Why not?" said Hattusilis, "We learned of this place from a trader, he must have spoken with them somehow. It would make good sense that the common language is known."

"Perhaps," Connal muttered. "Still, I was not expecting one so young to address me with such boldness. He was not afraid. I learned much about the city from this boy and found that he was out in search of special plants used to soothe the welting caused by insect bites."

Connal sent a sideways glance toward Telio. "I made my way into Najahmara with this boy and saw for myself how unprotected the village truly is. They are a simple people, my lord, and do not seem to fear invasion. They did not question my presence, but offered me food and a place to sleep. I was free to roam at will, even into their sacred temple. They will fall to us without a fight."

"Their queen?" Hattusilis' eyes were aglow. "What of their queen? There is no guard for her?"

"If there is a queen, I did not see her. I saw only the priestesses of the temple, but I can assure you, that is where the power lies. Everything revolves around the women of this temple and all paths lead directly to it."

Hattusilis heard again the voice of Benor describing how he fell before the feet of a woman on a throne and from that moment on, could not cheat any with whom he traded. Hattusilis had not understood the note of deep regret in Benor's tone, for he assumed it was only in Najahmara that Benor played fair.

Now Hattusilis was less certain of the queen or priestess who was not what she seemed. Regardless, there existed a great power at the heart of Najahmara, of that he was convinced.

Though they appeared unarmed, Hattusilis carried the shrewdness of many battles beneath his belt and would not continue on without a revised plan. Connal drew in the dirt as much detail as he could for them and, from there, they began to see an effective approach.

To soothe the soreness of their travels, and to celebrate their imminent victory, Hattusilis ordered the slaughter of beasts for a feast. They would offer prayers to their god, Teshub, and on the morrow, they would ride toward Najahmara.

SEVEN

The legion of soldiers set about hacking and trampling a large clearing, to make a suitable encampment. Tents went up and, for the first time since passing beyond the Maendre Falls, there was a sense of anticipation in the men. With wood for fires gained from the thick growth of trees along the Maendre's banks before dusk settled, the smell of roasting meat brought a ferocious hunger to every man.

The wafting greasy smoke rising from the fires that licked skewered carcasses prompted a renewal of wild urges that had sent most of them on this journey. Sparring matches sprang up as brute strength attempted to win out over cunning and agility.

The clanging of weapons and the grunts of men struggling in mock battle could be heard throughout the encampment as could the shrill laughter of the women who did trade with their bodies. These women followed the army on their own beasts and at their own risk. Their voices rang out in lewd suggestion to the winners. Scraps of music, the sounds of drums and high-pitched wooden pipes, along with sudden bursts of song wove through the noise as night deepened.

Fueling the festivities was the discovery of a mysterious cache of beyaz. Bags and bags of skins filled with the fermented drink were found amongst the provisions without explanation. All that was proffered were shoulder shrugs and grunts, for not one of the men who kept the pack animals could say why or where the beyaz came from. Regardless, the supply was met with loud approval from the soldiers.

"A gift from our god!" Rang out as the skins were quickly passed. "Teshub honors us before battle."

Hattusilis ate his share of meat then withdrew from the merriment, taking with him a skin of beyaz. He sat alone by the edge of the Maendre and watched the river flow with the barest hint of moonlight on its waters.

The shadow play reminded him of a woman's long hair drifting across the surface. Every now and then, he took a drink and each time the tart flavor filled his mouth, he wondered again how the beyaz could have stayed hidden so long from discovery.

The more he drank, the more there seemed to be in the skin. Yet after awhile, he no longer cared. He sat alone, drinking and stared morosely out across the water. As king, he should join the men in their revelry, but Hattusilis could not tear himself from the Maendre's spell.

Elongated phantom fingers danced along the edges of the darkened shores while the moving waters held him captive. He was reminded of the silken skin and long black hair of Azhar, his wife.

How he had loved to entwine his fingers in her hair, combing down through it to reach the treasures beneath. Stretching out his hand, Hattusilis imagined the dark water before him to be the body of Azhar, and he reached out with the tenderness he held only for her. He thought of how he made love to her.

How he planted the seed of a child in her belly and watched the burgeoning life grow inside her. He remembered the kindling of happiness begin to glow in the depths of her dark eyes as she waited for the babe and how joy spilled over onto him in a faint show of affection.

He reached and met nothing, not even the wetness of the Maendre. "Azhar," Hattusilis moaned and lifted the skin of beyaz to his lips again. "My beautiful Azhar."

Azhar was dead, and with her their child. His son, born perfect, with the blessings of Teshub branded on his back in the shape of tiny horns above one hip. His son, born perfect, but without life.

His mother soon followed him into death. Azhar could not bear for the babe to go alone. The boy would have made a great ruler, a proud man with a proud father. Instead, his son was ash and Hattusilis had only Telio to take the throne should he perish.

Hattusilis stared into what would have been and drank more beyaz.

'Take another wife. That was the command of the high priest of Teshub while Azhar lay withering away. *Take another woman.*

But Hattusilis could not, for he loved Azhar and wanted to save her. He begged her to get well, told her there would be more children. But she looked at him with her lovely sad eyes and shook her head. She would defy him and return to her people, one way or another.

Hattusilis had captured Azhar when he defeated the sand-dwellers. It mattered not that Hattusilis made her queen, gave her wealth and comfort, and bestowed upon her the gift of his own heart. She was a princess of the mightiest tribe and her greatest shame was that she had become chattel to the invader.

Lifting the beyaz, Hattusilis drank until he was winded, and still the skin was full. He stared at it, thinking vaguely it should not be, but his mind was foggy and his awareness was mired in the past. He did not hear the footsteps approaching through the brush but did not feel surprise when Deimos sat down beside him.

"What are you doing, Hattu? Why do you not celebrate with the men?" Deimos beamed as he saw the beyaz and smelled the drink on Hattusilis when he spoke.

With slurring words, Hattusilis answered. "I think of Azhar."

"Ahh, yes," Deimos murmured. "Azhar."

"We overtook them at night, by the light of a full moon." He waved at the sky that held the waning sliver of a moon as if in his blurry-eyed state it was the same. "The desert shone so brightly it was almost as if it were day. I will remember, always, how it looked."

"The battle was a great triumph."

"We left no man standing." Hattusilis went on, a tinge of sorrow in his voice. "And took all the women and children as slaves. I saw her as the others cowered around her and knew I would claim that one for my own."

"Azhar was very beautiful."

"Like the sky filled with stars, a beauty that steals away your breath. Even in her grief she was magnificent. She did not fight me." Hattu's chin dropped to his chest.

"What was there to gain? She did not want to die."

"No, but she never forgave me for the deaths of her father and brothers." Hattusilis sighed heavily. "I have long wondered if it was avoidable. We overtook them by surprise, could we not have held them captive?"

"It is doubtful, Hattu. Though Azhar was a gentle soul, her people were fierce and merciless. Had they come upon us first, they would have slaughtered every last one of us."

"But we crossed into their lands and destroyed them."

"They threatened your borders. It is the way of men, to creep across the land and take whatever they can. Soon, the sand-dwellers would have been at the gates of Ankira and you would have been destroyed. Women and children would have suffered far worse than those taken by you."

Deimos lifted the skin of beyaz, sniffed it, and pretended to drink. Hattusilis scarce noticed, taking the beyaz from him when offered and drinking of it. Wiping his hand across his mouth, he belched and then groaned.

"Perhaps, but I am thinking differently of this Najahmara. I think there does not have to be such bloodshed."

Deimos shrugged. "With careful planning, it is possible."

"Possible, yes. I sorely wish Azhar had seen what was possible. Did I tell you about Azhar?"

With a smile, Deimos settled into a more comfortable position. "No, Hattu. Tell me about Azhar."

Telio emerged from the tent of his favorite whore buckling his sword belt, unconcerned that the moans behind him were not of pleasure. Even though he hurt her, the wench called out for him to come back, fearful that if she could not withstand his pleasure he would seek another.

Instead of being reserved for the nephew of the king, she would be passed among all who wanted her. A life far worse than his little games. For her endurance, Telio made certain she was well fed. He did not want her weak and listless, for that would not suit his needs at all.

More often than not, her pitiful cries would arouse him again and he would return to her to put his shaft inside her, but rarely between her legs. Then she would scream for him to stop. Cursing his mother, cursing the day he was born, tearing at her hair with threats of a knife into his heart while he slept, and Telio would just get harder and stay longer.

Telio never slept beside any woman. He was proud of the fear he invoked. His chest puffed with pride knowing as far as his little whore went, he would not go back to her in spite of her wailing. This time, he had brought her blood gushing out and that filth he would not touch.

It did not matter, anyway, for he would not want her again. They were to take Najahmara very soon and there he would find new delights. He licked his lips in anticipation, one hand resting on the hilt of his sword. The plan was drawn. At the earliest dawn the army would move forward. They would fulfill their quest and his uncle would have his new domain. With the advent of new territories to worry about, Telio hoped Hattusilis would send him back to Ankira to rule.

Lost in thoughts of power, Telio almost failed to notice a quarrel breaking out. A group of men fought over a full water skin, each pulling at it with demented determination. Telio strode over to the band and snatched the skin from their grasps.

"Shut up, stupid swine. Save yourself for the morrow, when a true battle is before you."

"Aye, and there jus' might be blood drawn now if ye do not return my drink to me," snarled one man.

"Stand down before I gut you." Telio did not recognize any of the soldiers, but they were of the common rank and did not sit a mount. They were footmen, thus, in the rear of the legion.

In the flickering of the torchlight, Telio knew something was awry, for the man's eyes were glazed and he was barely able to stand. He stunk of beyaz and sweat as he swayed forward and backward, pawing at the skin in Telio's hand.

With narrowed gaze, Telio took a closer look at each face and saw the same thing: drunken incomprehension. He lifted the skin and sniffed. The sweet-sour scent of fermented mash stung his nose and he jerked it away. He had seen none of the big, black barrels used in brewing the drink.

"Where did this come from?"

The men shrugged, their gazes sliding away as if there was some secret to the beyaz.

"Where did this come from?" Telio grabbed one by the front of his leather vest and shook him. The soldier wobbled back and forth as if his bones had turned to water and giggled.

The boldest of the three said, "If you want some, then take it.

No need to make a racket." He nudged his companion and winked. The man who did not want to give up his share lunged toward the skin, tripped over his own feet and went sprawling face first into the grass. He did not get up.

Telio released the soldier he held and he, too, fell over backwards and did not get up. The last remaining soldier stared blankly at Telio.

"Where did this drink come from?" Telio asked again.

The soldier shrugged. "They found it."

"Who found it? Where?"

He shrugged again and gestured with sodden vagueness toward the ring of campfires behind them. Telio stared toward the central encampment and, for the first time, heard the sounds of merriment all over the clearing. Without thought, Telio again lifted the beyaz to his nose and drew in the pungent scent of the drink.

A burst of raucous laughter erupted and sparks flew up from the central fire followed by a loud snapping and more laughter. Telio was suddenly entranced by the gaiety and longed to join the men.

Tipping the skin up, he started to drink. Just as the beyaz touched his tongue, the bag was ripped from his grasp. Startled, Telio jerked around in time to see the foot soldier stumbling away toward the campfires as fast as his clumsy feet would carry him.

Telio started to go after him, after the beyaz, with murderous intent. Two steps into the chase and Telio came to a halt, shaking his head. What had come over him? He did not even find beyaz appealing as he favored the sweet wines of his homeland over the bitter drink, yet he would have killed the man to regain the skin.

Angered, Telio strode through the crowded camp between fires and tents, sidestepping bedrolls and gear, only to see countless skins being passed by the men. He might as well have been invisible as he stalked through the ranks.

Not one paid heed to his order to cease. He was ignored as the men continued the mindless drinking and carousing. Each time Telio drew near a bag of beyaz, he was seized by an incomprehensible desire to consume the sour mash. Though he hated even the smell of it, the beyaz would be nearly to his lips before he caught himself and threw it aside.

He found even the captains of the army were inebriated, along with Zan who happily danced to the off key tune of a wind pipe.

To see the staid Zan kicking up his heels like a goat in heat left Telio in a furious state.

Telio's shouts to fall in were disregarded and, instead, he was cajoled to come join them. Backing away and breathing hard, Telio looked about for Hattusilis. Where was his uncle in all this madness? Surely, Hattu was not indulging with the common troops, yet he was not within the higher ranks.

What to do? Telio blinked and rubbed his eyes, trying to clear the fuzziness of panic from his thoughts. Turning, he caught sight of Connal staggering towards the wooded edge of the clearing and he raced after him.

"Connal! What is happening? Where did this drink come from? Where is King Hattusilis?"

Telio grabbed Connal by the elbow and spun him about only to encounter a stream of piss wetting his boots. Scrambling a safe distance away, further angered by the vacant expression on Connal's face, Telio shouted, "What is wrong with you? What is this madness that grips our camp?"

"What?" Connal stared dumbly at Telio, one hand still holding himself though the stream had stopped.

Telio spat in disgust. "Where is King Hattusilis?"

"Don' know." Connal fumbled to stuff himself back into his leggings.

"Think, Connal, when did you last see him?"

"Headin' toward the river." Connal gave a vacuous grin just before he fell over in the tall grass and began to snore.

The Maendre. Of course, Telio thought with vicious resentment, where else would his uncle go? Hattu was fascinated by that cursed waterway. Telio edged through the thick undergrowth beneath the trees until he reached the rocky shore of the river. Looking back and forth, he did not readily see his uncle.

Telio called out to him but heard no immediate answer. He began to walk downstream, scanning the indistinct bank, and wishing he had brought a torch to aide him.

"Hattusilis. Uncle, where are you?" Telio's voice echoed back at him, making the hair on his neck rise. It seemed as though he was entirely alone under the cloudless, star-filled sky.

The encampment noise was drowned out by the sounds of the night insects. The trees loomed over him with ominous darkness. Filled with foreboding, Telio marched along the edge, shouting out for his uncle.

Many strides down, he heard a responding call and knew it to be the voice of Hattu. With great relief, Telio hurried forward.

"Uncle, you must return to camp at once. The men have found a stash of beyaz and are all drunk beyond sense. It is as if the drink is bespelled. Even the watch guzzle the swill and Zan - you would not believe Zan. He dances."

Telio came to an abrupt halt as he saw two figures sitting in the dark. A faint hiss passed through his lips as one stood and he recognized the height and width of Deimos. Hattusilis remained on the ground, though he lifted one hand in greeting. In his uplifted fist was the familiar bag of beyaz.

"Uncle, no. Do not partake of that evil drink." Telio ran the last few steps, reaching out to seize the beyaz from Hattusilis, but Deimos grabbed it first.

Hattu grinned from his lounging position. The white of his teeth and eyes caught the faint light of the moon and appeared eerily disconnected from the rest of him. Startled, Telio looked from Hattusilis to Deimos.

"Uncle, there is something very wrong with that beyaz. It is bespelled, for the men are so drunk they will not follow orders. Our army is in great disarray."

"There is nothing wrong with it," Hattusilis said with a cheerful wave. "It is a blessing from Teshub for our future success."

"It is no gift from our god, Hattu. It is…it is…." Telio's gaze caught on the glint in Deimos' eyes. "It is sabotage."

"Nonsense." Deimos also smiled.

A sudden shiver of fear struck Telio as he watched Deimos. Deimos seemed to grow larger as he held out the bag of beyaz toward him. "It is not too late to enjoy a little drink, Telio. It will bring you closer to your men."

"Perhaps, just a small taste." Reaching out, Telio could think of nothing else but to drink. His hand was closing on the damp skin when he jerked his fingers back.

"No." He forced his head to turn away from Deimos. Closing his eyes, he regained his ground before once again meeting Deimos' gaze.

"You do not wish to celebrate our journey's end?"

"We have not yet arrived. I wish to put all celebration aside and bring these soldiers to foot for the march."

"And that is precisely why you do not make a good leader, my friend, for you do not allow them to step outside their misery for one evening."

Telio snatched the bag from Deimos as if a nest of vipers were inside and cast it into the depths of the river. Hattusilis protested with rude noises.

"Uncle, the men are near treason. They do not command their posts, but have abandoned all cause. What if we were under attack by Najahmara? We would be lying dead instead of drunk." Telio spat and ground his toe into an invisible enemy. "Now I find you also within the spell and you do not even realize it."

"I take offense at that." Hattusilis attempted to climb to his feet but instead went sprawling into the sand.

"Telio, will you not leave your uncle in peace, even for a moment?" Deimos moved to stand in front of Hattusilis.

"No. He is king and therefore should be held to a higher standard. It is disgraceful to have him rolling about on the ground like the common men. He should demand his army to desist and be ready to march at first light."

"I doubt he will do that." Deimos gestured at the still-flailing figure prone on the beach.

"Where did the beyaz come from?" shouted Telio. "It was you, was it not? You have purposely betrayed us! Uncle, uncle, listen to me. It was Deimos all along, just as I have said. He seeks to destroy our army."

"Nonsense." Weakness of limb forced Hattusilis to stay on the ground. He laid face up, wiping at the sand in his eyes. "Deimos is a loyal friend."

"Deimos is a traitor." Telio unsheathed his sword and rushed at Deimos before another word could be spoken. Telio's rage was beyond containment and he cared not what his uncle believed.

Telio chopped the blade hard and fast, with mortal injury his intention. The edge caught Deimos between shoulder and neck in a blow that should have taken his head off. Instead, Deimos grunted with the impact but remained standing, one hand pressed against the wound. Telio staggered backwards, blinking in disbelief. The blow should have brought instant death. He stared at Deimos with uncomprehending eyes, mouth open.

"Demon! Foul creature, what are you?"

Deimos lifted his fingers away from his neck and stared at the blood, black and sticky in the darkness. The pain of the wound ripped away his control.

"You are a fool," he hissed. In two strides Deimos was upon Telio. He swung out with a backhanded slap that sent Telio flying through the air. He fell hard into a cluster of rocks and lay in a silent, unmoving heap. His sword skidded down the shore until it came to rest with the blade buried in the soil, the hilt quivering a few inches above the ground.

Hattusilis made gurgling panicked noises in his throat but was unable to force words from his lips. He was on his knees, eyes wide as he stared first at Deimos and then at the body of his nephew draped over the rocks. All the befuddlement evaporated and left him quaking with terror.

"Hattu." Deimos started toward him.

Hattusilis scrambled backward on hands and knees. "Hattu, stop. I will not hurt you." Deimos held his palm to his neck to staunch the flow of blood. "I am not what you think."

"Te...Telio...."

"He is not dead. He will recover but he will not remember what happened."

"He was right, you are a demon."

"No."

"You are no mortal."

Deimos stopped, his hand outstretched toward Hattusilis. Did it matter if this man knew who or what he was? Leave now, he thought. Leave both Hattusilis and Najahmara to whatever their fates might be and return to the realm of your own kind. Go, before too much is revealed.

Yet, he did not go.

"You are right, I am no mortal. I am the son of Teshub, sent to fight at your side."

"What?" Hattusilis could not comprehend. He crawled further away and awkwardly climbed to his feet. "How can that be?"

"I do not come among you as traitor, but as the son of Teshub, to bless your battles." Though Teshub knows nothing of it, Deimos thought with sudden amusement.

Ares, Teshub, whatever name his father was called, would not approve of this pronouncement. Ares was not known for his benevolence.

Without warning, Deimos began to laugh and could not stop.

"Do you mock me?" Hattusilis wiped at his face with his sleeve, trying to rid himself of the nightmare he faced. "No, no, I did not mean that." Fright crackled in Hattusilis' voice. "I just do not understand why you laugh."

"Nor do I, my friend." Deimos' chuckles died away. "But I do not lie. I truly am the son of Teshub."

"Then it was you who brought the beyaz to my troops and it would seem Telio was right when he said it was bespelled."

"In a way, yes. I intend no harm, Hattu, I hope you can believe that." With care, Deimos approached Hattusilis until he could place a hand on his shoulder. He could feel Hattu flinch beneath his touch, but he did not pull away. "I am loyal to you for as long as I ride with you."

"Then why would you bring tainted drink into my ranks?"

"It was with selfish purpose I offered the beyaz. I wanted only to delay the invasion of Najahmara for a few days."

Shaking his head, Hattusilis repeated, "But why?"

"It is difficult to explain."

"I must know or I cannot…."

"Trust." Deimos nodded. He understood. "This land we stand upon belongs, heart and soul, to the most ancient goddess, the spirit of Earth. Here, she is called Gaea. She was believed to be dormant, sleeping. None have felt her energy in eons, yet the moment we stepped onto her land, I sensed her.

"Curious about her people, I went to Najahmara to observe them. At the dark of the moon, they will hold a ritual marking their harvest and Gaea's bounty. I do not wish to dishonor Gaea by destroying the celebration." Deimos did not add he wanted very much to be present.

"You have been there? How? How could you be there and also here? How?"

Hattusilis stopped. There were too many things he did not understand. Why should there not be one more?

Yet here was another who had been to Najahmara, this place he had dreamed so long of finding.

"Take me there."

Hattusilis spoke with sudden, fervent belief that it was possible. To see Najahmara was his one true desire. He was weary, heartsick and, with a jolt, Hattusilis realized he did not care if he ruled as king. He merely wanted to see it.

"Take me there, Deimos."

"No, Hattu, I cannot."

"Yes! I know you can, though how, I cannot begin to fathom. If you can go there, you can take me with you."

"It is not possible." Or if it was, Deimos did not know how as he had never attempted to move a mortal being through his own will and he would not begin to experiment with one he held in high esteem. "No, you must ride into Najahmara as planned."

"Ride? Then ride we will. Now." Hattusilis started back toward the encampment only to realize he no longer knew where it was. Deimos came from behind him and led the way.

"It is late, and you have drunk far too much. We cannot go now. I will collect the beyaz so that on the morrow, the men will rise and have the ability to go forward." Deimos chuckled. "They may be somewhat ill, but they will be able to move if I seize the drink and they sleep."

"And if you do not destroy the beyaz?"

Deimos shrugged.

"If they are drunk, they will not know we are gone." Hattusilis' voice was feverish with excitement. "How long will they stay under this spell if you leave them as they are?"

"As long as they drink the beyaz, they will never regain their wits. But, Hattu, sooner or later, they will tire of it and sleep."

"Yes, they will sleep, but if there is more to be drunk when they awaken, they will go right back to it."

Deimos knew this to be true even without his help. "We cannot ride in the dark."

"You can."

"This land is too dangerous for our mounts."

"Connal has shown us where a trade route joins up with our path. We can be on that roadway by daylight. If you are indeed a blessing from Teshub, then you will do this, Deimos. If I see Najahmara for myself, I will be better prepared to triumph over her people."

"I do not want them hurt, Hattu. Though I am part of War, these people have no defenses, just as Connal has told you. They cannot fight back."

"Let me see this for myself and no harm will come to any of them."

After a long silence, Deimos said. "If you swear it, then I will take you there."

"I swear." Hattusilis' voice was filled with joy. "I swear it."

Telio awoke to an insistent voice calling his name. He crawled from his tent, head reeling and stomach heaving at the strong scent of beyaz on his clothes. He scarce made it outside before the vomit rose. Wiping his mouth with the back of his hand, he reached for a water flask to rinse his mouth, spitting it on the ground before facing Zan.

"What do you want?" Telio croaked. His body ached and his head felt as if it would crack open at any moment. Touching the back of his skull, Telio winced at the painful knot. His left shoulder was on fire, his side was stiff and painful, and he gasped at a sharp jab in his ribcage. One side of his face hurt and his nose was swollen, but he did not recall how he came to be injured.

"I did not think you indulged in the beyaz last night, Telio, but it appears you have been bitten by the same bug." Zan waved toward an encampment that was eerily silent in the wash of daylight. The fires were out and there was no sign of activity. Still forms could be seen sleeping in the grass.

Telio blinked, his mind unable to gauge the time. The sun was high up in a brilliant blue sky, too far up, for they should all have been roused at the first sign of dawn. Even the animals were quiet as they grazed on the lush greenery all around them.

Scowling, Telio could not shake the fuzziness from the night before. Something plagued the back of his thoughts, but he could not remember what had transpired.

Indeed, he did not remember drinking beyaz, let alone enough to be sick. Yet here he was, bloated and slow-witted, puking his guts onto the ground while his men lay dead to the world wherever they had fallen.

"I have been touched by the heat sickness."

"Of course," Zan murmured.

But, Zan, too, awoke with a pounding head, a sour gut and unexplained aches and pains. Worse, he also had a ravenous desire for more beyaz. He fought the urge to root around for leftover sludge and, instead, plunged into the cool waters of the Maendre. When he emerged, the need was gone. His concern was not.

"Telio, when did you last see Hattusilis?"

"I do not know." Telio sat on a log and pressed his fingers into his temples. "I do not recall indulging in beyaz. I do not recall entering my tent, I do not recall anything."

Raising his head with a jerk that brought a moan to his lips, Telio remembered one small thing.

"Hattusilis, I went looking for him." Holding his head again, Telio stopped, for the pounding had become unbearable. When he remained quiet, it did not hurt as much.

Zan rubbed his chin. "I worry, for I cannot find Hattusilis anywhere amongst the men."

"It is a very large camp, he must be here."

"I have checked everywhere, even the riverbank and I find no sign of Hattusilis."

Telio shook his head as he stirred the ashes of last night's fire, adding twigs in the hope there was a spark left to kindle new flames. He badly needed a dose of the strong morning tea. In a moment, he was gratified to see fire springing up out of the pile of wood.

"However, I did find this." Zan held out a curved blade with a carved hilt inlaid with jadestone. The figure was of a great cat with ruby eyes, a design carried by no other than Telio. "Why was your weapon buried in the dirt?"

As Zan turned it side to side, he noticed dried blood caked into the grooves of the hilt and along the base of the blade. "Your sword appears to have been in play."

With an appraising gaze, Zan added, "And you look as if you have been in combat. How is it that you have received such a beating, and yet you recall nothing about last night?"

Bristling under Zan's tone, Telio reached for his weapon only to have Zan hold it a hair's width too far for him to reach. "I have done nothing. I too was looking for Hattusilis." Telio grimaced. Why had it been so important to find his uncle?

"Con said you were headed toward the Maendre last he saw you." With perverse enjoyment, Zan kept the sword from Telio's hand.

"Con." Telio rose with unsteadiness, staring down at the stained and scuffed leather on his feet. His gaze moved up along the torn cloth of his trousers and a deep cut, still oozing blood, along his left leg. His shirt was ripped at the shoulder and the leather vest was scraped and filthy. His fingers rose to touch the scratches on his face and swollen nose.

What happened to him last night? He should be able to summon up the night's events from the depths of his memory, but he simply could not. How was he battered and bruised, his clothes tattered and muddied without his knowledge? And why was his blade lying buried next to the river? Last he recalled it was at his side as he left the woman's tent.

Telio wiped his face with his sleeve, wincing as the rough cloth rubbed the bruises on his face. After he had taken pleasure with the woman, he noticed the beyaz, the drunkenness. He wanted to put a stop to it all. Yes, that was it. He went looking for Hattusilis to take command of the legions.

Con said he was at the river.

"He was sitting at the riverbank." Telio frowned.

"So you found him?"

"Yes, by the waterway." Squinting into the brightness of the day, Telio rubbed his forehead. "I was angry about the beyaz. Everyone was drunk." He cast a sidelong glance at Zan. "Everyone acting the fool."

With great pain, the moment presented itself, and Telio recollected. "Hattu was with Deimos. They were sitting together at the river's edge, drinking beyaz and talking."

"Deimos?" Zan scanned the encampment, muttering "I do not recall seeing Deimos either, though that in itself is not unusual. He is rarely where one thinks he should be."

"Deimos." Telio fumbled for the water flask Zan held out to him and drank with care as not to heave what little there was left in his belly. Splashing a handful of water on his face, Telio recoiled at the sting.

The sensation brought a new image, one of Deimos standing over Telio, his hand raised to strike. "Deimos."

Touching his swollen cheek, Telio met Zan's gaze. Zan gasped. "Deimos did that?"

Telio nodded with the slowness of one recounting dim memories. "We quarreled."

He reached for the sword and this time Zan gave it up. Telio held it balanced in his hands, staring down at the crusted blood around the hilt.

"What happened?"

Turning the sword over and over, Telio concentrated on the

dull glint of metal as if the secret of the night before could be seen in the reflection. He shifted the hilt to his hand, wrapping his fingers around it, hefting it into the air, demanding his mind recall what happened.

"I knew there was something wrong with the beyaz. I knew when I smelled it, the behavior of the men - it was all madness. I knew something was very wrong."

With a sharp nod, Zan agreed. Even as he drank last night, he realized still more when he awoke with an unquenchable thirst. "I wanted the beyaz very much this morning and would have drank it, but felt something was off."

Zan pulled at his bearded chin. "They will all want it when they revive." His gaze was pointed at the sword.

Telio ran his finger along the sharp edge, feeling the grit of sand and the clotting of blood. "The beyaz caused madness but I did not harm my uncle."

"I did not say such a thing."

"But you wonder."

"I wonder what evil gripped us and I know it will start again when they wake, but that you might harm Hattusilis?" Zan shook his head.

"Never." Telio spoke between clenched teeth. "He is my king, as well as my blood, and I owe him allegiance. We must find him."

"First we must destroy the beyaz, for as soon as the men come to, they will kill to have more. It is bespelled, I swear it."

"Bespelled." Unbidden, Telio saw the image of the ferocious swing of his blade at Deimos, only to have him take the blow and stay on his feet. In a nightmarish way, the scene unfolded before him again.

The strike should have taken Deimos' head from his shoulders, but instead left no more than a flesh wound. Telio saw the rage burst and fall over Deimos in a mind-numbing reign of terror, and then, nothing. Telio recalled only that he awoke fully clothed in his bedroll as if he had passed out from too much drink.

"Quickly, we must gather all the skins and burn them," Telio ordered. "Last night, Deimos as much as admitted that he brought the beyaz. To what evil purpose, I do not know, but he tried to make me drink it. We fought." Sweat ran down Telio's forehead as he stopped to take a deep breath.

"Did you kill him?"

"No. I wish I had. I wish I would have. No, Zan, Deimos is not what he leads us to believe. He is unnatural, a horror that walks among us. He is a foul wretch. An undead who insinuates himself into our king's good graces and, I fear, makes Hattusilis do his bidding."

"What is this you speak of, Telio? Though Deimos is a strange one, I will grant you, I have not seen him do an injustice."

"And you will not, for that wicked one is clever. I tell you, Deimos admitted he supplied the beyaz, bespelled with his own hateful intention."

"Even if there was a way for Deimos to bring in this quantity of drink, I do not see he could have made all this happen."

"It was charmed," Telio's voice rose. "I now understand. Deimos wished to spirit our king away from us. Yes, that must be it. He separates Hattusilis from us, keep us drunk and dizzy with his tainted beyaz so we remain unaware of our king's absence."

"But why?" Zan could feel some truth hidden in Telio's words, enough to make his gut clench, yet he could not connect with the reason. "What would he have to gain from taking Hattusilis from us?"

"Fool! Do you not see it?" As Telio talked, his eyes began to glisten and strength began to flow through his body. The soreness ebbed away as fury overtook the pain.

"Why did none of us see it? I have always known Deimos was not to be trusted. I told Hattusilis to be careful around him. Instead, Hattu brought Deimos into his confidence and now they are gone."

"Gone where?" Still somewhat dulled by the effects of beyaz, Zan heard Telio, but his words did not make sense. "Where would they go?"

"Where do you think?" With a smack to the center of Zan's chest, Telio pointed toward the Maendre. "Where we are headed. To Najahmara, of course."

"But why there?"

"Because that is where a trap has been laid. Where an army is waiting for us."

"Connal said they are a simple people with no army. You heard him. That is why we changed our plans. There is no need to attack, but rather to invade in a more peaceful manner."

"That is a ruse, a lie." Pausing, Telio threw out his arms into a wide circle. "Did you not wonder why Connal was away so long?

They bewitched him as well, and told him what to say to us. Did he not look different? Yes, he did. We all noticed right away. We were about to walk right into the trap. They are waiting for us."

Zan rubbed his forehead, frowning. "If that is so, why take Hattu from us? If we are to walk into their forces, would they not prefer Hattu to be at our lead?"

"Perhaps, before last night. But when Hattusilis saw the truth about Deimos, he would have changed tactics. We would have attacked under cover of night just as we had planned. Deimos could ill afford to have Hattusilis give away his secret, so he took him away while we all lay in a stupor."

Head bobbing back and forth, Zan tried to comprehend Telio's speech. Demons, plots, an army where there is no army - it was lunacy. With a growl, Zan said, "Wait. How would this have all happened without any suspicion? We are not stupid, Telio."

"I do not know, only that when I struck Deimos with my sword, he should have fallen down without a head but he did not. He had no more than a small flesh wound."

With closed eyes, Telio felt again the blow that knocked him senseless. "Then Deimos attacked me. It was he who put me in my tent and made it to appear as if I were drunk on the beyaz, to further cloud my mind. I tell you Deimos has taken our king and we must find them."

"This is all preposterous. They are hunting, or they walk in the woods, or they are hidden away as they take pleasure, some such thing. I do not believe what you are saying. Demons? Tricks? This is nonsense."

As Zan started away, Telio yelled, "Hold. I will show you."

He snatched up the skin of beyaz lying beside his tent and hesitated only a moment as the scent of the beyaz called to him to drink before he threw it into the fire. Both men were startled when the beyaz exploded into a ball of fire that shot into the air and reached a height as great as the trees surrounding them. They stumbled backwards, arms thrown up to protect their faces, mouths agape.

Zan stared, eyes bulging, when another burst of high flames lit the early dawn sky.

Shaken and pale, Zan said, "By Teshub's horns, I have never seen anything like that."

"Yes." Telio's eyes were as bright as the fire. "Let us gather the rest of the beyaz now and then awaken our captains. We must find Hattusilis. We must ride toward Najahmara, for that is where he is, I am certain of it."

"But we cannot mobilize the entire army," Zan mumbled. "It would be impossible, we would lose too much time."

"We do not need the entire army. We need only the mounted legion. The others can follow behind. Speed is of the utmost. We do not know how far ahead of us they have gotten."

"If they are on horseback."

"If." Telio spoke with curtness. "We must check for their beasts."

"How else would they go?"

"I do not know, but I now would believe anything to be possible. We must act swiftly and with stealth, for we do not want Deimos to know we are on his trail. Let us dispense the beyaz. We must gather our captains and plan our attack."

Zan looked into Telio's wild glinting eyes and sensed a powerful fear. Yet what choice was there? Hattusilis was gone and he was there only leader. Lifting his shoulders, Zan went to gather the skins of beyaz while Telio roused the sleeping men.

EIGHT

"The dark of the moon." Inni shivered, peering out the window at the deepening night. The stars were not yet in the sky and the gardens were no more than a blur of heights and dense shadows, heady with the scent of late flowering blooms.

She let drop the thin material that covered the opening and turned back to the candlelit room. "I dislike it when our rituals fall on moonless skies."

"Why?" Pallin tweaked Inni's blonde braid. "I love it. The darkness is so forgiving. It opens up its arms and holds everything to its heart."

"You have eyes like a cat." Slapping at Pallin's hands, Inni sniffed. "You see well in the dark. I do not. I do not like being out when it is so black. It frightens me. There is much out there that cannot be seen, waiting, just waiting."

"To what, eat you?" With a laugh, Pallin growled and leaped at Inni, grabbing her up in a hug and twirling her around until they were both breathless.

"Stop it." Inni struggled to free her arms. "You make fun of me, but the night holds more than you know. You would be wise to have respect and hold a decent amount of concern."

"Tonight I will stand at the right hand of Gaea and if you think I am not worried, I am." Pallin released Inni, facing her.

"I did not mean that." Touching Pallin's face, Inni marveled at her youth, both in body and in spirit. "I meant, be wary of the darkness. It can hold a terror that is unexplainable. Tonight, I feel it holds more than we expect."

"Is there any time we host Gaea that we do not feel some sense of uncertainty?" Jahmed pushed aside the curtain and stepped into the small room. "We bring forth the spirit of Earth in all her power. How can we not be afraid?

"Pallin, we have all stood where you will be tonight and we have all felt the way you do. Take heart, you have been chosen to care for Niala before, during and after. To act as her guide and see no harm comes to her. Do you understand?"

"Yes," Pallin's voice quavered. "But you will be close by? What if...."

"We will be with you," Inni said. "Both Jahmed and I will be in the cavern. I will be where they enter and Jahmed will be on the other side as they leave. You have been through this ritual many times, you know it well."

Nodding, Pallin took a deep breath. "I have, but never as a full priestess of Gaea, nor one who is invested with the care of her vessel."

"Speaking as the vessel." Niala entered the room, her hair loose and damp from washing, skin glistening from the bath. "I have no concerns, so release this nameless fear, all of you. Gaea would never take me further than I can go. And tonight, we will give tribute to her. The most I will suffer is a belly ache for all the honey I will eat."

Pallin and Jahmed laughed, but Inni gripped Niala's arm, her face serious. "Something is different tonight. I feel it waiting in the darkness and I do not like it. I wish this were a full moon so we could at least see around us."

"Well, it is not," Pallin countered. "There is nothing we can do to change the sky."

"No, but we can be more watchful."

"Inni, what is it you think will happen?" Stepping closer, Jahmed touched Inni's shoulder. "What is different?"

Shrugging, Inni said, "I cannot put my finger on it. There is just a heaviness about the night and it frightens me."

"I will say this." Jahmed paused. "I have felt as if we are being watched. I feel eyes upon me, but when I look there are none. It is an eerie feeling and one I do not care for."

Niala scanned the three earnest faces which only moments ago were filled with the joy of offering sustenance to Gaea. Now those faces held mounting concern. She knew it was the presence of Deimos causing them such distress, but she was reluctant to tell them of him. Niala invited him to their ritual for Gaea to speak to him.

It was what Gaea wanted, therefore it had been done. Whether Deimos would go before her remained to be seen. To tell the women of the possibility would only add to their fears.

Niala decided to leave well enough alone.

"Gaea is anxious." Niala gave a gentle nudge to Jahmed. "We must go for ritual is to begin soon."

"Yes." All three murmured in response. Jahmed placed a light robe around Niala's nakedness, arranging it with care with the curling strands of hair on the outside of the embroidered cloth. Pallin and Inni held back the curtain, allowing Niala to go first, followed by Jahmed. They brought up the rear as they walked along the deserted corridor toward the gardens.

The younger women were already stationed along the main path leading upwards to the cave and Seire sat waiting at the entrance. The temple was empty and the solitude brought forth a feeling of desolation. Grief welled up inside Niala.

For what reason, she wondered. Did the end of her time in Najahmara grow near? Deimos was what he was and Ares could not be far behind. She sighed and stepped out onto the trail.

The black night was filled with the rhythm of drums calling everyone to the cavern. They would give thanks to Gaea for the bounty of the harvest, both in their lives and in their hearts. The drums beat steadily and would not cease until dawn, until each member of Najahmara went before Gaea and received her blessing. In return, they would honor Gaea with honey and milk in a sharing of their wealth.

Soon Niala would host Gaea's spirit within her body. She would surrender herself the moment she became Earth's vessel. It could be for the last time. Unbidden tears slipped from her eyes and rolled down her cheeks as she heard the voices of her people rise in a wordless swell of song. The melody echoed off the side of the ridge, reaching down to caress her.

Niala stopped, her palms pressed to her eyes.

"What is it," whispered Jahmed.

"Tell them to go ahead." Niala stared up at the sky.

Without question, Jahmed bid Inni and Pallin to continue up to the cave on the priestess' path behind the garden. The two women glanced back once, but did not speak. In silence, they began to pick their way along the narrow, rocky trail towards the rear entrance into the cavern.

As the others disappeared into the gloom, Niala clutched Jahmed's hands. Jahmed could feel the tension in Niala's fingers, could see it in the slant of her body as she leaned forward.

"If something should happen to me, Jahmed, you are next to carry on Gaea's purpose."

"Nothing will."

"But if I am suddenly gone." Niala squeezed Jahmed's hands. "Tonight, tomorrow, within a moon's cycle, whenever it might be." Her voice caught.

"This will not happen." Jahmed's fingers were equally as tight around Niala's. "It will not. He will not come for you."

"He will."

"How can you know?" Jahmed's voice quivered. "It was just a vision, a dream, you have said so yourself."

How could Niala know? Because she knew Ares the Destroyer. Defeat pounded at her door and, though she fought it, Niala knew she could not win. Sensing Ares was close, fear pressed down on her from all sides. He would have her again. During all the years she had hidden from Ares, she knew some day, in some manner, he would find her. What Jahmed did not realize was that Niala would be the instrument leading Ares to Najahmara.

"I said what was necessary. I did not want to cause rampant fear for there is naught we can do to keep him at bay. He will come."

"Why? After all this time?"

"There once were wards in place to keep Najahmara safe, so Ares could not find me, but I lifted them long ago." With a wave her hand, Niala stopped Jahmed's questions.

"There was no other way to draw new people into our midst. We were on the verge of becoming addled by inbreeding or dying out. I could not allow that for my sake alone. The others who needed protection were already dead. I was the only one left and I would not sacrifice Najahmara to save myself."

"How long?" Jahmed bit her lip. "How long have the wards been down?"

"Before you arrived." Niala touched Jahmed's cheek. "Before Inni. Had I not brought down the wards, neither of you would be here. After Seire, there were few women who could, even if they would, priestess to Gaea. Our strength was waning and I could not let Najahmara go into the mists because of my own fears."

"After Layla, then."

"Long after Layla died. There came a point when I saw no reason to keep us hidden."

Watching the star-laden sky, Niala made a small sound in her throat. "I had no heart after that. I thought to myself, what do I care if Ares finds me? I had lived far beyond my expected years and, forgive me, Jahmed, I even thought his punishment, even death, would be preferable to a life without Layla. I was empty then."

"But Seire?"

"I had not yet birthed a child, for I did not lie with any men after Ares until Layla was gone. I did not believe I could bear a babe at that age. Who would think it? And yet, I look no older than the day I arrived in Najahmara."

Bemused, Niala paused. "My only child was conceived at a spring celebration while Gaea was called into me. Through her, I became pregnant."

"And that was not enough to want to restore the wards against Ares the Destroyer?" Jahmed was trying to understand, but in her fear, she held an anger she did not want.

"No."

"But why? Now we are on the brink of...of...."

"War." Niala nodded. "Yes. I spend every night on the plateau praying, pleading, hoping it is only me that Ares seeks. Hoping he does not want to punish me by destroying all of what we built. I pray he will take only me and leave Najahmara alone."

"But it has been so long, why would he find you now? How would he know where to look?"

"Because there is one who walks among us that carries the mark of War."

"Here?" Startled, Jahmed's mouth hung open. "Why have I not seen this one?"

"He is immortal, just as his father is immortal. He can move amongst us unseen. You have felt the disquiet gripping our city - it is because of this one."

"And he will bring Ares to you?"

"Sooner or later, yes, he will bring his father here."

"But what of Gaea? She is a most powerful goddess, can she not stop this Destroyer?"

"She cannot, dear one. She is Earth, but she cannot control War."

"This is wrong. So wrong," Jahmed choked. "We must stop him."

"We cannot. Hear me, for soon...." Niala swallowed hard.

"No."

"Yes." Niala touched Jahmed's cheek and felt wetness. "Jahmed, you must take my place."

"No!" Anger dissolved and Jahmed's wail sent an echo up the side of the ridge.

"Shhh." With her fingers laid against Jahmed's lips, Niala whispered, "You are the only one who can. If I must go, then let it be in peace. I need to know our people are in good hands."

"Niala, no, I cannot." Shoulders shaking, Jahmed buried her face in her hands.

Niala held Jahmed in her arms and spoke into her ear. "If I am to go, you must carry on."

"Not tonight."

"No, not tonight. I offer myself again to Gaea and to our people, but it may well be for the last time. I may not go tomorrow or the next day, but there is no doubt, it will be soon." Niala kissed Jahmed with tenderness. "Say yes, for I need to hear it."

"How can you ask this of me?"

"It is not I, dearest, it is Gaea. She bids you lead our people."

"It is not possible. Death I could accept, but not this."

"It is to save you. Say yes, Jahmed, for you are her chosen one. Accept her grace. Give me peace and say yes."

"Ahhh."

"It is the way it is, Jahmed, you must accept this. Say yes."

"No."

"You must take my place. There will be great confusion and the people cannot be without someone to lead them, someone to call Gaea into their midst. Say yes. Please."

Jahmed sighed long. "For you, yes."

"For Najahmara. For Gaea."

"For you," Jahmed answered with firmness. "Only for you."

Niala touched her arm. "You must not speak of this to any other. It is between you and I and Gaea."

"I will not speak of it, but I will pray it does not happen. Tomorrow may it seem like a bad dream."

"Tomorrow," Niala responded with sadness. "May bring our goodbyes."

Jahmed threw her arms around Niala and clung to her with all her might. "If this must be, then take with you my everlasting love and never forget us, for we will never forget you."

Niala nodded, unable to speak. Slowly, they began their ascent to the cave.

NINE

Hattusilis lost track of time. They could have ridden hours or days. He did not remember more than it was night when they left and now night once again. He did not know if he dozed, or if Deimos bespelled him, but when he opened his eyes they were poised at the edge of a forest ready to cross a meadow.

He knew in his bones they arrived at Najahmara. The Maendre still wound by their side, for he could smell it and hear its rushing waters. It was so dark he could scarce see his hand in front of his face, but ahead there were pinpoints of light. As they rode in silence across a field of newly cut stubble, Hattusilis strained forward in his saddle trying to make out the rooftops against the deep night.

"It is Najahmara, is it not?" Hattusilis spoke with a whisper even though there was no wind to carry his voice. There was only a faint humming in the air. "But I see no one."

"Yes, we have found Najahmara."

As they drew closer, Hattusilis reined in his mount. "What is that I hear? It sounds like singing, but I cannot make out the words."

Beneath the chanting, drums echoed off the sides of the ridges. It was then Hattusilis noticed the walls of stone that rose on both sides of the wide valley. They were but a speck in the middle of the small mountains, heading toward an unknown people. Fear chased down Hattusilis' spine and he held up his hand.

"We should go no further, Deimos. I dislike this feeling I

have. Something dangerous is in the air."

"Come, Hattu, this is your dream. You wanted nothing more than to see Najahmara and so you shall."

"I did not intend to ride in alone in the dark."

"But you did intend to bring your army in this way."

"At first, but as you know, we have not yet decided if this was our course of action. Are they, indeed, weaponless?"

"They are."

"Then why do I sense a threat?"

"Because, though you are a warrior, what you see ahead of you cannot be fought with sword or dagger. What you feel is the work of their goddess."

Deimos put a hand on Hattusilis' shoulder and pointed with his other toward the far side of the valley, above the darkened depths of the city.

Hattusilis watched with wonder as many more points of light wound serpent-like up the side of the rise. Hattu squinted, shading his eyes with his hands even though there was no moon.

"What are they doing?" Hattusilis did not see the smile on his companion's face.

"They go to honor their goddess and we, my friend, have been invited to go along. However, we must leave behind our weapons if we are to enter."

"Leave ourselves without protection?" Hattusilis swung his head from side to side in doubt, but the siren song of Najahmara called him.

At Deimos' urging, the king shed the heavy sword and twin daggers with no more protest and left them where he dropped them. The thick leather tunic and trousers fell atop the blades. With surprising suddenness, Hattusilis felt light of mind and body, clad only in his shirtsleeves and thin leggings.

The chanting wove in and out of his mind, calling his name, and the drums continued to beat out the rhythms of the earth. Urgency shivered through him as if a cool wind blew upon his neck, yet he sweated with the need to join the people.

"Come Deimos, we must hurry." Hattusilis started to run, leaving behind his mount.

"Stop, Hattu, there is no need to go afoot. We have a distance yet to cover."

"Yes, yes, of course." Hattusilis scarce noticed the horses, too.

were relieved of their domain colors along with the leather pieces that fit over the head and down the neckline for protection against stray sword slashes. He knew only that he must be part of the flowing tide moving upward.

The streets were deserted but the energy that pulled at Hattusilis ran through the narrow passages whirling dust beneath his feet in a teasing dance. It fairly swept him along, so light did he feel, and he followed along behind Deimos with a sense of childish glee in his heart.

As they grew closer, Hattusilis could see the play of shadows from the torches being carried up the side of the mount. He longed to skip, to run as fast as he could, until he could fall in beside them.

Outlined in the torchlight, people trod a well-worn path that shone yellow beneath their feet, a glowing serpent alive and weaving up the gentle slope. They danced where they stood, lifting their arms with a joy Hattu had never before seen. They moved in answer to the many drums, their voices rising and falling with the beat.

The music rose to a lofty pitch then fell back like tide's answer to the shore, a glorious ebb and flow of melodic humming. There were no words, just a swelling of emotion that burst up and rained down on him, sending a quiver throughout his body. When he finally reached the path, Hattusilis stood mesmerized, not knowing why they celebrated, knowing only he must be part of it.

Deimos was jostled by those nearest him. He bumped Hattusilis, but neither noticed. The singing rose and swelled with each added tone. Loud, then soft, and then loud again. Waves and waves, like water, all their joy and grief rolled into one, released by the power of their own voices.

"It is Gaea." Deimos inhaled a deep breath. "She - the most ancient one among us - calls her children to join her. Listen, Hattu, they answer with their entire being."

"Gaea." Hattusilis was entranced, his eyes captured by the flow of light and people. "I have never felt such power."

Hattusilis' words trailed off as he was pulled forward into the crowd by unknown hands, an expression of utter bewilderment on his face. Deimos watched Hattusilis merge with the people of Najahmara until he could no longer tell which was Hattu and which were the native folk.

The line was not moving forward but energy rippled up and

down the path in anticipation of what, he did not know. He, too, was being sucked into the coils of the serpent as it snaked toward the mouth of the cavern.

Deimos would not join them in song, but his emotions sailed along with theirs, up and down, lost in the vast universal call. To never hunger, to never thirst, to always have home and hearth. Catching sight of Hattusilis ahead, he saw that he sang with them, his body angled into the crowd as if he could burrow into the joy headfirst.

Hattusilis appeared as if he sang with his heart, in spite of the fact he could not know what it meant. There were no words, but their voices sang to Her and their bodies called to Her; their faces were filled with Her bliss.

Deimos was with the worshippers, yet apart from them. In that separation, he felt an abiding loneliness. He lived on for eternity but did not have what they had. Life as life. For them it mattered not that death might be around the corner, for they embraced the moment.

Around him, the line began to move forward and Deimos was pulled with them. He lost sight of Hattu again as he rode the tide into the opening. Gentle hands pushed at Deimos, urging him forward. At the mouth of the cavern, he paused, struck by a humbling sense of emergence from a world of light into darkness. He could feel the power of the goddess more strongly than ever before, calling him inside.

It required Deimos to bow down to enter the cave and walk along a narrow path. The walls were damp. In some places water trickled in a zigzag pattern down an uneven surface. People crowded in front of him and to the rear. He could not slip past them.

The Najahmara folk urged him on with firm hands, as if these humans could read his mind and see he wanted to leave this place. Deimos brought Hattusilis to experience the people so that Hattu may not wish to destroy them. It was not Deimos' intention to be part of their ritual himself. He wanted only to observe, to see Niala again.

Hattusilis would laugh long and hard if he knew how unnerved Deimos was to journey into the depths. The fear of entering Gaea's very womb with no escape was very real.

Deimos forced himself to breathe in rhythm with the drums

and hold onto the rocky wall. At his touch, it seemed as if the entire cavern inhaled, held its breath, then released it with a trembling, secret expectation. Did She wait for him?

Did Gaea know he, god of Terror, the god of utter despair, did She know he entered her body as willingly as a lover, but without any right to be there? Would Gaea know him as the son of War? Did She know Deimos was ruled by his father, a god whose purpose was pure destruction? Would She reject him, knowing he did not contribute to life, but took life?

Deimos' head ached with these thoughts until dizzy and he could think no more. He could only follow along behind one who led his way. At some point he realized the torches were extinguished and all made their way in the dark. He could not turn back, but only go forward in spite of the abject terror in his heart.

*****

Within the cave, Niala sat upon a throne carved from rock in the center of a towering natural chamber. She was clothed only in a heavy necklace made of black stones in the shape of a great bird.

On her left leg, a serpent was tattooed. Its tail began at her ankle and wound from calf to thigh where the triangular head looked toward her own dark opening. Her back carried the mark of the Corvidae, the winged one that carried Earth from her solitary existence deep in her core to the surface and into the body of her waiting priestess.

The air pulsed with the energy of the masses waiting outside, a nearly unbearable and rising urgency built inside the cavern. With a sigh, Niala leaned forward, listening to the voices of the drums calling the people of the village, calling the Spirit of the Earth, calling, calling.

Their voices rose as one, calling Her.

Niala drifted, aware only of the rise and fall of the majestic euphony. She retreated as far as she could, yet from a small corner in herself, she was still aware when the spirit of the Great Mother came into her.

Tears coursed down Niala's cheeks. Words were whispered inside her head. The thoughts of Gaea entwined with Niala's own. She could not stop the tears. An immense love consumed her, love of all life, an expansion that swirled her into the depths of the earth.

Niala's limbs grew heavy as if weighted by a thousand stones and her breathing grew shallow. She could still feel, still hear, but her body was no longer hers with the exception of the strand that held them together.

The chanting grew louder as the masses began their journey into the cavern. Their voices reverberated off the walls of the narrow channel leading them to her. Niala could feel her tribe's hearts beating and their lives ready to begin anew.

Her soul was filled with such longing that it caused pain. Exquisite pain. She wanted children - her need was great. She wanted children created from her body. Many, many children. To have something other than herself.

Something made from herself.

Something to fill the yearning.

Gaea could not be the solitary one who breathed, who saw beauty. As she had been created out of Chaos, thus she would re-create herself. Her womb contracted. She screamed with the pain. With the desire to give life.

Hers...to have....

Gaea gasped and clutched her belly, breathing into the pain, pushing mightily. As her shrieks echoed in the chamber, the first of her children arrived.

Pallin slipped through the tunnel entrance, crossed to the throne and knelt before Niala. Four torches, anchoring the elements of life, flickered along the curved walls and domed ceiling. They gave light and heat, yet Pallin shivered, her eyes still accustomed to the darkness of the passageway and the chilled air that filled it.

She stayed quiet, head bowed, hands held to her fast-beating heart. Though Pallin had gone over and over the sacred rite of honoring Gaea, panic brought blankness to her mind and she was unable to speak.

With lips trembling, Pallin raised her head, ready to confess she could not go through with her duty, for the words were no longer there. Tears threatened to fall, for this would be a failure Pallin could not bear to live with. It seemed she felt the disapproval before she could even tell of her humiliation.

As Pallin met the steady gaze of the woman seated on the

throne, she was shaken by the change. No longer did Niala Aaminah look back at her. It was Gaea who saw through the warm amber eyes into hers. It was Gaea, not Niala, who smiled and nodded, Gaea who filled Pallin with exquisite joy and love.

Pallin was uplifted, breathless with a desire to serve and serve well. Gone was her fear. Gone was the tongue-tied girl whose knees shook and palms sweated. She was a Priestess, accepting Gaea's power.

"I am blessed to be your firstborn." Pallin kissed first one foot and then the other of the goddess before her. "I pray I may follow the wisdom of your footsteps."

"With each step, you will discover the secrets of the Earth," Gaea said.

"From you, all things flow. I am blessed to be blood of your blood." Pallin leaned between Gaea's legs and kissed her belly.

"And from my blood there shall be growth and goodness."

"Your bounty is full and rich. Through you, I am fed." Pallin kissed each breast and as she drew back, milk began to flow.

"I am the fountain which springs from the soil. Through me, all life will be sustained."

"And to you, Great Mother, I return the fruits of your labor. Taste the sweetness of my promise to serve you." Pallin dipped her finger in a pot of honey set to the right of the throne and touched it to Gaea's lips.

Gaea licked a drop of the golden liquid and closed her eyes. A low purr of pleasure came from her throat. "It is good and it binds you to me. Your promise now lives within my body. Do not forsake me."

Bowing her head, Pallin whispered, "I pray you will always love me as I love you."

When Gaea answered, it was with a deeply resonating tone, strong and vibrant. "My love is boundless."

"Blessed are we that have the Great Mother to call our own. To death I am yours and after death I become one with you."

"Rise my faithful one, stand beside me in life and I will take you after death."

Pallin rose to stand at the left hand of Gaea. The tight little knot of drummers behind the throne slipped from the thrumming call to gather into the steady beat that beckoned the others into the chamber. Slowly the beat - boom, boom, da, da, da, boom, da, da, boom, boom, da - echoed and was answered by the drummers who sat outside the cave entrance.

Gaea's children came forth one at a time, slipping through the crack in the rock wall, as if they were entering the womb of the Great Mother, readying themselves to be born into the world once again. Silently, Pallin watched as each member of her village came into the chamber to kneel before Gaea.

Pallin watched as the young ones came first and then mothers and fathers who carried infants. She listened to their stories just as Gaea did, even though Pallin already knew them. She knew each person, each joy, each sorrow as if it was her own, but she did not waver in her duty to stand by Gaea.

Pallin listened as Yena sobbed on Gaea's knee and told of her only daughter passing into the shadows, a daughter who was a mere babe at her breast. Why? How? She asked the Great Mother, how could this little one be taken away from her and into the coldness of death? Why had not Gaea chosen Yena to be the one? She would have gone happily if the child could have lived.

"Death is a return home. It is not a punishment, but a renewal," Gaea responded. "Life is woven as a piece of cloth, some threads are long and make strong the edges and others are the bright patterns that play within. Your babe was one small pattern. Take heart, for she may yet return to you."

Yena was comforted in Gaea's presence and made peace with her loss. Yena dipped her fingers in the milk that flowed from Gaea's breast and took the blessing. In return, she fed Gaea with honey and thanked her.

Pallin felt sorrow as Ramad told of an unfaithful love and was blessed with the milk of the Great Mother to soothe his pride. Then the unfaithful lover came forward and told of her unhappiness in the union and she, too, was blessed.

Each who touched their fingers to Gaea's belly and drank of the milk returned the gift with honey on the lips of the goddess. Pallin heard all the stories and watched them all receive from Gaea, no matter who they were or what they told.

Every one left the chamber with gladness written upon his or her face. Not once did Pallin waver though she stood for many hours. Not once did she turn away from a story, for if Gaea could listen and hold counsel she could do no less than stand as witness.

Midway, Pallin noticed an unfamiliar face. A slender, strongly built, dark-skinned man stumbled into the chamber as if pushed and stared wildly about. He looked as one first awakened by a loud noise, dark eyes unfocused and uncertain, body tense as if prepared to flee. Pallin's first thought was to challenge him, for he was not one of them and did not belong.

Pallin felt a gentle nudge against these thoughts and knew Gaea heeded her to remember her place. Pallin held silence and waited. The man began to speak, but she did not understand what he said. His tones were sharp and rapid, and not altogether pleasing to her ears.

"Where am I." The man turned a slow circle. "Who are you?" He spoke to Gaea in a choked voice. "Are you the Queen of these people? I do not recall how I came to be here."

His gaze swiveled away from Gaea to look about the cavern. "I do not know what is happening."

His eyes lit upon Pallin and he stared long and hard at her and she at him.

The man was unlike the men of the village. He had hair upon his chin, cheeks and above his upper lip. His brown hair was long and matted. His clothing was made of dark cloth, shiny from wear. On his feet, he wore boots made of hide. She took all this in quickly, certain now that he should not have come into the cave.

This man was a stranger who could cause harm to both Gaea and Niala. Pallin went to step in front of Gaea, to protect the body of Niala, when a hand touched Pallin's arm. It was Gaea.

Her expression was filled with compassion and directed Pallin to stop. Pallin bowed her head and returned to her post, but she did not take her eyes from the stranger's face.

"Who are you?" Hattusilis asked in a faltering voice. His panic subsided, but his confusion had not.

"I am Gaea."

Her voice held the lilt of the winds across the treetops, and she spoke to Hattusilis in his own language with ease. Hattusilis fell on his knees before Gaea, staring in wonder as milk flowed from her breasts down across her belly. She was naked before him, smelling of soil and sun-warmed grasses, a deep, rich scent mixed with the sweetness of milk. He could not take his eyes from her.

"What do you want of me?"

"It is not what I want from you." Gaea held him within the embrace of her gaze. "It is what you want from me."

"I do not understand."

"All who come before me seek something."

"I seek…." Hattusilis spoke with hesitation. Never had he been filled with such awe. Words would not find their way into his mouth.

"I do not belong here," Hattusilis whispered. His god required blood sacrifice for any favors and even then, a favor from Teshub was hard to come by. To merely ask and receive was too much for him to grasp.

"All belong to me. My blessings flow for any who would come before me. You are before me."

"But I am a follower of Teshub."

"Teshub. He who holds the reins of conflict. He chooses to be as he is, just as you choose to be as you are."

"I am a warrior, a king. I can be nothing else."

"Even Teshub is more than he seems." A rumble of laughter flooded the cavern. As the echo of it faded away, Gaea said, "Speak your heart's desire."

"To overcome my enemies."

"We are not your enemy."

"No, I did not say it was so"

"You seek to overcome my people."

"To give just rule, and protection. Nothing else. I do not intend harm."

Gaea nodded as if in deep thought. Her face was calm, her eyes bright as she kept her gaze upon Hattusilis. She seemed to search his very soul, reaching in and touching even the most secret places.

"Say what is in your heart, for if what you seek is not within, you will not find it without."

"Azhar, my wife," he whispered. "Azhar and her people."

"Azhar."

Hattusilis shuddered as Gaea's immanence flowed over and around him. An offering of forgiveness, a willingness to ease the pain, but he could not accept it. Head reeling, Hattusilis met Pallin's gaze.

His mouth trembled as he tried to form a question, for still, he did not understand what was expected of him, yet he could not. He turned back to the goddess who sat before him. She smiled at him with a radiance that made his heart hurt.

The priestess leaned in, ran her finger through the glaze of milk and lifted it to his lips. As he licked her fingers, he felt fire running though him, a brilliant flash of knowing all, of seeing clearly the choices before him.

And then it all faded away. He was left weak and near fainting as he watched the priestess scoop honey from a pot and press it to the lips of the goddess. Someone took him by the arm and led him away. Next he knew he had emerged into the night.

Above him, the sky was shot through with tiny specks of white light, as if all the secrets of the universe were on display. Hattusilis was beyond thought, beyond reason and could only stumble down a sloped pathway toward the valley floor, following others to the shores of a glimmering, star-filled lake.

Movement slowed as the passage narrowed and the line of villagers became a single file. Deimos knew they were close to their journey's end and, just as certain, he knew the most ancient goddess of all time waited within the deep recesses of the cavern.

Gaea's vitality washed over him in waves and the pounding of his heart was not his, but hers as she reached out to him. Those who were before him also felt her, for their singing slowed and finally halted, though the wordless song continued to carry on behind them.

Gaea had birthed the first immortals, splitting them from her own spirit and causing them to have conscious thoughts. She called some of those beings into body and there they lived as mortals again and again. Some she called to a higher sacrifice.

To become the unconscious memory of the masses. He, like his father, War, and his mother, Love, was of that nature. They were the patterns that existed because the mortal world could not hold the form alone. This was whom he waited to see, She who was the mother of all.

Dread swelled inside him. Dread that grew into fear and expanded to a trembling, high note of terror. Deimos fought against his nature, fought to control the fear, but it rose up and burst over those around him in a sea of terror that brought a sudden onslaught of screams and flailing arms. In the darkness, Deimos brought them something unexpected and without willing it, he destroyed something innocent.

Shame clawed at his spirit, yet he could not help who he was.

Deimos knew he should step out now, move from their world to his own and leave his quest to be in Gaea's presence trampled beneath the oncoming feet. He had done what he always did, caused despair and grief.

What could one such as Gaea have to say to him?

Leave, he told himself, leave now. Go back to your own realm where, at the least, you are understood. By what right are you here?

Deimos' thoughts came in a panicked hiss. *"None. Go. Flee! Before it is too late."*

Too late for what?

And into his thoughts came a clear voice, *"Stay."*

Deimos found his limbs weak and his will overcome. A sense of calmness descended and those who felt terror were now quiet, moving forward again as if nothing had happened. Ahead, Deimos could see wavering shadows cast by firelight through a narrow doorway.

It was the first light he saw in the many hours he was inside the passage. The glow beckoned him to enter the domain of the goddess. He had to step up over a rim of stone and lower his head to squeeze through the opening.

The cavern was large. He was able to stand up straight and look around at the white stone awash in the colors of the torchlight. He saw the group of drummers whose eyes were closed even as their hands moved, enthralled by the beat as if it emanated without their help. In the center of the cave was a natural rock formation creating a throne-like arrangement of the same white rock.

A naked woman was seated upon the stone chair. As he approached, he could see hair streaming around her lush body in a tangled, prolific growth. She sat at ease, with her arms resting upon the sides of the cloth-covered throne, her legs slightly parted, her head tilted back. Her eyes held an unnatural luminosity and her lips curved into a knowing smile. As he drew closer, he saw the body was Niala's, but it was not Niala who looked out at him.

Beneath the presence of Gaea, he could still feel Niala Aaminah, but she was distant, as if she surrendered herself to the power of Earth and now humbly waited to return. Deimos wanted to reach out to her, to be comforted by her gentle spirit, but he could feel Gaea's vitality pouring forth like a thundering fall of water sweeping all into her path.

Deimos was drawn to Gaea by her will and as her consciousness connected with his, he gasped and fell to his knees before her. Niala Aaminah slipped away from him and all he could do was accept Gaea's power as it flowed over and through him.

In front of his eyes was a patch of brown hair, the secret, hidden entrance to the dark cavern of women's mysteries. Though he yearned to know those mysteries, he dared not consider such a thing and instead lowered his gaze to hide his thoughts. He found himself staring at a likeness of the Blue Serpent, Kulika, winding from ankle to thigh upon Niala's left leg.

Kulika's triangular head appeared to weave back and forth as his tongue flicked toward the treasures that lay within the earth. Only Kulika, Earth's consort, was allowed to slither into that dark, moist place and mate with Gaea to create the abundance of the world.

The bounty of their mating flowed from her generous breasts to produce a river of milk, thick as cream with a succulent, sweet aroma. It made Deimos' head swim with the desire to press his face into Gaea's bosom. The milk dripped down her belly and ran into the creases of her thighs. Without thought, he laid his finger along the serpent image, tracing the blue lines with the milk from Gaea's own breasts.

A loud hissing filled his head and the tip of his finger stung as if fangs had sunk into his flesh. Eyes wide, he jerked his hand back, but too late, for a surge of heat slammed into him. Deimos' thoughts swirled with serpentine energy as his body roiled with sexual intent upon the crest of Kulika's power. Flames rose up in a wave and engulfed Deimos, scalding his flesh, stealing his breath, dragging him into the red-hot throes of instant passion.

Deimos fought back, casting outward for a way to pull free. Just as suddenly as it came, the sensation was gone. Deimos sagged, arms limp, legs frozen, head bowed. His breath came in ragged spurts as he knelt in front of the throne.

"Deimos." Gaea spoke his name.

He could not answer; he could only nod.

"You have aroused Kulika."

"I am sorry."

"He seeks now to mate with me through you."

"I did not intend it."

"Kulika has his own intentions, but he is not invited to this ritual. Do not touch me again or you will call him into being."

"Yes, my lady."

Gaea nodded with deliberate slowness, her gaze shifting to a place above his head. "Swear, then, no harm to my people, for to harm them is to harm me."

"Harm?"

"Turn your legion away."

"It is not my legion."

"They must not find my people." Her tone was firm. Behind her words was the hissing of Kulika's forked tongue.

"They will not." Deimos shrugged, for what else could he say?

At this, Gaea smiled, a simple curving of lips that once formed oceans and land that spoke of mountain peaks and sandy deserts. Her smile brought forth the images of lush greenery, of fecund earth and fertile soil.

Deimos exhaled, with downcast gaze.

"Look upon my face and see the love I have for you."

With effort, Deimos lifted his head and once he saw her shining radiance, his heart began to ache. "How can you love one who is Terror? One who brings fear and loathing, despair and desolation?"

"How can I not, for life is made of many things."

"I am of the dark side."

"You are both dark and light. You search for peace when it lies within you."

Deimos shook his head at the simplicity of Gaea's observation. "Unveiled, I cannot walk the earth. If I cannot show my true self, then I will never find peace."

"Terror, you must bear for all time. Despair is not your burden." Gaea paused to touch his face with her fingers, to smooth his hair. Her touch was like snow kissing the ground. "All things must balance,"

"I have no balance. I am no more than I am."

"Invoked with your name is Survival. When terror strikes, survival is ignited. You embody both, Deimos."

His lips parted to deny her words, but instead, Deimos was caught up in her gaze. There, in those clear and shining eyes, lay the ancient wisdom of Earth. She alone, could look past the god and see the man. All he was and ever would be was reflected back at him. He saw the cocoon of confusion that had gripped his past, and from that, he saw himself emerging into the greater self of his future.

Deimos was not alone, as he supposed he would be. Another stood beside him, though he could not see her face, and the ache of loneliness that had forever been in his heart was lightened. Hope lay in the depths of Gaea's steady gaze.

He reached toward that future moment only to hear the warning hiss of a serpent. Brought back, Deimos withdrew his hand from midair. He could not stop the trembling of his limbs and fought the tears welling in his eyes. Blinking, he dipped his head in a slight bow, for he could not speak past the tightness in his throat.

Gaea lifted two fingers to his mouth and fed him the bounty that flowed from her body. In return, he stood and kissed her sweet lips with a gentleness he did not know he had.

"Thank you." The taste of milk and honey lingered on his mouth as unshed tears stung his eyes. Blinded, he stumbled back only to have his hand taken by another. He was led across the cavern into the shadows where he found a wider passageway that took him out into the cool, crisp air of the night.

Deimos made his way along the path skirting the ridge. It seemed important he put each foot in front of the other and walk down the side of the mount rather than carry himself away. Once he reached the bottom, he stopped. Sounds of water and wind, the scent of fires and raw earth were all around him, but all he could do was to fall exhausted upon the ground and stare up at the vast universe.

How long he lay in the grass, he could not say. People passed him, some weeping, some singing, some silent, but they passed him, unseeing. They steered away from his resting spot without realizing they did so.

He pushed them away.

Yet he longed to be seen. To be seen, really seen.

As what? Not as Terror, that frightful image that drove some mad. What then? A warrior? A god? A lover? A man?

He did not know. Tears finally broke free, for the emptiness that seemed always to be part of him was back. He hurt, though he could not understand why. As he wiped away the wetness from his cheek, he held his hand up and stared at it, realizing the tears were part of Gaea's gift. Tears were a sign of weakness not allowed in his father's house.

Not if one wanted to survive. Deimos stared up at the starlit sky. Survive. Yes. He survived the terror of his initiation into the House of War.

Deimos stepped into his fate rather than hid from it. And those mortals who faced their own terrors? They, too have a choice. They could survive, or they could die.

Gaea was right.

He was Survival as well as Terror.

The cave began to dim as the torches burned down. Outside Niala knew the sky was becoming a murky gray as dawn approached. Still seated on the throne, wearier than mere words could express, without the infusion of Earth's ecstatic energy, she was mortal once more as she slumped against the stone back. The last few people passed through the cavern gateway onto the trail some time ago, including the faithful drummers and priestesses who stood sentry.

Pallin waited with patience for Niala to rally, offering food and water to sustain her, to anchor her back into her body. Niala would not yet accept anything and waved away the handful of nuts.

"But Niala, you must eat," chided Pallin. "You will not regain your strength if you do not."

"I am fine. I just need a moment to rest."

"Drink, then."

A small jug of water was held to her lips and Niala swallowed, for if she did not, the water would have spilled down her front. She smiled to herself over that, for she was sticky from head to toe with both milk and honey, and a little water would not hurt a thing.

"Niala?" Pallin's tone was anxious for she saw a slight smile. She knew Niala would open to Gaea and let her be present once more if she believed that is what Earth desired, yet Pallin also knew Earth should not return that night. But something else might.

Pallin was expressly forbidden to let that happen. The last thing Inni said to her before the ritual: *Do not let Niala drift away afterwards. It is very dangerous to leave her unattended, even for a moment. There are other spirits who would take advantage of her weakness.*

That caused Pallin no small amount of alarm, for she understood the 'other spirits' seeking a body could mean demons. She badgered Inni to near madness in her desire to know what she should do to prevent such a thing.

Make her eat and drink, it will keep her out of trouble.

"Trouble, trouble, trouble," Pallin chanted the word over and over under her breath.

"No trouble, no trouble, no trouble." She amended her mantra with a touch of panic. She did not want to draw a demon to them.

"No trouble." Pallin spoke with the emphasis on the 'no'.

"What?" Gaze bleary, Niala lifted her head.

With relief, Pallin saw no more than Niala looking back at her.

"It is nothing. Do you feel you can walk now? We should try to move a bit. Moving is good. Your feet upon the ground would be the best thing. Eat a few dates. That would also be good."

"Pallin."

"Really, Niala, I know what is best right now. Let me help you."

"I am fine."

Niala groaned as she allowed herself to be dragged from the hard seat. Her legs and feet felt as if a thousand thorns were imbedded in her skin. Clutching at Pallin's arm, she tottered a few steps and then paused to drink again from the jug.

"You do not look well." Peering up at her, Pallin steadied the water jug in Niala's shaking hand.

"It is the torchlight," Niala scoffed, though she felt more lightheaded than usual after such a ritual. She held herself upright as Pallin wrapped a robe around her, lifting her arms through the holes as if she were a child in need of being dressed.

Pallin wiped Niala's face with a damp cloth, for which Niala was grateful, then gathered her hair back into a stringy loop and tied it with a length of cording.

"There." Finished, Pallin surveyed her work. "You look more like yourself."

"I am feeling more like myself."

Niala allowed Pallin to help her across the dirt floor of the chamber and through the exit.

Fresh, cool air greeted them as they emerged, whipping away the staleness of smoke and sweat. Pallin shivered but did not release Niala's arm.

"You are well?"

"Yes, yes, of course." Niala smiled. "Let us go to the lake."

Pallin hugged Niala before they began the descent. They, too, would bathe in the lake before retiring, just as all the others had done, to wash away those things no longer useful to them for the upcoming year. The water would take away the wounds, the grief, the pain, and leave behind the start of new growth. The water would nurture the seeds planted for next year's harvest.

Somewhere along the valley bottom, a few distant refrains of song could be heard wafting up to where they stood. Niala cocked her head to one side to listen and then began to hum along with the singers.

"Who is that, do you think?" Niala tapped her fingers in the air.

"Why, I do not know. It could be anyone, I suppose."

"Anyone?" Niala continued humming.

"Everyone," amended Pallin. It was not the song they used to call Gaea, but another, more joyful tune sung afterward by those gathered at the water's edge. "You know it well, Niala."

"Of course." Niala hummed louder and began to move her feet in a little dance.

"What are you doing?"

"It is such a pretty song, I think." Niala broke away from Pallin's grip, skipping along the path, humming to herself.

"Stop, you will fall down the rise. This path is too rough to go so fast." Pallin chased after Niala, trying to grab at Niala's arm.

"Where is everyone?" Pausing, Niala peered over the edge toward the black waters of the lake. The singing had ceased and the spell broken. Niala relaxed and let Pallin take her elbow again.

"They have gone home to sleep." Pallin was breathless. "As we should, as soon as we have bathed."

"Oh, of course."

They walked in sedate companionship for a few moments, nearing the bottom of the ridge. The last bit of roadway was steep and rocky and needed great care to clamber down. Pallin let go of Niala to steady herself on a jutting piece of stone, calling out to her, "Be careful you do not slip."

"Do not worry."

A bit of song drifted up toward them again, just a burst of enthusiasm, one last refrain before retiring. It came from somewhere closer to the homes on the outskirts of Najahmara, clear notes carried on the light breeze.

Niala's head snapped up as she listened. "There it is again."

Pallin groaned and slid faster along the sharp bends of the path. They were almost to the bottom. Only a few more steps to catch up with Niala, but she was too late. Niala began singing again, loudly, and danced quickly down the slope onto the grassy meadow near the lake.

With arms spread wide and head thrown back, Niala twirled around and around, singing and laughing. Pallin ran behind her, shouting, "Niala, stop! Where are you going? The lake is this way."

Ignoring her, Niala continued to sing and dance her way through the meadow toward a bank of trees near the lake. With merriment propelling Niala, she spun around, loosening her hair and letting her robe slide off one shoulder.

"Niala, please." Breathless, Pallin begged. "Come back."

"Play with me!" Niala dodged back and forth between the tree trunks as if in a game of hide and seek.

"No, let us not." Pallin snatched at Niala's hem.

She missed and fell down on one knee. When she stood up, Niala had disappeared.

"Oh, no. Oh, mercy. Oh dear." Pallin wrung her hands. "I have lost her. What am I going to do? Niala? Niala!"

"Boo." Leaping up from behind a thick bush, Niala lunged at Pallin, slapped her back and then ran away.

With a startled shriek, Pallin went after her, but Niala was faster. This time she headed for the lake, her hair bouncing behind her. Pallin had nearly caught up to her when Niala tripped and went down into the grass, arms flailing.

"Niala."

Niala sprang back up, shouting, "Demons!"

Aghast, Pallin began screaming. "Demons? Demons? Jahmed, Inni, help us - we have been attacked by demons."

Pallin knew Jahmed and Inni waited for them beside the water's edge and they were close enough to be heard. She shrieked again, "Jahmed, help us!" before she reached Niala's side and grabbed at her arm to drag her back.

"Come, come away, Niala, please."

Pallin could not see anyone at Niala's feet, though Niala stretched her hand out as if she reached for someone. Frantic, Pallin, pulled at Niala. "It is a demon, we must get away."

"No, no, not a *demon*," Niala giggled. "It is Deimos. Why do you lie here all alone, Deimos?"

"There is no one there," cried Pallin, aghast. "It must be a demon, for you talk to the air!"

Pointing at the ground, Niala answered, "It is Deimos. Show yourself, for she thinks I am mad."

Before Pallin's disbelieving eyes, a young man appeared, sitting on the ground with his head in his hands. He murmured something she could not hear, but his words sent Niala off into yet another gale of laughter.

"Gaea had her way with you." Niala clapped her hands in delight. "I was hoping it would be so."

"And why is that?" Deimos shifted with irritation.

He lifted his head to glance at the woman next to Niala. She was very pale, with strands of straight black hair pulled free from a long braid. Her eyes looked wild in the shadows as she clutched at Niala's arm. He had seen her before, in company with Niala and tonight, in attendance beside the throne of Gaea.

"It is Gaea's secret." Niala threw her head back and laughed.

"What is wrong? What has happened? Where have you been?" Jahmed and Inni sprinted up, wheezing and scarce dressed, for they had been in the water.

"Niala was talking to no one and then there he was, out of thin air." Pallin's relief at their arrival was clear. "She acts possessed, for I cannot calm her. She ran away from me."

Jahmed stifled a laugh and Inni looked away with a suspicion of a smile on her lips.

"Oh, you make fun of me, but truly, she has invoked a demon into our midst." Pallin jabbed one finger toward the figure on the ground. "I saw him appear myself."

"Niala, what is this about?" Jahmed placed a hand on Niala's shoulder.

"I am no demon." Deimos rose to his feet. "Though there are some who would swear I am."

He was a tall one, taller than Niala and Jahmed, head and shoulders above Pallin and Inni. He was powerfully built and upon standing, seemed more a threat than when he sat. Jahmed's breath caught as she edged back, pulling Niala with her. His face was in the shadows, but the sky was light enough to see the intensity of his body. Inni bristled beside Jahmed and Pallin trembled next to her.

"You see," Pallin babbled. "He is not what he seems. First he was not there and then he was. He is a demon."

"Hush." Niala raised a palm towards the women. "He is no demon, but one who needs our care."

There was no hint of the silliness that touched her earlier. Niala had collected herself and now took the young man's hand. He did not resist her, but allowed himself to be drawn into their little group.

"Deimos has not been into the water and neither have I. Let us go there now, for I think I have reached beyond myself tonight."

"That is clear enough," muttered Pallin. "Though what was I to do about it? She would not stop."

"I told you that you could not afford to lose control." Inni frowned. "Feed her, dress her and bring her directly to the lake, I said."

"Hmmph." Walking fast, Pallin led the way with Inni close behind. "I tried, but she would not come with me."

"You did not try hard enough."

"What was I to do? Wrestle her to the ground and tie her in knots?"

"Whatever it takes."

"Stop," chided Jahmed. "It takes practice to tend one as strong as Niala after a ritual such as we had tonight. We should not have left you alone with her."

"It is not that I am unable."

"No, it is not that you cannot handle it," Inni interrupted. "It is that you did not."

"Inni." Jahmed shook her head. "Do not be so harsh, or I will have to describe your first Spring rites to Pallin and let her see what foolishness you were up to."

Inni did not answer, but Pallin saw the ghost of a smile on her lips. It seemed that would be a story Pallin would like to hear some day, for Inni often took the high road on matters of ritual, or anything else she could scold about.

Pallin glanced back at the young man and caught his gaze. She blushed and dropped her eyes for she saw raw hunger on his face, though it was not directed at her. She felt as if she peeped into a coupling, for his desire was reaching out toward Niala as surely as his fingers touched her palm.

There was no recollection of this man before tonight. Pallin could not think how Niala knew him, though Niala was not above keeping secrets from her sisters.

'However,' Pallin mused. *'Perhaps he is from before I became a priestess. Still I should remember him, for he is far too enthralling to forget.'*

She cast another quick glance at Deimos, only this time, he stared at her as if he could hear what was in her thoughts. For the first time, Pallin noticed a fair amount of blood at his collar and as he tipped his head, the edges of a raw wound.

"You are hurt."

"It is nothing." Deimos dropped Niala's hand to bring his up to touch his neck.

Pallin watched his fingertips as they moved across his skin in a near caress. She licked her lips and could not tear her gaze from that lean, strong hand.

"What is your name?" Deimos' voice was kind.

"Pallin." Her answer was abrupt and belied the tightening in her belly. She walked faster, away from them, and was the first to drop her robe and wade into the warm waters of the joined rivers.

"I think Pallin was overburdened by this night." Inni sent a keen glance at the bare backside of the younger woman as she slide into the rippling lake. "She does not seem right."

"It is my fault," Niala answered. "Gaea did not completely release me. It seems she wanted to…umm…dance a bit."

"Dance?" Jahmed burst into laughter. "No wonder Pallin is distraught. So, tell me, Niala, has Gaea gone to her rest?"

"I believe so, dear one." Niala inhaled and felt the weariness settle in. "And I am worn out from her play."

"Tell me, also, did you receive your promise?" Jahmed lowered her voice as Inni beckoned Deimos to shed his clothing and go into the water. She could hear their murmured words and see the doubtful shake of his head.

"Yes." Niala watched Deimos hesitate before he threw off his clothes and follow Pallin into the water.

Jahmed gathered Niala into a fierce hug. "Thank the goddess."

"Still, sister, should I suddenly be gone from your midst, it is your duty to step into my place. I have your agreement on this."

Nodding, Jahmed exhaled with relief. "Yes, you have my agreement."

"Good." Niala turned away from the shore. "I do not feel like swimming."

Jahmed frowned. "You should wash."

"I will bathe at the temple. Call Inni and let us leave them to themselves."

"But...." Jahmed looked back at the two in the water.

"It is as it should be." There was finality to Niala's words and Jahmed argued no more. She hissed Inni's name and her response was immediate and without question; together they escorted Niala back to the temple. Neither Pallin nor Deimos noticed their retreat.

TEN

"Deimos, wake up." A voice hissed in his ear. "Deimos!"
The voice was urgent.

His shoulder was gripped and shaken by a calloused hand. With a start, Deimos came fully alert. For a moment, he did not remember where he was, for the voice and hand forcing him to awaken belonged to another place. He rubbed his face and gave a low growl.

"Go away."

"Deimos, you must get up."

Deimos would not open his eyes but tried to turn away from Eris, his brother. It was then Deimos realized he rested in a low-slung hammock not at all like the high, heavy bed in his quarters at Athos.

Nor was it the hard ground of an encampment with the dampness of the morning spread like a blanket over everything. Pallin lay in his arms, her body nestled against his, her cheek resting on his chest. As he shifted, she gave a soft moan.

Touching her eyelids, Deimos whispered, "Shhh. Sleep, Pallin."

She stopped moving and fell back into deep slumber.

"Go away, Eris," Deimos repeated.

"I cannot." Eris' voice was high-pitched and more grating than usual. "You must return home immediately."

"Why?"

"Ares commands it."

There was too much self-satisfaction in the boy's voice to suit Deimos. "Return and tell Ares I am occupied at the moment and cannot attend to him."

"Eerk." A strangled sound squeaked from Eris' throat as he stared at Deimos in horror. "You do not mean that, Brother. Ares calls, you must answer."

"I do not feel like it this morning. I bid you go back to Athos, or wherever Ares is, and tell him I will attend him later."

Through half-closed eyes, Deimos watched Eris flush to a darker shade of green and sputter with angst. "I will tell him no such thing. If you refuse to return, then you must tell him yourself."

"But if I do not return, I cannot tell him. Since you are the messenger, it is up to you to relay my words exactly as I have said them."

"I will say you purposely disobey him. That is what I will do if you do not disentangle yourself from that mortal and return home!"

Eris danced back and forth, glaring at Deimos, his sharp, pointed teeth bared in a grimace. Though he was a son of Ares the Destroyer and a true warrior, every attempt to look fierce failed, for Eris resembled his mother far too much. Eris had the same delicate features and small stature as the one who bore him, a Sylph woman named Aglauros.

His skin was very pale, like hers, with a light tinge of green. His hair was a mop of rich brown curls straggling to his shoulders while his eyes were wide, anxious and the golden-brown of turning leaves. Eris was as pretty as his mother, but as opposite in nature as a wild boar to a tender fawn.

He was also known as Strife. Therein, it took little effort to stir Eris into a state of natural frenzy. There was no question Deimos would have to return to Athos. He knew he should not further torment the boy, but he could not help himself.

"I am quite comfortable right here." Kissing Pallin's forehead, Deimos made a show of smoothing the hair away from one bare shoulder. "What does Ares want?"

Voice rising, Eris answered, "I do not ask why, I just do as I am told, as should you. Do not defy our father, or you will find yourself locked within the bowels of Athos."

"Is that what he did the last time he was displeased with you?"

Eris flushed again. "You know how I hate the underground. Rock and dirt, stale air, dark, creeping, crawling things."

He shuddered and hugged himself across his unclothed torso. Clad only in a loincloth, the rest of his body lithe and smooth-limbed, Eris appeared a harmless creature.

"I am not inclined to return. It seems you will revisit the dungeons for failing him again."

"I warn you, do not ignore Ares."

"My father should be proud I seek out his favorite entertainment."

"Our father," spat Eris. "Is angry and you are the source. Whatever you have done, it has upset the Ages."

"The Ages?" Startled, Deimos eased himself free of Pallin's weight and climbed from the woven-reed hammock. "What has the Council to do with me? I am scarce allowed into their hallowed halls."

Eris licked his lips, staring at Pallin with great interest. Frowning, Deimos picked up the light cover that had fallen to the floor and tucked it around Pallin's nakedness. She sighed, still deep in sleep, and rolled to her back. Long strands of black hair stood in vivid contrast against the sheeting and one slender arm was thrown across the space he just vacated.

Deimos stepped between Eris and Pallin, blocking his view. "What has disturbed the Council?"

"I do not know." Eris shivered, his resolve gone. He balanced on his toes and shook his curls from side to side, staring intently at the deep wound on Deimos' neck.

"I do not want to know. Whatever the cause of this madness, it is your doing. Early this morning, Ares was summoned to the Greater Realm to stand before Zeus and the rest of the Council. He was not happy."

"No, I imagine not," Deimos muttered. "But I have no idea what lies at the root of this upheaval. Ares told you I was the concern?"

"More than told, brother. He was in a fury over the summons, and truth, it was better you were not at hand when Hermes arrived."

"What was said?" With growing concern, Deimos dressed himself in the lightweight tunic and leggings he had thrown aside the night before. "I have done nothing to warrant all this interest."

"I was not allowed to listen, though I tried. Hermes is a sly one and took care I did not overhear. All I am certain of is you must return to Athos, and better it is before Ares arrives back from the Greater Realm."

"Perhaps you are right. I should make haste to Athos. I do not understand what this is about."

"Yes, we must go." Eris cocked his head to one side. "What has happened to you?"

"What do you mean?"

"Did someone try to cut your throat?" Eris pointed to the already healing gash made by Telio's sword.

Deimos frowned. "Never mind that. It was no more than a battle wound. Now, let us begone, if that is what we are to do."

"Yes, of course. I will follow you."

Deimos turned a lingering gaze on Pallin's sheet-covered form. "There is something I must first do."

"No, Brother, I am bid to bring you back. If you stay, I stay." Eris, too, watched Pallin, an eager expression on his face.

With a snap of his fingers, Deimos brought Eris' attention back to him. "It is not about her, though I loathe to leave her side. It is about another I brought here last night. He was left to fend for himself in a strange place and I must first check on his safety."

"There is no time, Deimos. How long the Council will convene over this matter is hard to say. You do not want to keep Ares waiting, for he will...." Eris swallowed hard. "He will punish you."

"I do not fear his anger as you do." Deimos' tone was harsh. "I have suffered at his hand more than I can say. There is nothing new in either realm that could cause me further wounding."

"Bold words, but I would not voice that thought too freely." Eris met his brother's flat stare with a knowing nod. "Further, if you are not at Athos when he returns, he will seek you out himself."

A tiny trickle of sweat crawled down Deimos' forehead. Though he spoke the truth when he told of penalties served, he lied when he said he did not fear his father. Only a fool would not fear War.

"Is he aware of Najahmara?"

"Of course, and of the army that lies in wait beyond the forest. He was curious as to what battle might happen between these hapless folk and a hardened legion. To what purpose do these men come bearing arms? Is it to be a full-scale slaughter? Such violence is bound to draw him, this you know full well."

Deimos lifted a hand as if in protest, then let it fall to his side. "It is to be a peaceable takeover. I have convinced the king who leads this army to infiltrate rather than attack."

"That should please Ares, should it not?" Scorn laced Eris' words. "A bloodless invasion."

"It does not always have to be about bloodletting." Deimos touched Pallin's cheek one last time. "These people have done nothing to deserve annihilation."

With a derisive hoot, Eris said, "I will see you in those dungeons yet, my brother."

"Why would that be of any concern?"

"Why? Already, Ares thinks you move too freely in the mortal world, that you have become lazy in your duties to the Greater Realm. Should he get wind of this, you will roam the mortal realm no longer."

Eris' glee was more than Deimos could bear. He lunged at the youth, grabbing him by the hair. A loud howl was his reward.

Deimos hissed, "Say nothing of this to Ares or, I warn you, he will not be the only one you have to fear."

Eris stuck his tongue out and disappeared before Deimos could snatch at another handful of curls. Without further thought, Deimos left Najahmara for Athos, intent on catching Eris before he caused more harm.

It took but a moment for Eris to tumble into the dank corridor outside Ares' private quarters at Mt. Athos, with Deimos on his heels. He leapt away, holding his forefinger to his lips.

"Shhh." Eris pointed at the heavy wooden door leading into the chambers.

It was ajar.

Deimos fell silent, watching the crack between panel and jam as if Ares would burst through the space in a rage. They stood long moments in silence, breath held, waiting for his appearance.

Nothing happened.

Deimos gave a light rap on the door. When there was no response, he pushed the door open.

"Father?" Deimos called out.

A strong breeze blew through the room, stirring the dead ashes in the arched fireplace. Double doors leading to the outer walkway stood wide and the damp, cold air of the mountaintop laid claim to the interior. No sunlight broke through the heavy mantle of clouds and it seemed as if even they sought entry to the fortress as wisps of fog hung low on the ceiling.

"Delightful," muttered Deimos. Louder, he said, "Father, I am here. What is it you want from me?"

"I do not think he has returned from the Council."

"Apparently not."

With quick steps, Deimos crossed the room and rapped on the double doors to the bedchamber. When there was no answer, he grasped the brass handles and pulled the doors open.

Peering into the darkness, he called in his softness voice, "Father? Are you resting?"

His voice echoed in the emptiness. The doors leading to the courtyard were closed, the one window shuttered. No lamps or candles burned and the hearth was as equally lifeless as in the outer chamber. Deimos could just make out the shape of the four posts of the massive bed reaching up into the gloom.

The frame was made to support a canopy and thick draperies to shut out the chill breezes of Athos, but Ares had neither hanging from the bed. It was barren, other than the coverings.

Deimos withdrew and turned in time to see Eris close the bathing room doors across the way. Eris was shaking his head and mumbling to himself.

"What are you saying?" Deimos retreated from the inner chamber. "Speak up, I cannot hear you."

Shrugging, Eris said, "He is not here."

There seemed no answer to this and they both knew it. Deimos drew closed the last set of doors which would take him out onto a narrow walkway circling the fortress. Even with all secured the room became steadily colder. The inlaid black and red spiral on the floor was coated with mist, dulling the colors.

Everything was drab and lifeless, sucked dry of any vitality. Everything was inanimate except the long sword hanging above the mantle. Deimos paced the room, going more than once to stand in front of the yawning fireplace and stare up at the blade.

Deimos reached as if to touch the shimmering tip but withdrew his fingers before he made contact with the metal. Always, he had been fascinated by Amason. As a child, he yearned to hold it. During those miserable years, it seemed Amason called his name, with quiet, dulcet tones so its true master would not hear. Or perhaps it was just the dream of a young boy. But he had heard more than once, *'Deimos, take me up in hand, for I am the mightiest sword in either realm'.*

He never did, for Ares allowed no one to handle Amason. It took great strength and agility to wield the sword and, as a youth, Deimos had neither. He did not even ask if he could lay his hand against the metal, for the answer would have been painful and he lacked courage.

Now as Deimos stood staring at the sword, he thought he heard it beckon him once more. And why should he not take it from its place and wrap his fingers around the leather hilt? The opportunity was ripe, for he had never been left alone in Ares' private quarters with Amason unattended.

Deimos fought the urge to lift the sword down, for his courage failed him. With certainty, Ares would know Amason had been disturbed and his ire would be no less dreadful than in times past.

Turning toward Eris and away from the hearth, Deimos said, "We might as well sit as it appears we will have a long wait."

Neither went toward the chairs beside the fireplace but retreated to the corner table. After long moments, Eris pleaded for warmth.

"I am quite frozen. Can we not have a fire to take the chill from the air?"

"If you want a fire, then make a fire."

"I am not as adept at such things, as you are," Eris wheedled.

"You are as able as I. You just prefer I incur the trouble it might bring."

Eris ducked his head and refused to look at Deimos. Instead, Eris sat shivering, arms wrapped around his bare torso.

"If you would but clothe yourself while you are at Athos, you would not find the cold so unpleasant."

"You know I cannot stand to have that weight upon me," Eris chattered. "Indeed, I can scarce stand the chill of this place." He looked about the cold dreary walls with contempt. "I am born of warmth and timber, not of ice and rock."

For a moment, Eris was taken back to his native forest, the land where he was birthed. He could even smell the damp earth covered in layers upon layers of leaves, the bottom of which was melting back into the black soil.

The trees created a steaming canopy for the Sylph women who made their homes among the twining boughs or within the hollow trunks. As a child, Eris never touched even a toe to the ground until he was old enough to defy his mother's ways.

Little did he know that first step upon the ground would deliver him into his father's grim world. Had he been told what was to come, would he have ever left the serenity of those treetops?

He remembered playing with the other children, darting across the outstretched limbs as if these skyward bridges were built only for their silly games. The scent of flowering trees rose strongly in his nose, along with the sense of flying freely through the air on vines.

Would Eris have dropped to earth as swiftly as he did, tumbling head over heels in a gale of laughter while the other children watched from their perches, silent and frightened? Would he have teased his mother when she scolded, had he known that in a few short years Ares would come to claim Eris, and his beloved forest would become a forbidden pleasure?

Sighing, Eris leaned on his elbows.

"Fine." Deimos scowled, waving a hand at the barren fireplace. A blaze ignited. Warmth spread throughout the room, dispelling the dampness. The fog cleared, giving way to a reddish glow. "It appears we must wait, therefore, we shall wait with a bit of comfort."

Eris relaxed with a smile and was wise enough to stay silent.

*****

"There." The ashen-faced girl pointed at the hammock pushed into a corner in the medicinal quarters. "I found her there. She will not awaken."

Inni strode over to the bed and stared down at Pallin. "So this is where you took him," she muttered to herself. "Better here, I suppose, than in your room with Seire."

Though Inni was puzzled by Niala's insistence on leaving Pallin with Deimos at the lake, she was not stupid. She knew there was intention there, but did not know why. She was pleased Pallin had shown Seire respect by not returning to their joint area but for

Pallin to still be lying abed when the sun was up was disgraceful.

"Wake up, lazy one." Inni shook Pallin with more roughness than necessary. The hammock jiggled and its four-cornered frame scooted up against the wall with a slight thump. Pallin did not so much as flicker an eyelid.

With hands to her hips, Inni frowned.

"You see," began Laida. "She will not wake up."

"Nonsense." Inni shook Pallin again and then patted her cheeks. Her skin was cool and clammy. With a growing sense of alarm, Inni bent over the silent girl and put her ear to her chest and her fingertips to Pallin's lips.

"She breathes, but scarcely." Straightening, Inni now noticed Pallin's waxy complexion and the dark smudges that stood out beneath her eyes.

"Go and fetch Niala." Inni pushed Laida toward the back exit. "Hurry."

The girl scurried to the rear and left through connecting quarters that would take her into the kitchens. Inni went to a long high bench and rummaged amongst the earthenware jars until she found the one she needed. It held bitterroot and the moment she removed the lid, the pungent odor of the herb filled the room.

Extracting a small piece, she carried it back to Pallin's bedside and snapped it in half beneath the girl's nose. The freshly opened root released an evil smell, enough to make Inni wrinkle her nose and lean away from it.

The herb did not affect Pallin at all. She was as still as death. Lifting each lid, she saw the dark center of Pallin's eyes nearly covered the green outer edges and did not contract to a finer point as the light touched her.

What did Deimos do to her? That he had been with her was certain, for the smell of a man was on her, or had been, before the bitterroot overrode it. Inni flicked the coverlet back and viewed Pallin's nakedness. There were no bruises or blood, no cuts or scrapes, no signs of force. Relieved, Inni tucked the sheet back around Pallin's slender body.

"Had he violated you," Inni muttered, "I would kill him."

"He would not have forced her." Niala spoke from the doorway.

"Do you know him that well, then?" Inni wiped her face with her sleeve. "Look at her. She lies as if she is dead."

"I know what little pleasure he allows himself is not drawn from violence." Niala touched Inni's cheek, brushing back a stray strand of yellow hair.

Inni came to them from a childhood of slavery, where cruelty was an everyday occurrence. She was forced to submit whenever her master demanded and if there was so much as a whimper, there was another beating. Only an odd stroke of luck delivered her to their doorstep. Her master died abruptly and none questioned too closely how he met his death.

A trader took pity and hid her away in his wagon, thinking he would turn a nice profit on the girl. It was Inni's good fortune that on the return trip to his homeland, the trader made his way into Najahmara. Niala made him an offer he could not refuse. Niala smiled at her now, forgiving both her suspicions and her sharpness.

"Deimos would not harm Pallin. If I thought so, I would not have left them together."

"Of course." Inni drew her shoulders up. "I did not mean to insult you, but I could not help but wonder if he caused this."

"Hmmm." Nodding, Niala glanced down at Pallin. Inni edged aside so Niala could move closer. She held her hands above Pallin's sleeping form, feeling the ebb and flow of energy. It was sluggish, as if dammed like a river to form a quiet pool. There was peace about it, like an oasis, and Pallin drifted aimlessly in its midst.

With a deep breath, Niala plunged her hands into the slow current of energy and touched her fingertips to pulsing points. Immediately, warmth began to flush Pallin's body. A moment later, Pallin's eyelids fluttered and she stared at them without understanding. Niala withdrew and smiled at her.

"Niala? Where am I?"

Pallin rubbed her throat and swallowed hard. "I am so thirsty." Pushing away the sheet, she added, "And hot."

Inni muttered, "Thank Gaea." Then she ducked her head and went to get a jug of water.

"What happened?" Pallin stuttered. "Where am I?"

She looked beyond Niala, to the dried herbs hanging from the ceiling, over to the cluttered benches, then down to her unclothed body. "Oh."

Pallin pulled the sheet to her breast, flushing to the roots of her hair. A light film of sweat covered her upper lip. "I did not mean to be found here, Niala, I am so sorry. I just...I just....”

Inni returned with the water and thrust it at her. Pallin gulped until it spilled down her front, wetting the sheet, then returned it to Inni. “Thank you. I should get up.”

“Yes, you should.” One brow arched in disapproval as Inni held out a hand to help her.

“Not just yet.” Niala stopped them. “Give yourself a bit more time before rising.”

Pallin nodded, for in truth, her legs were wobbly and her middle felt queasy. She lay back with her eyes closed, one hand shading her face. She did not want to look at either Inni or Niala.

“Get up when you are ready.” Inni left Pallin’s side with brusque relief . “Niala and I have work to do.”

“Do not rush.” There was a hint of concern in Niala’s voice, though she kept her tone light.

Pallin nodded but did not open her eyes. She heard their footsteps retreat and was grateful they dropped the curtain at the outer door, cutting off the stream of bright sunshine. Within the cool and quiet chamber, Pallin sighed and wondered of Deimos’ whereabouts.

Why did he leave her without saying goodbye? Without a kiss. She went hot again and then cold. Shivering, she drew the damp sheet up to her chin and curled on her side, fighting the urge to heave up the drink she had swallowed.

In the dawn, the water made her bold. The cool, smooth lake with its tiny, lapping waves that stroked her naked body and made her tremble with carnal thoughts. As Pallin dove into the water and swam beneath the surface, as she felt it slither along her bare skin and caress between her legs, she could think of nothing else but the way Deimos looked at Niala.

When Pallin surfaced and found him there right beside her, when she discovered they were all alone, she could not stop herself.

Pallin groaned and pulled the sheet over her head, but could not shut out the memory of him.

Instant, burning desire gripped her. She stood there, staring at him in wonder, at how his skin glistened like a jewel in the early morning light. She saw how strong his body was and how beautiful his face. How the droplets of water glided along his lean sides and

*fell into the lake at his hips. She remembered how much she
wanted to see the rest of him.*

*She embraced him, kissing his chest, licking at the trickling
drops, tugging at him until his lips met hers. She remembered how
slow he was to respond and the flush of humiliation that gripped
her.*

*"I am sorry. I know it is Niala you truly want." Pallin could
barely speak as she turned away.*

*He did not answer to her charge. Instead, he said, "Are you
afraid of me?" Deimos made Pallin look at him, look into dark
eyes brimming with a strange sadness.*

"No, no, never."

*He pulled her tightly against him and whispered, "Then it is
you who shall have me."*

*His kiss, though tender, lit her body on fire. She slid her hand
between them and stroked that member which was so foreign to
her. His groans of pleasure led her further into the mysteries of
man and not long after Deimos lifted her, she eagerly wrapped her
legs around his waist. When he went into her, she cried out and
could not help shrinking away.*

"You are virgin."

It was an accusation.

"Do not stop, I beg you."

"You are virgin." He said it again as he stood frozen in place.

*"Yes, but not by order," she gasped, wishing only that he
would speak no more.*

"I would not defile a priestess of Gaea."

*"You do not." Pallin clung to him, kissing his mouth, his face,
his neck, as her body pleaded with him to continue. "I am innocent
only because I have not desired anyone. There is no other reason, I
swear it."*

*"Why me?" His breath was hot on her cheek, ragged in her
ear. He held back, waiting for her answer. "Why?"*

She shook her head.

"Tell me why."

*Pallin met his gaze and saw torment of a kind she had never
seen before. "Because I cannot help but love you."*

"Pallin." His sigh was long and filled with an aching need.

*Then he carried her to shore, into the soft grass beneath a
canopy of trees. She brought him back to the healing hut as*

daylight further brightened the sky, knowing everyone in Najahmara would sleep late, even the priestesses of Gaea would not rise early after the night's ritual.

Now Pallin was alone, without even knowing why Deimos was gone. She loved him. She knew this from the core of her being. But did he love her? Sighing, she turned her face to the wall and closed her eyes.

"What did he do to her?" Inni asked, the moment they stepped into the street, beyond Pallin's hearing. "Do not say it was nothing, she was like death."

Niala held up her hand and Inni fell silent, but her blue eyes were reproachful. "It was as if he caused her vitality to slow, but it was not death he intended. He did not hurt her, only made her sleep more deeply than normal. Why he did it, I do not know."

"Would she have awakened on her own?"

"Perhaps not."

"Then he intended to hurt her. If not death, then something else."

"I think he meant to return to her side."

"Then where is he? And how does he have the power to do such a thing?"

Niala shrugged, for her fear went far deeper than Pallin's state.

"I do not understand what this is about. Why did you leave them alone?" Inni paused, her freckled face reddening.

"His need was great. And it was time for Pallin to become aware of her own needs."

"You decided that?"

"They decided. If it was not meant to be, then it would not have been."

"But a stranger?"

"No, Inni, a god."

"What?" Inni stopped in her tracks, mouth agape.

"Deimos is not of our world. He is an immortal."

"And you let him couple with Pallin?" Inni was fairly hopping up and down in anger.

"I let Earth have her way, for she brought them together. I merely offered them the opportunity."

"I do not understand."

"It is important that we bind Deimos to us in a way

that he becomes protective of us."

"So that is why." Jahmed stood behind them. Her long braids were tied back with a yellow cloth and she carried a bag slung over one shoulder.

With a sharp warning glance, Niala said, "Jahmed, I did not know you were out. Has there been a birth?"

"No, it was Mirma's youngest. A twisted leg. Next time he will not leap from so high a ledge. These boys, they climb the side of the ridge as if it were a tree." Though Jahmed chuckled, there were two lines of worry between her brows. "This Deimos, dare we hope he will do as you wish?"

"I pray it is so, Sister. He seemed agreeable by the lake, did he not?"

"He seemed distant, unsure," Inni said. "Perhaps I understand better why that is, but there are things that still make no sense to me. Was Pallin aware of this…ahhh…arrangement? And why was he here in the first place?"

"Pallin knows nothing other than what she heard during the ritual. It was by chance that she was the one, there was no conspiring."

"You are certain?" Inni cast a glance back at the healing hut. "She is not in danger?"

Niala shook her head.

"You still have not told me why he is here."

"He is curious about us. About Gaea."

"And why do we need his protection?" With hands to her hips, Inni saw the sideways look Niala and Jahmed exchanged.

"Enough of this," she snapped. "I am not stupid. I can both see and hear that there is more going on than meets the eye. Do not think for a moment I have not felt the upheaval.

"Since your vision, you have pretended all is well but I know it is not. Jahmed scarce sleeps for worry and I know you leave the temple to sit all night upon the plateau. Do neither of you trust me enough to say what is on your minds?"

The words quivered in the air between them. Jahmed moved closer to Inni, placing one hand on her stiff shoulder. As Inni shrugged away, Jahmed threw a pleading glance at Niala.

"I trust you with my life." Jahmed spoke with sweet tenderness. "You know that."

"Then why does this secret hang between us?"

"Because I have sworn her to silence," Niala answered. "There is little we can prepare for and I did not know until last night." She heaved a sigh.

Beyond Inni and Jahmed, Niala could see the brilliant blue sky. It was so clear, so achingly beautiful. Around them was the scent of fresh, flat loaves of bread baking in the outdoor ovens. Children giggled in the distance. Carts clicked along on the rocks and the low murmur of conversations swirled through the breeze.

Everything was as it should be. Everything except the legion of warriors who sought Najahmara for their own.

Now Niala fully understood both Deimos' presence and Gaea's intention. Why he needed to stand before her in the cave. She knew everything would change, and there was naught they could do about it. And she knew, irrevocably, that Ares the Destroyer would come for her.

"What did you not know?" Inni cast a sharp eye between them.

"We cannot talk about it here." With one last sweeping gaze at her beloved city, Niala led the way into the temple.

It was time everyone understood.

ELEVEN

Ares entered by way of the outer doors, speaking not a word. He neither cast a glance at Deimos nor Eris as he moved in front of the hearth. Ares' angular shadow stretched along the floor, reaching toward them with a silent threat. Eris shrank away and out of his chair to hover behind Deimos.

With an involuntary shudder, Deimos rose to his feet. His father was dressed in the formal white and gold tunic required at Council and, though he chose to wear his cut above the knee rather than the ankle-length of the more decorous, it was no less disturbing. Across his shoulders he wore a warrior's mantle of blood red and black, the colors of War, which made it very clear the gathering was not of a trifling nature.

"Father?"

"Eris, leave us." Ares' voice was thick.

With a squeak of relief, Eris was gone.

Ares turned to stare at Deimos, his expression less angry and more appraising

It was an odd mixture, thought Deimos. He would not give voice to such observations for Deimos did not want to make things more difficult. He approached Ares with wary steps.

"Father, what has happened?"

"That is for you to tell me." Ares' tone was soft, dangerous. "I was called to Council to account for your actions."

Deimos raised his hands in confusion. "I do not understand why. What have I done that could possibly cause the Council grief?"

"What, indeed?" The glint Deimos knew so well was in Ares' eyes. "I do not like being called in front of the Ages for any reason."

"Why has there been upheaval?"

"I particularly do not like being made the fool by my son." Ares scowled as he yanked the cloak from his shoulders, tossing it onto a low, backless couch against one wall.

"Not I." Deimos watched the play of muscle along his father's bared arms as Ares clenched his fists. Deimos knew what strength lay within that grip. Though he fought against it, Deimos' nature was his own enemy, for terror made his knees weak and his breath short.

"But you have."

Ares paced back to the hearth and stood in front of the flames. To Deimos it seemed most deliberate, for that hulking shadow loomed over him once again. With the fire blocked, the chill of the room closed about him. He forced himself not to cringe and stood his ground.

"Father, I would not intentionally bring you misery. Tell me what has caused this trouble so that I might answer to it."

Deimos wanted to add, *And if what I have done has caused such concern with the Council, why do they not call me instead of you?*

He already knew the answer. Deimos was not allowed at Council. Though he was son of Ares and Aphrodite, grandson of Zeus and Hera, he was no more than a minion of War, born to preserve Terror in the mortal world. The Council did not want to be disturbed by Terror or have such angst within their narrow world. Yet, was there not a hint of fear behind this demand?

"What is it you find so amusing?" Though Ares spoke with harshness, but some tiny bit of the tension had lessened.

Deimos watched as Ares dropped into the oversized chair to the right of the hearth and stretched out his legs. He made no sounds of relief, but the weariness was most apparent now that the light reflected upon his features.

Exhaling , Deimos moved closer to the hearth and sank down, cross-legged, in front of the fire. "They do not want Terror in their midst, but they are afraid."

"Truth. You have brought the Council your gift of fright and they are unhappy about it." A tone of grudging respect laced Ares' words. "They prefer I keep mine...." he snorted, "...to myself."

"Then that is their error in judgment, for there is more to me than terror."

One black eyebrow arched up as Ares viewed his son. As always, Deimos stood before him with courage and brutal honesty, yet something was different. Ares saw it in his stance and felt it in the very air around him. This change held Deimos a little straighter, a little less yielding. His gaze was more direct and there was a hint of defiance in its depths.

Ares was not certain Deimos realized the altered state with which he presented himself. Ares made no comment, for he did not yet know if he approved.

"They agree it is their job to judge." Ares leaned his head back and closed his eyes. "Though I disagree. I prefer to ignore the Ages, but I am bound to answer my father's call, just as you are bound to answer mine. And so, from him to me, from me to you: what dealings have you had with the earth goddess Gaea and her consort Kulika?"

Startled, Deimos blurted, "Gaea and Kulika? How did they know?"

Ares blinked and then pinned his dark gaze on Deimos. "How could they not? They reside in Olympus, within the boundaries of the Sky."

"Yes, of course, but these events did not affect them."

Ares held up his hand and Deimos fell quiet. "As opposed to those of us who choose to live in Earth's Realm?"

Deimos held his silence. Ares continued. "There has been a rumbling in our world. I have felt it, but sometimes it is that way with Gaea. On occasion, she feels the need to be heard, however, that does not give any of us permission to interfere. "

"I thought they believed Gaea was dormant." Deimos could no longer contain himself.

"By those who live in a realm differing from ours." His tone was heavy with scorn. "We are of the earth, brought to life by her children. Your mother and I, you and your brothers. Look around and see how many of us endure this existence because of Gaea's creation." Ares stopped with a grunt. "That is of no concern now. What have you done to disturb Kulika?"

"Ahh, I engaged with Gaea."

"Engaged, how? Kulika has made himself known. Last night he sent a sign across the Sky realm in such a manner that Zeus could not deny it. And it led right back to you."

"Last night." Deimos relived the mad moment when he reached out and stroked the image of a serpent etched onto Niala's thigh. He remembered the instant response of the Blue Serpent and could again feel the scalding heat eat along his skin.

Deimos turned away from Ares' gaze. "Father, I cannot deny this, for it is true. I had no idea Kulika's response went beyond myself."

"Tell me everything."

After Deimos finished his tale of Najahmara, after describing the band of priestesses, after telling of the army drunk on bespelled beyaz, of their king who now wandered somewhere within the city he wished to rule, and of the ritual invoking both Gaea and Kulika, Deimos fell into distraction.

He did not speak directly of Pallin, or how he left her, or that he feared for Hattusilis. Most of all, he did not inform Ares of his promise to Gaea to turn aside the invasion. These concerns were his alone. Lost in thought, he failed to notice Ares had risen from his seat or that he changed from Council clothing to warrior's leggings, tunic and boots.

Deimos did not notice the flat, ugly expression on the face of one who has discovered betrayal. Not until he was jerked to his feet did he see this and then it was too late. Deimos fair dangled in his father's grip and could only answer in a strangled voice after Ares demanded, "By what name did you call this priestess who leads?"

"Niala."

"Niala Aaminah," Ares' eyes glittered with malice in the firelight. "Niala Aaminah."

"Yes. She is the one who bears the mark of Kulika. Who brings Gaea into body. She is most striking, extraordinary. I cannot say for certain what she is."

Without ceremony, Ares released Deimos. He staggered backwards and just avoided falling into the flames by grabbing at the high mantel.

"She is one of us."

Deimos stared at his father. "She says she is not."

"She lies," Ares snapped. "Oh, she is a clever one, Niala

Aaminah, wearing her innocence like a shield, pretending to please, and then...." He stopped, breathing hard. "Still, I do not know how she achieved this."

"Achieved what?" Deimos took care to stay as far away from Ares as he could. Deimos had seen that expression before and it was not a pleasant one.

"Escaped me, hid from me, denied me." With each word his voice sank lower until it was no more than a rattling hiss. "Najahmara?"

Deimos could only nod in response.

"Where is this place?"

"I will take you there."

"No, you will not." A cold smile touched Ares' lips. "You will tell me where to find this one and that is all. You will stay here until I say you may go forth again."

"I cannot." Deimos held up his hands in protest, though fear made him weak in the knees. "I must return."

"Your obligation is only to me. I forbid you to leave these walls until I next call you. Is that clear?"

Their glares locked. It was Deimos who first looked away.

"Yes, father." Deimos' heart was heavy, but he knew he had no choice.

"Now tell me where I will find Niala Aaminah." Ares' fury bored into Deimos until he surrendered.

*****

Five hundred men. Telio was not pleased, but they were all that could be rallied. The rest lay in drunken stupors unable to comprehend that their king was missing. Together, he and Zan gathered every drop of beyaz and threw the skins into the fire. The explosions rocked the camp and sent balls of flame skyward, while most of the men remained dead to the world.

Telio was forced to leave the majority of the legion behind with no more than two captains to prepare the encampment to move out. They would be days behind.

Smiling a thin, mirthless smile, Telio thought, *We will either have King Hattusilis back by then, or we will all be dead.*

Telio hoped he would not only rescue his uncle, but that, under Telio's command, Najahmara would be captured. Only then would he be able to garner the respect he so badly desired. His uncle had grown soft in the head on this journey, favoring sentimentality over calculated maneuvers. Was it no wonder he had been taken during the night by one such as Deimos?

By Telio's estimation, Hattusilis had been outsmarted. Favoring this outsider, in spite of the warnings, Hattusilis gave Deimos free rein. In return, Deimos brought in bespelled beyaz to thwart the invasion. How did he do it? Why seemed clear enough. Deimos intended all along to steal Hattusilis and lead him into a trap, befuddled and off-guard.

But how did he do it? That question plagued Telio throughout the grueling ride. How did Deimos bring in such quantities of beyaz without anyone seeing? Somewhere, in the back of Telio's mind, was hidden the answer but he could not summon it, could not voice it. When he tried, his words came out jumbled and Zan did no more than look strangely at him and mutter that madness ran within their family.

Telio glanced at Zan, as he sat forward in his saddle, squinting toward Najahmara. They were in close proximity. They need only cross the mown field in front of them to arrive at the outskirts of town. Behind them, five hundred men sat their steeds in eager silence, waiting for the order to charge forth.

The ride was grueling. With little time to rest their pounding heads and churning bellies, the men were relieved their reward was now before them. Aches and pains were forgotten, they were about to move forward as one, with stealthy intent, practiced so well that not even a hound would bay at their shadows.

Their mounts would be left behind, protected in the heavily wooded area near the Maendre, while the men went by foot into the city in search of their king. They waited only for Connal's signal, for he had led them across the countryside to this place and would lead them further in and up to the temple doors.

Each man was armed with sword and dagger, with orders to slit any throat they came upon.

"Spare no one," Telio ordered, and the whispered command was passed man to man until every last one knew this night was to be a blood offering to their god.

*****

Deimos was right. Ares had only to wait on the plateau with the five white stones until Niala appeared. It really was too simple, after all the time he had searched for her.

Years. Many, many years he had looked for her, but her tracks were so thoroughly covered he found no sign of her. He believed their connection, the energy they shared, would lead him to her but when it did not, Ares believed Niala was dead.

He thought he was wrong about her, that she was no more than mortal after all. And then, as the Fates would have it, she was delivered back into his hands. There was order to the mortal realm and if the Fates decreed their paths would cross again, it was with reason.

Ares needed no other cause than his desire for her.

Deimos said Niala came to the plateau every night after Najahmara slept. He spoke the truth, for Ares watched her now. She came from the rear of the temple, crossing through the gardens behind it, then started her journey up to pray to her goddess.

It was too easy. He should have to plan his approach, to wage a battle to capture her. At the very least, there should be a small skirmish before he could retrieve her. He should have to threaten punishment. He should have to destroy her surroundings before she would come to him.

Ares should have to kill everyone.

He wanted to make them suffer, those who stole her away. He glanced toward four of the markers. Seyyal. Mahin. Edibe. Layla. He should have known those accursed witches were involved in Niala's escape. Now they were long dead and past his revenge.

But Niala Aaminah was not. In all the years Ares sought her, it never occurred to him that she would walk right into his arms.

Niala climbed the path with head bowed, without once glancing beyond her steps. Ares watched her struggle upwards, placing one foot in front of the other with care. He watched and he waited, without bothering to cloak himself.

Not that Niala would have seen him, had she looked up. It was very dark, no moon to give away his presence. She climbed the path slowly, as if she carried the weight of the five stones upon her back.

He waited until Niala topped the mount and stood uncertainly at the path's end. She scanned the length of the plateau and back again to stare at the stones without taking another step. She brought her arms up to hug herself as if she were chilled and still did not venture any further onto the grass.

Ares wanted light so he could better see her, see her face when she realized he was there. Or just to see what she had grown into.

He could make light.

No, he would not, not yet.

Niala was scarce more than a child when he last saw her. She was now a woman, her face in shadows, garbed in a hooded, loose wrap falling to her ankles. He could tell nothing by this sight, but he could feel the waves of energy pulsing from her body and, from that, he knew it was indeed Niala Aaminah who stood before him.

"Deimos?"

She spoke in a hushed voice, her head tilted to one side, listening. "Are you there?"

When he put his hand to her throat, she screamed. It was quickly stifled as he tightened his grip. He could feel her heart pounding beneath his fingers, feel her swallow with painful effort, but she did not fight. She just stood in his grasp, eyes closed, lips parted as if she would beseech his forgiveness.

He wanted to hear it.

Begging.

Pleading.

Crying.

Anything.

Niala did nothing.

Nothing except say his name. "Ares."

She was tall, so much more than she had been, but still not as tall as he. He had to lean to whisper in her ear.

"You expected my son? He gave you away."

"He had no choice." Her voice was choked, breathless.

"Are you certain? He is what he is."

"I know what he is."

Ares' fingers flexed and he thought of how easily he had taken her innocence, of how he used to bring her to endless pleasure, and how that same hand was now poised to snap her neck.

He thought of the young, budding body of a girl transitioning to woman, of small breasts and slender hips, of long, coltish legs that gave her an ungraceful gait. He thought of luminescent amber eyes and honeyed skin, of curling autumn hair cropped short in spite of his urging to let it grow.

Ares wondered what was beneath her cloak, what time had done to her. Should he act out of anger, the opportunity to find out would be lost. But, like a black cloud on the horizon, his rage moved closer, ready to consume him.

After all, she had betrayed him.

"Why, Niala?"

Barely audible, "You know why."

Niala's breath was shallow, wheezing. Ares could feel her body going limp and for one tiny second, he was willing to let her suffocate. It would be his revenge. Sweet, satisfying revenge. Niala would know with her last gasp that he delivered upon his pledge.

But he did not want her to die. He was not even certain she could die. All that time he spent wondering if what he sensed about her was true. Was she Ilya returned? Was she an immortal like him, born into the world because the vortex of human greed desired it? If she was another immortal, what was her purpose and how was it she had come to him if she was not Ilya?

Niala Aaminah was too young to answer when last he saw her, too unformed. Her trials might have driven a lesser being into madness, or a goddess into awareness. For Niala, it was neither.

She remained closed, unwilling to believe there was another possibility. To her, she was only a shepherd brought into the fortress of a god by mischance.

Ares knew there was no such thing as chance. All threads of life, be it human or animal, immortal or inanimate, all life carried a destiny. The trick of the Fates was whether one carried through to fulfillment.

Some never did. Some denied it. Others embraced it.

Forcing himself to loosen his fingers on her neck, Ares heard the dry, rasping cough and felt the shuddering of her body as the cool night air flooded into her. She tried to pull away, but he held her chin, lifting it up, feeling the smooth line of jaw.

He ran his thumb across her lips, touched the sharp edge of a tooth, the curve of her cheek and the dampness beneath one eye. Rapid blinking lashes brushed against his thumb, soft and delicate. It made his heart quicken.

"I thought you loved me." Ares spoke next to her ear.

Unhurried, Niala raised her hands and pressed his palm to her lips.

"I will not forgive you for the sake of a kiss," Ares growled.

"Of course." But she kissed his palm again. For a moment, his anger lessened.

"Why, Niala?" She turned, then, folding closer into him, elbows drawn up between them as if she desired some kind of barrier, however small. Ares could not help how his arm crept around her, bringing her nearer so he could feel the heat of her on his chest.

"I was afraid."

"Of what? I would never have hurt you. Not then."

"What if you grew tired of me? I thought you might pass me to the men in the warrior's quarters."

"Why would you think that?"

"You told me you would."

Ares remembered. "Once. An idle threat to get your attention." He could not see the expression in Niala's eyes for the darkness, but there was something in the way she held herself. "No, it was not about fear."

"It was."

"Not about the men." He dug his fingers into her collarbone, pleased at the way she flinched. Her hood fell back and he could see her hair was long now, woven into a single, thick braid partially hidden beneath the cloak. "You were afraid I would discover your deceit."

"My journeys down the mount were not dishonest. I needed to have my feet on the ground again. I had to have contact with the earth, with living things."

"You should have told me."

"What would you have done? Taken me back to my homeland, where I longed to be?"

"A garden, perhaps."

"A garden? In that frozen wasteland? Even in summer months there was snow."

"I can do many things that seem impossible."

"Many things, yes, but the one I needed most, you could not do."

"A garden."

"No, Ares, I speak now of your heart. I was young, alone, and I needed someone to love me. You gave me no one, not even yourself. You left me no choice. I had to seek out others to befriend, to care for me."

"To take as a lover?"

At Niala's sharp intake of breath, Ares laughed without humor. "Did you really believe I would not have you watched while I was away?"

"I did not see anyone."

"It was not a creature you would have delighted in."

"If you knew, then why?"

"Why did I let you go to them? What harm could it bring? A handful of women whose sole purpose, it seemed, was to act as healers to those in need. They did not concern me, not even when...." He paused for a second. "...not even when you took to one's bed."

"You said nothing."

"Why bother? There was a certain enhancement that occurred. I enjoyed it. I just did not consider the possibility you would fall in love with her, that you would run away from me."

"If there had just been someone there with me."

"Do not make excuses, Niala. You know there was to have been someone."

"A child," Niala said.

"Yes. A child that somehow never was. Somehow, in spite of my attempts."

"They...." Niala inclined her head toward the stones, a fierce, prideful tone in her voice. "They made it go away. I could not face a birthing, not alone, not there. I could not do it. They made certain there would be no other."

His face twisted as the connection was finally made clear to him. What arrogance that he never thought of outside interference. He just believed her to be too young to carry a child and, in due time, she would.

With a bellow of rage, Ares dragged Niala half the length of the plateau, careless of whether her feet hit the ground. Niala stumbled more than once as her cloak caught on her toes and wrapped around her legs. She uttered not even a whimper, allowing him to propel her to the base of the five stones.

There he shook her as if she were weightless, until her head wobbled and she was again gasping, until the wrap came loose from her shoulders and fell away and she was left in her thin dress. Still he shook her, pointing to the etchings on the face of the rocks.

"These women, priestesses, they called themselves, healers.

Witches! I let them stay in my land, never thinking they would dare steal from me."

Pain shot down her right side and her knees buckled as his fingers dug deeper into the hollow of her shoulder. Niala slid to the ground, her forehead resting against his leg. The pressure released as he let go, but her arm was numb and she could not get up.

"It is too bad they are dead, for I would enjoy inflicting torture upon them."

"They are beyond your reach."

"But you are not." Ares wrapped her braid around his fingers and forced her to look up. "How did they convince you to go with them?"

"What does it matter now?"

"I want to know."

"It was my decision. I begged them to take me away. They did not want to. I made them."

"Lies!"

He pulled Niala's hair until she gasped. "Did you ever think you would be left behind to serve your punishment? That I would someday find you? No, you thought you would be dead yourself by now. But, I think, you are very alive."

Ares pulled harder, until tears streamed down her face and she rose to her knees. "Have you not wondered why you still live?"

"Yes, " Niala said. "I wondered if what you told me was true."

"So you remember."

"Yes. Ares, please."

"Begging...." Ares leaned forward and spoke into her ear. "...will not help. Tell me now how you got away and perhaps I will spare you some suffering."

"It does not matter."

"It does."

He twisted her braid until she cried out. "...a spell...of concealment...."

"That would not be enough."

"Layla covered me with her own spirit. I retreated and her essence filled me. She hid me from you."

His voice held a tiny bit of admiration. "When I reached out to find you, there was nothing. I tried, you know. I cast out over and over again, hoping I could find one trace, one shred, but there was nothing."

He gave one, last vicious yank to her hair and then threw her down. "My hounds could not even scent you. At the time, I knew the women had left the seaport, but there were only four who had gone. Even if I suspected them, there were only four."

"There were five," Niala whispered. "Five aboard ship."

"They planned it. For how long, Niala? And you knew you were to go. Of course you did, for you would have to learn the art of suppressing your own spirit. You lay with me knowing all along you were to go."

Ares paced back and forth, passing from one stone to the next, glaring at each as if they mocked him.

"Yes."

"I hoped they forced you. I should have known they did not. Where did they take you?"

"I cannot tell you."

"Why? They are all dead now." He turned to glance at Niala. "Or are there others?"

She buried her face in her hands. "If anyone is to be destroyed, it will be me alone."

"There are others. Where are they? Where did they hide you? For how long, Niala? Long enough so I would think you were dead. Long enough so I would think I was wrong about you?" Reaching out, Ares traced the name etched into the surface of the furthest white stone.

"I thought your stories were only to serve your purpose. I was frightened."

Fingers clenched, Ares shouted, "Treacherous, deceitful, unfaithful witch!"

With his fist, Ares slammed into the rock and a crack as loud as thunder echoed into the night. The stone split at the base and fell over.

"Ahh...no...please...." Niala moaned.

"Please? Please, what?" His fist shot out again and the next stone tumbled backwards.

"Please, please do not do this."

Another stone snapped in half. It crashed to the ground, on top of the one that went before it and broke into pieces.

"This one." Ares stood before the fourth stone.

"Layla." Niala whispered, "Do not. I beg you."

"Why are you so distressed, Niala? They are just rocks,

nothing more. Rocks with names." Ares looked between the two remaining stones. "This is a monument to them."

He nodded at the stumps sticking up from the earth. "It is their burial ground, is it not?"

Niala's tone vibrated with sorrow. "It was all I could do to honor them. I did not think they would all leave me, but there they are. I will do anything you want, but I beg you, please do not destroy what little I have left of them."

"Your love was so true that you do not want this grave disturbed?" His voice sank. "You would abandon me, lie to me, steal from me and now you wish me to leave this grave alone? Niala, did you learn nothing about my nature while you were with me?"

Ares plunged his hand into the earth as if it was water, down, down until he found the body of the priestess Layla. She had lain long enough in the soil that there was nothing left but brittle, stained bones and it was this he brought to the surface.

He wrenched a handful of crumbling bones from the bosom of the earth and held them aloft. The ground rocked beneath his feet but he did not care.

"This is all you have left, Niala. It is all you will ever have left of any mortal you chose to love."

"Stop, stop!" Niala struggled to her feet, no longer the staid and humble priestess, but a clawing wild woman with fire in her heart. She threw herself against him, reaching for Layla's bones. "You are wrong, I am mortal born as well."

"Born of whom, I do not know," Ares answered. "But that you carry the spark of one whose feet are set upon an immortal journey there is no doubt. I see it, I hear it, I taste it. You are who I say you are."

The earth rumbled and shook and the once star-lit night began to grow heavy with clouds. As Gaea protested, Kulika, responded. A chill wind curled around their feet, lifting skirts and hair alike.

"Do you hear how angry Gaea is? Return Layla to her grave."

"Perhaps it is you who angers her." The old bones crunched in his fingers. "You deny the grace she gave you, for she was the beginning of our journey. She breathed life into both of us and, now, you deny her."

Niala snatched up a splintered piece of stone and raked her palm until a dark line of blood welled up. She slapped her hand across his face, smearing blood on his lips. "Taste this, Anyal, and know you are wrong. I am mortal born and always will be. I have always honored Gaea. It is you who turned away from her."

Ares froze, one arm pushing Niala back as she fought to reach the remains of the priestess still within his clutch. "You called me Anyal."

"Yes. I have known since my initiation into Earth's mysteries. I know I was once called Ilya, during the dawn of humankind. That was my name brought forth with me from spirit. It is who resides deep within me, but is not me in this life."

"Then you know the pact we made, you and I and Elche." Ares grew quiet, though Niala still assailed him.

"It was *your* promise. You and Elche. Elche was always forgiving of your transgressions. But I could not forgive you and what you have become is not my concern. I do not have to be like either of you to fulfill my destiny."

"So you turned away from us and hid in the mortal realm. You let us both go on with the shade of the past casting both our futures while you linger here, denying your part in it." Ares' voice was tormented. "You were First Woman. You were my wife."

"It matters not what happened during the beginning of ages, only what we have done from there. That, too, I have learned." Niala dropped back and gazed at him for long moments. "Ares the Destroyer. Why did I not see this before?"

In answer to herself, she whispered, "Ares the Destroyer. You are what you have always been. You deliver pain and humiliation, you cause such grief that no one wants to look upon your face, however beautiful it is."

Louder she said, "You did this to yourself. If it is my forgiveness you seek, then you have it. There, I have said it. I forgive you. But that will not absolve you of your guilt. You must first forgive yourself."

"You speak of forgiveness? You, the deceiver? And what a hideous deception it is. First then and now again, you seek to cloak yourself in something you are not. At least I show my true face and do not lie to either myself or to others. My traits are well known. I do not hide behind the façade of a humble priestess."

"I am Niala Aaminah, nothing more and nothing less. I acknowledge what has been in the past, but it does not determine my future."

"Stubborn even to the end," Ares answered. "You will live this pain over and over until you step into your true self."

"I do not see that your true self has ended your pain. I only see more of the same." Niala turned and walked away.

"Where are you going?" Ares held the bones above his head.

"Back to my people. I am a priestess to Gaea and that is what I will remain until the last breath is squeezed from me. Do not try to force me into your mold."

"Do not walk away from me."

Ares hurled the bones after Niala. They flew through the air and rained down on Niala, striking her head and back with cruel intent, some shattering, others bouncing away into the night. She was knocked to her hands and knees as the bones scattered across the grass and rolled over the side of the ridge.

The earth groaned and thunder echoed her distress in the distance.

The wind picked up as Ares strode over to Niala. All the horrors of the world buzzed about him, gathering in a furious storm. Niala heard the howling of hounds and the shrieking of his creatures as he towered over her, seeming bigger and broader than before, his face as dark as the sky. Lightening shot through the clouds overhead and a rumble shook the earth.

"I will crush these bones and all of those in the city below so you will have nothing to go back to."

Sobbing, Niala scrabbled in the grass and dirt to gather Layla's bones, reaching beyond the rim for those that had tumbled downward. Dried brush snagged her clothes, scraped her arms and legs and tore at her face. The cut on her palm began to bleed again, dripping into the soil. The earth heaved and Niala fell halfway over the edge.

Ares caught her and yanked her back to sit on her heels. He released her but his hand hovered over her head as if he would snatch her up at any moment and carry her away. Wordless, he stared out over the valley.

Niala could scarce see him for the tears. She sat cradling the bones in her arms. The splintered, broken bones of a woman once alive and warm, a woman she had once held with love. Rocking back and forth, all she could say was, "Please."

"It is too late." Pointing toward Najahmara, Ares smiled but it did not reach his cold eyes. Though his anger had dissipated, he could feel the pull of the violence unfolding below. "And I have yet to lift a finger in its destruction."

Blindly, Niala looked toward her home and saw nothing but shadow. As she was able to focus, she saw small, moving lights spread out along the narrow streets. She saw a half circle of the same light ringed around the temple.

She began to hear screaming - human screams. Not the creatures of darkness that hailed to Ares the Destroyer, but the terrified shrieks of her own people.

"It is a vision." Niala closed her eyes, shaking her head from side to side. "No more than that - a vision."

"It is an invasion. The handiwork of my son."

"Deimos promised. He swore this would not happen."

"He is what he is." Arrogance laced Ares' voice. "Come away with me now, for there is naught you can do to stop it. Your people are doomed and soon, Najahmara will be no more."

"No…no…." Panting, Niala dropped Layla's bones, unaware that they tumbled down the ridge, further shattering as they struck a half-exposed rocky ledge. "It cannot be."

"But it is. You do not have to watch." Ares reached for her just as a tortured wail rent the air, rising from the valley floor like a wounded thing carried off by sharp talons.

"Ahhh…." Niala began to keen in tandem with the awful sound. "Ahh…ahhh…."

Before Ares could prevent her, Niala began a sliding, scrambling descent from the plateau. She did not take the path but rather went from boulder to boulder in a skipping drop that took her rapidly downward, uncaring that her gown was ripped and blood began to ooze from deep scratches.

She felt no pain other than in her heart. She had no desire other than to cast her fate with her sisters. They would not die without her.

TWELVE

Crouching low to the ground, the men crossed the field with practiced stealth and scattered across the city. They first came upon crude, lean-to structures and those who slept within were cruelly silenced before they could wake.

As they went further into the streets of Najahmara, Telio's army found sturdier buildings and even less resistance, for no one stirred. There were no walls to bridge, no sentries to shout a warning, no beasts to set upon them. They found a silent, slumbering, defenseless city.

With Connal in the lead, Telio made for the center of Najahmara, to the sprawling temple with many doorways. There, he lit a torch and held it high, the signal they reached their destination. The men around him pulled sticks wrapped in waxed cloth from their belts and began to pass the flame back, from torch to torch, until a pinwheel of light spread out over Najahmara.

"The good citizens will now pay close attention, will they not?" Telio spat upon the entrance to the temple. "They will regret the capture of our king."

Amidst cries of alarm that began and ended abruptly, Telio waved Connal forward.

Connal whispered. "This is where the holy women live."

"Are there no men here?"

"Men come and go, but I do not think any stay."

"They have no husbands, these whores? Do they have any men to please?" Telio licked his lips, a sly smile turning up the corners. "Perhaps they shall have one they will not forget, eh, my man?"

Connal blanched, for he knew within these walls were young girls. Better their throats were cut than to fall prey to Telio and his evil ways. "Tonight there may be guards, for this is where King Hattusilis will be, if he is here."

"Then pray we find him within these walls." Telio stood just inside the arched entry, savoring the moment. He held no fear over his decision. Rather, he could imagine how his uncle would weep for joy to see him.

Telio would free Hattusilis from his imprisonment and defeat the demon that captured him. With fingers tightened on the hilt of his sword, Telio could not wait to run through the flesh of that filthy traitor. Blood and entrails would spill as he slit Deimos' gut. After a slow painful death, Telio would slice off his head and mount it for all to see.

What was left of Najahmara would kneel before him, grateful to be alive. And who, in the end, would claim the queen but he, for Hattusilis was already beaten.

"Come," Telio hissed, "Let us find our king."

He led the way along a short, narrow corridor, motioning a group of men to follow. A few stayed outside the temple to guard the other entranceways. There would be none running to assist the temple whores and there would be none escaping.

The men emerged into a large, rounded room with a domed ceiling supported by four pillars. In the center was a fire pit banked low with coals. Wisps of sweet-scented smoke curled up and as Telio followed the trail, he saw it disappear up through a grate open to the sky. The slats were tilted so that only a glimmer of the stars could be seen, but on a full moon, light would shine down as if it were atop the building.

"Clever," Telio muttered. As he stood staring upward, a streak of lightening shot through the darkness, followed by a loud roaring of the heavens that shook the building.

"Teshub is with us." Telio's gaze rolled heavenward. "Now go, check every room, every corner, every bed. Bring everyone you find here without delay and do not kill any, for I have been waiting for these women."

He grew hard with excitement and when the first of the girls was dragged in, he went to her with lustful intent. The smell of fear was strong and only heightened his desire, but he no more than touched her thigh as she struggled against the hands that held her when Zan interfered.

"My lord, this is not the time. We seek Hattusilis. He is our sole purpose."

Face ugly, Telio whirled on Zan. "Do not tell me my purpose. It is my blood who is lost, and it is my blood we will find."

"As you wish, my lord." Zan did not flinch. "There is naught more important than Hattu's safety."

"Yes. Yes." Telio cast a regretful glance at the girl who was now on her knees, weeping, then turned his attention to the others being herded into the chamber.

There were twenty-three, all young and tender, rumpled from sleep, in flimsy, sleeveless gowns. Telio stared at them, mouth agape.

"Is this all of them?" His voice was hoarse, eyes darting back and forth amongst the trembling, silent women.

Zan nodded toward another doorway where voices were raised. Within moments, four more women were shoved into the central area. A very old woman with kinky white hair and brown skin lashed out with gnarled fingers, pinching anything that came too close, all the while madly shrieking.

Following her was a woman scarce taller than the bent, old one. She held her gown tightly wound between shaking hands, black hair falling down her back in a straight curtain, her eyes wide with terror. Behind her was a tall woman with long braids, a piercing gaze and tightly clamped mouth. She refused to be pushed, turning a glare upon the soldier who put his hand on her arm. His hand dropped away as if he had been cut.

The last woman caught Telio's attention above the others, for she was unlike any of them. She was small, slender and very, very pale. Tiny dots of color stood out across her cheeks, nose and across her forehead. Hair glowed yellow in the torchlight creating a halo around her head. Even her eyelashes were pale. She stared at him with unblinking pale blue eyes.

Telio had never seen blue eyes before. He had seen yellow hair only once. Entranced, he reached out to touch the golden aura only to have the woman slap his hand away. Flushing, Telio hit her with the flat of his palm, knocking her to the floor. A wave of squealing rose up from the girls, the old one continued to shriek while the small dark one began to weep

As Telio reached for the pale one. "Silence them."

Before a hand could be lifted or a dagger flash forth, the tall woman shouted words in her tongue and a sudden quiet fell. She turned her fierce gaze upon Telio and spoke to him in the common trade language.

"What do you want?" Jahmed held herself still, though inside she felt witless. A legion of soldiers, Niala had told her. Nearby, searching for us. But after the cave ritual, she had said not to worry, the soldiers would not find Najahmara.

Keeping her eyes turned toward this strange bearded man, Jahmed fought down rising panic, for if she looked at Inni, she, too, would begin screaming. She knew the girls watched her and waited, for if all were to be put right, it would be up to her.

Niala was not with them.

What had they done with Niala? There were awful sounds coming from outside. They could all hear the wailing, the moans, the muffled screams. They could smell the smoking torches along with the acrid scent of fear. They could feel the waves of terror coursing through Najahmara and could do nothing. They were trapped here, in their own home, with the hard hands of rough, stinking men tossing them about like hunks of meat.

"Is this everyone?"

The man spoke to her using words she could understand. Before he had ranted in a coarse, guttural tongue that made her twitch. Even though she did not know what he said, his tone made it amply clear that before the night was out, death, or worse would be upon them.

He grabbed her throat. "Is this everyone?"

"Yes." She dared not let her gaze rove across the huddled group of girls, nor into any corner searching for Niala.

"There are no men?"

"No."

He released her but not before he slid his hand down to touch her breast. Jahmed bit the inside of her cheek and refused to squirm away. If he would rape, she would rather it be she than any of the others.

But there were many men. Despair made her heart pound, yet she spoke with calm. "What do you want?"

"My king. Where have you hidden him?"

Jahmed shook her head, dumbfounded. "There is no king. We have no ruler."

The smack across her face was unexpected. Jahmed stumbled backwards into the arms of another soldier. Inni cried out as she clung to one pillar, trying to stand. A bruise blossomed on her right cheek.

Seire began wailing. "What happens? Where is Niala? Niala? Niala!"

Pallin wept as she held Seire's shoulders and tried to quiet her. The young girls set up a high-pitched wail as they clung to each other.

Jahmed straightened, shrugging away the soldier's grip. "I do not know who you seek, but you will not find him here. There are no strangers among us."

"There are, there are," cried Pallin, in her own tongue. Though she knew some of the trade language, it was not enough to describe the one who had knelt before Gaea. "Tell him about the bearded one in the cave...and...." But she could not tell him about Deimos. Instead, she repeated, "There was a bearded one who visited us last night."

Telio looked askance at the small pretty girl who rattled on to the tall one. She waved her hands and nodded, and it did not take much to see that she had knowledge of something.

"What does she say?" Telio stared at the girl.

"Nothing. She is afraid."

"She says you are worse than a donkey turd and we will tell you nothing," shouted Inni. She knew the common words better even than Jahmed, for Inni had taught the trade language to her.

With a futile gesture, Jahmed warned Inni to be silent, but Inni's face was flushed with outrage and her thin frame strained forward as if she would fly into the beast.

To Jahmed, Inni said, "I do not care if they beat me senseless, I will not let them hurt you."

"Be still, Inni, for these savage ones are likely to kill us all," Jahmed pleaded. "Do not aggravate him further."

"Where is Niala?" Seire groped outward with her hands, reaching in hope that Niala was nearby. She found only the slick, sweat stained leathers of a soldier who shoved her away. "What have they done to her? Aaiee - have they murdered her?"

"Be quiet, old one." Pallin wept openly. "We do not know

what has befallen Niala. She is not here."

"She is not with us? Aaiee." Seire's wail rose to inconsolable heights.

"Kill her." Telio pointed to Zan.

"She is but an old woman," Zan protested. Faithful warrior that he was and loyal to his king, he did not approve of Telio's approach.

"My lord, it is clear Hattusilis is not in this dwelling. It has occurred to me that perhaps we are wrong. Perhaps Deimos is not of Najahmara, but from beyond this land and leads a counter-invasion inward from the sea. I think we waste our time here."

Zan's declaration ruffled throughout the body of soldiers. Murmurs rose and grips loosened. One grizzled soldier muttered, "This is not a battle, it is grievous error."

"King Hattusilis is not here." The call rose up and spread outward.

"Silence. I am your king now. Hattusilis is lost to us and you will do as I say," Telio shouted. "Show your allegiance or die a traitor's death."

"Telio." Zan held up one palm to stop the madness.

"King Telio. Show your respect." Telio drew his dagger and shoved the point into Zan's broad chest, piercing only the outer layer of the thick leather vest.

It was enough for Zan to raise his hands and give a quick dip of his head.

"King Telio." There was a dangerous glint in Zan's eyes as he viewed their newly proclaimed leader.

"Now, kill the old one. It will teach these whores a lesson that they may not lie to me. They will follow my rule from this day forward."

The entire room had grown quiet at their raised voices, all but Seire who continued to wail, in spite of Jahmed's sharp "Be still!" or Pallin's soft begging, "Seire, please, stop."

"Do it, Zan, or you yourself will die." As Telio swore, his face darkened with outrage.

"Then so be it," Zan answered. "But be prepared for mutiny. I am all that stands between you and these men, for they would sooner cut your throat than do your bidding."

"They have followed my command."

"They seek their true king. If Hattusilis is dead, then Teshub help you, for they will not, unless I am by your side."

Though rage boiled through him, Telio knew Zan spoke well. Telio could not afford to lose control of his men. With a shout of frustration, Telio leaped forward, seized Seire and with one quick chop, slit her throat.

The old one did not even know what happened, he gloated, for her film-covered eyes never saw him. She died at his feet, her blood soaking into the woven rug.

The women set up a shrill howl as one. They began to strike out at their captors, all of them, with a sudden rush of courage that began when the yellow-haired one attacked Telio.

Her eyes narrowed into animal slits as she went for his face, clawing and shrieking like a banshee. He struggled with her as the soldiers fought to subdue the other women, beating them back into a corner with fists and dagger hilts. Here and there a blade flashed forth and one fell, and then another, while the grief and horror rose to a higher level.

Jahmed was snatched from her feet, bashed in the head until she was dizzy, and then thrown into the corner with the others. Spots danced before her eyes and she could not see what befell Pallin.

Her only thought was of her beloved Inni, but Jahmed could not best the rough hands that kept shoving her back. It was when she finally made it to her feet again in the melee that she heard Inni's agonized scream slice through the madness.

Telio fought with Inni. His already scabbed face ripping open with each swipe of her nails. Rivulets of blood and sweat ran into his eyes as he throttled her, shaking her like a beast. Still she kicked and punched at him until he heaved her away. His fingers caught at the neck of her gown, shredding it from her body. She went face first into the pool of the old one's blood, retching and naked, red staining her skin.

Telio kicked her once in the side and then again feeling her flesh give way beneath his foot. Her cries brought lust rising up in Telio like a storm. Tossing the torn gown aside, he fell on her from behind and loosed his trousers. He jerked her arms into an impossible angle behind her shoulders and felt the snap of bones as his rigid manhood impaled her.

All else faded as he rode the woman, enjoying her agony. Near release, he withdrew and entered that forbidden, filthy place he liked best. He liked the cruel pain it caused and the tightness that gripped him as he thrust into her over and over, grunting out curses. Her screams became shrieks until she fell silent as he spilled into her.

He pulled free and the pale woman lay still, arms and legs at wrong angles. Dead or not, he did not care. The yellow hair she had not allowed him to touch was pulled free of its braid and swaddled her broken body in a golden blanket. The tips soaked up blood from the floor, a mixture of the old and the young.

Telio looked for the short, dark haired girl, for he was not ready to stop. There were others who took his lead and lay on top of a limp body and, then, there were some who watched, indecision and a hint of revulsion in their eyes.

He saw the traitor Zan, along with his brother Connal, had herded as many of the girls into a corner as they could and they set themselves up to guard against their own legion.

Telio would not forget nor forgive this action.

All the women would die after they served their purpose. The road to Najahmara had been long and this was their just reward. From the corner of his eye, Telio caught sight of the dark haired one and set off after her before another spread her legs. His hands were on her when he heard it.

A venomous hiss and the dry rattle of scales rubbing together. The building shook and the noises died down as all turned towards a dark corridor at the far end. Telio felt the hair on the back of his neck rise but all he saw was a single, disheveled woman appear framed in the smoky torchlight. One hoarse word was cried out.

"Niala!"

It was a name, a prayer, a plea, a warning.

Telio dropped his hand from the trembling girl and turned his full attention on the woman who now advanced into the room. He stepped forward in challenge, his lip curled, ready to draw the dagger once again, but he did not want to kill this one. A sly and calculating thought occurred. This one held authority. This one was their queen.

Take this one and all else became his.

As Niala passed through the gardens, she gave no regard as to whether Ares followed her or not. He would have to crush her to keep her from this battle. Win or lose, those she loved would not stand alone against this evil tide of destruction. She ran madly along the path toward the temple, frantic to get inside.

Oblivious to the cuts and scrapes caused by her descent, the twisted ankle upon her landing, and the bruises that would cripple her on the morrow. There was no one there to stop her but she could hear the murderous rampage on the outer streets of Najahmara. She could only fear the worst inside.

The ground continued to shake and the heavens rumble and groan as Gaea mourned. Deimos gave his word. He swore to stop the invasion and yet he did not. Gaea's people were dying and she could not prevent the slaughter. Why did he not stop them?

Niala felt Gaea's torment. It filtered up from the soil and pushed through her body until her heart pounded unmercifully against her chest. Do something, Gaea said. Do something.

Do something, do something. Stop them.

Stop them. Stop them.

How could she?

War had marched into their midst and War was stronger than all of them. But Kulika reared up over the betrayal of his beloved. He hissed, coiling ever tighter in his desire to strike out. He forced Gaea back into the earth and he, himself, pulsed with deepest fury up through his image and it was as if Niala's thigh was on fire. He pressed against her, eager for revenge, fangs set for the taste of meat.

Niala fought to suppress him, for he could not go forth unless she let him and she was not willing to release him. Once unleashed, he could not be withdrawn until he was satiated.

There were no words to describe the horror as Niala stepped into the temple chamber. The altar had been destroyed, the girls beaten and used. Fresh blood and waste filled the air with a stench that brought vomit into her throat. She stared in wordless sorrow at the bodies strewn across the drenched rugs.

Zahra. Fatin.

Others she could see lying so very still, beyond the legs of the soldiers, but not their faces. She could see no more faces.

How many were dead? How many would bear scars, on the surface and below, because of this? How many were yet to be tortured before it was over? Tears streamed from her eyes as she viewed the carnage.

And this man who stared at her with such conceit. How much

blood was on his hands? He looked at her with a hunger that should have brought fear, but instead it was loathing that twisted her mind.

Hatred. Icy hatred.

Bright blue, like the sky at midsummer.

Like the Blue Serpent who lay over the earth and gave shelter to ungrateful mortals. To those who would rape his beloved and strip away that which she adored.

Kulika's blue flame shot through Niala and seared from the inside out. Her skin felt as if it were disintegrating, dissolving away into scales, into the undulating coils of the serpent. He peered through her eyes, the black slits turning her vision into double and triple, blurred, for Kulika did not see well. But he felt the heat and he smelled his prey standing before him without even the sense to be afraid.

Free me. Kulika's voice hissed in her ear. *Free me, and this will end.*

"I cannot," Niala cried.

And then she saw the empty eyes of her daughter. A soldier shifted and Seire's face became clear. Next to her, a golden shrouded body, naked, broken. There was only one who was that fair among them.

Inni. Seire. Dead.

With a tormented shriek that sent a shudder through the chamber, Niala collapsed within herself and Kulika was released. His energy swirled upward in a great column and reformed her body into massive blue coils and a flat, elongated head with a blunt snout.

His tongue whipped out, forked, red as blood, and those he touched died screaming from his poison. He breathed fire and smoke and shot it out through the corridors of the temple until the flames engulfed anything in its path, flesh and object alike.

Blue fire roared along the streets of Najahmara taking over the yellow flame of torches, consuming and destroying everything and everyone it touched.

Fangs bared, he shifted to the cowering human who tried desperately to run from him. He could feel the frantic beating of his prey's pulse, the blind panic as he dodged back and forth, thinking if he could escape the temple, he would be safe.

Kulika cornered Telio as he screamed with terror and begged

for his life. Kulika waited until his bowels emptied and gut spewed and then he bit into him. Pierced his heart with wicked fangs and tore him apart. Blood sprayed in a delicate, dark pattern onto fabric hung on the wall. It was all that was left of one who would give no respect to his beloved Earth.

Then Kulika turned his attention to the others in the room, for the taste of prey was strong in his mouth and he desired more.

Ares stood on the brink of the plateau and watched as Niala was swallowed by the dark valley floor. He did not chase after her. He did not need to. She did not run from him, but rather to them, and all he had to do was follow along and retrieve her when he was ready.

He wanted to take his time, to think about what she said. Did he believe her? Had she journeyed far enough into the depths of her soul to see what hid behind her mortal existence? Or did she mouth back his own words, mocking him with the story he told her of Anyal, Ilya, and Elche?

He wanted to think but there was more pulling him than old wounds.

There was violence erupting in Najahmara. It began with fire sweeping across the city. At first it was no more than a trickle, catching his attention as it became a bobbing light that jumped here and there, spreading out like thin fingers along the paths between rooftops. He was held in thrall by the sight, as if he watched the earth crack open and reveal her hidden self to him.

But Gaea groaned in protest, shivering beneath his feet.

Ares knew it to be the torches held aloft by a legion of soldiers who came to conquer Najahmara. The army Deimos had spoken of. They were no longer in the throes of a bespelled brew, but ready to launch an attack. His son would be most unhappy over this turn of events, but such was the way of mortals. They had an uncanny way of worming through any obstacle to get what they wanted.

It seemed they wanted Najahmara.

The prospect of violence always excited Ares, drawing him into the thickest part of the battle with no care as to which side he fought on. He pursed his lips and gave a slight shake of his head.

This was not a battle. It was a deliberate massacre. Screams were beginning to drift upward. Not shouts of courage to urge men on, but the shrill keening of women and thin wails of children. Still, the spiral of energy brought on by aggression wrapped about him and his breath quickened.

The shriek that sent Niala racing down the mount came again, worse this time. A high, pinched cry of pain that willed death to end it.

If Ares did not take care, the detachment would leave him altogether and he would descend to the valley and become part of the bloodletting. The call to kill for pleasure was strong, yet he fought it, not ready to become the mindless warrior again.

Already, he could see Enyo, that frightful specter of death, scooping up souls and consuming them into an everlasting torment. Even those who worshipped Gaea were not immune to Enyo, for they died in pain and confusion and were ripe to harvest. She did not ride alone.

With her were War's minions, the Keres and the Erinnyes, those foul creatures whose greatest joy was to wreak havoc for their master. He could also see Eris darting in and out with lurid glee, the slathering hounds at his heels, creating further confusion.

And his mother demands him back, Ares thought with amusement. Aglauros would no longer recognize her son. He should send Eris to visit the Sylph and see how fast she returned her pride and joy to Athos.

Why is it that females were so stubborn? They will not listen, therefore, Ares was forced to demonstrate. Time and time again.

Yes, he would send Eris back to the woodlands for a visit. Aglauros would beg to have her blood-thirsty son gone from her gentle forest in a matter of hours.

Ares' thoughts had drifted far enough away from the commotion in the valley that he could almost leave without entering the fray. But then a column of hot energy exploded upward and outward, shooting in all directions. Energy he saw as blue flame and white smoke. Flame that burned bone to ash.

Someone interfered.

Immortal interference.

Kulika.

The silken web of brutality grew stronger and Ares could no longer resist. Thus, Ares was drawn down to Najahmara where the piteous cries of the dying and the stench of the already dead got War's full attention. He left the plateau just as a hard rain began to fall and the thunder that preceded it was now overhead.

Ares entered the temple with the awareness that Kulika had ended the skirmish. The Sky god had receded nearly as fast as he had advanced, leaving behind devastation. The walls were shadowed where flames licked along the corridors and charred bodies lay unrecognizable on the floor. Ares followed the acrid scent of smoke and burned flesh to the common area.

The fire had erupted and belched out from the central chamber. The walls were blackened and the floor gritted beneath Ares' feet, even though he tread with care. Blood and entrails created gory patterns across the ruined walls with bits of bodies tossed about.

On the other side a handful of women were spread out upon the floor but untouched by either flame or frenzy. A few men lay sprawled across them, whether caught in the midst of attack or protection, he could not tell.

One lone figure moved.

Niala. Her face was buried in her arms as she huddled on the floor. She was on her belly, unclothed and slick with sweat, her hair loosened from its braid, thick, wet and matted to her back. It was clear Niala had hosted the demented Kulika. If Ares doubted before, he would not do so again. Niala was not of the mortal caste. He squatted and touched her shoulder but she would not lift her head.

"Niala, it is done. Look at me."

"Go. Leave me alone."

"What happened here?" Ares turned her over and brushed the hair away from her swollen eyes, his fingertips lingering on her scratched cheek.

"What happened here was war, you should be proud." Red tears tracked down Niala's cheeks and in her eyes was bitter remorse.

"War is not always about power. It, too, is about protection." He scanned the chaos again. "Or pleasure."

"Yes, yes, I wanted them to die. Helplessly, horrifically. Gaea, help me."

"She cannot, but I am here." Ares propped Niala on his knee. She lolled back, too weak to hold herself upright. "I will help you."

It was an odd offering for War to make but he was compelled by the past, determined there would be a future.

"Then slay me," Niala begged, clutching at his shirtfront. "Please, slay me. End my misery."

"No."

"Dispatch me," she wept, wiping one hand across her forehead. The rain of bloody tears grew harder. "You want to kill me, I know it."

"I never wanted you to die." Ares kissed Niala's bloody forehead. "Never."

"I cannot bear this life a moment longer. I have destroyed the enemy but along with them, my own." Niala shuddered and then began a trembling that would not stop. Her teeth hit against each other and her eyes rolled up. Her face took on a flattened appearance and there was the slightest undulation.

Kulika. He did not want to leave. Niala forced him out, but now he tried to return.

Ares saw then the image of Kulika drawn on her leg and placed his hand upon Niala's thigh, his fingers around the blue, scaled neck. As he tightened his grip, Ares commanded Kulika to leave.

"You have done your duty. You have protected your mate. Now I bid you go in peace. There is no more threat here."

An angry hissing echoed in his ears. "Go, Kulika."

Beneath his hand, Ares felt the power of the heavens shifting, merging in an attempt to stay, to convince him it was good and right that the Sky have form.

"No," Ares spat out between clenched teeth. "She is mine."

And Earth responded with a grinding rumble of dissent.

"You have had her all these many years," Ares said to Gaea. "Give her to me. I will care for her now."

Gaea grew quiet, as if in contemplation and then Kulika withdrew. Ares could feel the energy of the serpent fade and Niala lay quiet, staring up at him. Tears continued to run from the corners of her eyes.

"You can send him away, but it does not change what I have done." Weariness was etched into every angle of her face though she finally grew still. "I ask for your mercy. It is not to rid myself of Kulika, but to let me have peace."

"Death by my hand will not give you peace. It would put you into the grips of something much worse. It is better that I leave you with breath, even if you must see the damage."

"And what hateful world do you inhabit that death becomes punishment rather than reward?"

"For most it is neither." Ares lifted her to her feet, felt her knees buckle and all vigor flow away as she saw the girls strewn across the floor.

"Gaea, forgive me, I have delivered them into your hands, may they be safe now from harm." With a sudden lunge, Niala reached for Ares' sword. "Give me your weapon and I will join them, for I cannot live knowing what I have done."

"Stop, Niala." Ares stayed her hands and held her tight to his chest. "You could not wield Amason even if I would let you, for you have not the strength. Be silent now, they are not all gone, some are only without their senses."

"They are dead."

"Some live on and so shall you."

Niala broke away from him, wobbling, reaching out to hang onto a pillar. Her gaze riveted on the gore-smeared walls and once more she felt the surge of exultation, the pure joy of slaying them. Their blood was again in her mouth, in her nose, and in her eyes. Their screams echoed in her ears. Clamping her hands to her ears, she sank to her knees.

"How could I?" Niala cried. "How could I do this?"

"How could you not?"

"I am no better than you. I killed for pleasure."

"It is not as simple as that."

"Life is sacred, even those men." She gestured at the half-eaten bodies.

"Perhaps Kulika has a different sense of life."

"It is wrong." Niala swiveled to look at the rest of the temple chamber. It was then she saw Seire and Inni lying next to her.

Crawling to Seire, Niala fell over her, weeping. "Aaiee. I cannot bear it."

Niala kissed the old one's face, then laid her forehead against Seire's lips as new tears rained down. One hand crept over to stroke Inni's hair, but she could not look at what had been done to her. As her hand moved down the wet strands, she touched cool metal.

A dagger, its blade darkened with blood. Niala's fingers closed around the ornate hilt and she drew it closer. Rolling to her back, Niala lifted the dagger and held it between both hands.

She had no fear of death.

More, she feared to stay alive. Closing her eyes, Niala stabbed downward with all the strength she had left. The blade struck and pierced. She felt it catch and slide through, but there was no pain and still she breathed. With swollen lids barely able to open, she looked up.

Ares had placed his hand on her heart. The dagger was embedded in his flesh. Blood seeped around the wound and dripped down between her breasts. With a grimace, he plucked the blade free and tossed it aside.

"You see, Niala Aaminah, you are not the only one who bleeds." With no further words, Ares gathered Niala into his arms and left Najahmara.

THIRTEEN

"I owe my allegiance to War."

Deimos spoke only to himself, for there was no one else in all the upper reaches of Athos. He paced the confines of his quarters, moving with restless concern from corner to corner and back again. Thinking Athos had never seemed as suffocating as it did in that moment, he would even welcome the company of Eris, however annoying the boy could be.

The command to remain within the walls of Athos had turned Deimos' place of retreat into a prison. He paused mid-stride to take critical note of all around him, looking for the one thing that dissatisfied him most, the thing he could destroy without punitive measures.

Deimos used only a single long room with a hearth at one end and a bed at the other, although there was an adjoining chamber beyond those walls containing a bathing area. A tall cupboard sat empty next to the arched doorway that led to the corridor.

Opposite them were matching doors that would take him outside to a narrow walkway overlooking the sea. A table, devoid of any objects, and two chairs sat to the left of the fireplace. A low, backless couch was to the right. Everything in the room was simple except for the ornate, seven-pronged candle stand, dark with tarnish. It was not even his, but remained after the last inhabitant.

Except for a large oval rug woven in shades of the sea - blue, green, pearl, sand - there was nothing of particular value or sentimental reminder. He brought nothing with him into Athos over the long span of time there. He realized he did little more than survive in the harsh world of War, taking each moment as it came, never looking beyond the obstacle before him.

Without realizing, Deimos let himself slip into the same bleak pattern that beset his father. His surroundings were severe and colorless, except for the rug. Even the neat bedcovers were cold unbleached cloth along with neutral woolen blankets. The mantel was barren, the table clear, the chairs and couch empty.

There was no need for luxury.

Indeed, where in all of Athos could opulence be found? And Deimos encouraged that by closing off any option for cheer or comfort, even in his private quarters. He could have lived any way he wanted, surrounded by color and warmth, by servants who would provide him with both pleasure and company. Instead, he chose to live in dismal darkness, mirroring his inner state.

Deimos exhaled, staring at the rug. It was the only reminder of his mother's world. The only memento he would permit himself to own. It was too painful to allow those memories to intrude upon his function.

Not even Deimos' reflection gave hint to his mother's side, so much did he resemble his father. There was nothing that spoke of Love, though he was born of Aphrodite and Ares together.

"Should I not bear some witness to my mother? I owe my allegiance to War but do I not retain some semblance of Love?"

With minute detail, Deimos recalled playing along the shores of Cos, his mother's isle. He could feel the way the fine white sand grabbed at his bare feet as he ran up and down the beach. The way it packed solid as the sea rose and then was sucked out from beneath him as it receded.

How many hours did he and his brother, Anteros, stand at the edge letting the water flow over and under their feet, waiting to sink further and further until they would lose their balance and fall giggling into the waves?

Even now, the strong scent of brine filled Deimos' nose and he felt if he reached out, he could again pick up a handful of the delicate foam created from nothing more than the incessant pounding of water on sand.

He and Anteros would fling foam at each other until they were covered in it, then chase each other far out into the turquoise expanse beyond the breakers. There they swam with a multitude of brightly colored fish, explored the reefs beneath the surface, and teased sea creatures that could have crushed them.

Their favorite games involved the dolphins, the sentient beings that stood guard over them, and who would intercept the two small boys who often strayed further out to sea than was prudent. They never told Aphrodite of their foolishness. Unlike the hounds of War that slunk around the corridors of Athos, the dolphins were fitting pets for Aphrodite's sons.

Deimos tried to befriend the hounds when he first arrived at Athos. Now he would sooner kick them aside than look into the relentless, yellow, vicious eyes that recognized no one but their master. When Ares was about, the dogs whined and groveled at his feet, but in his absence, they turned to slathering mindless things bent on terrorizing a little boy.

The hounds no longer frightened him, still they refused to do his bidding. Deimos lifted his shoulders in a shrug. It was doubtful the dolphins would either. It was a pretty picture, his short life on the Isle of Love, though he knew he did not belong there.

Still, he was born of Aphrodite. Unlike Ares, he carried some sense of love and duty in his heart. He had sworn to Gaea during a sacred ritual that her people would not be harmed, yet here he lingered while Ares went alone to Najahmara with an old grudge foremost in his mind.

Ares could destroy Najahmara out of spite, with or without Hattusilis' army. Would Ares defy Gaea, even with the grim reprimand from the Greater Realm hanging over his head? Zeus was not without the means to punish the entire House of War should Earth and Sky demand it.

"And Grandfather would be quite happy to carry out his threat." Deimos threw open the outer doors. A cold breeze engulfed him. "And most certainly, with the blessing of the entire Council."

For once, it was a clear night. The earlier fog had dissipated and the clouds lifted, exposing a heaven full of brilliant stars. The sea was near invisible in the darkness, but the unmistakable noise of the surf could be heard as it crashed over the rocky base.

It was not the gentle tides of Cos, but the battering of one element against another. The sound served to remind Deimos of the bitterness of the conflict between Ares and Zeus. Would Ares allow Zeus to gain control just for the sake of revenge?

From the moment Ares repeated Niala's name, Deimos knew the answer was yes on all counts.

"Ares commands me to cease my efforts with the mortal world and yet, with all recklessness, he rushes in." Deimos leaned on the stone barrier between himself and a headlong dive to meet the sea below. "Ares cares not what his father decrees. Should I then heed what my father demands of me?"

Zeus would penalize all, but Ares would direct his wrath towards only one.

Deimos sighed. "I cannot prevent Ares from lifting his hand against Najahmara, but I can halt the army."

With this came startled thoughts of Hattusilis. What had become of him since the ritual? After a momentary spurt of guilt, Deimos contemplated the worst that could have happened, and that was Hattu without a woman to make love to him.

Najahmara bore no rancor towards Hattusilis, for they did not know his intention. He would be treated with the same kindness Deimos had experienced.

"I hope he lies abed with a Najahmaran woman. That would do him good," Deimos mused. "It may not be with the queen he sought, but both coupling and sleep will help abate his grief for Azhar and allow him to see the truth."

Najahmara's pursuit had been conceived to bury Azhar, but if the dead did not want to rest, there was naught mortal or immortal could do about it.

Deimos would seek out Hattusilis once this score between Ares and Niala was settled and reunite him with his army. He would divert their steps towards the western reaches where a battle would be welcomed and Najahmara would be left in peace.

"There will be none amongst them who will even remember such a place exists when it is all done. None but myself." For though he could not have Niala Aaminah, there was still sweet Pallin to consider.

"And she is well worth whatever happens, although with any luck, Ares will be in contention with Zeus and I will not suffer through his fit of temper."

It was Niala who most concerned Deimos but Ares would bear no interference. Whatever had occurred between them must stay between them, yet it was a mystery of some magnitude. Truth, there was much about his father's existence that remained hidden, most Deimos would rather not know. But Niala?

How did a gentle priestess of Gaea become that which Ares the Destroyer wanted so badly he would risk further disfavor to have her?

With a shake of his head, Deimos put those thoughts aside. If he hurried, there was a chance he could uphold his promise to Gaea and not get caught. He moved with swiftness, going first to the army's campsite, hoping he could return to Athos before Ares knew he was gone.

That hope deserted him as Deimos saw the barren landscape. The army was gone. All that was left of the encampment was trampled, muddy ground and the filth of many humans and their beasts. Here and there faint glowing coals from a few remaining fires told him they had not pulled out that long ago.

Why did they break camp just before nightfall? How far could they go and, more to the point, how did they shake off the effects of the beyaz?

Cursing, Deimos called Synod, one of the winged steeds from the Greater Realm, and threw himself upon the back of the stallion. Synod was able to fly over the land rather than leave Deimos to guess and guess again with a tedious margin for error.

When they caught up to the army, Deimos' eyes widened, for it was little more than half its number. The men below straggled forward in the flickering fickle light of weak torches. The group was comprised only of foot soldiers with two captains on horseback to keep them moving. Even further behind were the pack animals and the women who followed them.

Where was the mounted legion?

Deimos nudged Synod forward into a frantic flight along the curling Maendre, but there was no sign of them. Light rain compounded the darkness as he closed the distance to Najahmara.

It became a steady downpour by the time he reached the forest's edge. He brought his mount into a slow spiraling descent just beyond the tree line where a herd of horses were tethered. He took a moment to thank the winged one and bid him return home, for his work was done. Snorting contemptuous vapor at the earthbound, four-legged creatures just beneath the canopy of leaves, Synod lifted his head, gave a shrill warble, and disappeared.

"Telio. Zan. We must wait." Deimos froze as he realized there was naught but the beasts within the forest. Five hundred mounts restively waited, grazing on anything within reach.

Those closest stomped their hooves and laid their ears back with soft whinnies at the sound of his voice. These were warhorses and they longed to be in the thick of battle, not safe and out of the way tied to low-lying branches.

"Shh - shhht." Deimos held the nearest bridle and scratched behind twitching ears. "Why have they gone on foot? What has Telio done?"

As if in answer, there was a great clap of thunder and the earth shivered. Then nothing. The rain muffled all other sounds yet terror filtered through the air. He caught it as if it were a tangible thing that slammed into him with the force of a tumbling boulder.

Massive, overriding terror, the kind that would be present if he rode with War, if he released his power from its boundaries within himself. The times when Deimos sought to make a mortal die from sheer fright.

Terror lay across the valley like a pall, held in place by the water gushing from the sky. And then in the distance, he heard the unmistakable shriek of Enyo as she delivered souls into an eternity of torment.

Deimos took the reins into his hands and leaped astride the pawing beast. The mount needed no encouragement to race into the deluge, his hooves throwing clots of mud behind them. As they crossed the fields, Deimos could make out some movement ahead, indistinct black on black shapes.

He could not tell what it was until he was nearly upon them and then he found them to be part of Telio's legion. They ran at Deimos, stumbling, falling, flailing in the rain and mud, too shocked to speak.

He caught one man to get some word from him, but the whites of his eyes glowed with panic and his words were slurred and nonsensical. Deimos released him and he melted away with the others. He came upon pockets of these mindless men but the closer he came to Najahmara, the more disoriented they were.

Less running than wandering and, more often, accompanied by natives of Najahmara. These folk were dressed in their nightclothes, light colored and easier to spot, but still indistinct in the darkness and heavy rain.

The wet choking scent of burned buildings and scorched brick hung low over Najahmara. Behind it came the stench of charred flesh and bone. Upon arrival at the first line of small huts that hailed the beginning of the city, the smell became overwhelming. He slowed his mount, for bodies were strewn all around.

The moans and cries of wounded and dying people echoed in darkness thickened by smoke. Deimos could scarce see where he was going. Once, his mount stepped down and a shriek of pain rose up like a lance, then gurgled out in a rasping gasp.

Deimos slid from the horse and felt for the one beneath its hooves, but it was too late. With one slap to the beast's flank, he let it go on its own and went by foot into the town. With each step, his horror grew, for there were more dead than he could count. Shapeless, faceless shells in the night.

He could not tell if those whose bodies littered the streets were soldiers or the folk of Najahmara. He could not tell if they were men, women, or children, for the corpses were no more than black smudges against the night.

Enyo's howling grew louder and the wild snarling of her minions rose in nightmarish tandem to the moans and cries echoing through the streets of Najahmara. In the background, Deimos could hear Eris laughing with the madness brought on by blood-letting, as if it were all provided just for his entertainment.

It was more than Deimos could bear. Hot rage shook him with such force he lost all thought. He sought out Enyo and her snapping beasts, striding past the devastation with one purpose, until he found her. He plucked her from the carnage, his hand at her throat and throttled her until she regurgitated those souls that did not belong to her.

Though Enyo's beasts gnawed his legs, he kept shaking her until she spewed forth all that she would. Hatred burned in her hollow eyes and her skeletal face twisted with the effort. Bony hands clawed at his arms and neck and her thin legs whipped about trying to kick him as she fought, but he remained steadfast, strangling her, wishing it could be to the death.

Nothing could kill Enyo. She could be locked away and starved for all eternity and still, she would not fade away. Deimos did not have the power to do such a thing, yet it would be a long while before she showed herself when he was near. When he threw her away from him, she flew up into the air with a hoarse shriek.

"You will pay for this, son of Ares."

"Begone you monstrosity." Deimos brandished his weapon. "I will not have you feeding from this place. Begone before I make you beg for mercy."

Weakened and bruised, Enyo cursed at him and then fled, her whining beasts at her side. Eris was no fool for he witnessed this insanity that possessed Deimos and made his escape before Deimos' wrath could be turned toward him.

"It is well and good you, too, leave, Brother," Deimos ranted. "For you knew this place was not to be disturbed. But you cannot hide from me, I will finish with you later."

The city fell into an eerie silence, as if there was not a whisper of life left in it. Dawn was not yet forthcoming; rain kept falling with a steadiness that spoke of hours more before the clouds lifted.

Deimos made his way toward the temple, that crouching black hulk in the center of town, the heartbeat, the center, the guiding light for all of Najahmara. It, too, lay charred and lifeless, with not a sound emanating from inside. All who fled, and those who could not, did not bear contemplation.

He refused to think of Niala lying unrecognizable amongst the rubble. Instead, he questioned how much of this was at Ares' direction. Could he, would he, have hastened the army's descent onto Najahmara to satisfy his own bloodlust against Niala Aaminah? To irretrievably destroy that which she loved so much before her very eyes?

Yes, it was something Ares would do.

With clenched fists and lips pressed tight, Deimos entered the temple. Here he found the overriding stench of burned flesh and bone, of defecation and urine, of death clasping hands with unimaginable horror. He continued on until he saw flickering light against the corridor walls.

A single torch remained lit in the smoke-filled central room, casting bizarre shadows upon the gruesome scene. Blood-drenched walls scorched black by fire, shredded entrails and bits of flesh flung across the floor mixed with shards of pottery and splinters of bone. There were bodies and more bodies, some obviously dead, some intact but very still, some with breath.

Gaea's altar lay smashed, statue on the floor, coated in blood.

Stunned, Deimos turned in circles as he viewed the butchery. He was overwhelmed with the wild emotion that remained locked within the walls. It whirled about him in a frantic, unstable force, battering against his mind. The fear that remained gave vivid sensations. He could see the rising up of some beast, its massive head swaying. He could feel the fire as it burned across his own skin, smelled the smoke and felt searing pain.

Screams tore from his own throat as he felt teeth rip his flesh and heard the death rattle of his own breath. He reached out with blind eyes to fight against this monster but came back with no more than a bloody stump of the victim. He heard the shriek that issued from his own mouth and tasted the sweat from his own body as his blood pooled on the floor.

Grunting, Deimos pushed away the tattered and tortured imprints of the dying. Opening his eyes, he drew in deep breaths even though the air was putrid with blood and waste and smoke. It was not until he turned again that he saw movement.

In the corner, upon a heap of bodies, one shape began to detach itself from the others. First with hands that clutched at anything near, reaching upward to push a body away. Then a man rolling away from the pile to stare up at the ceiling.

The man's mouth worked but no words issued forth while he clawed at the space above him, still fighting against an attack. Deimos made his way to that side of the chamber and stared down. He realized it was Zan who still lived. Crouching beside him, Deimos clasped one of Zan's hands, grateful for the feeling of the calloused warm skin against his palm. He squeezed Zan's still moving fingers.

"Zan, what happened here?"

With a hoarse cry, Zan struggled to pull free and scoot away.

"Zan, it is I, Deimos. Do not be afraid. It is Deimos. There is nothing left here to fear." He repeated the phrases over and over in a low voice until Zan grew still. "Tell me what happened, Zan, for I do not understand what did this."

Finally, Zan turned swollen red eyes toward Deimos. His face and beard were streaked with soot and his parted lips were dry, cracked and moving, but unable to make a sound. He blinked in recognition. It was not joy that appeared there; it was loathing. One word hissed through his teeth, "Traitor."

With a start, Deimos realized the last Zan had seen of him was during the drunken revelry at the campsite, before he had taken Hattusilis away. They had rallied enough to attack Najahmara. They would have understood that the two missing men were together. They would have thought Hattusilis was here. They would have sought to save their king.

Deimos recognized it was his fault the army advanced into Najahmara. They did what any loyal legion would do; they went forth to rescue their king. If Deimos had not been drawn away by command of his father, Hattusilis would have been returned to them and this slaughter would not have happened. Deimos was sickened with remorse.

"No, Zan," Deimos spoke, his heart heavy. "I am no traitor. I did not intend this harm."

"Hattu." Zan's voice croaked out the single word.

Shaking his head, Deimos hesitated for if his assumption were true then Hattusilis was probably a charred corpse along with the rest of Najahmara and his troops. "I am sorry, I do not know."

He pulled Zan to a sitting position, steadying him as he swayed.

"I did not betray you, I swear it." Again, Deimos paused. He did not want to say that his true self was revealed because of Telio's action. No other knew of it but those two and now it appeared they were both dead.

"Telio commanded our attack." Zan coughed hard, spit blood, and coughed more.

Deimos reached behind his back and summoned a flask of water to his hand, offering it to Zan as if it had been with him all along. Zan drank long, choking some, but swallowing more.

"What happened here?" Deimos asked again. "This fire, it did not start on its own."

"No. It was unbelievable." Zan passed a filthy hand across his forehead. He told the tale as best he could, of their discovery that Hattusilis was gone, the beyaz. Here he paused and looked askance at Deimos, but then went on with his story in halting, half-finished phrases. When he was done, he sagged with exhaustion and resignation.

"Are all the men dead?" Zan's voice cracked.

"Not all, for I saw some running, headed toward the woods." Deimos rocked back on his heels, his gaze sliding over his shoulder towards the body parts that littered one side of the chamber.

"The horses are tethered in the forest."

Deimos nodded, his thoughts returning to the giant serpent. He felt the energy of the beast lingering within the walls. The specter loomed up, blood flowing from its fangs, madness in its gold eyes, before fading away into mist. A blue serpent.

The image drawn on Niala's thigh.

"It was Kulika." Deimos spoke in an undertone, as if the Sky god could hear him.

"I do not know this monster's name, but I saw with my own eyes how it tore Telio to pieces and then turned on the others."

"On all but those." Deimos nodded towards the women of the temple. With a jerk and a widening of his eyes, Zan pushed away from Deimos, calling to his brother. On hands and knees, Zan crawled to the pile of bodies and began shoving them aside.

"Connal - Connal."

Deimos helped drag Connal to one side and turn him over, gratified to see he still breathed. A deep gash was across his forehead, and his face was slack, yet he was alive. Zan supported Connal's head and dribbled water between his lips, all the while calling to him to awaken. It was then Deimos saw Pallin was beneath Connal.

Deimos pulled her free of the other bodies and cradled her in his arms. He could see the slightest rise and fall of her chest and there were no visible wounds. She lay silent and pale, her head falling forward against his chest.

"Pallin." He touched her cheek. "Pallin, awaken."

It was long moments before she opened her eyes, with time enough to consider taking her away, except there was nowhere to go. The temple was in ruins and most of Najahmara destroyed. He could do naught but wait until her lashes flickered.

Pallin came awake with a shriek and immediately, violently, threw up. Her vomit splattered his clothing and onto the other bodies as her hands beat against the air around her.

"Stop. Stop." Deimos' tone was rough, for he did not know what else to do. Pulling at Pallin's hands, he called her name until she clutched at him, weeping. He poured water into his hand and wiped her face, then scrubbed at her skin with his shirttail.

"Drink." He held the flask to her lips.

Pallin swallowed once and then heaved again, pushing away the water.

"Niala," she sobbed. "Seire." Words dropped from her lips in a babbling rush, as fast as the tears fell from eyes wide and filled with terror.

She fell into spells, shuddering helpless wails as she tried to speak. He could do no more than rock her back and forth while he searched as far as his gaze would reach to find Niala.

Even though dazed and unable to comprehend what happened, the young women began to return to their senses and struggled to sit up. There were dead ones and those whose faces he could not see. From the length of the bodies, the hair, the gowns, whatever it was he could glimpse, none were Niala.

Could it be she was not there? That Ares had taken her away before the soldiers reached Najahmara? For a moment, Deimos was filled with relief, until the dread thought occurred she might be one ripped apart by Kulika.

His gaze was drawn to an arm lying in a pool of blood. The arm was thick with coarse, dark hair and a scarred hand attached. It did not belong to a female and, yet, she could still be spread amongst the pieces littering the temple.

Deimos was accustomed to death in the mortal realm, but this carnage sickened him, and he could not stand to look upon it for another moment. He thought to leave them all to their misery, let them sort it out on their own.

But, as he gazed into Pallin's eyes, Deimos knew he could not walk away, for no one had ever looked upon him with such desperate need. No one had ever moved him like this woman, like Niala and her people. Deimos could not abandon them to such a cruel dawn as they would find, though he was certain to pay a very high price for staying.

FOURTEEN

The wound through Ares' hand burned hot as water splashed over it. Palm down, he stared at it, allowing the tingle of pain to spread. Pain reminded him he was alive - immortal, but not invincible. Subject to error, he was just as much a fool as any human when it came to matters of the heart. He should have let Niala feel the very real pain of a blade sinking into her flesh. It might have eased the pain that now ate away her soul. But Ares would have run the risk of being wrong.

Niala Aaminah had grown up, but not grown old. That alone convinced him she was of his race, born to serve the mortal world. He admitted with grudging reluctance that seldom, yet possible, was a deity born of the Greater Realm unaware of lineage.

It had happened. They did not know of Aphrodite until she rose from the sea, her appearance causing a startled ripple throughout the Greater Realm.

It happened.

Ares had searched for Ilya for so long he almost missed her. By a mere fluke, she turned up at his feet, a captive of his worshippers, who were blinded to the true jewel they so rudely brought him. A goddess in disguise, one raised with such humility she could not accept her true bloodline.

How could Niala Aaminah deny it now? She had hosted the spirit of Kulika, the Blue Serpent. Shape-shifting to accommodate a god, she had done murder for him. No mortal could withstand such punishment.

But if she had pierced her flesh with that dagger and Ares was wrong, not even he could retrieve her from the halls of the Shadowland, for he was denied entrance to Hades' realm.

Could Ares be wrong? Closing his fingers into a fist, he looked at the ragged edges where the dagger left its mark. Shifting his gaze to Niala, he knew that though she suffered, the proud sweep of forehead to chin gave testimony to her indomitable fortitude, the shining strength that attracted him from the beginning.

It was Niala's fierce courage that held him hostage when he would rather it did not. He reached out to touch her face while rivulets of water made tracks in the blood on her skin. With a dazed expression, Niala rested against the marble, shoulder deep in the steaming bath. She had uttered not a word since he caught her up from the wretched bedlam in Najahmara and carried her home to Athos.

She made no protest, not even when he paused in the outer chamber, again looking upon her with desire much like now. Although she had been shaking, lips blue, eyes rolled back, and the remains of her enemy's dark stains upon her body, Ares still wanted her. With unaccustomed tenderness, he cupped her cheek in his palm.

"I am sorry." Niala turned her face and pressed her lips against his palm. Two fat tears rolled down her cheeks and joined with the drops of moisture gathered on her chin. "So sorry."

She squeezed her eyes shut and shrank away from him. Sorry she hurt him. Sorry she ran away. Sorry he found her. Sorry so many died. Sorry she lived on.

Sorry....sorry...sorry.

Her head ached so much she could not think other than to know she did not want him to look at her, to touch her, to console her. She would slip below the surface of the water except for his watchful eye pinning her to the side of the pool. But, should he look the other way, she would breathe her last.

Niala buried her face in her arms, too tired to cry more.

"It was a willing sacrifice." Ares jabbed a finger into the gash. He was rewarded with a hot jolt that made his hand twitch. Blood oozed out and thinned into the wet creases of his skin, then disappeared into the greater pool of water.

The wound would heal and be gone within a few days time.

With the exception of Niala, there would be no reminder of the carnage. He studied her as she hugged the edge of the pool knowing she would rather take solace from the cold marble than from him.

"Just as yours, too, was a willing sacrifice." Ares laid the injured hand on her shoulder and felt her flinch. "Niala, you must face what happened and not turn away from it."

"You think I do not see it every moment?" Sliding further along the cool marble rim, Niala answered in a strangled voice. "In every ripple and drip of water, I do not see reflected there the faces of those I killed?"

"They were your enemy."

"They were human, alive. Someone loved them."

She sagged deeper into the hot water, becoming aware of the scent of sandalwood that rose up around her. Her gaze went to the familiar ceiling, the erotic playful figures, and the graceful arches from dome to the four corners. The glimmer of polished stone surrounded her. Beauty meant to soothe, to arouse, to insulate from all the hate that beckoned violence to erupt.

It was the one place from which Ares could turn away from the world, forget who he was and what his role was to forever be. He told her that long years ago. She remembered his every word. She remembered it was the first time she felt something deeper stirring, something beyond the carnal. She had begun to understand him, to love him. Only to turn around and betray him, just like she had betrayed those who lost their lives in the temple.

"You protected your own." Ares followed her along the edge of the pool.

"I killed my own. When I released Kulika."

The rush of heat consumed her, swelling outward as though Kulika would burst through again with fire and smoke. "I sent his energy swirling into the corridors. I wanted the enemy to die. I did not know he would take my own with them. Kulika still seeks to join me."

Ares dipped his hand beneath the water and touched her thigh. There was an immediate cooling as the throb evaporated with the steam. "Yes, he hovers nearby waiting, for he enjoyed far too much the sensation of his own physical form. He has never been allowed it before."

"I have only called him into being during ritual, when his host would not give up self. This time...."

"He took control. The destruction belongs to him."

"I was with him, always aware. It was my fury that fed him, my hatred. When I saw Seire lying there, her throat cut like an animal, I would have ripped her killer's heart out if Kulika had not destroyed him.

"Seire, my beloved Seire." Niala covered her face with her hands. "I have no one left."

"She is dead and, with her, the rest of Najahmara."

"Then it is true," Niala wept. "When the fire swept through the corridors, it reached into the town. I knew it did. I felt it. I felt it eating everything alive. But I thought...I hoped. Is there nothing left?"

"Nothing." Pausing, Ares dwelled on his deceit. Najahmara was not dead, though over half wiped out. They would build again, breed and gain back their strength, but it would not be the same. Better she believed it was destroyed, for Niala would never return. "Najahmara is gone."

"Aaiee, I cannot bear it." Niala beat her hands upon the side of the pool and would have brought her forehead to the same end had Ares not stopped her.

He turned her from the marble rim and held her locked within his arms so she could not further hurt herself. He did not bid her stop, but allowed her to cry until the wracking sobs slowed and she sagged against his chest.

Only then did he loosen his grip enough to draw a work-worn hand up to the candlelight. Across her palm was the ragged cut she had made with a stone while they were atop the ridge above Najahmara. Blood trickled to her wrist, for she broke it open anew with the frantic pounding.

Lifting her hand, he kissed the wound. "You are not alone, Niala."

He ran his tongue over the welt, tasting salt. She carried the blood of two worlds in her body, though she did not want to acknowledge it. They had come to this standoff. He, wishing to claim her for the immortal realm, and she, fighting to stay within the bounds of mortal decay.

She deceived him, hid from him, struggled against him, and why? Because she did not want to face her destiny.

For the first time, Ares saw it was not because of him that she ran away; it was in spite of him. The pull to be human, to struggle blindly with no more than what could be seen with the naked eye, the pitiful, overwhelming attraction to be part of the god-forsaken mortal condition had always been with her.

As Ilya, as Niala, as anything in between, she sought the fragility of human life for no other reason than it ended. There was the finality of death to liberate her from a life grown too heavy.

Unlike his existence.

Ares released a sluggish breath, his gaze moving across Niala's miserable countenance.

She tried once to escape her pain. She would try again. Now he was convinced that she could, and would, relinquish her life, but he would not let her. Niala had the gift to move between the worlds, to walk on either side, yet all he had to do was look into her despairing eyes to see she did not want it.

With deliberate slowness, he licked her wound, thrusting his tongue between the torn edges of skin, probing deep into Niala's flesh until she moaned in protest, but she did not pull her hand away.

He sucked at the wound, biting with seductive intent, until fresh blood welled up. Warm and fluid, her essence filled his mouth. He could forgive her anything right then, anything, if she would reject her mortal side and step fully into his world.

"Let them go, Niala. They are fragile beings, here for only a short time. Let them go. Be who you are meant to be."

With a small shake of her head, she shuddered, trying in vain to reject his caresses. She would not look at him, but kept her head down.

Ares felt her desire beneath the reluctance like a thin veil thrown over a solid block. Beneath the opaque surface of grief, he knew she wanted him to bring her solace, to push away the hurt even for little awhile. She needed him, but would not ask.

Lifting her chin, he sought her lips, sucking and biting at their fullness, as if to break open that tender skin, as if he could siphon off the pain and replace it with pleasure. He knew what it was like to suffer the torment of regret, to wonder what would have been had he chosen another course.

He knew the spiraling darkness that could consume even one such as he, if those choices were dwelled upon. The chasm yawned before him all too often; he would not afford her the opportunity to sink into oblivion.

Pressing her mouth open, he exhaled into her. Niala gasped and arched backward, eyelashes fluttering. He blew his breath into her again and felt the quiver pass through her from head to toe. It was then he began to kiss in earnest, yet her lips scarce moved beneath his.

As his ardor grew and his kisses became more urgent, she moaned, "I cannot do this."

"It is what you need. To forget."

"I do not want to forget."

"You must or it will drive you mad."

"Too late. I have already reached the brink of madness. I can think of nothing else." She drew away from him, arms crossed over her breasts as if she just noticed she was unclothed. "I cannot pleasure you now."

"Niala." Ares shook his head. "I do not ask that. Though I am a bullheaded beast in most things, I know your great need at this hour. Let me give your body relief so your thoughts can take respite from this horror."

"I know you too well. Generous acts are not in your nature. You want this for yourself."

He shrugged. "Sexual pleasure is my only hope to turn away the tides of aggression that flow from the mortal world. I have confessed this many times."

"You have, when your only thought was to mate."

Ares stared at her for a moment. "You are right, you know me well. I have missed you, Niala, for there has been no other with the attractive mixture of sweet tenderness and coarse talk. Though in your role as priestess, I would think you had found some measure of balance between selfishness and kindness."

Niala flushed and bit her lip. Without thinking, she had lashed out with the childish retorts of old. Her gaze wandered the chamber again, breathing in the scented vapors, allowing the water to rock her, and listening to the crackle of wood burning to heat their bath.

Had Najahmara been no more than a dream? At that very moment, death seemed distant, as if Najahmara was the vision that evaporated into the mists instead of Ares, from whom she was separated all those years. She had lived in fear he would find her, but now it seemed she had never gone, and the present fear was merely a shadow of life to come.

Ares reached for her. "You must heal your grief, Niala."

She shoved him. "What do you know of grief? You bring it without care."

"You are as stubborn as I when it comes to what is in front of you. I did not bring those soldiers to Najahmara. It is the mortal condition to take, always take. Take, take, take."

He struck his fist upon the marble rim. "Woe to me I am attracted to their greed, but that is my due. You accuse me of not knowing grief, yet you claim you remember our lives as Ilya and Anyal.

"If that were true, I would not have to defend how I mourn or what I have become. If you truly remembered, you would understand. You would agree I deserve what I am."

"As usual, you talk nonsense."

"Do you really remember, Niala?"

"Yes, though it is like looking at the sky wrapped in clouds. I cannot see with any clarity."

"Then you do not remember it all." There was defeat in his voice, but his face was impassive, unsmiling, the close-cropped, dark beard adding another layer to the sense of brooding, keeping the lower half of his face hidden. "And so it will be with Najahmara. In time, its memory will retreat into the far distance."

"I do not believe that. I stand here, still covered in my enemy's blood and it carries not a single candle to the filth blanketing my soul."

"I understand more than you know, but I cannot help if you will not let me."

"How can I allow passion when my heart aches so much?"

"How can you not?"

With his answer came a gentleness Niala did not expect. Nor did she expect him to pluck a square of white linen from a stack along the rim of the pool, dip it in the water, and begin the task of wiping the blood from her face. It stained pink until he rinsed it and continued scrubbing at the gore. He paused once, at her neck, where his cruel grip had left bruises.

He spoke no apology, but pressed his lips to the marks. She felt his tongue slide across her skin, felt his mouth close over the pulse at her throat, felt her heart skip a beat and her knees weaken. He then withdrew and went on washing her.

Hot water flowed over her shoulders and chest, the whisper of cloth brushed her nipples and below, to the line of water at her waist. But there he stopped, though the hint of a smile lifted the corners of his mouth.

Turning her, he scooped handfuls of water to wet her matted hair and, when completely soaked, poured soap from a small pitcher until it became thick frothing foam. Niala stood silent as he worked the lather into the tangles, slowly combing the strands out with his fingertips, pulling every now and then as fingers caught in a web that would not loosen.

She could not see the expression on his face as he lifted her hair to rinse it and discovered the winged tattoo across her back, but she felt his curiosity as he traced the feathers along one shoulder.

Curiosity turned to suspicion as he asked, "What is this?"

She knew without seeing, he thought of the serpent on her leg and how Kulika lived through it. Without answering, Niala sank into the water, swimming beneath the surface where his voice was no more than a vibration. When she came up to breathe, he was next to her, all signs of affection having disappeared. His countenance was stern, as if he saw a threat.

If there had not been such emptiness inside her, she would have chuckled, but the numbness kept her quiet.

"What is it?" Ares brushed her hair to one side to better view the black wings sweeping over her shoulder blades. They were wide and rounded, with finely detailed feathers fanning out along her sides, reaching to her hips. The bird's body was robust, the head turned sideways with a long thick bill, slightly hooked and partly opened. The tail feathers were long and forked, spreading down below her waist onto her buttocks.

"Who does this one call?" His tone warned he would not bear untruths.

"The Corvidae."

"The Corvidae," he repeated, with a certain awareness.

"He is a creature of Air, gifted to me upon my initiation into Gaea's service." Niala shivered as Ares caressed the fine lines that made up the Corvidae's body, his hands trailing downward.

"What does he do for you?"

Ares spoke next to her ear, through a curtain of hair that fell around her face. He was blocked from sight and she did not want to look at him, to see the lust as it filled his eyes. Already, it was in the timber of his voice, in his touch, different this time from a moment ago when he sought to take her pain away. This time there would be no tender coercion.

"What does he do for you?" Ares stroked her back, following the smooth line from neck to waist. As he passed the beak of the Corvidae, it seemed to snap at him and ruffle its feathers, but he kept his hand steady until he reached the curve of Niala's hips. The water rippled over the roundness of her buttocks, lapping toward the final dark strokes of the tail feathers.

"What, Niala? What does he do for you?"

His breathing was harsh as he leaned over, forcing her to grasp the side of the pool to keep from falling. He pressed down upon her back, rubbing along her with the length of his body, his hardness pushing between her legs.

He did not yet enter her, but placed his arms on either side of her, gripping the marble. "Does he protect you the way Kulika protects Gaea? I have heard of no one who has command of such a creature as the Corvidae."

"I do not command him."

Niala gasped as Ares thrust between her thighs, but not into her. His member pulled at the small hairs and hit upon the place that made her writhe with instant and fiery desire, yet still, he withheld.

"Then what do you do with him?" Ares licked her back, along her spine, teasing the Corvidae with his tongue and lips. "Does he give you flight, Niala?" He pushed her further up onto the marble side until he could open her legs to his seeking mouth.

"No," Niala whimpered, "I swear."

Shamed, she struggled under his torment. Shame because she wanted to let go of her grief, to forget those who died, abandon everything to the excruciating pleasure he gave her.

There was no help for it, she wanted him, wanted him to make her forget. Weeping, she prayed he would ease all memory with his body, that she might open her eyes on the morrow and be content in his arms.

"I will not leave you again," she whispered through her tears.

"No, you will not." Ares rose up over her and this time he penetrated her innermost place. Niala cried out as swift release swept over her. It took no more than that, for the frenzy he drove her to was now welcome.

*****

"Long have I awaited this day, Zahava! To find you still abed with the sun fully up and everyone looking for you. It is too lovely."

Pallin bent over Niala, face split by a huge grin. Giggling, Pallin brushed the end of her braid across Niala's upper lip, and then danced about as Niala tried to pull herself out of her hammock.

"It is well into the morn. Why did you wait so long to wake me?"

"Seire said to leave you alone, you were tired."

"Then why are you here?" Niala retorted.

"Because, Seire says, now you have laid abed too long."

Pallin bowed her head, put her hands behind her back and balanced on her toes like a child in trouble. Her eyes held a sparkle of mischief that could not be disguised as she peered coyly at Niala through long lashes.

Niala frowned for a moment, disoriented by the daylight streaming through the window, and then inhaled deeply. She had been dreaming, of course. An invasion by foreign soldiers, murder and destruction. Ares the Destroyer amidst it all, ready to punish her with a swift and terrible hand. Najahmara burning. Death all around.

So real, yet it was no more than a dream.

Niala smiled with relief as she watched Pallin's antics. Outside the open window, she could hear the distant laughter of children playing and, nearer, the chirping of the many birds that fed in their gardens. Wafting on the warm breeze was the scent of newly baked bread. It smelled so good, Niala realized just how hungry she was.

She had lain in bed too long, for her head and body ached mightily with every move, even her face, when she smiled. She would have Jahmed give her a powder for the pain and it would soon be gone. But if she did not first get up, they would all think her ill. Niala threw the blanket to one side, struggling to climb from the hammock..

"Pallin, help me up. I am sore from climbing. Pallin. Pallin...."

"Pallin. Pallin...." Niala opened her eyes with a start. She could hear her own fretful voice calling out, but there was no answer. She lay still with her breath caught in her throat, staring up at a dark ceiling. Her face was chilled, for the air around her was cold, but she sweated beneath the heavy layers of woolen blankets that covered her nakedness.

Her gaze drifted over the high thick beams above her to the faint line of daylight easing around the doorframe across from her. The sunlight found every crack and chink that the wide double doors had to offer, outlining the edges and cutting down the middle between them. It was the only illumination in the chamber, but it was enough to see Ares beside her.

She bit her lips and brought trembling hands from beneath the blankets to cover her mouth so she would not shriek aloud. Panic beat within her, trapped inside the prison of what was no more than a dream.

Niala whimpered.

For now the bloodied faces of her loved ones floated before her. Inni's raped and broken body, Seire's nearly severed head. Pallin and Jahmed hidden from her sight. Dead or alive, she did not know. The cries of the younger ones...beaten...violated....

Niala held back her screams, swallowed hard, unable to catch her breath, twisting to stare at Ares, and to watch for a sign she had awakened him. It was rare that he slept - when he did, the slightest sound or movement would bring him springing up as if prepared for battle. She did not want him to wake up.

'Please,' she prayed in silence. 'Please.'

Upon the death pyre of her people, she saw herself wallowing in pleasure, abandoning them in their agony to couple again and again with Ares. Her body went hot, then cold, then hot again with shame. How could she have done such a thing?

Scalding tears ran from swollen eyes as her chest tightened and she thought, surely, this time Gaea would strike her down. Niala had killed. She had tasted the flesh of her enemy and reveled in it. She had destroyed Najahmara with flames and forsaken any that were left. She had made love in their shadows.

She did not deserve to live.

Niala looked again at Ares, peacefully asleep, the barest hint of a smile on his beautiful face. He never slumbered, but there he was, and why not? He had won. He slept as the triumphant conquering warrior who had claimed the ultimate prize. Her.

Weeping in silence, Niala slipped from beneath the covers and stood naked against the chill of the room. She felt nothing, nothing but the trickle of his seed as it rolled down her leg. It began warm and wet, then slid down into icy, desolate drops clinging to her ankle.

There was no hope at the end. Newly planted, the seed would seek to make life, to bring forth something good from the pleasure that set it in motion, but afterwards, when life did not spring forth, it became useless.

A burden to be washed away. Cleansed of this life.

Niala went to the doors and pulled them open. Frozen, fresh air poured over her. Pure and sweet. She breathed it in until her chest burned. She stepped out onto the balcony, scarce noticing the snow beneath her feet as she went to the railing overlooking the sea. It was stark and beautiful, just as she remembered. Vast and green, continuing on in endless, rolling waves that finally tumbled upon the shoreline below.

She had forgotten how loud the surf was, how brutal the sharp rocks appeared from above. She had forgotten how evil life could be.

One deserved the other.

Niala climbed onto the narrow railing and balanced there for a fleeting moment as she took one last breath, one last look at the shining sea. Then she leaped into the air and felt herself falling, falling down to meet the earth.

FIFTEEN

Jahmed crouched beside Inni, one hand hovering over a grotesquely swollen arm, too afraid to lay even a finger upon Inni. It was unbearable for Jahmed to see her beloved lying in such pain.

Inni's face was unrecognizable, her eyes no more than fevered slits within bruises. If Jahmed heard again the low animal cry that escaped through Inni's cracked lips, Jahmed would lose what fragile hold she still had on herself.

Inni's arms were nearly torn from her shoulders, her wrists snapped, her legs broken. Her torso was a mass of black and blue. From hip to neck there were still-oozing cuts where broken ribs protruded through her skin. But the worst, the absolute worst, was the rape. He had pierced two places, ripped the flesh, and left her bleeding from his vile attack.

It was too much to bear.

And, yet, what choice did she have? Jahmed heaved a sigh, too numb to weep.

"She will recover." Deimos stood just inside the entrance to the medicinal quarters, appearing as calm as if he spoke of the weather.

Jahmed found his presence an odd comfort and tried to smile in agreement, but merely managed a nod. Her throat was tight and her eyes burned, yet she kept her composure and slowly rose to her feet.

"Though her wounds are terrible and may heal, it is her mind I fear will not survive."

"Often there is no memory after such horror."

"She is aware. I see it in her eyes."

"What you see is the desire to survive. She knows she has been wounded and must now retreat to live. I have seen it often on the battlefield."

"You cannot possibly understand. If only you knew the indignities she suffered before she came to us." Jahmed's voice trailed off. She sounded harsh but did not mean to.

Without the young man in front of her, all would have given up and waited for death to claim them, so terrible were the scars across the face of Najahmara.

In the early hours of dawn, Deimos was the strength they were lashed to. He pulled them together through sheer will, lifting them up from the wreckage as he barked commands to any with wits.

Jahmed thought of her first sight of him in the smoke-blackened temple - tall, untouched by the fire, garbed in the rough leathers of a warrior. He spoke with a few battered soldiers as he supported an unsteady Pallin. A ferocious expression on his lean face, Jahmed thought him an invader out to do more harm.

In her fright, she did not know him for the youth who had been at their ritual. But, as she lay dazed and afraid to stir, she saw the way Pallin cleaved to him, moved with his every move, as if she could not stand on her own or even breathe without him.

Pallin's head was bleeding, her gaze unfocused and her chin wobbling, yet however mindless, she did not let go. It was then Jahmed struggled up from the bodies around her, uncertain if he would strike her dead or help her.

Deimos came to her aid, dragging Pallin with him. He pulled Jahmed to her feet without ceremony and spoke in a sharp guttural language to one soldier who immediately supported Jahmed's weight against his shoulder. Jahmed did not have the might to shove him away. She could not even stand alone at that moment.

Though she did not want to accept the kindness of one who helped terrorize her people, she could do no less. Deimos then called her by name and bid her not be afraid. To her his tone was soothing, his gaze unflinching amongst the horror that surrounded them; she let those men who survived assist her.

They, too, were dazed, glad to have direction, to work without thought. Deimos brought order to the turmoil. He sorted the living from the dead, the hopelessly wounded from those who might survive, the able-bodied from the addled.

To see what damage was done to the rest of the temple, he left them for mere moments, though Pallin cried for him the entire time. While he was gone, it was as if all hope was sucked from the chamber as they waited with a listlessness that could not be thrown off. When Deimos returned, they breathed again and waited for his instructions.

He discovered corridors heavy with damage, but other rooms minimally so, and the kitchen and upper floors intact. Only the entrance to the gardens was scorched, while all beyond the grounds remained untouched.

To the front was a different story, one Deimos would not detail, though the grimness of his expression told Jahmed it was worse than she could imagine. She did not press him. She knew she would find out soon enough. Their task at hand was daunting and it was all she could think of.

There were too many dead and too much suffering. So many she loved were beyond help, but Inni was alive and Deimos carried her to the medicinal quarters at the far corner of the temple. It was blackened on the outside, but undamaged on the inside. There he placed Inni on a low hammock to be watched over at all times.

Niala had not been found.

Outside the temple, rain drenched everything, turning roadways into mud and damaged houses into pools. The dead lay unrecognizable and the living wandered like ghosts, hollow-eyed and coated with mire.

They could not rally. They could not even weep, not until Jahmed stepped forward. In private, she grieved, but she kept her promise to Niala. She went out into the streets and called to her people, walking amongst the horror with Deimos at her side. With his help, she was able to gain what little semblance of order was possible.

Jahmed could not now be disrespectful to him. "I am grateful for everything you have done, it is just that you are not aware of her beginnings." She shook her head and glanced down at Inni. "She was enslaved, beaten, defiled. She would rather have died."

"I do grasp what you are saying. I pray for her sake she does not remember."

Jahmed nodded. With another sad glance at Inni, Jahmed

faced Deimos. Her voice wavered when she spoke. "Is Niala dead?"

He hesitated, his gaze shifting to one side.

"She was with us in the temple. She came in after...." Jahmed could not even speak the words to describe the evilness. "I saw Kulika rise, and...and then...."

Shuddering, she stopped. "It was too awful. I fear he destroyed her. He must have, for if she were alive...." With grief clouding her gaze, Jahmed whispered, "She would be here."

When Deimos said nothing, Jahmed took the silence as agreement. Her shoulders sagged. "It is done, then. Niala has given her life to protect us, yet we do not even have her body to mourn. What will become of us?"

"You will survive, though I cannot stay here to shepherd you along the way. I must return to my own world."

"You would abandon us?"

"I have no choice. My father will demand my presence."

"Your father?"

"Ares. He will command me to Athos." Deimos stopped, a bitter smile at his lips. "As soon as he realizes I am gone. You see, Jahmed, you will not be the only ones to pay a price for Telio's recklessness. I, too, will suffer the pain of War."

"Athos." Jahmed grabbed his arm. "Niala spoke of being there, in that place. It is where Ares lives." Her eyes widened. "It is where he would take her. Mercy. She is not dead. He has her."

There was no denial ready on his tongue, only a turning away, as if Deimos could not face her with the truth.

"It is true, then. He has her."

"She is dead to you." Deimos stood with his back to her, one hand lifting the curtain to escape. "You must lead your people through this alone."

"No, I will not accept that. You allowed this to happen, now do something, return her."

"There is nothing I can do."

"Or nothing you will do." Jahmed darted forward to block his path. She cared not that he was immortal or that he could slay her with a single blow.

"Niala told me of the promise you made to Gaea to stop the army, but you did not. Would he have come here without the threat of violence? She did not think so, nor do I."

For long moments, Deimos met Jahmed's gaze. Then he looked away. He could not stand to see the condemnation in her eyes. "There is much you misunderstand about our world. I did not purposefully betray you. My intention was to prevent the army from invading, but I found I could not. " He shrugged. "It was too late."

"He did it. That hateful warmongering beast!"

"No, Jahmed. Ares is drawn to violence but he did not create this. What became of your people can be laid at the feet of one whose greed bested him. Even I will not accept the burden of his behavior, for it is what brings about the worst in the mortal world. I would have directed them away from Najahmara had I arrived before, and now there is naught to do but heal the wounds."

"But why Niala? Why? She is not one of you, she does not belong to him."

With his jaw tight, Deimos answered, "Oh, but she does, in ways that sting me. I cannot change what has happened, or alter her course."

"Then some day she may return?"

"Do not cling to that thought, for it is doubtful."

"I can hope."

He nodded. "I must see to the work before darkness falls again. There are many more wounded."

"And more dead." Jahmed slumped, her exhaustion bearing down like a boulder upon her head.

"And more dead," Deimos agreed.

He left her sitting on a low bench, eyes closed, hands clasped between her knees. Rubbing his forehead, Deimos, too, felt weary. Of all the battles he had seen, he had never remained for the aftermath. He was not prepared for the complete and utter devastation of Najahmara and her people.

Stepping outside, he let the drape fall back into place. The immediate contrast between the softly lit room and the blackened blighted walls of the town struck him. Some buildings had their roofs caved in or a wall crumbled to the ground. Others stood intact but with the bleak soot-streaked stain of fire across their surfaces. An undeniable stench hung over everything.

Once the fire reached the streets, it ignited every blade of grass, every tree, every bit of flesh to which it came in contact. The scorching heat popped mortar from between bricks, buckled walls and turned belongings to ash.

From all appearances, the fire moved rapidly through the streets, destroying everything it touched from the center out but the flames diminished as it reached the furthest edges of Najahmara.

Deimos made his way as far as the forest, covering every corner and every space in search of Hattusilis and maybe, just maybe, Niala. In the back of his mind, he thought she would be better off dead than imprisoned at Athos. To find her body would be crushing, yet her people would have a chance to say their prayers and send her off in their tradition, rather than believe a god had stolen her.

Believe? The people of Najahmara would have no sense of the likes of Athos. He was the only one who understood how harsh Athos was. Niala was there, of that he was certain. To her people, she was dead.

Deimos could not bear to think of her in Ares' grip.

Or in his bed.

A branch broke off in Deimos' hand, its sharp crack bringing him back to awareness. It was from a tree the horses were once, but no longer tethered. All the animals were gone, either taken by the remnants of the army, or frightened away by the smell of smoke and the threat of fire.

How many soldiers survived? Deimos could not even begin to count the dead close to the center of town, nor the additional bodies littering the mown field. Some fled; others lay injured and dazed, and at the mercy of the Najahmaran people.

He could not say how many were left, or where they would scatter, running madly away from a giant, fire-breathing serpent, or regroup and join up with the rest of the forces. Would they turn away, or would they rally and return? They had no leader unless they found Hattusilis. Anyone else, except Zan, was not strong enough to control the mass of battalions.

Hattusilis was alive, Deimos was certain of it. He could feel him out there, somewhere, injured, perhaps near death, but still alive.

Why could he not locate Hattusilis?

Deimos left the forest, certain no one hid there. Those alive had disappeared like smoke. The dead were not his concern. Soon, the entirety of Najahmara would not be his concern; surviving his punishment for leaving Athos would be the only thing on his mind.

Though the fire seared the rails, all bridges were intact. By mid morning, much needed help arrived from the outlying lands. These folk were able to shoulder the burden and begin the grievous task of removing the dead. All except the slain priestesses were taken to the fields surrounding the lake where pyres were built and the bodies continued their journeys into ashes.

"It is not our custom." Pallin wept into her hands as the night began to darken and the orange glow from bonfires dominated the southern horizon. "It is not our custom to burn our dead. Our bodies are to be returned to the Earth, not flung to the winds."

"There are too many."

"Mixed with the filthy soldiers who meant to destroy us - to burn alongside these creatures would be wrong."

He grasped her upper arms and held Pallin away from him. "What does it matter now? Their body holds naught their spirit, and the fire cleanses flesh and bone. It is the ash that will nurture Earth and bring new growth."

"We have had no ceremony, no blessings to send them on their way. They go alone and unlamented."

"They go together." Deimos' tone was gentle. "All of them. They go beyond their mortal bonds and see new truths. They are at peace."

"You say these things to help, but they do not. I feel the restless souls of my people as they wander about. They have no peace."

"Pallin, you are too weary to see anything but your own pain. It is the living who worry if the dead have had due respect, but the dead do not care."

"They do."

"Shhh." Placing two fingers on her lips, he said, "Enough. You must rest, for more difficult days lie ahead."

"I cannot sleep. I can think only of what has happened and wonder what it is we are to do."

She strained to press against him and Deimos let her bury her face in his chest as her arms went about him. Pallin was warm and pliable, molding to him, wanting him to blot out the horror that she could not. He held her with a light touch, on guard, for he feared he would once again give into his own needs without thought.

"I cannot bear it," Pallin's voice was muffled. "I simply cannot bear it. I wish I had died with the others."

"It was not your destiny. There is much yet for you to do in this life. Grieve, Pallin, but forgive and grow wiser. Rebuild Najahmara."

"Forgive? I am not strong enough to forgive. I would rather kill them all myself."

"You are too gentle a creature to harm another. It is the reason...." Deimos bit off the rest of his words.

"You what?" She lifted a tear-streaked face to look up at him.

Deimos could feel her trembling under his hands, trembling with exhaustion, grief, and the unspoken desire for him to love her. With both hands, she held his face, her luminous eyes glittering with unshed tears. "What, Deimos? What?"

He shook his head, his hands closing over her wrists, pulling her fingers away. Pallin was his opposite, the root of his attraction to her. Where he was darkness, she was light. Where he was distrust, she was innocence. He was terror; she was tenderness. His loneliness was an abiding void that drew him to her, but he could not give her what she desired.

"You must sleep or you will become ill." Deimos pushed her toward the temple.

"I will only go to my bed if you go with me," she answered, fighting the force of his arms, reaching for him.

"No."

"Do not deny me this small comfort. I do not ask one such as you to share my life, or even to love me the way I love you, but on this night, this dreadful night, you can be with me."

"Pallin, I must go. I have stayed overlong as it is."

"Please," she sobbed. "Do not leave me like this."

"There are others who will help."

"Do not leave me!"

"Ahh, Pallin, do not weep anymore." With his reserve shattered, Deimos took her into his arms and kissed her.

What harm if he stayed one more night?

*****

"Deimos!"

Ares' bellow shook the very foundation of Athos. Like the cruel tidal waves that could sink a sailing ship, his anger sucked the life and energy from the fortress. Time froze as his voice echoed through the floors, across the chambers, and exploded out onto the mount. His call demanded an immediate answer, for none could hear it who did not realize the wrath behind it.

An uneasy quiet fell throughout Athos, even in the lowest reaches where drunken warriors held vigilance. They felt, rather than heard, the thundering of Ares' voice and, though they did not know why they paused in their revelry, they stared at each other with alarm.

Soon enough, their voices rose in strident turmoil, each describing the doom they felt hovering nearby. There was panic in their eyes but a certain laxness to their limbs that left them unable to act upon their fears.

Eris crouched low to the floor, hugging the mug of ale he had just begun to drink. He would find the growing discord of the men amusing if it were not for his own foreboding. His eyes darted back and forth for some manner of escape beneath the tables, among the many legs and feet.

There was none.

When Deimos did not answer, and Eris knew he would not, Ares' next snarl was predictable.

"Eris!"

With regret, Eris dropped the mug onto the filthy straw-strewn floor and took himself to his father's quarters. He arrived in the sitting chamber to find Ares scowling at a young woman who stood before him with a guileless smile on her dimpled face.

She was a lovely rounded thing with plaited yellow hair wrapped about her head like a crown. She wore a soft blue chiton girdled with a silver belt, her plump feet in silver sandals.

Eris was captivated and could not help smiling back at her. Her cheeks were rosy and glowing, her lips pink, her teeth a shining white. The best of all were her sparkling, mirth-filled blue eyes, as blue as the cloth draping her figure. He knew her, of course, everyone knew Thaleia. She was from the House of Love, a Grace who served Aphrodite in the same manner he served Ares.

"My Lady," Eris murmured, with a small bow.

Thaleia smiled. "And to you, Sir."

"Enough." Ares' growl brought them both about, facing him. His countenance was foreboding, eyes narrowed with distrust.

"What is it, Father?" Eris' smile disappeared.

"Where is Deimos?"

"Deimos?" Eyes widening, Eris felt heat rush to his face.

"Yes, Deimos." Ares cast a dark look at Thaleia. "It appears his mother would have a word with him. Where is he?"

"I...uhhh...." Eris ducked his head. "Ummm."

He could hear Deimos' furious curses still ringing in his ears and it would not do to add more fuel to that fire, if he could help it. "I do not know."

"Do not protect him, Eris, it will only bring you grief."

"No, no, I do not."

Cold silence fell and held until Eris peeked up at Ares through brown curls. He cringed at the look he received. "Truly, he could be anywhere, now." He offered in a faint tone, "anywhere at all."

"Anywhere being Najahmara."

"Ummm, perhaps."

"I forbid him Najahmara."

"I will gladly search for him." Eris made move to leave but was stopped by a firm grip on his shoulder.

"No." Ares cast a glare at Thaleia as she stood with hands folded demurely in front of her. "You will stay here."

"But I..." With a futile gesture towards the lower reaches of the fortress, Eris grimaced.

"Yes, I know, you would drink ale and then cause mayhem amongst the warriors. It is just as well you remain here. It appears I may have to visit Cos."

"*May* have to visit? Master of Misery, what makes you so reluctant to accept an invitation from my mistress?" Thaleia spoke with an air of innocence. To Eris, she whispered, "Aphrodite bids him join her at Cos, but he refuses."

"You refuse Aphrodite?" Eris blurted.

From beneath her lashes, Thaleia watched a flush work its way up Ares' neck. She took great delight in his irritation, safe in the knowledge that she would not suffer under his hand.

It was a law of the Council that no punishment was meted out by one House on those of another House. Ares would have to take his complaint to Aphrodite and, there, it would fall on deaf ears.

Ignoring Eris, Ares addressed Thaleia. "You speak out of turn. I have not refused. You said only that your mistress has concerns about Deimos and I shall find him so she may ask him herself."

"My Lady wishes for you to attend to her, not Deimos."

"Is this about him, or is it not?" Ares gave a sharp slap of his palm against his thigh. "I have no patience for this."

"I have yet to see you in a proper mood, do you even have one?" Thaleia laughed.

"Watch yourself." Ares' scowl promised bad things.

"Or what?"

"I am known for breaking rules, Thaleia. I would take a great deal of pleasure in handing you over to the warriors who wait below."

Thaleia's smile faded. "You would not."

"Oh, I would."

"Aphrodite would never forgive you."

"Aphrodite is playing games. What is this about?"

"Oh, la." Regaining her composure, Thaleia lifted one hand in a languid wave. "There is only one thing my mistress wants from you and you know well what it is."

She turned and walked without concern toward the towering double doors on the far side of the hearth. She trailed her fingers across the heavy bronze handle and threw a wink over her shoulder. "Or should I detail it, lest you have forgotten? It has been a long while since Aphrodite requested your presence."

Ares' lip curled. "Tell her I will consider her request."

"Do not tarry too long, there are many others who would gladly step in."

"No other would dare."

"Are you that certain, Master of Misery? There are many who clamor for her favors."

"I care not what she does in the mortal world."

"Mortal?" Thaleia cast a sly glance at Ares. "Did I say it was only mortal men who seek her company?"

"There are none stupid enough in the immortal realm to go against me."

Shrugging, Thaleia hummed a lighthearted tune to herself as she toyed with the latch, wanting very much to peek inside the next chamber in the hopes it was Ares' fabled bathing pool. "Not stupid. I would say he is rather clever."

"What?" Ares' nostrils flared. "Of whom do you speak?"

"I am sorry. Your forgiveness, please." Thaleia did not sound a bit sorry. "I speak out of turn. Do you wish to attend to my mistress? I am bid return with a yes or no."

With thumb pressed to the smooth metal, Thaleia wondered if

she dared pry further into Ares' private quarters. She had heard many stories of his pool and all that went on there, so much so she just had to see, even if it angered him.

Smiling to herself, she admired the polished wood of the door. "Of course, if your answer is no, then you will have a very difficult time regaining Aphrodite's favor."

"I do not take well to threats."

Thaleia shrugged again, her attention on the latch.

"There is more at stake here than Aphrodite's passion. Tell me what it is she wants with no more of your twisted humor."

"Truly, she did not say, only that she desires your wretched company." Thaleia grinned at him and threw caution to the wind. With a sudden shove, she flung the double doors open. She saw first a darkened chamber lit only with flames from the oversized hearth.

When her eyes adjusted, it was clear there was no reflecting pool of water, but only a massive high bed dominating the room. With a tiny thrill of excitement, she glided into Ares' bedchamber.

"Thaleia, halt. You go too far." Ares reached out to throttle her, Council law or no.

Laughing at him, Thaleia darted away from his outstretched fingers and caught her foot on the bedpost. Stumbling, she clawed at the frame to steady herself and came up with a handful of blanket.

As she straightened, she saw a naked woman lying on her back. Thaleia blinked, clutching the blanket to her chest.

"Mercy." Thaleia jerked as Ares' cruel fingers clamped down on her arm. The woman appeared as if dead, her face ashen, slack jawed, and streaked with scratches. Dried blood left tiny black dots all along the reddened lines across her cheek.

She had but a moment to study the woman before Ares yanked the covering from her lax hands and dragged her away, but in that moment she saw temporal splendor beneath the damage. Was this woman mortal or immortal?

Thaleia could not tell with so quick a glance, but there was no denying the tender mouth and thick dark lashes, high cheekbones, and strong chin surrounded by a tangled riot of brown hair burnished red by the flames from the hearth.

One leg was inked with lines winding around calf to thigh. As her eyes were drawn upward, straining to make out the markings in the dim light, she saw the slightest rise and fall of chest, and then the torn flesh and blossom of a dark stain at the woman's side.

What have you done? Mercy, what have you done to her?"

"Get out." Ares shoved Thaleia toward the doorway.

"Who is she?" Eris stood frozen at the entrance. "I have seen her before."

"You have not," Ares thundered. "Leave, both of you. She is of no one's concern but my own."

"Let me help her." Thaleia struggled within his grasp.

"Go, now."

"She will die. I must help her." All mirth fled Thaleia's face. She grew pale and pinched. "Is this what you would have me tell Aphrodite? I teased, earlier but now, truly, I have a dreadful tale to pass. Do not let it be so, Lord Ares. I beg you."

Ares paused, his face grim. "You cannot, Thaleia, she is beyond you. I will care for her and she will live, but not a word of this to your mistress. Do you understand me?"

"But who is she? Is she of immortal seed, and if so, how?" Thaleia's gaze remained riveted on the chamber doors, pulled shut after them. "And if she be mortal, then she will surely die."

"She is neither. And she is both. I request you do not bear this tale to your mistress, for it will only distress her."

"Aphrodite will ask how you are and I must answer. I dare not lie. I will not lie."

He nodded once. "It is for me to tell her of this one, not you. Return to Aphrodite and advise her I will attend to her, whatever her desire."

"When can she expect you?"

With a sharp glance toward the double doors, Ares said, "Soon. Now, go."

Thaleia did not hesitate. Upon her release, she fled Athos.

Eris ducked his head, his gaze on the floor - he too would flee but his courage waned and so he waited. He heard the double doors swish open and not close. He feared to look up. He remained downcast until Ares called to him. With care, he crept into the warmth of the inner chamber.

Ares stood with his hands behind his back, a pensive expression creasing his forehead. When he spoke, his deep voice rumbled through the quiet room. "It seems Love is troubled and would hold council with War without delay."

He mumbled a few curses beneath his breath. "With Deimos absent, I must trust you to guard this one while I am away."

"Guard her? Is she a danger, then?"

"Only to herself."

"I do not understand."

"She has suffered a great tragedy and is mired in her loss. I have tried to help her, but alas." He glanced toward the set of doors leading out to the stone veranda, now frozen with a thick blanket of snow. "She could not bear her grief and threw herself over the railing."

"She fell to the rocks?" Eris pictured the giant, jagged boulders at the bottom of the mountain.

"Not quite, but it was her intention. She sleeps now, suspended between the worlds where she cannot harm herself. I have placed her there to heal both in body and soul."

Ares' gaze fell to her torn side. "Have no fear, she will not awaken until I command it, but still, I do not want to leave her alone. You will sit with her until I return."

"But Deimos would be better suited for this task."

"Deimos is not here."

"I could find him."

"You will do as I say, Eris."

"Yes, Father." Eris dipped his chin to hide his frown.

"Keep the fire steady, she needs the warmth."

"Yes, Father."

"Do not leave this chamber."

"Yes, Father."

"And above all else, do not touch her."

"No, Father, I will not."

"I will know if you do. So be warned, do not touch her."

"Yes, Father." Eris pouted, the edges of his sharp teeth pressed against his bottom lip. "You can trust me."

Ares snorted. "Just remember what I said."

"Yes, Father," Eris muttered, but Ares was already gone.

SIXTEEN

Aphrodite waited for him in her favorite pavilion. It did not take Ares long to find her there, for her quarters were deserted and he could hear the sounds of play outside. He paid no heed to the children who raced along the white sands of Cos, or to the women who sat at the water's edge keeping watch over the young ones.

He went to the grassy hill where the white pillars of Aphrodite's temple were outlined against the crystal sky. The tall columns swept up to support a rounded ceiling cast of fat cherubs, demure young maidens, flowing fountains and flowering foliage.

Ares glanced at it once and frowned, for he found the scene fraught with ridiculously idyllic emotion. Three steps up led to a shining marble floor laid in the pattern of an underwater landscape.

Exotic fish in bright colors of yellow, orange, green and red swam in a lush sea of turquoise water painted in shades of aqua and cobalt blue. In the center lay the open pink clamshell that brought Aphrodite to the surface, a fully formed goddess representing Love. The floor was so delicate to view that he was reluctant to soil it with his heavy boots.

At the opposite end of the pavilion was a raised pool. Sweetly scented steam rose from within the marble sides of the spa, waiting for Aphrodite to immerse herself in luxury. Small blue and green tiles swirled in a soothing pattern that mimicked the swell of waves on high tide. Together, they had spent many hours in that pool, their wet bodies entwined in passionate embrace.

Ares restrained instantaneous lust. Instead, he looked toward his wife and her retinue. Aphrodite reclined in dazzling beauty on a wide, silver-wrought couch lined with a myriad of pillows while the Graces fanned her with jeweled feathers. Aphrodite was dressed in a shimmering rose gown that clung to every curve, opaquely hinting at the mysteries just beneath its surface.

One smooth sensuous shoulder was bared, as were her perfect feet, which rested on an embroidered cushion. Like treasures at the bottom of the sea waiting to be discovered, she held forth the gentle temptation to plumb her depths.

It was all so sickeningly benevolent.

Everything about her spoke of her oceanic birthright. Her soft skin glowed like the pearlescent underside of a shell while her flaxen hair fell about her in long frothy waves like newly created sea foam. Her turquoise eyes sparkled just as moonlight dances across a glassy sea and, as she smiled, it was with the brilliance of sun on golden sands. Her power surged across the space between them, washing up and over, caressing him like the tides across the shore.

Ares hated Cos. It was unbearably hot.

He seethed inside his leather tunic while Aphrodite did not claim one bead of moisture on her face. She appeared as cool as the green ocean glittering in the distance beyond her left shoulder, and her demure expression told him she knew his discomfort.

It would take but a split moment to re-clothe himself in a loose robe more fitting for the island retreat, but he would not give her the pleasure of knowing he succumbed to her damnable climate. Instead, he sweated and grew belligerent.

"What is so important I must drop everything to be at your side?"

This brought a sly smile from Aglaia, the oldest of the Graces. Euphrosyne, the youngest, blushed and continued to swirl the feathered fan in slow strokes. Thaleia was silent. Ares cast them a menacing glare and all three looked away.

Aphrodite extended one elegant hand and beckoned him forward as jeweled bracelets dripped from her wrist, jingling ever so slightly at her movement. Ares frowned at the sight, for he knew the craftsman behind the exquisite cuffs. Ares was not pleased to see the work of the Forge God, Hephaestos, adorning his wife, though he did not speak of it.

He let it pass for the moment.

"This is a pretty picture you have arranged, but I am not impressed. What do you want?"

Though he spoke with sharpness, Aphrodite was not fooled. She knew his lust was ever-present.

"My love, how prickly you are today." Aphrodite laughed and the world stood still while the clear, silver-belled sounds echoed against the roof in a glorious riot of melody.

"As opposed to any other day?" Aglaia whispered loudly. Euphrosyne giggled but Thaleia remained silent. Her distressed gaze said she could not forget the one in his bed.

Ares raised an eyebrow in warning and saw her pale.

"Shhh, good sisters." Aphrodite admonished, though she smiled as she spoke. "You neglect me, Ares. Come and kiss me."

Ares hesitated at the edge of the pavilion, feeling as though a trap was set and he the hapless prey. Yet he could not fathom what she wanted. Aphrodite called to him again with more than her voice. She called with her body and with her soul.

Desire wound around him and he could not help the responding hunger that reared in return. Closing his eyes, he tried to resist, but she battered against him with the wiles of Love and he shamelessly weakened. When he could stand no more, he crossed the white floor and knelt at her side.

As he pressed his lips to her hand with pretended politeness, Aphrodite murmured, "Much better, my love."

Aphrodite captured his black curls in her fingers and pulled him forward, rising up to meet him. Her lips parted as she kissed him, her tongue a gentle probe against his.

He meant to take no more than what she offered, a generous show of affection, a greeting fit for a long-absent husband. He reminded himself there was time. He need not rush. Though they might be apart for great lengths, though they might argue bitterly and revel in accusations, suspicions and swear never to forgive transgressions, they would still make love.

They always did.

He had been away too long and his lust was fully aroused at her first touch. When she attempted to draw back after one kiss, he would not let her. With a harsh indrawn breath, Ares gathered her into his arms. He caught her hair in his grasp and she cried out, but there, in her oceanic eyes, was reflected his obsession.

Aphrodite liked pain.

It jarred her balance and made real her presence. It reminded her that Love was not all about lightness and good, beauty and harmony. Love was gritty and real, causing grief and heartache. Love hurt yet the mortal world could not survive without her. Without Love, there would be a vast and empty plain, void of all feeling.

She liked to be reminded.

He was naked beside her, his kisses demanding. Gasping, Aphrodite cradled one palm against his cheek and with the other, signaled the Graces to leave them. They were gone before her fingers dropped to stroke his manhood, and with them, the children and their nursemaid. They were alone and Cos was silent except for the shrieks of seabirds drifting overhead.

Gone, too, were her gown and the cursed bracelets. She was resplendently unembellished except for the pink of her nipples and the silky golden triangle below her rounded belly.

Ares lay over her like a shadow, his darkness in direct contrast to her fairness, his fire cast over her water. They were opposites attracted by their differences, driven apart by the same, and drawn back together again, as it always had been.

Ares rubbed a calloused palm across one breast, over the tender and taut tip as he bent to kiss her. Aphrodite shuddered, her hand tight to his hardened phallus.

"Do not wait," she whispered. "For I am ready. I need no teasing."

"Yet," Ares breathed into her hair. "That is half the pleasure."

"You would have me squirm and wail and beg you for relief?" Though her voice was choked with desire, there was a hint of humor.

"Yes, for that is what I enjoy." He moved his mouth to the same tormented breast, his hand between her legs, touching the wanton wetness that waited for him.

"Not...." Aphrodite moaned. "Not this time, my love. I want you now."

With a strength no mortal woman could ever have, Aphrodite pulled him atop her.

"Now," she commanded.

Ares smiled and did as she bid him.

It was not until they lay satiated and content, entangled in each other's arms and legs, a salt-laden breeze cooling their sweat, did

Ares again wonder why he was there. When he said as much, Aphrodite laughed aloud.

"Could it not merely be that I missed you?" she asked, tickling the short, coarse hair on his chin.

"No." Ares brushed away her fingers with impatience.

"But I do miss you. Why have you stayed away so long?"

"Why have you not called me?"

"Why must I always be the one?"

"Because you hate Athos and will not travel there."

"As much as you hate Cos and do not come here."

They went silent, aware that tension once again grew between them. They each took a breath and vowed to savor the sweetness of the moment and not mar it with a fight.

"Still, why did you send Thaleia?"

"She means no harm. If you did not take offense, she would not taunt you so."

"You are angry when I send Eris to Cos."

"Eris was born to you by another. It is not the boy himself that bothers me, though he does rather alarm Euphrosyne. I do not like being reminded of your infidelities. I would far rather you sent Deimos."

"Deimos declines to visit Cos."

"Why?" Aphrodite sat up, her hair in glorious disarray around her state of undress.

Ares was quite taken with the sun shining through her strands, turning it into a golden halo. So much so, he reached for her to make love again.

Aphrodite swatted his hands away. "My son does not want to see me? I do not believe it."

"No, no, I do not mean it that way," Ares protested. "You cloud my mind and I do not think straight." He reached for her again.

"Stop." Aphrodite fixed a chilly gaze on him. "What is wrong with Deimos? Therein, is one reason I bid you come here: I am worried about him."

"It is nothing. Truly, do not be concerned."

"What has transpired with the Council? Father Zeus is angry. He said Deimos has disturbed both Earth and Sky."

"I know what he said." Ares sighed as his desire faded. "But it is not through fault of Deimos that Kulika has stirred. He was ill advised to be there in the first place and continues on the same path in spite of my warnings."

"Where is he now?"

"There."

"Where?"

"Najahmara. It means nothing to you. Deimos is enamored of a simple mortal place, although I do not understand why."

"Why? Because he yearns to be loved, as any would." Aphrodite frowned at Ares' snort. "Any but you."

"Love?"

"Yes." Aphrodite tickled Ares' chin. "He was a sweet child until you took him."

"There was to be a battle over Najahmara. He was there for War."

"He was there for Love." She spoke with a sense of wonder, for she had thought her connection to Deimos was broken. Ever since the bleak and despairing day Ares took him from Cos, she believed Deimos lost to emotion. He had grown cold and distant, refusing contact even with his twin, Anteros.

Lost.

But there it was before her, the shining thread that connected them, and it strummed with desire. Deimos loved again. Aphrodite leaped from their cushioned nest and danced with joy, arms over head, twirling to music only she could hear.

Ares, propped on one elbow, watched her show of abandon with a mixture of appreciation and confusion. "Surely Deimos is not the only reason you requested my presence."

"There is something else." Aphrodite jumped on him, kissing him with the soundness of a woman on a mission. Straddling him, she clapped her hands together. "I had a dream, a vision. There is one who waits."

"Waits for what?" Caution filled Ares' voice.

"To be born." Aphrodite leaned over and whispered. "A child, Ares. I have dreamed of her over and over. She waits for us. A daughter. We shall have a daughter."

Mouth open, Ares stared at her. "You jest."

"Not at all. Do you not see it is time for another? And this one," she sighed. "This one is to truly be one of my heart. A daughter."

"You did not...."

"Trick you?" Laughter flowed from her like water through a sieve. "No, but it would be a simple task, would it not? You are too easily blinded." She kissed him and felt the lust rise again.

Ares rejected her passion and set her aside.

"Look at who speaks. Who would not be blinded by your beauty, taken in by your sweet charms? But enough of this." He rose from the couch, clothing himself. "I do not consent to another child. We have yet to settle over Phobos."

"Phobos has nothing to do with this. I dreamed...."

"I do not care what you dream. Phobos must come to Athos. His time draws near and you do not want him here when it happens."

Aphrodite glared. "He may refuse it if he wants."

"You would have him turn away from his godhood out of your own selfishness?"

"A mother's love is never selfish. I am afraid for him. Ares, he is not like Deimos. He has neither the courage nor the constitution for the House of War. I beg you, leave him here with me."

"He is mine and I will claim him whenever I decide it is time."

"You promised you would wait until he is old enough."

"He is old enough now. You have had him far longer than you had Deimos."

"He is not ready."

"Then make him ready, for I will claim him soon."

"I will not let you have him."

"You cannot stop me," Ares growled. "And there will not be a daughter between us. Not now."

"She will not wait. Would you make me look elsewhere for a father?"

Ares froze as his gaze fell upon the pile of trinkets that had been around her wrist. "Do not threaten me, Aphrodite, for though you hold my affection, I will not tolerate unfaithfulness."

"You talk to me of unfaithfulness? You, who would send another woman's child to my house and then deny me my own son?"

"Eris' mother is a Sylph, but she is not immortal."

Hands on her hips, eyes blazing, Aphrodite retorted, "She is neither immortal nor human. By those standards, you claim it does not matter? You believe a child does not count unless it is a child born of two immortals? What would you say if I were to bear a mortal man a babe? What then, beloved?"

"You would not."

Aphrodite fell silent, appraising. "Perhaps not for this child." Turquoise eyes blazed. "For this child, there must be an immortal father. Will it be you?"

Their gazes locked and held, Aphrodite waiting, but Ares gave no answer.

*****

Eris shivered. The room was freezing even though he fed the fire. The arched hearth was nearly as high as his head with flames licking the roof, yet he was still cold. He stood in front of it, hugging himself, thinking the mug of hot ale he left behind in the warriors' quarters would be enough to warm him.

Would it cause any great harm if he were to leave his charge alone long enough to visit the hall for ale? How could Ares object to a small mug, especially when there was nothing else for him to do but stand idle and watch this female sleep?

He turned his gaze upon the woman, wondering again who she was. There was a certain familiarity, but not even her name brought forth a memory.

"Niala." He tested her name on his lips.

Shaking his head, Eris crept closer to the bedstand. Niala had not moved a hair since Ares departed for Cos and, for this, Eris was grateful. He would not know what to do with her should she awaken.

"Ares said she would not." Eris spoke aloud. "Then she will not."

His thoughts returned to the spilled ale and his longing for a bit of libation. "Ares said she would sleep - that she cannot awaken. I would be gone for only a moment." Eris rubbed his hands together and held them toward the flames, his back to Niala. "It would hurt nothing."

He could just as easily bring the ale to himself without leaving the room, but it was the men's quarters, the games, the quarreling, the excitement that drew him as much as the drink.

But Eris would get caught up and forget about this one lying in his father's bed. And then where would he be?

"In more trouble than Deimos." Eris laughed, a sound that

echoed like a rushing woodland stream. For once, he was not the focus of Ares' wrath and Eris preferred to keep it that way.

He turned to stare at Niala. In the hours Eris had been with her, some color had returned to her face. The parts of her he could see - face, arms and shoulders - glowed warmly in the firelight. She reminded him of his Sylph home and of the rich woods he grew up in.

It had been long since he had seen a woman so perfectly in pitch with the Sylph for Ares would not let him visit his people. This one did not have the green tint of his tribe, but still had the look of deep forest.

Eris was very curious about Niala, about the wounds on her side, about the markings on her leg, about the reason Ares brought her to Athos. There would be no answers, of course. Ares had already told him more than was his nature.

"A certain sign this one is different."

If he stared at Niala too long, he was afraid he would become entranced and forget his place. He was afraid he would lift the coverlet to see where the serpent's head rested. He was afraid he would climb beneath the covers to lie next to her.

Do not touch her. He could hear Ares' command as if he stood in the room.

"Not to touch her. No. Never."

Eris wiped that thought away. He was not interested in her as a mate - even if he was, he shuddered to think of the punishment for one who would lie with Ares' woman. Still, Eris would like to see the rest of Niala.

Just a little peek.

But fear kept Eris shivering near the fire, with his back to her and only an occasional glance to be sure Niala had not moved. Eris found it puzzling as to why he found her appealing. Niala was like the Sylph, it was true, but it was rare a female who could catch Eris' attention so thoroughly.

He knew many women, some so glorious in their radiance they could scarce be looked upon and Eris paid them no attention. He was far more content with the men, so then why did this one pique his interest? He shrugged, as if to answer himself, and glanced her way once more.

Eris paid great detail to her face and the long red-brown hair lying in a snarl around her. It was like she fell into vines and was caught within the foliage. Her face, though, was what attracted him most, for there he understood what it was he liked. Though Niala was ill, with scratches along her cheek and dark circles beneath her eyes, she reminded him in some ways of his mother.

Eris blinked.

Niala stirred, he was certain of it. He rubbed his eyes and put his back to the fire so he could better see her. For a long time he stared and she did nothing.

"She cannot wake up, Ares said so himself. When he has placed one in stasis, there is no way out except through his power. She will not wake up."

And yet, Eris could not help the rising concern as he continued to squint at her, afraid to go near the bed. He stared until his eyes watered and grew heavy watching for movement.

Niala was as still as death. With a sigh of relief, Eris settled into one chair, choosing the opposite of Ares' favorite. It would not do to have Ares return to find Eris in War's chair. The warmth of the fire began to lull Eris into a stupor. Finally, he dozed.

How long Eris slept, he did not know, but when he opened his eyes, he saw movement.

No, it could not be. But it was.

Niala's fingers curled up and her head turned to one side.

"It is a mistake. I am seeing things."

He fixed his gaze on her for long moments. Who could defy Ares and break free of his hold?

"None."

But Niala moved again.

This time he was certain. Only the tiniest bit, only her fingers and the barest flutter of her lashes, a faint sigh and Niala lay still again. His heart pounded as he crept closer, circling the bed, checking every angle to see if she would make the slightest change in position.

He stared until dots danced in front of his eyes and his mouth became dry, but she was as before, silent and as still as death. Blowing out a noisy exhale, Eris collapsed cross-legged upon the floor next to the bed and leaned his forehead against the wooden crossbeam.

Eris must have dozed again, because when he next opened his eyes, he was surrounded by a whirlwind of shrieking and moaning. The sound of a thousand tormented souls descended upon him. He yelped as he scrambled to his feet, reaching for the small dagger he carried strapped at his waist.

Little good it would do him, though, he knew what the awful noise meant. Enyo was dropping by for a visit. Although Eris was often in the thick of battle with her, he had never been alone with her. He never wanted to be.

With frantic haste, Eris looked about for escape, but there was none. He must protect Niala, or life would not be worth living. He hunched his shoulders against the incoming tide of a demented howling storm.

Enyo was neither divine nor human. She was an elemental creature, a specter with all the horrors of the dead upon her face. She rose with the winds of War and receded when the battles were done. Devourer of Cities, she was called.

She consumed the souls of the dying and what she did after that, Eris did not want to know. As for those two blood-sucking monstrosities that went everywhere with her, he would sooner twist his dagger in their evil little hearts than look at them.

With no other choice, for he could not flee and leave his charge at her mercy, Eris steeled for her onslaught.

The shrieking subsided when Enyo appeared. She was a walking nightmare; dark, gaunt, skeletal, nearly insubstantial, as if a hand would pass right through her. Her face constantly changed expressions: mouth stretched in a silent scream, teeth bared, pursed in pain, eyes wide in terror, slack with shock, on and on, never resting.

Perhaps it was all those she swallowed trying to get out, a different soul every second battering at the gates. What would happen if she could no longer contain them and they all rushed forth at the same time?

Eris trembled at the memory of Deimos throttling her in Najahmara, forcing souls to spew from her mouth. He remembered how angry Enyo was and how she swore her revenge.

Was she here in search of Deimos?

Enyo reached a bony hand toward him. He shuddered, drew back, and felt the solidness of the bed behind him.

"Deimos is not here," he blurted.

"Deimos, that cur." Her voice squeaked in a breathless gasp.

"He is not here." He kept one eye on Enyo's companions, who squatted at her feet snapping at the air near his toes.

"I do not seek Deimos." Enyo came closer, her face ever shifting. Wispy hair floated in the air as she wagged her head from side to side. "Though when I do, there will be a reckoning, but now I seek Ares."

"Ares is not here."

Cold damp fingers brushed his skin as she leaned closer. "Tell me where he is." Rancid breath enveloped him.

"I do not know!" Frantic to escape her touch, Eris climbed up the bedpost and leapt to the other side. "I swear I do not know."

His dance across the bed jostled Niala and she rolled toward him, the covers slipping off. Enyo's gaze drifted past Eris and went to the woman. Her eyes seethed with hatred.

"Who is this who lies abed waiting for Ares?"

Eris would have laughed at her jealousy if he had not been so frightened. He clung to the furthest bedpost, nose twitching, watching Enyo stare at Niala.

"Blood...." Taking in air with a whistle, Enyo repeated, "Blood. This one is near death and fair game." She stretched out her wasted arm, claw-like nails poised to rip flesh.

"No, do not touch her." Eris, taking courage in hand, dove at Enyo. As he flew across with dagger drawn, he saw the outline of a bird with great wings outstretched upon Niala's back. His attention was scattered just enough that Enyo batted him to the floor as if he were an insect.

Eris hit the stones with a crushing thud.

Enyo turned back to Niala, her talons descending.

With darting speed, Eris attacked and sunk his sharp teeth into her leg. He nearly gagged at the taste of rotten flesh but did not release her. Enyo squawked with rage and whirled about, trying to throw him off.

Eris held on, clamping down harder as black blood spurted over the rug. Her two minions now joined the fray, chewing at his feet and ankles. One jumped at his throat, but Eris was quick enough to block its fangs and knock it head over heels into the corner. Enyo shrieked again and beat at Eris with her claws until he dropped away.

"Loathsome creature," Eris howled, "Begone from this place before your master returns and cages you for eternity."

Enyo lunged after Eris, bloody foam dripping from her lips drawn back over blackened teeth.

He scrambled away from her, screaming, as her nails pierced the flesh on his arms, and her two minions bit at his heels. They tore through the chamber, causing rents to appear in the drapes, upturning chairs, ripping apart the rug. In the struggle, they broke every piece of earthenware in sight.

A statue carved of rare black stone fell and cracked in half. Tall candleholders tipped over, extinguishing the flames and caused the tallow to seep into the cracks between the stones. The bedding fell partway onto the floor and Niala slid dangerously close to the edge.

Eris paused in panic and attempted to push her back to the center, all the while hearing the refrain, 'Do not touch her, do not touch her.'

Tears of pain and frustration ran down his cheeks as he wished that Deimos, or even Ares, would appear to stop this demon, for Eris surely could not.

"Halt!" A female voice rang out. "Or I will slice you through with Ares' own weapon."

Silence fell upon the room. Eris whirled around, mouth agape at the site of Thaleia standing in the doorway, the hilt of the mighty Amason clutched between her hands.

The sword, longer than she was tall, dragged upon the floor while its sharp blade glowed with ominous malice in the firelight. He knew she could not possibly wield it much less imagine how she had taken it from its place above the hearth. Yet there she stood, bristling with indignation, her eyes ablaze.

Enyo gnashed her teeth, looking back and forth between them, as if weighing the injury Amason could cause. Did she believe Thaleia could harm her?

Eris prayed she did.

With a sudden howl of rage, Enyo became a whirling wind spout. She gathered her beasts to her sunken breast and left, but not before sucking the life from the flames in the fireplace and spewing hot ash across every surface.

Streaked with soot, bleeding profusely, but grinning from ear to ear, Eris said, "Thaleia, thank you. I do not know how you came to be here at the exact moment of my need, but I thank you."

"I could not stop thinking of her." With eyes huge and round, Thaleia glanced over the room and then down at the sword in her fingers.

"I have never seen anything so hateful." Thaleia stumbled backwards into the sitting chamber, releasing the blade. Then she passed out cold.

Amason clattered to the floor, its hilt striking sparks as it fell. Thaleia lay beside it, as pale and shining as the blade.

Eris sat next to her, head in his hands, whimpering, "This is bad. This is very bad."

*****

Niala floated in a warm, dark cloud of silence with no thought and no memory, no sense of being other than a tiny flare of awareness in the void. Somehow, somewhere, she existed. She could not move or speak. She had no desire to; she had no reason care. She simply floated, drifting in and out of alertness.

A sound. She heard a faint sound as something else caught her attention. Something aglow, something crisscrossed her body from chest to toes. Her body. She had a body. She was not a faceless being suspended for endless time in the void of silence. With wakefulness came the desire to move. She tried to get up.

The softly glowing golden ropes held her in place.

Niala could not feel them. The bindings were feather-light and did not cut into her. She could not feel them but they held her securely, as if placed there with deliberation. Were they to keep her floating in the void, drifting, as if there was nothing above or below her but darkness?

She did not remember anything. Not her name, or where she came from, or why she was here in this place. She did not know how she got here, or why she was bound in such a fashion, or by whose hand. She did not know if she was alive or dead.

If this was death, it was an easy one. Peaceful. She drifted without aim, contemplating her death. How did it happen? Why was she dead? She thought she frowned trying to remember, but she could not be certain anything moved. Beneath was the tiniest bit of recollection.

A flutter, a brushing of feathers against her skin.

Falling…falling…falling.

Niala jerked and felt a stab in her side. Blood-stained feathered wings wrapped her in the desire to flee. Her heart pounded.

But no more pain. Just peace. Do not question, a little voice said. It is better not to know. She relaxed. No need to question. No need for answers. Just lie still.

Sleep. Yes, sleep. And she drifted more.

But then there came violent motion and fear. The wings returned to protect. In the far distance she could hear muffled voices, shrieking like the call of a giant bird. She attempted to fight back, to hear the voices, but they fell silent and she once again drifted.

The bird was gone. But she found she could move her head and fingers. With her breath, she could sigh and the sound reached her ears. She pulled against the ropes and felt them tighten. Fear covered her awareness.

Niala struggled to free herself. But the more she struggled, the tighter they held her. She recognized the one who placed them did not want her to throw them off.

Who? Who made her prisoner? Why?

Why?

Why?

Was it the giant bird that flew against her?

But she could not think why. Only that it was so. All the while she lie lost in a cloud of darkness. She heard her breath rasping and saw the glowing ropes. With fear pounding in her ears, she forced herself to breathe with deliberate slowness, expanding and contracting. In the darkness around her, the bindings relaxed and again were weightless.

If she refrained from the fight, the bindings stayed loose.

SEVENTEEN

Eris shook Thaleia and hissed, "Wake up. Please wake up."

Thaleia groaned, her fair lashes fluttering. "What happened?"

"What happened? No more than you threatened Ares' minion with Amason." Eris held his hands to his head, "Not that I am ungrateful, but Amason? How did you get it down? It weighs more than a grown man, and I myself cannot lift it. How did you do it?"

Regaining her senses, Thaleia sat up. "That horrible creature, is she gone?"

"Yes, gone, but do not say her name for she may think we call her back."

"I do not know her name and do not want to know, now or ever." Thaleia passed a hand in front of her face. "Do not tell me her name."

"No, I will not." Eris stared at Amason, lying with belied innocence beside them.

"How did you get it down? How are we ever going to put it back? Mercy. Ares will kill us over this."

"I could not stop thinking about the one in there." Thaleia nodded toward the doorway, the corner bedpost in view. "I slipped away from Cos so I could...."

"Could what? What did you intend to do? Ares has said to leave her alone and that is what we must do."

"But Ares is not here. He is with my mistress." Thaleia winked. "He will be otherwise engaged for some time. I thought perhaps I could help her."

"We cannot touch her."

"I only want to help. There is something about her that draws me. I do not know what it is, but I must help her."

"We cannot touch her!"

"But...."

"No. We must put Amason back where it belongs above the hearth. How did you get it down? I do not understand."

"Once I saw that dreadful creature, I was frightened out of my wits. I saw cruelty, and I...." Thaleia paused to stroke the blade beside her, and it brightened like a shimmering star.

"I think it likes you," whispered Eris.

"I think it does," Thaleia whispered back. "For I found it in my grasp without knowing how it got there."

"Ares will be very angry. No one is allowed to touch Amason, not even Deimos. What are we to do?"

"What if I ask it to return to its place?"

"Yes. Yes, do that."

"Amason." Thaleia again stroked the blade. "Please return to your place of rest."

The sword did not move.

"Please?" Thaleia repeated. "Please go back where you came from."

"Pleeaassssee," Eris begged.

Amason lay where it had fallen with the two crouched over it.

"It is no use." Thaleia held up her hands. "We must try to lift it ourselves.

I will take this end." She pointed at the hilt. "And you take that end."

Eris stared at the wickedly sharp tip. "Umm, no."

"We cannot drag it. It will dull the edge."

"But...."

A clatter from beyond the doorway brought them both to their feet. "What was that?" Thaleia lifted her skirt in preparation to run away.

Eris held her arm. "I do not know, but we must find out." He could feel Thaleia trembling beneath his fingers.

"What if it is that thing?"

"Then I must protect Niala, or die trying."

"Truly?" Thaleia gazed at Eris with new respect.

"Truly." He hitched up his loincloth and strode into the inner chamber with Thaleia at his heels.

The room was dark but it was clear the big bed was empty.

Frantic, Eris shrieked and sifted through the covers before dropping to his knees to look under the massive bedstead. From there he scanned the room and still did not find Niala.

"I am doomed," he howled. "Doomed!"

Thaleia stood with her hands on her hips frowning as she watched him skip about the room. "Wait. Let us think a moment." She lifted one hand and a blaze began inside the hearth. The room took on warmth as she scanned the four corners.

"Think? We have no time to think. If you would help me, then help me," he shouted. "If she is gone, I will not see light of day for eons."

"She cannot be far away." Thaleia remained calm once she was assured Enyo had not returned. "She did not pass us into the other room."

"Then where is she?" Eris stopped as Thaleia gestured toward the outer doors.

"Aaack." Eris choked. "Not outside. Not there…oh no…"

He raced to the heavy doors, now seeing one cracked open. In his panic, he did not feel the wind creeping through into the chamber.

They found Niala lying in the snow, just beyond the doorway. Eris felt her forehead and found it cold and damp.

"She is dead. Woe to me, for Ares will never forgive this." But at his touch, Niala stirred and opened her eyes.

"She lives. What shall we do? I am ignorant as to what to do with her. He said she would not awaken, but here she is and I do not know what to do."

While Eris babbled on, Thaleia took firm hold of Niala's arm and sat her up. Niala wobbled, her head falling forward at first, before leaning against Thaleia's ample chest.

"We must bring her inside before she freezes."

"Yes, yes, of course."

Together, they half led, half dragged, Niala back into the quarters and sat her on the rug before the fire.

"Bring that blanket here," Thaleia ordered. "Then find food and drink. Hot drink, for she is weak and needs sustenance."

Wringing his hands, Eris stared at the naked woman who could not focus well enough to see him.

"Do you not hear me?" Thaleia stomped her foot. "We must warm her and feed her. Do as you are bidden. Now."

Eris scurried away after tossing the blanket to Thaleia. By the time Niala was wrapped in the blanket, Eris was back with a platter of meat from the spits below and a cup of steaming wine. He set them with care on the floor before Niala.

Thaleia looked over his offerings with distaste. The meat was charred on the outside, raw and bloody on the inside. Congealed grease drippings floated in a thick layer over the juices and the smell was abhorrent.

"This is what you call food? Could you find no fruit or cheese?"

"But this is all there is. I brought wine rather than the ale."

"Ugh, that is revolting. And what of plain water? Could you find no spring to dip from?"

"Water? There is only the water that fills the bathing pool. I know of no other."

"I suppose this will have to do."

They froze as Niala lifted her head, gasped, and then spewed vomit down her front and across the plate of food. She then collapsed face down in the platter of meat, her limp hand knocking over the wine.

It spilled into her hair, staining her skin, before pooling on the rug. The blanket slid off Niala's shoulders into the red puddle. The gash in her side began to bleed again.

"Oh, mercy." Thaleia put a hand to her mouth as Eris stared in horror.

"By the Fates, we are truly doomed," Eris whispered.

"This time, I believe I must agree." Thaleia nodded at a point behind him.

Without looking, Eris knew Ares had arrived. He could feel the icy fury spread throughout the room with the finality of a smothering blizzard, frozen and strangling, without any of the peaceful beauty of snow. Eris groaned and faced his sire with fingers clutched together in prayer.

"I can explain," he began. "It is not what you think."

"Oh, I am certain it is far worse. It never occurred to me that my private quarters would be destroyed, and the woman I said not to disturb is now lying in a pool of vomit."

Ares turned to stare at the sword, his voice more strident.

"And you dared to take Amason down?"

"It was Enyo," Eris whimpered.

"Enyo did this?"

"Most of it. If not for Thaleia, the female would be dead."

"You," Ares snarled. "I just left Aphrodite and already she sends you?"

"I am no happier to see you, Master of Misery." There was no humor to her words. "But it is not at the bidding of my mistress I am here."

"Then why? What have you two done?" Ares stared at Niala, shaking his head. "How did you awaken Niala?"

"I...I...did not, sire. She did it. I do not know how."

"Impossible."

"I swear, she twitched and then...." Eris wiggled his fingers.

"And then Enyo, she...." Eris made howling, whirring noises.

"And then...." Eris pointed at Thaleia and pretended to hold Amason. "If not for that, this one would be swallowed up by Enyo, for that was her intention."

"Enough." Ares lifted his hands in disgust. "I will hear this story later."

Ares plucked Niala from the filth. "Before you go, make right this room and everything in it. I demand it in its rightful order. Bother me no further."

"But what of...?" Eris followed Ares into the sitting chamber, sidestepping the sword with care as if it would slash out at his ankles.

Thaleia obediently brought up the rear.

"Clean it up," Ares thundered as he carried Niala into the bathing chamber and, with one vicious kick, the thick wooden door slammed shut.

"Amason?" Eris finished, only to see the broadsword was once again hanging above the hearth where it belonged.

"Is there no end to the woe offered me?" Ares looked down on the limp wretched form in his arms. "I am surrounded by fools and, worse, a myriad of idiots who prey on my good grace.

"First Deimos, who ignores my orders for the sake of a mortal town, and Eris, who has not the sense to pay attention, and then Aphrodite. Another child. A daughter, she says, for her. It takes nothing from me, oh no, just give her a daughter."

Ares glowered at the bathing pool. The water was dark and

murky as he had not prepared it for use. With a glance, he brought the torches along the walls to life and fire in the hearth at the far end. In moments, the chill was gone, but the pool itself remained dark.

"And you, Niala." He shook his head with annoyance. "What am I to do with you? I grow tired of picking up your pieces."

There was no response. Niala lolled slack-jawed against the front of his leather jerkin. Sniffing in disdain at the sourness wafting from her hair, Ares raised his eyes again to the pool. "You, too, must learn to do as I tell you. This is for your own good."

His smile was grim as he tossed her into the cold water.

Water splashed high as she sank to the bottom. Ares stood by and watched, waiting for her to break the surface. If she did not, he would go after her. He waited and soon enough, she staggered up, coughing and gagging, hair streaming over her face and body. Her visage dull and dazed, Niala stared at him without spark. She did not even lift a hand to part the hair from her eyes.

Ares' breath caught at the site of her, for with her long hair floating behind her like an auburn drape, she looked ever more like his beloved Ilya. Droplets slid down her skin as she held as still as a statue. He watched in fascination as a drop of water glided from shoulder to breast and hung at the nipple, a tentative caress that soon fell from grace back to the pool.

It was as if the element of water attempted to make love to her while she remained aloof and unmoved. Niala seemed not to notice she was waist-deep in the cloudy water even when she began to shiver. Eyes wide in a drawn ashen face, she began to gasp, as if she could not catch her breath.

The wound dripped pink with watered down blood. Niala's blue-tinted lips moved as if she tried to speak, but he could not hear her. She brought her hands in front of her, shaking with cold, but did not move to get out. She simply stared at him as if she had lost her wits.

Cursing, Ares slid into the water. As he did, the pool cleared to a crystal green and the water became hot and fragrant with steam rising in scented strands. He was now clad only in the lapping waves, his skin and hair dampened by the heavy air.

"What do you say? I cannot understand you." He reached to take her hand, to pull her down into the hot water but she jerked away as if stung.

"You punish me." Niala's voice cracked, a strangled shadow of her usual rich tones.

"Yes, and you well deserve it." He stroked the curls lying thick and wet along her back, clinging below her hips.

She shuddered under his touch. "What have I done?"

"What have you done?" Ares was incredulous as he circled her shoulders with his arm and cupped her chin to examine the scratches and bruises on her face. "You jest."

Ares felt Niala flinch, as if she would break free from him, and tightened his grip. In her eyes, he saw an uncommon panic. It was the fright of a snared bird, wings beating with frantic fear against the net. He found it a strange reaction for Niala, the defiant one who pretended to obey and then did as she pleased.

Voice quavering, Niala whispered, "You are hurting me."

"Am I? It is your own fault that you are pained." He slid his other hand to her hip, and dug his fingers into the wound. At her gasp, he said, "This you forced me to do. All was well between us. I had forgiven you, Niala. Truly, I had. And then you throw yourself off the side of my fortress."

Niala clutched at his hand.

"You would rather lie dead than lie with me."

Niala shook her head, moaning against his palm.

"Do not ever attempt such again, or you will suffer the torment of a thousand excruciating deaths and still breathe to beg for my mercy."

He released her and let her stumble backwards until she caught her balance against the corner, one hand pressed to the gash. The imprint of his fingers was visible on her face but she remained wordless with an unblinking stare.

With an impatient wave Ares frowned. "It is only a flesh wound and it will heal quickly. Do not look at me as if I intended to hurt you. You left me no choice."

"I do not understand." Niala's voice quivered.

"Nor do I." Ares sank neck deep in the steaming water and rested against the side. "You have lived too long as a mortal, Niala. Like them, you believe death will solve all your troubles. It is a foolish notion. We must all live out our destinies, whether in this life or another."

"Is this my fate, then?" Niala's gaze roved from one end of the room to the other, taking in the rich carvings that decorated the ceiling. Her arms crept across her bared breasts as her eyes returned to meet his. "To become slave to you?"

"Slave? I cannot seem to keep you in one place, even when I bind you, let alone force you to my will."

Ares tapped his chin and mused, "Yet another reminder of Ilya, for so it was with her. She would defy me at every turn, and yet sneak back to lie with me while poor Elche covered her face."

Lifting a forefinger, he pointed at Niala. "Be careful, for Elche has changed."

"Elche." Niala repeated.

"She is no longer accommodating or innocent. And now I see, falls prey to the same foolishness that besets you. I had not thought of this before."

Trailing off, Ares closed his eyes and inhaled the sandalwood scented air. "You are more alike than either of you will admit. How did you do it, Niala? How did you break free? The sleep was for your safekeeping, you know. No other reason. How did you do it?"

When there was no ready answer, Ares opened his eyes to see that same odd expression on Niala's face, a cross somewhere between panic and bewilderment. Ares could see her searching for escape, her gaze skipping past him to the only doorway, then back to him with a startled, fearful breath when she saw he watched.

"How did you do it?" Ares repeated. "Tell me. I am quite curious. No other has ever been able to throw off the sleep. But then, you always seem to do the impossible. Is that not correct, Niala? You always find a way around me."

"I...I...." She turned, arms still held across her chest. "I do not know what you speak of."

"Do not toy with me, Niala. I have no patience for it. And do not hide yourself from me." Irritation flared his nostrils. "There has been too much pass between us for you to grow modest now."

"I cannot help it." Niala did not drop her arms, instead brought her head down and a curtain of thick hair fell between them.

"Look at me." Ares reached for her, turning her about to gaze at her face, but she would not meet his eyes. "What is it?"

She lifted her shoulders. "How did I come to be here? I cannot remember where I last was, except it was dark and I was bound hand and foot."

"Yes, that is right. I put you there to rest, to sleep."

"But why?"

"Because you would dash yourself upon the rocks below us."

"Why would I do that?" Panic again. "What did you do to me?"

"It is not what I did, but what you did that drove you into madness."

"What was it?" Niala pressed her hands to her eyes. "Why can I not remember?"

"You should not be troubled that you cannot recall these things, Niala. They were not good. Perhaps it is for the best that these moments have slipped from your mind."

Ares rubbed one thumb across his short beard while contemplating her escape. "It must have been your rapid awakening. Not all of your awareness has returned, but it will, I am certain." He saw her fear and more, her helplessness at his words.

Dreaded tenderness began to creep into him and Ares did not want it. "You will remember everything in time." He spoke more harshly than he intended. "And if you do not, so be it."

Niala brought her elbows together, her arms once again covering her nakedness. "I do not even know my name."

"It is a temporary state."

"I do not know my name or yours, or any of the others you have said." Her voice rose even as her gaze traveled to the top of the domed ceiling. "Or this place, or why I am here. Or even how I got here. It is all gone."

"Stop." Ares put his hands on her shoulders, ignoring her flinch. "You will recall it soon enough."

Niala wagged her head back and forth. "What if I do not? What will I do?"

Ares gazed past her head, at a spot on the far wall. "Perhaps, then, you will become what you were intended to be, rather than what you chose to be."

"What does that mean?"

"It means…." He smiled, but it was not one of kindness. It was a smile of superiority. "It means you reside here."

"But where is that?" Niala covered her face with her hands as Ares wrapped his arms around her. She could hear the rumbling of his voice through his chest and it made her knees all the weaker.

"Athos is my fortress and below us, are my warriors. They come to worship at my feet like the fools they are, asking for my favors and doing battle in my name. I am War, Niala. A god among the mortals. You are meant to be a goddess among them.

"Not one of them, but above them. That you cannot remember your mortal existence tells me you are finally ready to accept this truth. You ask what you will do? You will step into your immortal journey and leave behind the life you once led."

"You talk in circles." Niala tried to break away from him. "And I think I do not believe you."

"Oh, believe it. You lived generations past any other. You are not of the mortal caste and now there is opportunity for you to move on. You are no longer tied by human strings."

"I think you lie to me."

"I tell you the brutal truth and still you do not listen. Your family is dead, your life there is over. It is well that you cannot remember it."

"You are cruel." Niala looked away from him.

"Sometimes, yes, War is cruel. And ugly." He gave a short bark of laughter. "And sometimes, a beautiful temptation."

"I am not tempted."

"It does not matter. You belong here and here is where you will stay." With one arm around her waist, he lifted her chin and kissed her. "Do not fight me, Niala. Let me show you what you really are."

"But why? Why does it matter what I am?" Niala strained to free herself from his grasp. "I have no past. I am nothing."

"Far from that." Ares' tone grew hoarse. "I am your past and I will be your future. Come, Niala, let us celebrate your homecoming."

He leaned in to kiss her again when there was a rapid series of knocks on the door and then it was thrown open. Thaleia scurried in, head bowed, carrying a tray of delicate pastries.

"Lord Ares." Thaleia held out the tray. "I thought you might be hungry."

"Get out, Thaleia."

"But are these not your favorites?" With a sly gaze toward Niala, Thaleia went on, "As weak as she is, she would need food. It would not do to engage in lovemaking, only to have her faint, now would it?"

Ares frowned. "Leave it, then."

"Certainly." Her smile dripping sweetness, Thaleia squatted at the edge of the bathing pool. She could scarce keep her gaze down, so magnificent was the chamber.

It was everything she heard it was, but Thaleia kept a dutiful expression on her face and continued. "But, in her desperate state, I would think I should check her wounds, for they seemed quite severe. Just look at the bruises on her lovely face and see how she lies listlessly in your arms. She could well drown if you were to continue."

"Go away," Ares growled. "Her injuries are not life-threatening."

"And how do you know? Have you turned healer in recent months?" Thaleia's tone was scornful.

"I need not be healer to know that this one is…."

"Is what, my Lord?"

"Fine. She is fine. Now, leave us."

"If that is your desire, Lord Ares. But she seems quite ill to me. And weak. Very, very weak." Thaleia arched her brows toward Niala and gave a slight nod. "Do not hold me at fault if she drowns."

"She will not drown." Ares released Niala and struck his fist on the edge of the pool. "Thaleia, your impertinence annoys me. Leave us."

"As you wish." Thaleia cast another grimace at Niala.

Niala's eyes widened and then she began to moan. With hands to her temples, she whispered, "My head, it aches so. I feel ill."

"What?" Ares dark brows drew together.

"I do not feel well, Lord Ares." Drooping, Niala let herself sink further into the water. "I think I may up heave."

Ares viewed both women with suspicion.

"Here, my dear, let me help you." Thaleia pulled Niala from the steaming bath and wrapped her in toweling.

"Wait." Ares lifted a hand but let it drop to his side as he watched Thaleia escort Niala from the chamber.

"Perhaps it is just as well," Ares muttered. "After all, we have no limit to our time."

But still, his mistrust of Thaleia's motives would not let him linger further in his bath. He dried and dressed with swiftness, exiting the bathing room in long strides. The central chamber was empty, the doors to the bedroom closed.

Sighing, Ares settled into his chair and waited.

EIGHTEEN

Pallin awoke with a start, alone on the narrow cot. Eyes burning, she thought Deimos had once again left her without a word, but as her sight adjusted, she saw him standing at the window.

His tall frame no more than a dim outline in the predawn light, regardless, she knew it was he and she was relieved. Deimos stared out with an intensity that frightened Pallin, for he did not respond when she called his name, but continued to hold the drape to one side as he looked toward the plateau.

Rubbing the sleep from her face, Pallin sighed. It seemed only a short time since they had crept up the stairs looking for an empty bed in the women's quarters. Every other possible place was taken by the wounded, with pallets covering the floors and stretching out into the gardens in makeshift tents. There had been only this one small place in a hidden corner.

Deimos looked askance at the slumbering forms filling the quarters, but not for long. Pallin flushed at her remembered boldness, at her consuming need to be with him. He was solid and warm, his breath sweet on her face, his weight comforting against her.

He moved with the same frantic desire that gripped her, stifling her moans with his mouth while his body strained to give her pleasure. It was desperate and quick and then she fell asleep wedged between him and the wall, with his arms locked around her.

For the first time since the horror descended, she felt safe.

To think that in such a short span of time, the room could go from housing exhausted, happy young women learning the healing arts in the name of Gaea, to a place for the brokenhearted and homeless was hard to fathom.

Pallin could not contain a second heavy sigh. It was sad, so very, very sad, and she could not see how they would ever recover. The sadness was followed by a pang of guilt, for she should be downstairs, side by side with the others. Throwing the blanket off, Pallin sat up.

Deimos turned at the creaking of the wooden frame.

"I hoped you would sleep longer." He was dressed in his warrior leathers, his face somber, as he took the few steps between them.

"I can rest no more. They need me." Pallin stood up, swayed, and was gripped by a swell of sickness. Deimos grabbed at her, but she shrugged away his hand and knelt to wretch into a bowl at the foot of the bed.

Done, Pallin sat back and wiped her mouth with a trembling hand. Deimos offered her a cup of water and she took it, not asking where he found it.

"You are ill."

"I have not eaten since...." Pallin brushed the hair away from her face. "I do not recall when. I just need food and I will be fine."

"What would you like?" He held one hand behind his back.

"No, do not use your magic to feed me," she protested, though she was pleased.

"It is not magic, I merely draw to me what I want. Choose, or I shall choose for you."

"No, really, stop." Pallin stifled a laugh at a complaining growl from the far end of the room. "I will find something downstairs, I swear it."

"Eat this." He held out bread and cheese as if it were a bouquet of flowers.

Taking the bread, Pallin pushed the cheese away. "All better. I must go, Jahmed will be wondering where I am." Pallin swallowed a few crumbs.

Deimos watched her pull on a gown, tie it at the waist and then slip sandals onto her bare feet. At one point, she paused to ask, "What were you looking at out the window?"

"Nothing." He lifted his shoulders. "Everything. The mortal spirit surprises me. You have come so far in so short a time."

"Odd," Pallin answered. "I was just thinking how far we have fallen. Less than two days ago, not one of us would have dreamed this could happen."

"A few hours ago, I would not have thought it possible for you to survive. And yet you have."

"Because you helped us."

"I have done what I can, but Pallin," Deimos stepped closer, one hand on her arm, "though it pains me, I must leave you."

Pallin opened her mouth to plead with him to stay, but she did not. She knew Deimos was not meant for her. He was a god, an immortal, someone whose boundaries were so far beyond her that she could not imagine them.

To try and hold him there was wrong, so she said nothing, merely nodded, and heard a sound of relief from him. In the rising light of the new dawn, she could see the regret in his brown eyes.

"I understand, your duty calls."

"It does. My father calls, but not just this moment. There is something I must do and, I swear, I will leave you with no less than a kiss of farewell." Deimos touched her cheek and smiled. "If you will still accept my favors."

"Always." Pallin kissed his palm. "For I love you. You do not have to say the same to me, but I want you to know I love you."

Deimos opened his mouth to speak, but she shushed him. "No, do not say anything. Accept it, just as I must accept your leaving."

He looked into her eyes for a long moment before agreeing with a slight bow. Words failing, they left the women's quarters the same way they arrived. At the foot of the steps, Deimos parted company with Pallin.

She was enveloped by the sight of overwhelmed helpers crying for her assistance. He watched her walk away, unnerved by the tenderness in his heart.

"It is not love," Deimos muttered, "but lust, and I should put that aside, lest I become as Ares."

A sobering thought. Lust was one Deimos would not indulge at the moment. While he stood staring across the makeshift infirmary of the gardens, with no more on his mind than seeing the patterns of the torches as they flared against the darkness, he became aware of a different energy.

Beyond the wretchedness of the gardens, beyond the grounds, expanding up toward the plateau, Deimos felt the stirring of Hattu's energy.

From nowhere, it seemed. It was not there and then it was, as if Hattusilis awakened from a long nap and now stretched. At first, Deimos could not determine from where it was came. He reached out with his mind, pushing his own energy toward the rock wall behind the gardens.

He believed Hattusilis might be one of the wounded, lost within the shuffle of people, but then it became clearer. Hattu was further away, higher. Deimos probed the field of energy in each area with patience until he hit upon the place pulsing with Hattu's presence.

It was Gaea's cave.

Dismayed, he did not think to look there, Deimos was eager to go and on the verge when Pallin awoke, so he waited.

There was nothing to stop him now.

Deimos stood at the mouth of the cave certain Hattusilis was inside. He called, and there was no answer. The passage was dark and silent, his voice returned to him with an eerie echo. Plucking a torch from beside the entry, Deimos brought it to life and stepped inside.

He could feel Hattu's terror latch onto him and stretch out like a rope leading the way. With each step, Deimos was reminded of his first journey into the depths of the cave and he slowed, as he felt reluctance build. He did not want to go into the main chamber again.

Why?

It seemed Gaea spoke to him, but it was only the wind in the tunnel, something he did not notice when it was filled with the noise of rejoicing. The breeze cooled his face and he breathed with forced slowness, leaning on the damp wall for support.

Were it not for Hattu, Deimos would not enter Gaea's domain for a second time.

Why?

The whisper came again and the hair stood up on his neck.

"Why?" Deimos straightened. "Because I failed."

There was no response, neither to forgive nor to castigate. Deep, profound silence followed and Deimos thought he imagined Gaea's voice in the wind. He paused and then said softly, "I am sorry."

One word seemed to whistle through the stone corridor, one word, real or imagined. *Survive.*

"Yes, they will survive, but they are changed."

In that statement, Deimos found some bit of peace. He had brought Najahmara terror, but also the will to survive. He knew returning to Najahmara would be worth whatever price Ares demanded of him.

Pushing forward with a determined stride, Deimos arrived in the main chamber. Empty, it seemed so much larger than before. His boot heels struck the floor in loud echoes as he crossed patches of rock. Within the stone room, he could feel Hattu's terror and, beneath that, panic.

Flashes of a man.

In such complete darkness he could not see his hand before his face. Lost within the Earth's womb, with no way out. Running, stumbling, falling into walls, and in the end, into something that crashed down upon him, and then sinking into utter blinding panic.

Deimos listened. Panic was being called into the mortal realm with greater and greater strength. He saw it on the rise in Najahmara, felt it pressing down, again, now with greater force in Gaea's cave. Soon, Panic would be challenged to take his place among the gods. He prayed Phobos was ready to accept his place within the immortal caste.

With a sense of urgency, Deimos circled the chamber. Behind the seat carved from natural stone, he discovered a honeycomb of openings. Some shallow niches, some corridors leading deeper into the hillside, and two deep cavities where the harvest was stored.

As the torchlight flickered over row after row of huge urns in the next largest chamber, he was amazed at the wealth of food. Drying bunches of fruits and vegetables hung suspended from racks as the strong scent of medicinal herbs mixed with their flavors in the cool dry air.

The chamber was filled with enough stores to keep all Najahmara fed for months. And there, lying beneath one overturned urn and a pile of spilled grain, he found King Hattusilis.

He was in a faint, his face gray in the flickering light. He was not dead, Deimos knew without touching him, for he could still feel his energy and the cocoon of terror that bound him.

Placing his torch into a holder along the wall, Deimos righted the stone urn and brushed away the mounds of grain covering Hattusilis. One glance was enough to see bone pushing through a ragged tear in Hattu's trousers.

Blood dried the linen and traces of grain to his skin, but, even with this, Deimos could see one leg had been crushed by the weight of the urn. It was swollen twice beyond the normal size and his foot twisted at a wrong angle, nearly severed from the ankle. The other leg suffered injuries at the knee and thigh, with much blood loss.

Hattusilis' face was cut and bruised, and, from the labored breathing, Deimos suspected more broken bones within his torso. Deimos could not know how long the container laid atop Hattusilis, but it had served as a tourniquet, keeping most of his blood inside him. Though his injuries were severe, it could have been much worse. He could have bled to death.

"Hattu?" Deimos touched Hattu's face and felt the clammy skin. He may not yet be dead, but he was very near. "Hattu. Hear me. Open your eyes. Wake up, Hattu."

With tiny grunts of pain, Hattusilis' eyelashes flickered. Deimos continued talking to him until a hoarse moan issued from Hattusilis.

"Deimos."

"It is I, Hattu."

"I thought...I...would...die...here."

"Not today, my friend."

"I thought I would die." Tears trickled from the corners of eyes gone glassy.

"You will be alright, now, Hattu. We have been searching for you, Zan and I. We have looked everywhere but here. I did not think to look in the cave."

"Zan is here?" Hattusilis gasped and then drew in a wheezing breath that brought a grimace of pain to his drawn face.

"Yes, Zan is here." Deimos held a flask of water to Hattu's parched lips and let a small amount dribble into his mouth. Hattusilis choked and began coughing. His coughs brought up water tinged with blood and made him cry out.

"Speak no more, Hattu. I am going to take you out of here. It will hurt when I move you."

"Worse....wounds...in...battle." Hattusilis protested, but the moment Deimos lifted him, he passed out.

Hattusilis could not focus. Every jostle brought him immense pain, each attempt at a deep inhale brought a grinding in his chest that kept him mindless for long moments. He breathed with shallow pants as he tried to concentrate on his surroundings.

He had gone numb, remembering nothing from the moment Deimos lifted him until he opened his eyes and saw a roof and the walls of a tiny room. He lay on a narrow cot, shivering in spite of the ✓ thick blanket tucked around his shoulders,.

Hattusilis was so cold he could not bear to have even his arms outside the blanket. And, though his mind wandered, he was aware that he was clean. He no longer could smell the acrid scent of sweat and his own filth.

Should he be humiliated that unseen hands had stripped and bathed him? Perhaps, but he could not muster the strength. He could think of nothing more than to be grateful. He was even without concern over the continuous dripping of tears from the corners of his eyes.

Fitfully, he slept. In and out of a dreamlike state, he was aware Deimos spoke to him about his caretakers, but it seemed as if from a great distance, and he was unable to respond. He was also aware Zan stayed by his side, murmuring prayers interspersed with stories of his army and of Telio, but again, there was no sense to it.

In his dreams, Azhar haunted him, calling upon him to reunite with her, reaching out to him with specter arms, holding up a son long dead, no more than bones. She called to him to relinquish his hold on life, to die and be with her again. He wept as he wandered in the mists looking for the way home.

"We have done all that can be done. Now we must wait," Pallin told Deimos, as they gazed down at Hattusilis, whose violent shivering rattled the cot. "He has a fever which means there is disease in his body. His legs, I think. I pulled as much poison out as I could, but the wounds are deep."

She shook her head. "We can only hope now."

Zan sat in a corner, pale and shaken after he had assisted Pallin in her duties. He heard his king scream in agony while the woman cut open Hattusilis' legs and poured medicine inside and then pressed both hands into his flesh to set the broken bones. Zan came near to fainting when she took needle and thread and sewed the torn flesh of Hattusilis' foot back to his ankle and then tied his legs to strips of wood to keep them straight

If that was not enough, the woman wrapped layers of bandage around Hattusilis' chest until Zan thought the cloth would strangle Hattu, but the woman smiled at Zan's worry and spoke that it must be done in the trade language.

Zan nodded and looked away as she bathed the king, lifting Hattu when she asked. After all was done, Zan carried Hattusilis into a tiny room where he did not have to share a pallet. Hattusilis was laid on a hammock strung to a wooden frame.

"It is Niala's quarters," Pallin said. "I had to move ours out to the main healing area. Jahmed was very displeased, but it was done. Niala would want it so. I remember this one." Pallin cast a quick glance at Hattusilis, "From the cave."

"Yes, he was there." Deimos smoothed his tunic. "I do not yet understand why he went back."

"We may never know." Pallin settled a blanket over Hattusilis. "Lesser have died from such a fever as his. Even if he survives, he may well lose his foot or his entire leg."

"Hattu is strong. He will fight it off. I ask only that you take good care of him, for he is a friend. He will be able to help Najahmara once he has recovered."

"In what way?" Pallin eyed Hattusilis with suspicion. "He is one of them, I can see it in his face. He is dark like them and he wears a beard and long hair. He looks just like the evil one who raped and killed Seire."

Anger sparked in her eyes. "Do not try to convince me he is not a soldier."

"He is a warrior, yes, and more. He was uncle to the bloodthirsty one - he is their king."

"King?" Pallin gasped. "But then he...."

"No." Deimos rubbed a hand across his face. "After he came to Najahmara, once he saw how it is here, he did not intend violence."

"An invasion anyway you describe it."

"Perhaps, but, please, Pallin. What is done is done and it will do more harm to reject Hattusilis. He can help in ways I cannot."

"I do not understand what you are asking me to do."

"Care for him."

"I have already promised what I can, is that not enough? What else is there for me to do?" Pallin looked away from Deimos, her jaw set. Tears came unbidden to her eyes. "You are leaving."

"Pallin." Stroking her cheek, then turning her face back towards him, Deimos said, "I must. I have heard that trouble arises in my father's house. I must attend to it."

"Of course." She was unable to meet his gaze.

"Please, Pallin." Deimos lifted her chin between thumb and forefinger, forcing her gaze upward. "What I ask of you now, you cannot understand, but it is important. I ask that you open your heart to this man, to Hattusilis, to a king. He will have great need of you in the coming days."

"I will do what I can."

"You do not hear me. I ask more than that. He, too, has suffered much grief in his life, and he does not yet know what his nephew has done. It will cause him pain for he did not wish to destroy Najahmara. He will restore it, and he will need you to accomplish it."

"Why? Why me, why not...."

"Because Niala is no longer here. She would have done this for the greater good, but she is not here. I ask you in her stead."

"Niala," Pallin choked.

"It is what she would want you to do."

"You are cruel and unfair." Pallin buried her face in her hands. "To invoke Niala. She is lost to us and in her name, you ask me to be kind to her tormentor?"

"More than kind."

"You go too far."

Leaning forward, Deimos whispered in her ear, "Niala is not dead, but is at my father's fortress. I go to see about her."

"Are you certain?"

"Shhh." Deimos held a finger to his lips. "This cannot be known. I will strive to bring her back, but in return, I ask this one thing. Open yourself to Hattusilis. Give him what he needs to heal and he will lead Najahmara back from this darkness, I swear."

"What does he need?"

Mouth pressed against her ear, Deimos answered, "Love."

"But...."

He placed a brief kiss on her lips, spoke a few quick words to Zan in his own tongue, and then was gone. Pallin was left staring at Hattusilis, panic welling up in her heart.

NINETEEN

The uppermost level of Athos was silent.

Deimos stood in the corridor outside Ares' quarters, head cocked to one side, listening. There was nothing. Not even a sigh, unless his own breath counted. Deimos knew this could not be good.

Eris sought him out in Najahmara with a convoluted tale that brought him home as soon as he could muster. He sighed again and raised his hand to knock. When there was no answer, he pushed the doors open and went in.

What he saw brought an immediate snicker, for it was a picture too reminiscent of mortal existence. Ares sprawled in his chair beside a leaping fire, one arm thrown across his face, as if he was at peace in his rest. Eris lay curled on the rug in front of the hearth with a content expression on his face, and a tray of empty dishes beside him. Thaleia sat prim and proper on a stool on the opposite side in deep concentration over a delicate piece of sewing.

At Deimos' chuckle, Ares lowered his arm. He was anything but peaceful and came to his feet.

"What do you find here that is so humorous?"

"Nothing." Deimos bit back a smile.

"You smirk."

"No, it is only because this is so unlike you."

"How so?"

"I am surprised to find you here at all, let alone…"

"What?" Ares advanced to stand toe to toe with Deimos.

"Thaleia." Deimos gestured, afraid he would dissolve into a fit of laughter.

"She will not leave." Ares' voice dropped lower.

"I do not understand. Command her back to Cos, if you do not want her here."

"She will not go."

"She must obey you."

"She says she does not have to."

Ares fell into a whisper as he gripped Deimos' arm. There was a certain madness to Ares' eyes that Deimos had not seen outside a battle, and it did nothing to help contain his mirth. He bit his tongue and nodded as Ares continued.

"I have told her to return to Cos, but she refuses."

"Father, you can force her, if you wish."

"Yes, but then we would have no agreement."

"What do you mean? Why would War need an agreement with a Grace?"

"Why?" Ares gritted his teeth. "I cannot have her at your mother's side without an oath of silence."

"Niala." Deimos' gaze darted past Ares' shoulder. In the moment, he had forgotten about her, but now his concern resurfaced.

According to Eris, Niala was injured, ill and at Ares' mercy. "What have you done with her?"

"She sleeps." Ares jerked his head toward Thaleia. "And that one has decided to be nursemaid."

"Nursemaid?" Deimos could not quite see the mischievous Thaleia in such a role. "And you allow this?"

"It seems not to matter what I allow, for she does what she pleases." Ares added in an undertone, "Just like your mother."

Louder, he continued, "I do not want Thaleia here and yet whatever holds her here remains a mystery."

"What holds me is curiosity," Thaleia announced. She rose from her seat and came to stand behind Ares as she spoke. "You brought a mortal woman to Athos, a place females are not allowed.

"No, do not deny it, for I have heard it bragged upon by those filthy creatures who worship your sorry hide. No female would dare enter into these hallowed halls, not even Aphrodite herself, which is laughable. They obviously do not know Love, for she will go into the most miserable hovel if she is so called, and often does, though I chastise her."

"Enough." Ares swung his hand backward, narrowly missing Thaleia. "Do you hear this drivel? I have listened to it for hours."

Thaleia took a deep breath and then smiled at Deimos. "You are well, Deimos? It has been too long since I have seen you."

"I am well." Deimos returned the Grace's smile. "I am surprised you take time away from Aphrodite to torment my father."

"He does not mind the distress he causes my mistress, therefore, is it so odd I might cause him an uncomfortable moment in her name?"

"It is unusual, and I think it is less about my mother and more about the woman who sleeps in the next chamber." Deimos lifted one eyebrow in question.

Thaleia smiled again and the deep dimples in her round cheeks gave her a most innocent appearance. "I confess, I am drawn to her and I cannot say why. When I first saw her lying there, bloodied and unconscious, I could not help the compassion that called me back to her side."

"Bloodied and unconscious?" Deimos turned to Ares. "Eris spoke only of Enyo's attack, not of another."

"It was before Enyo." Thaleia's eyes were bright. "Aphrodite sent me to invite Ares to Cos. I saw her, then. Enyo came later."

"Enyo?" Eris stretched and yawned from his place on the rug. "I would be most happy to see her cast into oblivion."

"As would I." Deimos frowned.

"Do not toy with Enyo," Ares said. "There is more to her than you can see."

"She is a worthless hag."

"Even a hag has purpose."

"Do not let her cross my path or her purpose will end," Deimos growled. He would not forgive Enyo for attacking Najahmara.

Ares looked at the loathing on his son's face but did not pursue it. For now, he would be pleased to rid himself of Thaleia, as long as he had assurance she would not speak of this to Aphrodite. If he could not have that pledge, he would be forced to keep her at Athos, but in what capacity? Nursemaid to Niala?

No. Ares would not tolerate any more interference.

Turning a speculative glare on Thaleia, he received a

beguiling smile in return. At that moment, Ares knew well he could never trust her to keep still.

"If it was not Enyo who caused such wounding to Niala, then who was it? I want to see her."

Deimos started toward the inner chamber.

"And why is your interest so keen?" Ares blocked Deimos from entering the room.

"I am responsible for the fall of Najahmara, I can scarce feel less of a burden for Niala's ills." Deimos intended to step around Ares, but Ares moved in front of him.

"Niala brought this upon herself." With a slow inhale and a sidelong glance at Thaleia, Ares continued, "From the moment she opened herself to Kulika's power."

"But it was I who first caused Kulika to stir when I laid a hand to his image." Deimos turned his head away from Ares' hard stare.

"You had the opportunity to touch her where the serpent begins?" There was a dangerous undertone to Ares' words.

"It was not what you imagine. It was during ritual and it was Gaea who was before me."

"Worse yet, you laid a hand on the most ancient of us all? Now I begin to understand the attention you received from the Council. You did not speak of this detail before."

"I could not." Deimos raised his eyes to squarely meet those of his sire. "Let me see her. Please."

Ares stood silent for a moment, his gaze unblinking. With a curt nod of his head, he said, "Thaleia, what say you? Should Deimos be allowed to visit your precious charge?"

They both turned to Thaleia, Deimos tense with a silent plea and Ares impassive, impossible to read. Thaleia scanned between them, her heart racing. Ares intended for her to choose, and if it was the wrong choice?

She did not want to cause Deimos further pain, wishing more than anything to wipe away the haunted expression on his face, even though it gave rise to a tiny twinge of jealousy in her heart.

Thaleia saw how much Deimos longed to be with this woman, the desire behind his concern. And then there was Ares, whose yearning for the same woman was crystal clear though he sought to hide it behind his conceit.

Deimos was Aphrodite's son and Thaleia would do anything for her beloved mistress. She should let Deimos have his way. And further, if she were to serve Ares and his wicked ways, it could only bring more heartache to Aphrodite for she would be very unhappy to hear of this liaison.

Yes, Deimos should see this one, this mortal whose pull was so strong. In the end, fear won out. Thaleia could pretend Ares was of no consequence, but he was, and he could cause them all greater harm should she cross him too readily.

"I am sorry, Deimos, but no. I have kept Lord Ares from her side and I will keep you away as well. She is weak and sick and must rest with no interruption."

A fleeting yet powerful sadness passed over Deimos and he slumped, suddenly exhausted.

"Perhaps later," he mumbled.

"Perhaps." Thaleia was unable to watch the smug and satisfied curve to Ares' lips. "You must both leave her alone."

With those parting words, Thaleia tugged open one of the double doors into the bedchamber and slipped through it, letting it click shut behind her.

Deimos stared at the doors as if a deep chasm had just split in front of him. There was no hope of getting past either Ares or Thaleia, this much he knew. Resigned, he turned to go. Before he could reach the far side of the room, Ares spoke.

"I am not finished with you."

Those were the exact words Deimos spoke to Eris at Najahmara. And there was Eris stretched out like a hound basking in the heat of the flames, belly full, unconcerned with any reprimand.

Anger swept up like a tide, staining Deimos' neck and face with red. It roared out into the room, a typhoon of futile resistance. Wordless, he faced his father.

Ares reacted to the wave that washed over him with his own force, pushing back with a thunderous fury. There was a momentary struggle, as the clash became a torrent of colliding energies and War and Terror locked together in deadliest conflict.

It receded as quickly as it began.

"You dare." Ares raised one fist, ready to strike. Deimos remained cold and silent, not at all remorseful.

Ares watched his son through narrowed eyes, his blow paused at Deimos' guarded stance. "You have grown arrogant since I allowed you free rein in the mortal world."

"I have grown more like you, is that not what you wanted?"

"What I want is obedience. We do not live in the pretty world of Love."

"And what do you call your obsession with Niala Aaminah?"

"I call it none of your concern."

Deimos made no move as Ares paced a few steps then turned with abruptness. A chill chased along Deimos' spine for no longer did Ares show menace on his face. A more frightening, tight-lipped smile had taken the place of his snarl. With one forefinger, he beckoned Deimos to his side.

"If you would be like me, then I have a task for you. You will go to Cos in my stead and bring Phobos back to Athos."

"What?" Deimos' jaw dropped. "Take Phobos from his mother, my mother's, arms? You would send me to do so cruel a thing to my own brother?"

"Oh, and that I would." Ares' tone was soft. "If you aspire to be War."

"I do not."

"Then you must learn the consequences of your actions are often harder labor than the task itself."

"This is not a lesson I need."

"You would rather I lock you away in darkness? A punishment fit for a child, Deimos." Ares nodded, deep in thought. "No, you will do this."

"And if I refuse?"

"You will not."

The devastating power of War shook Deimos though Ares made no move toward him. The nightmares of Deimos' childhood pressed down and dark spots danced before his eyes. His knees grew weak, his breath became no more than a gasp. When released, he kept to his feet by sheer will.

"Go now to Cos, and do not return without Phobos."

*****

Deimos stood before his mother, expressionless in the face of her anger. He would not have her see his inner anguish, or doubt that he meant to follow through on Ares' command.

"How can you do this?" Tears shone in Aphrodite's eyes.

"I do as Ares bids, Mother. It is all I can do." Deimos spoke in a monotone, scarce able to keep his gaze affixed to hers, also unable to look about him at the place he was born.

The moment he set foot on Cos, he could feel the contrast to Athos. Love emanated from the very ground Aphrodite's dwelling sat on, reaching out to him, a cherished child welcomed home.

It wrapped around him like fur, curling upward to stroke his face with unseen hands. There was an absence of recrimination, no reproach, only an embrace of his entire being.

Acceptance.

Deimos had once been part of this bright world Aphrodite lived in, he and his twin, Anteros. He was a happy child, content and secure until Ares came for him, as Deimos now came for Phobos. It was a time of great pain, confusion, and of a wound so deep he could scarce think of it, yet his father insisted there was no other way.

Ares' harsh words still haunted him: *'You are made of my darkness and nothing you do will ever make you part of her light. To stay will leave you an empty vessel with no purpose.'*

Joy, once taken for granted, was now too foreign for comfort. Deimos pushed the sensation away, but could not escape so easily from the surroundings. Everywhere, there were reminders of what had been.

It was in the air, in the flowering vines, in the warmly scented grasses, in the salted breeze that had once dried the ocean from his skin. The rush of memories of laughter and play, so pained him, that he squeezed his eyes closed and held his breath against the onslaught.

Shame.

Deimos was surrounded by unconditional love and in return, he was to commit thievery and take away a jewel from Aphrodite's crown.

"Deimos?" Aphrodite touched gentle fingers to his face, tracing the strong line of his jaw. "You, too, are my son."

He jerked, eyes flying open. "Yes, I am flesh of your flesh, but I belong to War. I must do as he bids."

"He bids you take Phobos from my arms because he lacks the courage to do it himself." She withdrew in a swirl of sparkling blue-green silk.

"It is not lack of courage, Mother. You know him better than that."

"No, I do not. Not anymore. He has changed. When Phobos was born, Ares swore he would not force me to give him up like…like…."

"Like me."

"Like you. I know you believe I willingly let you go, but I did not. I begged. I pleaded. I would have given him anything he desired if he would only have left you here a little longer. But he would not."

"It was not your fault."

"But you do not forgive me for letting you go."

"You do not forgive yourself. There was nothing you could have done to stop him. I have taken my rightful place in the world, just as Phobos must."

"But are you happy with what you have become? Could you not have been just as happy staying here?"

Deimos shrugged. "To stay would have been to watch my brother take his power while I had none to offer. No, Mother, it was the right thing for me as it is now right for Phobos. He must discover his true purpose."

"Phobos is too young, too delicate. He cannot survive in your world, Deimos."

"He is stronger than you believe."

"And how would you know this? You have not been to Cos since the day Ares stole you from me. Why have you not returned?"

"I could not mix the two worlds."

"Why?"

Deimos licked his lips and turned away from Aphrodite's accusing gaze. "You would not understand."

"A trite answer, my son. The truth is you could not bear to see what you left behind."

"I left behind my innocence, but one cannot live in that insulated place of childhood forever. It is a pretty place to visit, but now it no longer serves."

"You are just like him." Aphrodite wiped at a tear that trickled down her cheek. "Cold and uncaring."

It was true. Deimos carried the darkness of his father, but there was that hidden light of his mother lurking deep within him, unchallenged, unexamined, waiting for him to delve into its watery depths.

But not on this day.

Although Deimos held some of her light, he had no place in the Realm of Love. He was what he was. And beyond any doubt, Phobos was just like him. He could not stay, or he would be no more than a shadow in his mother's world.

"It is for the best, Mother."

Deimos shrugged away the past and with it the desire for love. Instead, he held out his hand to the youngster who half-hid behind a couch woven of sun-bleached reeds. The pile of pink and gold pillows afforded Phobos a peep-hole. Only huge, frightened brown eyes along with a fringe of black curls gave him away.

"Come, little brother, I will not hurt you. I want only to bring you to our father's knee."

Smiling with encouragement, Deimos wiggled his fingers. "Please, brother, do not make this more difficult on our mother. It is time for you to take your place beside our father."

With reluctance, Phobos emerged from behind the cushions. He was a thin wiry child, wearing only a blue loincloth that showed off bronzed skin. His legs were just beginning to grow longer and looked too gangly for the rest of his body. It gave him an awkward appearance, one that Deimos remembered well from his own childhood.

Phobos did not smile. His face crumpled as if he tried not to cry. Deimos faltered for a moment – the boy was so very young – but Deimos knew he went to Athos at a much younger age than this and survived. He hardened his will and took the boy's cold hand into his own. "You will not mind so much when you are accustomed to us."

Phobos nodded, speaking just above a whisper, "I am afraid, Brother."

"I know, but I will be with you the entire time."

Phobos did not speak, but leaned against Deimos' leg. His head came chest-high to Deimos and the gesture made him seem even more vulnerable. Deimos let his hand rest on his brother's shoulder.

"Let us go, then."

"No!" Aphrodite came from the corner where she was standing with her face buried in the edge of her robe. "Phobos is not leaving here."

She snatched the child from Deimos and brought him into her

arms, fingers digging into his thin back. No amount of force could take him from his mother's embrace. Phobos clung to her with equal strength, his face buried in her neck.

"Mama," Phobos cried, his voice muffled.

"It is all right, my darling. You will stay here with me."

"Mother, please, do not go on so." Deimos reached for Phobos. "He will come to no harm."

"No harm? Just as you came to no harm?" Aphrodite wrenched away, taking the boy with her.

"I? I am better for the experience. You must give him to me." He followed her across the room, toward the doors that opened upon a wide veranda.

"Absolutely not. You have never spoken to me of your coming of age trials, but now you are so different. I do not like the change."

"How could I be as you remember? I was a boy and now I am a man. I create Terror in the world, unlike you, who brings eternal Love. Why would I not be different?"

"Indeed. You were once innocent, like Phobos, who went with trust to your father. And what was brought back to me?"

"I am grown now, Mother, not a timid child."

"Nothing," Aphrodite shouted, "nothing was brought back to me. My precious son, now a warmonger, and why? Because you went with trust and did not look back. I will not have the same from Phobos.

"Now begone. Do not make me more angry than I am, or you will see who can exact more vengeance, myself or your father."

Phobos wailed as she clutched him tighter and his shrill little voice cut through the air. Another boy dashed into the room and threw his arms around Aphrodite's waist. Aphrodite crouched down and clung to them both, rocking back and forth.

"My babies." Aphrodite kissed the tops of one dark head and one golden.

"Mother, please try to understand that what I do is for his protection, it is not to cause him harm."

"Leave him, Brother, for he does not want to go with you."

Deimos turned to see his twin, Anteros, standing in the doorway. There was no glad greeting on his lips, but a pinched, angry expression that took nothing away from his beauty. He stood every bit as tall as Deimos, for they were head to head, and a mirror image except for their coloring.

Anteros was of his mother's lighter skin, with hair the color of golden sand, with eyes as blue as the sea. Deimos wore his thick black locks shorn above his shoulders, while Anteros' was to his waist in a flowing silken mass.

Their clothing, too, reflected their differences. Deimos dressed in drab leathers, a hip-length jerkin, heavy riding trousers, boots made for rough terrain, and a long sleeve coat that fell below his thighs.

Anteros wore a sleeveless knee-length white tunic edged in blue, along with laced sandals. The only thing they shared now was their anger.

Once they had been inseparable, two boys who plotted endless ways to torment their nurse. Two brothers who ran naked and laughing upon the heated sands and played in the warm tides, who slept cuddled in each other's arms. Now they faced each other with anger and distrust.

"How is it you have come to this, brother?" Anteros said. "Once aligned with this house, now turned against us and willing to steal a babe from his mother's arms? To cause our mother such hurt, truly a deception of the heart."

"Anteros, you know what lies at stake. I cannot leave Phobos here to suffer through his rites of passage with no one to guide him."

"And I cannot do the same for my brother? How little faith you have in me, or mine, that you do not trust us to see him safely through his journey."

"It cannot be, brother." Deimos waved a hand towards the tumbling sea. "Not all can be healed by water. Some take fire as well. Do not make this task more difficult than it already is."

As Deimos dragged Phobos from Aphrodite's arms, Anteros also grabbed hold of the boy.

They fought, each claiming one side of Phobos, who screamed as they pulled at his arms and legs.

"No, no, you will not do this." With her head tilted back, Aphrodite shrieked, "Ares! Ares, hear me now. Coward that you are, come forth and face me yourself. Ares, I command you to come here, now."

There was no more than a second of silence before Ares spoke. "Well, well. This is quite a pretty sight, is it not?"

Great clouds covered the sun and an instant pall fell over Cos. Both Deimos and Anteros released their share of Phobos, who skittered to his mother's side. Ares strode up to Aphrodite ignoring all others. He towered over her, his face dark. Aphrodite hugged both Phobos and Eros to her as she glared up at her husband.

"Coward? You would accuse me of cowardice?"

"Yes, again and again. What other name is there for one who would take a defenseless child from his mother?"

"Defenseless? Even now, I feel his power approaching. It swells up from the mortal world, growing day by day."

"He does not have to accept it."

"If he does not answer its call it will burst forth uncontrolled and sweep across both realms. Is that what you want?"

"She wants to keep her child." Anteros came to his mother's side in a protective stance.

In turn, Deimos stood at his father's side, one hand upon the dagger at his belt.

"And you," Ares growled at Anteros. "Are you prepared to fight War? You are no more than a pretty shell upon your mother's beach. You would be crushed beneath my boot before you knew what happened. Begone, for this is not your fight."

Anteros refused, standing fast. When he spoke, it was with a strangled voice. "Just the same, I see, there is no compassion in your pitiless heart. You will see the death of Phobos' innocence and think nothing of it, nay, celebrate it as a victory against Love."

"Victory? Victory does not exist. It is too high a price for any to pay. But a pitiless heart?" Ares barked a short laugh. "Yes, I like that. A pitiless heart. But, then, you misunderstand me, and why would you not, having spent your life here."

With great disdain, Ares waved his hand toward the sun-washed shores of Cos. "I will take him and there is naught either of you can do."

His gaze fell on Phobos and a dark stain wet the front of the boy's loincloth, dripping down his legs.

Ares' lip curled. "You see what you have done to him? He cannot even look upon his father's face without losing control. How will he be able to assume his role in the world?"

"Why must he? There is nothing writ, no law, no rule, not even a standard, that would force him to accept something he does not want."

"How do you know he does not want his power? Have you asked him?"

Aphrodite twisted her fingers in the cloth of her gown. "I have tried to explain."

"From your mouth comes an explanation of my world? It would not give fair chance to the boy. Why would he want to step over?"

"Yes, Ares, why would he? Would you want what he is destined for?"

"I am already all that he will ever be. Who better to guide him into that fraught role? Would you have him discover his real nature alone?"

Aphrodite knew Ares spoke the truth, for she was all that her sons were as well. Each child born of them took a piece of each, blending it into his own shape. Just as Deimos took Terror from War, he took Survival from Love; just as Anteros took Response from Love, he took Manipulation from War. Phobos and Eros would also step into those pieces that would become a whole. All said, it did not make giving Phobos up any easier.

"I would not have him discover it at all." Aphrodite's eyes shimmered with unshed tears. "He is the sweetest child, so loving. He will not survive with you."

"He will be instructed."

She looked past him to Deimos. "I do not like your methods. Please, I beg you, do not take him from me."

"Phobos will grow up and face his demons sooner or later. If he is unprepared, you will truly lose him. You claim he has choice, but I say that is not so. His choice was made before he was born."

"It is not too late to change his destiny."

"Love speaks." Ares shook his head. "Who better than Deimos to escort him into the Shadowland and back? With us, he will be safe. It is with you he would not survive."

Ares touched Aphrodite's cheek. "Let Phobos go in peace with us and I swear, I will send him to visit you at the first opportunity."

"You promised to give me more time with Phobos. You swore it." Aphrodite slapped Ares' hand away.

"I have given you more than twice what you had with Deimos. Phobos is much older than Deimos was when he came to the House of War."

"Yes." Aphrodite's voice was brittle. "You took Deimos at a tender age and he scarce knows where he came from."

"He does his work well."

"Too well." Aphrodite laid sad eyes on her eldest. "He rejects Love."

"Would that I could reject even a small portion of Love." Ares' bark of laughter brought Aphrodite's gaze back to Ares' black eyes.

"Sometimes, I believe you have already renounced Love."

"I am taking Phobos with me."

"You are as cruel as you have always been."

"And you are as blind. I seek to save him from himself and you wish to sacrifice him on the altar of motherhood. It will not be, Aphrodite. He belongs to me and you can do nothing to stop it. This matter is settled."

Flushed, Aphrodite said through clenched teeth. "Not quite."

"What, then? You cannot change my mind."

Their voices sank as they moved further away from their children. "I have already told you what I want."

"A daughter."

"Yes, a daughter."

"You would exchange one child for another? Is this not bribery? And you call me cold."

"It is not in exchange, for I would have them both, but I know you will take Phobos no matter how I protest. You would not take a female from me."

"No," Ares mused. "I would have no use for a female."

"There, you see? Why would you deny me this pleasure? Give me a daughter, Ares."

"And if I refuse?"

"You would only refuse to spite me, for there is no other reason."

"I would refuse because it is not right. Always, we have discussed the purpose of our children before they are conceived. They are not brought forth from a dream, but from deliberation."

"She is not like any other."

"Then tell me what she is to be and I will consider it."

"I do not want your consideration. I want your agreement."

"I will hear the reason, or there will be no other children between us."

"You do not trust me?" Aphrodite's chest heaved with anger. "You take my son from me, two sons from me."

"And left you with two. You ask if I trust you? No, and with good reason. Our agreement was that I would have one of each set of twins and, both times, I had to fight you. I have had to endure your tantrums and insults to gain what we agreed upon. Why should I enter into yet another union that will cause me more misery?"

Although she trembled, Aphrodite spoke with dangerous distance. "Because if you do not, there will be no end to the grief you will suffer."

"Is that a threat?" Ares' dark brows came together over an ugly expression. "Never has a child been born of our blood that we have not decided together what that child would be."

"Yes, yes, I agree, that is true," Aphrodite interjected. "But this time it is to be different. You have no interest in females if you cannot bed them." She paused to glower at him and it was as if the ocean froze. "This child will be mine alone. There is no reason for you to have any say in what she will be."

"Yes, a child for you alone." Ares' voice lowered to a hiss. "Why is that, Aphrodite? So far, we have brought into the world two sets of twins, each having a balance of light and dark, each carrying a part of ourselves into flesh. Why, now, would you change this?"

"You have made it clear there is no place in your world for a female. Always you choose our children to be males, and whether they follow in your footsteps or dwell in my temple, they are still male and cannot fully understand what Love is about. No one understands."

"Not even your precious Graces?"

"They try, but they are not of my blood, and do not carry the same burdens. Our burdens, Ares." She took a deep breath and laid her fingertips on his arm. "Who but Deimos can understand your pain? No one, my darling. I ask for a daughter who will do the same for me."

Ares' anger began to ebb away as he gazed down at Aphrodite. She appeared to him like sunlight across placid waters, an open invitation to swim in the warm comfort of her arms. She only wanted someone to be with her, a daughter who would love her as she loved others.

Why not?

He blinked. Resist, a voice in his head cried. Resist.

Ares covered Aphrodite's fingers with his own hard grip and felt her try to pull free as his senses returned.

"Rise above petty trickery, Aphrodite."

Aphrodite managed to liberate her hand. "It is only because you are often as cold as the snow on your mountaintop and will not listen to reason that I resort to convince you in other ways."

"If there was reason to your plan, then I would not need to be convinced."

"I have told you why."

"And you do not think I am considerate enough to want you to have comfort?" A cutting edge returned to Ares' voice.

"I think." Aphrodite stood on tiptoe. "You do not value a female as much as a male and that offends me."

"Women are not made for war."

"No, women are made only for love?" A nasty silence held between them.

"I have given you two boys for Love's cause, does that not show equality?"

"But you have not taken a female for your cause and that speaks louder."

"You do not ask me to." Ares stalked to the arched doorway and stared out toward the sea. "You ask me for a daughter that will be yours alone."

Aphrodite followed him. "Would you agree if I asked for twins? Light and dark, just as our boys have been?"

"No." His tone was flat, unrelenting, even though the thought once occurred to him, now Ares would not have it. "Women should not be part of War."

"What of your sister, Artemus?"

"She kills to please herself, and then is held up as admirable. She has no concept of the horrors of War as a way of life."

"So you claim women should not take up swords to fight, yet we should be the victims, the chattel of those who do?" Outrage blazed in Aphrodite's voice, sending it to a higher pitch.

"For the mortal world, I do not care, but I will not contribute a daughter to the miseries of violence." Ares' jaw clenched. "It is grief, enough, that I see any of my children carry this burden of which you speak."

"Then we should not have brought forth Terror and Panic, nor even Response and Passion, for they also invoke violence at times." At the thought of her precious children never having been born, Aphrodite clutched at her chest above her heart.

"Perhaps that is so. Perhaps we should not have delivered children into this world for whatever reason." Ares turned away from Aphrodite so that she could not witness the pain of such a statement. Whatever beast he appeared to humans and immortals alike, he would never deny his love for his children.

"You are insufferable. How could you say that?" Aphrodite stomped her small foot.

"I would not want to disappoint you."

"Then we are back where we started."

Aphrodite looked toward the corner where a great bronze bed sat arranged before a row of windows. It was made to appear as a giant open shell with vines and flowers twined together, creating a canopy overhead. Plump pillows, the shades of deep water and brilliant sunsets were scattered across it.

"You are my husband and the rightful one to sire my child, but beware, Ares, there are others who take interest in me should your wicked nature keep you from consent."

Ares hated the instant stab of jealousy. He knew of whom Aphrodite spoke, the same who crafted her bracelets, and who gifted her with such a glorious bedstand.

Hephaestos.

Hephaestos would waste no time should he be given the opportunity, for he had loved Aphrodite since the beginning.

With one lingering gaze about the room, Ares took in the graceful pillars and white marbled flooring, the sweeping spaces with nothing to contain a spirit of the sea save the outer walls and roof that shaded her.

He saw the drawn faces of his four children, two so like their mother and two so like him, and knew they despised him for this aggravation. He swung back to Aphrodite and was captured all over again by beauty that made all else recede into shadow.

Hephaestos.

Ares ground his teeth at the thought. Would Aphrodite do such a thing? This child, this daughter, why was she so important? Abruptly, he nodded. At Aphrodite's quick smile, he held up a hand. "We shall speak of this later, when we are alone."

"Soon." Aphrodite smiled. "Soon, Ares."

"Soon," he replied. In two strides he reached Phobos and scooped him into his arms. With chin quivering and tears streaking his small face, Phobos appeared a babe against his massive chest.

Aphrodite moaned and covered her face with her hands.

"Mama," Phobos shrieked, and then he, Ares and Deimos were gone from Cos.

Spirit weakened, Aphrodite sought the reed couch and sank into its depths. She sat dry-eyed, her grief too raw to speak.

"Mother, how could you do this?" Fury stained Anteros' face red. "Why? For the sake of a daughter? One who you believe can understand far better than I, though I stand loyally at your side?"

"You are young yourself." Aphrodite spoke at last. "There are many things you do not know."

"I know he stole my twin from my side without care and now he has done the same to Eros. I know I hate him and I will never forgive him." Anteros shot one last accusing glare, turned on his heel and strode from the room.

With burning eyes, Aphrodite watched Anteros go without offering a word to soothe him. She understood his anger and let him have the moment to himself. There would be time enough to talk.

She turned to her remaining son. "Come to me, little Eros, and let me put my arms around you."

Eros ran to his mother and threw his arms about her neck, awkwardly kissing her cheeks. "Do not cry, Mama, Phobos will be back."

"Perhaps, my little one, perhaps. In any event, he will be fine with his papa and brother to look after him."

Eros went still. "Mama, why does Papa love Phobos more than me?"

"What?" Aphrodite held him out from her so that she could look into his eyes. "Why do you think that?"

"He did not want me to go with him, only Phobos. I do not think he loves me at all."

"Ahh, child," Aphrodite folded the boy against her breast. "It is not that he has no love for you, it is just...I cannot explain until you are older. Even then." She shook her head with sadness as she looked toward the path Anteros had taken. "Even then, it mocks all meaning of love as we know it."

TWENTY

Phobos shook with muted sobs as Ares set him down in the center of the red and black spiral. The boy hugged himself, tears tracking along his cheeks as his gaze shifted back and forth, taking in his new surroundings.

Ares stood before him with arms crossed, feet apart, staring at the child. Deimos waited behind him, with a firm grip on Eris, who viewed the boy with a great deal of curiosity.

"Do not scare him." Deimos gave Eris a shake.

"I just want to have a look." Eris leaned further around Ares to see the child. He was not much shorter than Eris, but skinny with bony arms and legs. "He does not seem like much, does he?"

"He has only just arrived."

"Quiet," Ares snapped.

Phobos jerked as if slapped and began to cry in earnest. Ares tapped his fingers against one elbow. "What are we to do with you if you wail at each turn?"

"What are we to do with him now?" Eris inched forward.

"I think a change of clothing would help. He is cold and wet." Deimos arched an eyebrow toward the soaked child.

At that, Ares looked down at the damp spot on the front of his tunic and frowned.

"No more of that," he growled. "There is no need to be frightened."

"There is every reason to be frightened." Eris grunted when Deimos gave him a sharp poke in the ribs.

"Take him to bathe and put on fresh clothes." Ares gestured at the boy. "And food, I suppose. For he still needs sustenance at his age. Deimos. Take him to your quarters and care for him.

Sighing, Deimos reached to take Phobos by the hand. The boy screeched and ran to hide behind a chair.

"What is he doing?" Eris watched with growing excitement. "Does he play a game?"

"No, and do not chase him." Deimos went behind the chair. "Come, Phobos, I will not hurt you."

Phobos squealed and darted across the room and dove beneath the broad table.

"He is timid, like a rabbit hiding in the wood." Eris crept forward, crouched low, ready to spring at the boy should he scurry off again. "But I have no trouble catching even the quickest beast."

"Do not chase him," Deimos warned. "Or I will send you to the dungeons."

"You would have to catch me first and you know you cannot." With a grin, Eris rose and sprinted past Ares, toward Phobos' hiding place. The moment Eris got close to Phobos, the boy began to shriek and backed into the furthest corner.

"Now see what you have done?" Deimos lunged for Eris and missed. "You may outrun me, but I will always find you, one way or another. Get away from the boy."

Ares did not move even though all three brushed past him in their mad dash, but stood with one fist raised, knuckles pressed against his forehead.

"What did I do with you at this age?"

"Ahh...." Deimos stopped in his tracks, as did Eris. "I was sent to Priapos."

"Yes, yes, so was I," added Eris. "Will you send him to the Centaur? Send him! Send him to the Centaur."

"Be still," Deimos hissed. "Father, Phobos is not ready for Priapos' cave."

"I agree. You must give the boy instruction first. We will wait awhile." Ares grimaced. "But take him out of here. Now."

"Yes, Father." Deimos crawled under the table on his hands and knees and dragged Phobos by his ankles, letting the boy's screams fall on deaf ears. If he were to instruct the boy, then they would have to come to an understanding of who was in charge. "I have said I will not hurt you, Phobos."

"What is going on here?" Thaleia stalked from the bedchamber doorway, hands on her hips. "Who do you torment now?" When she saw Phobos' forlorn, dirty face, she was aghast. "Phobos, what are you doing here? When did you arrive?"

She whirled to face Ares. "What have you done? You swore to my mistress you would not take Phobos at such a tender age. Does she know he is here?"

Ares turned such a look of malice on her that Thaleia flushed and covered her mouth with one hand. Phobos squirmed free of Deimos and ran to her, hiding his face in her skirt.

Thaleia put her arms around his quivering shoulders and bent to kiss the top of his head. "There, there, child. I will see no harm comes to you."

"*I* will see no harm comes to him." Deimos held splayed fingers up to stop her. "You are to take charge of Niala. She needs you more."

"She sleeps, but this poor lamb." Thaleia gathered Phobos into her arms, his coltish legs half the length of her. "Let me see to him, Lord Ares."

"No, she is to care for Niala," Deimos insisted.

Eris snuck up behind Thaleia and stuck his tongue out at Phobos. Phobos screeched and buried his eyes against Thaleia's neck. Thaleia staggered under his shifting weight.

"Be still," she scolded and then turned to Eris. "Leave him alone, green one, or I shall twist your pointy little ears right off."

"He is such a baby," Eris grumbled.

Deimos suppressed a chuckle with a loud cough.

Ares held up his hand. "Stop. Thaleia, take Phobos to Deimos' quarters the next floor below and see to his needs. Deimos, escort them."

"But, I…."

"Go." Ares pointed at the outer door. "Eris, leave the boy alone. You are released to find your own entertainment. Out, all of you," Ares thundered. "I am quite weary of this foolishness."

He watched them leave and waited for the door to latch before crossing to the bedchamber. Flames from the hearth kept the dimly lit room quite warm by Athos' standards. Thaleia had done well in providing for Niala.

"Niala?"

There was no response. She was deep in slumber, undisturbed

by the commotion. Ares stood over her, studying her for long moments. Her face was lovely in repose, the scratches and bruising hidden in the shadow of the flickering light, as if the mortal grief Niala suffered had indeed fallen away.

Ares was struck by the vast difference between the flawless delicate symmetry of Aphrodite, and Niala's substantial, earthy, imperfect beauty.

His thoughts returned to those ancient days when there were only the three of them on Earth. That story that continued through the millennium.

Aphrodite, who was once Elche, she who desired harmony above all else.

Niala, who denied ever being Ilya, but retained the same rebellious ways against conformity.

And himself, once the tortured and confused Anyal, always caught between them.

It appeared that some things would never change.

Ares exhaled with a heaviness brought on by the weight of the past twining with the present.

He was envious of Niala's rest, for sleep often eluded him. To be able to sink into that temporary state of oblivion, to release, even for a short time, the heavy mantle he wore, to have some peace from it all. What would he give? It was a question he frequently asked himself, but had no answer.

Ares' thoughts were ceaseless and they would not abate for even a moment, for all acts of violence found their way into his realm. No matter how small or inconsequential, every aggression fed the House of War. Every aggressive act of humankind against any living thing. There was no end to it.

There never would be.

Ares slumped forward, head bowed. He was tired and muddled. Tired of the disorder surrounding him, muddled by the same emotions he rejected out of hand. To simply lie down, to forget for just awhile, maybe even to sleep.

Throwing off his clothes, Ares slid into bed and settled next to Niala. He stroked her from forehead to cheekbone to chin, his fingers lingering on the unhurried pulse at her throat. She sighed at his touch, and though she did not wake, she rolled away from him onto her side.

Moving closer, he breathed in her scent while absorbing the

heat of her body. He stretched and molded his body around hers, enjoying the sensuality of her soft oiled skin and the coarseness of the coil of her braid as it brushed his chest. He kissed the back of her neck. Kisses intended to give rise to passion, for that was his need.

It was his way, to escape violence with pleasure.

"Niala." He ran his hand from her shoulder to the hollow between hip and thigh.

She sighed again and reached down to take his hand. Her fingers laced through his as if she would guide him on, but then went lax as sleep overcame her once more. Ares thought to wake her to take the pleasure he needed.

Instead, he found himself slipping away with her, falling deep into his own slumber. His last thought was not of violence or sex, but of forgiveness.

Niala awoke with a suddenness that left her chilled. As her eyes adjusted to the cold watery gray of the chamber, she could see the wan, early morning sun filtering through the cracks in the doorframe. It seemed as if she had awakened to the same view many times before.

The hulking hearth with its logs burned down to ember, the oversized doors with light seeping around them. The long beams above her, the profound silence, as if no other creature dared stir until the master rose.

She lay very still, listening. Even the wind made little noise as it slithered around the outside corners of her prison. Inside, there was only quiet breathing next to her. She knew it was Ares lying close, for his body was heavy against her.

One arm draped over her, his hand tucked beneath her as if he feared she would flee the moment he closed his eyes. Painfully aware of their nakedness, Niala was loath to move for fear of waking him, for fear of what his last words to her meant before Thaleia snatched her away.

'I am your past and I will be your future. Let us celebrate your homecoming.'

Past. Future. What about the present? Where had she been, if this was her homecoming? And to celebrate, to make love? It seemed clear her relationship with Ares was beyond flirtation.

And Thaleia showed her such kindness, first in escaping Ares and then soothing her injuries. Who was she? If Niala knew her, she could not remember, but it was a comfort to give in to her ministrations.

Thaleia had examined the cuts and bruises, clucking her tongue as she did so, but in the end, agreeing they were only surface wounds. She had combed out Niala's hair, neatly braided it, then rubbed sweet oil on her, paying special attention to the sorest places.

All the while, Thaleia had kept up a flow of chatter that lulled Niala into a peaceful state. Niala did not know what they spoke of during that time, only that it was pleasant and allowed Niala to fall into a natural slumber while Thaleia's voice droned on above her.

But Thaleia was no longer present. Instead of her friendly chatter, there was Ares, silent and frightening, yet so familiar. Achingly familiar. The heat of his body, the cadence of his breathing, his scent, all so familiar.

Even the protective arm around her waist. Niala had been here before, exactly like this a thousand times. She had lain here before, listening, just like she was now when the thought came unbidden: was he really asleep or in deep thought?

A miniscule piece of memory floated past Niala, one of Ares sitting for hours without speaking, lost in contemplation of forces she could not understand. She saw herself at his feet, wordlessly staring into the flames, glancing up at him once in awhile, waiting for him to break his reverie. It startled her to feel content in his presence, even in this tiny bit of lost past.

There were other things as well. Details like the erotic grandeur of the bathing chamber, the small private closet off it, and this room, with its heavy beamed ceiling and wide doors. Even the lingering smell of smoke from the hearth seemed known to her.

Had Niala any choice but to believe what Ares said was true? That Athos was where she lived? That she was companion to him? To a man who claimed to be a god?

Not just any god, but War.

A low groan escaped without intent and Ares stirred.

"What is it, Niala?" His voice was without threat.

Still, she twitched and tried to ease away from him. He let her go, but asked again, "What is it? Are you ill?"

"No." The cold air hit as Niala slid from beneath the warmth of the covers and she shuddered as the need for relief became immediate. Glancing around in confusion, Niala again had the sensation she had done this before.

"There." He pointed to a bench where both a gown and a wrap lay waiting for her.

Where her clothing always lay. The thought struck her even while she bent to retrieve the gown, aware that Ares watched as she struggled to put both on in a hurry.

A pair of slippers underneath, slippers that fit as if made for her. Niala pulled them on with trembling fingers and then rushed to open the heavy doors into the outer chamber. If Ares called to her to ask where she went, she did not hear him. She would not have answered if she had.

When she returned from the bathing room, a new fire was blazing and Ares was in the big chair to one side of the hearth. Niala's teeth chattered from the cold. He did not seem affected by the frosty air.

Ares sat with his legs stretched out, crossed at the ankles, feet bared, wearing only a long sleeved, lightweight tunic and loose trousers. His elbows were propped on the arms of the chair, his fingers tented together before him.

He did not smile or greet her, but nodded toward a low table set before the fire. It was filled with fruits, soft cheese, a flat round of bread, and a pitcher of clear water. A mug was already poured for her.

Niala looked at the arrangement and then at Ares, slumped with casual carelessness in his chair. Again, her mind stirred. She knew she had been here before, in this exact way, for it seemed a ritual to have breakfast laid out just so, just for her.

"These are things I enjoy?"

"Everything. Why would I serve you anything else?"

"To test me? To see if I remember what it is I prefer. To see...."

"If you have truly lost your memory, or if you seek to trick me?" A brief smile turned up the corners of his mouth, appearing more like a grimace than humor. "I am already convinced, Niala. But you will tell me if you begin to recall these things?"

His tone was light, yet carried a warning.

"Of course." Niala bowed her head. "There are things already."

"Oh?" His eyebrows lifted. "Such as?"

"This." She waved at the table "I feel as if I have done this many times before."

"Every day." Ares nodded in agreement.

"There is only one mug and one plate." Frowning, Niala knelt before the table. "Will you not eat with me?"

"I do not need food."

"How can that be? Do you not get hungry?"

"No, I do not hunger nor thirst."

"You never eat?" Niala paused with a handful of grapes lifted partway to her mouth. "Does that mean you cannot?"

"I can." Ares rubbed a spot on his cheek. "If I choose, but it would be out of pleasure, not need." He dropped his hands to the chair arms. "But I detest the end results. One does not cancel out the other."

Uncomprehending, Niala stared at him. Ares gestured toward the bathing chamber and the small closet within.

"Oh." A blush crawled up her neck and stained her face. "But it is what everyone does."

"I do not like it and I have a choice. As do you, Niala. You do not have to suffer through the humility of eating and discarding if you do not want to."

"Not eat?" Confusion colored her words. "I must, to live."

"Only because your body has been taught to crave food. You can retrain yourself to do without."

"But I would weaken, starve to death."

"You would at first, feel the pangs, but then it would stop and you would find you do not need anything. And if you did, there is ambrosia."

Ares could not disguise the scorn with which he spoke the word.

At the questioning look on Niala's face, he said, "It is a nectar drunk by many immortals and is said to contain a property called ichor, which keeps us invulnerable. In truth, it is much like the fermented drinks of the mortal world and those who partake become dependent upon it.

"I do not allow those in my House to drink of it, and we are just as indestructible as the others. Perhaps more so. For we do not carry the desire for ambrosia like a dead weight as do those in the House of my father who spend their time looking forward to the next offering of it around the table."

"I see." Niala grew thoughtful. "But you would not deny me that which I need, would you?" One hand hovered over the table as if she would snatch up the food and hide it away in case he would keep her from it in the future.

"No." The sound of his voice echoed around the chamber. "It is a choice and I will not force it upon you. Nevertheless, eating does not make you mortal. It is a habit to which you have become accustomed and nothing more. In time, we shall see."

Turning away from his scrutiny, Niala wanted very much to speak of something else. "Where is the woman, Thaleia?"

"Would that she had gone home," Ares grumbled. "But no. She is in another part of the fortress, attending to other duties."

"She does not live here?"

"No."

Niala could not keep the distress from her face, for Thaleia had been a bright spot in all the confusion.

"You like her."

"She is very kind." Niala spoke in a low, apologetic voice.

"I have never found her anything but irritating."

"It seems you find most things irritating. Perhaps that is why she does not live here."

Ares snorted and the sound bounced off the walls. "You assume it is her decision, when in fact, I do not want her here."

"Why? She seems most helpful."

"Let us just say I do not appreciate her interest and leave it at that."

Niala fell silent while she ate, keeping her head bowed over her food. There came a moment when she could no longer stand the quiet. "And what of the other one, the green one, does he live here?"

"Eris does indeed live here, though he dislikes Athos. He prefers the forests, but he obeys my wishes."

"Does everyone here obey your orders?"

"Everyone but you, and we must do something about that."

There was no humor in his voice. Niala lifted her head to look at Ares, to see the serious set to his features. A chill chased down her back that had nothing to do with the cold. This, too, was a familiar feeling. Fear was invoked by his intense black gaze.

"Whatever it is that I have done, I am sorry."

"Whatever you have done? You make it sound so innocuous,

so innocent, as if what you have done amounts to a tiny tear in the fabric, a misstep in the parade, a small lapse in judgment in the overall frame of things. It is not that simple."

"I see I have made you unhappy. That much is obvious."

"And quite an understatement as well."

"What is it that have I done?" With chin raised, Niala met his angry eyes.

"The list is endless, but let us just discuss the overriding point, and that is your refusal to see yourself as you are."

"That again," Niala sniffed. "I can neither agree nor deny what you say. Is that not quite convenient for you?"

She climbed to her feet, unable to stop her voice from rising. "Tell me who I am, or what I am, or what I was. Give me something…anything…anything but these vague accusations."

Ares started up in his chair, as if he would strike her. Niala held her place, though her knees shook. She would not look away from him. They stared at each other for long moments before Ares' mouth began to twitch and he fell back in a fit of laughter.

"There." He spread his hands out, palms up. "That is who you are. The wild one, the rebellious, delirious one. Not passive and certainly not modest. That is what I saw in you from the first moment and it is who I want now."

A bubble swelled before Niala, an incandescent image of a young girl with shorn locks and defiant eyes. She refused to bow down before a god in spite of the blood offerings that stained his altar.

Niala sucked in a gasp and took a step backward, one hand raised. As she blinked, the likeness disappeared and the present reasserted itself. With it came a bout of nausea. Niala coughed, trying to contain her breakfast. She sank down on the cushion before the table.

"How did I come to be here?"

"You were delivered into my hands by the faithful," Ares answered. "And they received their just reward."

He drew one finger across his throat. "Fitting, do you agree? Payment for the years of torture they put you through."

"What did they do to me?"

Ares shrugged. "Unpleasant things, I presume, but you did not speak much of it."

"Rape?" Niala could not look at him, for somewhere on the

fringes of her mind she saw the violent taking of women, heard the shrieks of terror, and relived the helplessness of one who could not stop the destruction.

"It would not seem so, at least not inflicted upon you."

"You spoke of my family, you said they were dead. Did these beasts who brought me here, did they kill my family?"

"It is what you told me, that these men massacred your tribe."

Eyes closed, Niala began to shake, for now it was more real. The screams, the smell of smoke, blood, bodies strewn about; the taste of death was in her mouth. With a moan, she covered her face with her hands.

"Niala." Ares drew her closer, so she leaned against one knee. "Those people, they were not your true parents."

"What do you mean?"

"You were not of their blood."

"Though I scarce remember their faces, I feel that part of my life." She touched her fist to her breast. "They loved me. I was their only child, their only daughter."

"And yet, you came to me as a boy."

Trying to clear her thoughts, to call back this piece of her past, Niala squeezed her eyes shut. "They wanted me to look like a boy, but I do not know why." She trailed off and pressed her face against his leg.

The trembling lessened with the strength of his limb against her and she took strange comfort in the large hand lying on her neck, absently plucking at her braid.

"To hide you, Niala. You were not born to them. You were found. I believe they feared someone would come looking for you, so they disguised you as a boy."

"But who?"

"After all these years, I still wonder."

"I think you have imagined such a tale, for it cannot be true."

"Oh, but it is. You have lived far far beyond your normal age, and look at you, you have not changed, not grown old and wrinkled. Your parents were immortal."

"If this were true, and I do not think it is, but if it was, why would they leave me?"

Ares lifted one hand for a brief moment and let it drop back to the chair arm. "I cannot say." His gaze centered on the far wall. "It is an unusual circumstance and I have not heard of such a thing before.

"Not that an immortal child has never been left with mortals, but that no one will own up to it. However, once you step into your power, I will know from whom you sprang."

"If I have not yet taken this power you speak of, why do you think it will happen now? There must be a reason why I am as I am."

Boldness made Niala meet his gaze. A slight thrill of defiance lifted the hair at her neck. It was quashed within a single glance, for what she saw in his eyes was terrifying.

"Because, Niala Aaminah." Ares' fingers tightened upon her flesh. "This time, I leave nothing up to chance. This time, I will make certain you accept your power when it is thrust upon you."

TWENTY-ONE

Hattusilis grimaced. He could not hold back the low grunt as Zan and Connal helped shift him onto his new bed. Hattusilis would rest far better on the wooden platform they had constructed for him rather than the cloth cot. But still, every move brought a jarring surge of pain in his chest and both legs.

He was grateful to his men for providing the solidness beneath him. As a warrior, he was used to sleeping on the ground and could not accept the too-soft and lax bed.

Saying as much, Hattusilis received quick grins from the brothers, Zan and Connal. Pallin watched the whole maneuver with arms crossed and a frown on her pretty face. The suspicion in her eyes was quite humorous, as if Zan and Connal sought to cause him damage rather than relieve the ache in his back from the sagging hammock.

"But how am I to keep such a thing clean?" Pallin spoke in halting words as she attempted to speak in Hattusilis' tongue.

She glared at the platform and switched to the trade language to continue. "No air can get to it and there could be insects crawling about in that dreadful hide."

Connal had found a fur to spread over the wood and, though it smelled a bit like smoke and a lot like a horse, it was good. Connal, always the shy one around women, ducked his head and mumbled, "I shook it out; there should be no crawlies."

"What did he say?" Pallin asked. "Did he say there are crawling things?"

"No." Hattusilis smiled and spoke with measured words so she could understand. "He said it is clean and should suit even your demanding nature."

Pallin snapped around to stare at Connal, who turned red at her scrutiny. "I could at least have put a sheet over it, but you were too eager."

"Would it make you happy to have it covered?" Hattusilis braced himself for more pain.

Pallin studied the hide-covered wood. "Yes, though I do not think you should be moved again."

"For you." Hattusilis gestured for the Zan and Connal to lift him while Pallin laid a clean linen sheet over the dingy fur and insisted that a few plump pillows be placed for Hattusilis to prop against.

As she tucked another sheet over him, she said, "It is better if you are not level."

Waving at the discarded hammock with its elevated end, Pallin shook her head. She did not approve of the flat, hard platform but these foreign men did not listen and would do what they would do.

"I will get your evening meal." Before retreating, Pallin threw a warning scowl should they think to come up with any further plans to disturb her patient.

"She is a difficult one, is she not?" Zan rolled his eyes. "It must be this way or this way, but not that way."

He mocked Pallin with gentleness, for he appreciated the attention she gave his king. To find Hattusilis alive after all that happened was a huge relief, though he did not understand how Hattu came to be in a cave half way up the ridge.

Zan was still distrustful of Deimos and how it was possible to discover Hattu in such an odd place, but there was no further discussion of it. Even once Hattusilis regained his wits, there was little talk of what took place there, for Hattu refused to elaborate. He said only that it was an accident caused by his own clumsiness - it was a miracle Deimos found him at all.

He doubted this tale, but kept it to himself.

Zan watched Hattu now as he rested against the pillows with closed eyes, his face pinched and melancholy in the lamplight. Perhaps moving him had not been such a good idea, after all.

"Hattu," Zan spoke in his own tongue. "Are you feeling ill?

Should we leave you to rest?"

"What?" Blinking, Hattusilis roused. "No, do not go. I have been thinking about what you told me, about this demon serpent and where it came from."

"I have never seen anything like it," Connal spoke up. "In all our travels, this beast was truly unbelievable and yet, I saw it with my own two eyes. I saw what it did."

He shuddered and offered a small prayer to Teshub in thanks for sparing his life.

"Telio." Hattusilis scowled. "Telio violated the sanctity of the earth goddess' temple and raped her priestesses. Is it any wonder she would invoke such a beast to destroy her attackers? We thought them to be defenseless, but they had a weapon far more powerful than any of ours. We would have clearly been spared had we arrived without harmful intent."

Hattusilis' breath caught as he shifted his weight and he groaned softly. "These cursed pillows."

"Must stay." Zan glanced over his shoulder at the doorway. "I do not want a tongue lashing from that one when she returns."

"But I would lie easier if my head were on the same level as my feet."

"She said you must be at an angle." With an uneasy expression, Connal also looked toward the entrance. "I see the healing work these women do and the many lives saved that I believed were lost."

"Neither of you will remove the pillows?" With one eyebrow arched, Hattusilis looked between his men. At the stubborn silence, Hattusilis laughed, and then cried out when a sharp jab of pain struck his side.

"Sire! If you really want them gone, I will take them." Zan reached for a pillow only to be stayed by Hattu's lifted palm.

"No, we will abide by the priestess' decision." Sighing, Hattusilis settled a bit deeper into the mound. "Going back to this serpent, I do not think he will return."

"If there is another threat to Najahmara." Connal stared at his king.

"And there will not be." Hattusilis' voice lowered. "However, I wish to know what has happened to the rest of our forces."

"They have turned tide and run," replied Zan. "Or they would have arrived by now. They were only a few days behind us."

"How many men are accounted for?"

"Half, maybe three quarters, most of them dead."

"And the others?"

"I do not know, Sire. It would be the outer most ring that survived and I would think if they are not here, they have fled."

"An act of cowardice against their king?"

"Yes. No." Zan bowed his head and stared at his hands. "If you had seen this thing and the fire that blasted outward - no man could stand against it. There was no hope to fight it; there was only one chance to escape. I would have done the same thing."

"No you would not. You would die rather than flee. That is apparent as you are here, by my side. And you, Connal, what do you think?"

"It was a nightmare. I cannot blame those who ran."

"And yet, you did not. How can either of you dismiss my charge?"

Both men shrugged and remained silent.

"I see." Hattusilis drew his brows together and nodded. "Where have they gone, then? To join the rest of the army? To warn them away from Najahmara? It would mean any hope of saving their brothers would be gone."

"My King, I do not intend insolence, but if you had been here, you would know there appeared no hope. This demon roasted everyone in his path. No one was spared, not even those who worshiped the earth goddess, for they burned in their steps along with our men.

"Najahmara, herself, is destroyed. Few buildings survived intact. Though largely made of mud brick, the bricks now crumble from the heat. The serpent spared no one, nothing. Our men were right to flee." Zan spoke each word with care.

"My question then is this, can you find them?"

Connal was slow to answer. "Perhaps. They would need to follow the same path out that we took in, but if they are not there, then they are lost in the wilderness beyond this valley."

"They should have the good sense to stay with the Maendre, should they not?"

"They should," Connal agreed. "But we do not know if they have."

"Then you must find out. I want to know what has befallen them." Hattusilis paused. "And if you find them, I want the army to return here, to me. All of them."

"What do you intend?" Zan cleared his throat and thought of the pyres that still burned out in the fields.

"We sacrificed many for Najahmara. We have the right to her now." Hattusilis grimaced as he took in too deep a breath. "This time there will be no violence, no harm to her people. If this is what the earth goddess does to her own, they should be well pleased to have a change. Go, Connal, see what has befallen them and bring them back to me."

Connal gave a quick dip of his head but did not meet his king's gaze. Nor did he glance toward Zan, but left the small room, brushing past Pallin as she carried in a tray.

Pallin stood in the doorway with the curtain held open behind her back staring after Connal. Beyond her could be seen the bleak, smoke-streaked corridor, the burnt scent still strong. As she turned, there was new wariness in her eyes.

"Where does Connal go in such a hurry?"

"I sent him on an errand." Hattusilis kept his gaze neutral.

"What is he to bring back?"

Hattusilis glanced at Zan, and Zan spoke for him.

"It would cause you deep embarrassment if my king were to say. Leave the food and return to your work. I will see he eats well."

"You are dismissing me?" Pallin's tone bordered on dangerous.

"Ahhh, it would seem so." Zan stood up and reached for the tray.

Pallin held tight. "Now I know Connal is up to mischief. The two of you misunderstand your king's sudden alertness. He is still very ill."

"Of course." Zan tugged at the tray. "But he does not wish you to know where Connal went."

"Why? Why do you hide this from me? Where has he gone?" She relinquished the tray to Zan but stood firm, hands on her hips. With a sudden arch to her brows, she added, "He cannot have wine."

"He is King, he may have whatever he wants."

"Do you wish to see him heave his guts to the floor and break loose all that has healed?"

"Of course not."

"No wine."

"Please," Hattusilis raised his hand. "Connal did not go for wine."

"What is he to bring back?" Pallin demanded.

"Do not ask questions you do not want the answer to," Zan's voice was sharp. "Go back to your work, woman."

Pallin stood with arms crossed, toe tapping the floor. "Where did he go?"

"Why is it so important that you know?"

"Why is it such a secret that I may not?"

Zan and Hattusilis exchanged glances. Hattusilis opened his mouth to speak but Zan cut him off. "If you must know, the King has needs."

"What does he need I cannot provide?" She tossed her head and her long black braid swung back and forth.

"Why do you guard him so fiercely?" Zan set the tray down and stood in front of Hattusilis. "That is my responsibility."

"Deimos bid me care for him and that is what I shall do."

"Deimos." Zan scowled. "Did Deimos tell you to pleasure King Hattusilis as well? That is where Connal has gone, to find a woman to pleasure his King."

Both Pallin and Hattusilis gasped, but Zan blocked the view and Pallin did not hear Hattusilis. "That is absurd. He cannot...he should not...tell Connal it is impossible."

"I beg to differ." Zan ignored the strangled protest behind him. "There is proof beneath the blanket if you wish to look."

Pallin pressed her lips together, shooting a glare at Zan. Without another word, she whirled, her braid lashing like a whip, and marched out.

"What have you done?" Hattusilis tried to sit up and he regretted his outburst as his side seared with pain. Clutching his bandaged ribs, he whispered, "You have angered her."

"Made her jealous, I believe," Zan snickered.

"Neither one serves a purpose."

"Would you have her know the truth, that you plan another invasion of Najahmara?" Zan's voice was low.

"No, but such a lie will haunt me."

"From the look in her eye, it may serve you."

"How?" Hattusilis grimaced. At Zan's sly wink, Hattusilis added, "Get out. Leave me to my misery."

"I think you must eat first."

"I have no interest in food. Now, leave me."

Zan bowed and left, meeting Pallin in the corridor as she stalked back toward the tiny chamber. He chose to leave well enough alone and said nothing to her. She did not address him either, but pushed past him.

"Ahh, my King, you are in for it now." Zan chuckled as he made his way out of the temple in search of his own dinner.

Pallin threw back the curtain at the doorway and stepped in. "I will not allow more visitors this night. You are too weak. And look, you have not eaten a bite of your food."

"I am not hungry."

"You must eat, or you will become weaker." Pallin lifted a spoonful of hot, cooked grain sweetened with honey to his lips. "Eat."

Hattusilis swallowed the cereal with grudging acceptance.

"It is not so bad. And it will help you get better, better able to do as you wish." Her face stained pink.

"Pallin," Hattusilis caught her wrist. "Zan teases you. Connal has not gone seeking a woman for me."

"Well, that is good. For he would not find one here."

"You do not think he would find a woman who would bed me?"

Pallin met his gaze, dark brown, nearly as dark as Deimos. She was reminded of her own lust and her flush deepened. "I do not mean that. The women here, they do not lie with a man when bidden. They choose the time."

Pallin shook her head with sadness. "And who is left? All who are able already work and scarce have time to sleep as it is."

"I am sorry for what has happened."

"It was not your fault."

"It was. I should have stayed with my men, instead of indulging a whim."

"A whim?" Pallin tensed at the glimmer in Hattusilis' eyes.

"Nothing." Hattusilis looked away from her.

"If Connal does not seek a woman, what is he supposed to bring back?"

Hattusilis weighed his words before he spoke. "He is to bring my men."

"Your soldiers?" Pallin choked. "Why? Why do you want

them here?"

"We are strangers in a strange land. I am their king, and they need me."

"So many of them are dead."

"All the more reason for those remaining to see I am alive."

"Are you planning more violence?"

"Look at me, my dear." Hattusilis held her hand between his. "I am dependent upon you for my care, what plan could I have?"

"I do not know."

"I will not say trust me, for how can you? But I swear I will never let harm come to you or your people."

After a long pause, Pallin said, "I believe you."

"About the woman as well?"

"Yes, that, too." She smiled, embarrassed. "You could not, anyway, with your injuries."

Hattusilis' grip on her hand tightened. "I could. For the first time in a very long time, I could."

He lifted her fingers to his lips and the warmth of his breath made her quiver. Pallin withdrew her hand but touched his cheek as she did. The hair on his face was gone, shaved clean while he was in a stupor and kept that way during his recovery.

Her caress lingered on his smooth skin as Hattusilis turned his face towards her palm with eyes closed. A sound escaped, a sigh filled with longing.

"I will confess something to you, only to you." His voice was husky. "I have not been with a woman in over a year."

"Why is this a secret? If you do not want to be with someone, it is your choice. Though, I thought all men thought of nothing else."

Hattusilis chuckled. "Perhaps not all men, but for warriors, it is a sign of vitality."

"You are their king, they should not question you."

"True, but it is not so easy to be a king. I must be above all failings to lead or the men lose faith. I have hidden it, but in truth, I had no desire."

"Why?"

"Azhar, my wife. She died and my son with her. It was a great tragedy, beyond any I have ever suffered. I have not had the heart to be with another since then. Until now."

"What happened to her?" Pallin's hand drifted past his face, to touch the coarse curling brown hair above his ear. This, too, she cut, for his hair had been matted and filthy when he was brought to her.

She had sheared his locks without guilt, for he was an invader and it gave her pleasure to strip him of these badges. When he awoke, she was surprised to find he had not minded at all.

"It is a tale that shames me."

"Do not tell me, if it distresses you so very much."

He appeared youthful and defenseless, his face creased with grief at the memory of one lost. Pallin knew and her losses swelled up in response. Tears stood in her eyes as she watched him. And then, she could not help that she leaned forward and kissed him.

"Pallin."

"You wish, now, to have someone in your bed?"

"You, my beautiful one." He touched her face with his fingertips. "If you are willing."

"I do not know how it is possible." She glanced along his sheeted form. Beneath the cover there were no secrets, for she bathed Hattusilis every day. She knew his injuries would prevent lovemaking in the only way she had experienced it, the way it had been with Deimos. He had lifted her up, had lain atop her. Hattusilis could do neither.

"My innocent one, this is not the way I would chose it to be for us, but it is all I have to offer." Hattusilis threw aside the sheet to show his arousal. "Come, lay on me."

Pallin's heart beat harder at the sight of his erection. He was glorious in his manhood, but it did not disguise the many deep bruises and unhealed wounds, or the swollen discolored leg and foot splinted with bandages and wood.

"But I will hurt you."

"Some pain has value."

"I could relieve you in another way." Pallin hesitated before reaching for him.

"No." Hattusilis grabbed her hand. "Not that way. Please."

Nodding once, Pallin stepped out of her sandals and climbed up beside Hattusilis. Lifting her gown, she sat astride him, feeling his eagerness pressing against her. She helped to guide him into her.

"Owww, by the gods," Hattusilis cried as she rocked back.

Pallin froze. "I have hurt you. We must stop."

"No! No. No, do not stop. Do not stop." Hattusilis' chest heaved as his face grew slick with sweat.

"I cannot," Pallin wept.

"I swear it is good pain. Do not stop."

"It is not right."

"It is…it is right." Hattusilis tried to reach for her, to grasp her hips, to hold her in place, but he could not lift his arms. His fingers flexed, clutching at the bottom sheet and that was all he could do, for he had not the strength to even help her. He could only plead, "I beg you do not stop."

With tears tracking down her cheeks, Pallin began to move again. With each downward stroke, she felt the tension building within her. Her breath shortened and a moan tore from her lips. Soon, soon, she would burst, she could not postpone it; she would burst.

"Ahhh, Hattu…."

"Yes, that is right. It is good." Hattusilis panted between his own groans, both from pain and pleasure. Spots began to jump before his eyes and he felt his chest constrict, forcing out the air in a whoosh. In that moment, his body jerked into a hot, white arc and he spewed forth his seed into Pallin.

Convulsing, he fell back in a faint.

It was as if a hand opened and forced Pallin wide, leaving her defenseless against the raging onslaught that consumed her. She was unable to contain the shriek, though she tried to stifle it at the last. It came out a muffled squeal as she fell forward, gripping his forearms, the last waves of pleasure flowing over her like the tide sucking sand out to sea.

When the weakness subsided, Pallin stepped to the floor on shaky legs. "Hattu? Hattu, are you all right?" She patted his shoulder. There was no response in his slack features.

"Oh, mercy, I have killed you."

Snatching up a damp cloth from a basin near the bed, Pallin wiped his face, calling to him with frantic fear. "Hattu? Please, do not be dead, I cannot bear to lose another. Hattu?"

With a grunt, Hattusilis opened his eyes.

"Thank Gaea!" Pallin kissed him several times over.

Feebleness numbing his body, Hattusilis found he could not lift his hand but could still speak. "I love you."

Jahmed bit her thumbnail as she sat beside the cot, watching Inni thrash about, struggling against unseen enemies. Weeks had passed and still Inni fought demons that were no longer there. She looked at, but did not see those who took care of her. Inni screamed and cried and lashed out before collapsing back into a vacant stare, repeating the cycle over and over.

Though Jahmed called to her, tried to talk to her, it was of no avail, for Inni did not hear anything but internal voices. Her lips moved, but it was to those voices she responded and nothing else.

What could they do but keep her contained in the healing quarters, tied to the cot for fear she would fall to the floor as she had already done once? With each fit of violence, Inni's wounds would bleed again and the broken bones were jarred, sometimes needing to be reset. She seemed not to get better, only worse.

There were no more tears for Jahmed to shed. She was drained, empty, and yet still unable to accept that Inni would never change.

"There has not been enough time." Jahmed spoke through her own grief. "My love, you can come out of this. You can, you are a strong woman. You have been through worse. You will survive."

As if to answer her, Inni gave a bloodcurdling shriek before dropping into hollow-eyed silence.

"You are exhausted." Pallin stood at the doorway to the greater temple, where the wounded and dying lay.

"I cannot sleep," Jahmed agreed. "Though I am weary, it does no good to lie down."

"You, too, will become ill if you do not rest."

"I try."

"Try harder."

"Why, because if I fall sick, it will be you who takes on the burdens?"

"Jahmed!" Clicking her tongue, Pallin came into the room and offered her a plate of chopped dates and nuts rolled into balls and dipped in honey. "I made these for you."

"For me? Are you certain it was not for the one you constantly coddle?"

"I gave him some, too." Pallin grinned with impish delight. "He said they were very good."

"I think there is little you could do that would not please him. His eyes follow your every move."

Pallin gave a delicate shrug. "I hope he will soon be able to leave his bed. It would be better for him to sit up in the sunshine. How I wish the gardens had not been destroyed."

"The gardens." Jahmed plucked a sweet from the plate. "They will have to be replanted once we are no longer using the ground as hospice." She bit into it and added, "Mmm, this is good."

Pallin smiled and laid the plate to one side. Jahmed ate another, staring up at Pallin with a questioning expression. "Are you not eating any?"

"These are yours."

"That has never stopped you before. I thought these were your favorite sweet."

"Yes, but I am not hungry." Pallin turned to look at Inni, now sleeping. "There is no change?"

"No. This is just the lull before another storm. What am I to do, Pallin?" The note of panic in Jahmed's voice brought Pallin's attention back to her.

"I do not know, but we will find a way to heal her, I promise."

"If only Niala were here. Niala could reach her."

"Yes, if she were here, but she is not. Really, Jahmed, you need to rest. I will sit here with Inni tonight while you sleep."

"I cannot leave her. It is bad enough that I must attend to duty during the daylight hours, but at night I cannot leave her."

"Then lie down beside her, sleep there."

"That cot is not big enough for two."

"I assure you, it is," Pallin chuckled. "If you cannot leave her, then be with her."

"No, she is too frail." Jahmed looked with longing at the quiet figure huddled on the cot. "I will hurt her."

"Sometimes, the pain is worth it."

With much trepidation, Jahmed eased onto the cot, molding herself around Inni. One arm crept over her and Jahmed buried her face in Inni's neck. Silent sobs shook Jahmed's shoulders as Inni relaxed against her with a sigh.

Pallin pulled the sheet up over them before putting out the lamp and leaving them to sleep. There was so much yet to be done but it would wait.

Everything could wait.

TWENTY-TWO

Something stirred on the edge of Niala's memory, like a flutter of wings caught at the corner of an eye. She tried to grasp it, even spread her fingers out as if to touch it, but it filtered through as sand flows between rocks, one tiny grain at a time. Left behind was an impression, a gritty feeling, something far bigger than she.

Clenching her fists in frustration, Niala stared across the open sea. The sky was dark with a storm, the third in as many weeks. Soon, she would not be able to stand out on the courtyard.

The wind already blew in a furious attempt to sweep her over the edge and toss her down onto the boulders below the massive building. Niala clutched her cloak and peered over the side at the sheer dizzying drop to the sea.

She could scarce believe she would have ever thrown herself over the side. It was too foolish to contemplate.

She did not believe him.

So many things Ares said were improbable, if not impossible. She simply could not take him at his word, and yet he was unrelenting, much to her frustration. He wanted her to remember and, though he said her memories would return in time, there was always that guarded expression in his eyes that spoke louder than his words.

Perhaps she would never know the truth of his tales.

Exhaling into the cold air, Niala watched as her breath puffed out and then dissipated. Turning, Niala paced to the narrow walkway that exited off the courtyard and circled the fortress.

Following the rickety wooden rail, she went to the other side to stare at the high wall of white-capped mountain peaks.

They stuck up like jagged teeth ready to rip into the purplish sky, making a route through impassable, or so she had been informed. There was only one way up and one way down.

Another quarter turn and she could see the beaten path to Ares' doorway. She watched caravans arrive with herds in tow and loud, cursing warriors who quarreled over who would be the first to enter Ares' sacred domain.

They appeared over the rise, made their way down a steep incline and disappeared somewhere under the fortress. She could still hear them when the wind was right, but could no longer see them once they had passed beneath the curved edge of a lower roof.

Niala had vague recollections of a filthy drafty room filled with smoke and the scent of burnt meat and fermented drink. Even thinking of it made her stomach lurch. She swallowed repeatedly to dislodge the taste of flesh that she had no recollection of eating. As the wind picked up, she could smell the scent of animal droppings and human waste.

And worse, death.

Gagging, Niala continued her way around the castle, returning to the courtyard where she had begun. The wind strong, but clean, smelled of saltwater and moss as the waves crashed against the filtering stone at the foot of the mountain. Though she was cold, Niala waited for the storm to come in, leaning against the low wall as if she could sail off the edge into the currents and fly.

When the storm broke, she was pelted with snow. Stinging hard dots of white stuck to her clothing, her hair, even her eyebrows and lashes. Her teeth began to chatter, her fingers and toes numb before she retreated into the chambers.

The wind chased her inside, blowing fiercely, lifting her skirt and hair with playful twists while the white clots covered the floor and the bed coverings. She struggled to close the huge doors as the storm increased in strength and was all but exhausted when she felt them swing shut without effort.

She was afraid to see who helped her, for if it was Ares, he would be livid. She was forbidden the courtyard, and most certainly the dangerous walkway, for the same reason she was not allowed to roam his fortress - Ares did not trust her.

If his claim of her attempted self-destruction was true, then his distrust was well-deserved yet it did not make her feel better.

Turning, with an excuse on the tip of her tongue, Niala was surprised to see not Ares, but a young man who very much resembled him. He was wide of shoulder and long of leg, just as Ares.

His face was as beautiful, but his black hair was cropped short and he wore no beard. The same black eyes watched her from arching brows drawn together in concern. As she studied his face, he appeared to study hers as well. It was then she realized she knew him.

But not his name.

Niala could not pull his name from the depths of her memory, no matter how hard she tried.

"You must be more careful, Niala, one misstep and you would fall to your death. The ice and snow make the walk slippery. My father would be quite unhappy if he were to return and find you broken upon the rocks or frozen to the walkway."

The timbre of his voice also rang true to Ares' deep tones, but the weariness that laced Ares words was missing.

As the youth took her elbow and guided her toward the fire, he smiled. A pair of dimples creased his cheeks and made him seem all the more unassuming in the wake of War.

"Do you suppose, beneath the hair on Ares' face, there hides a set of such pretty dimples?" Niala asked, staring at the young man.

Though he chuckled, he answered with all seriousness. "Yes, I think it is quite possible, but I have never seen Ares without the benefit of a beard."

"Perhaps that is why he wears it."

"Perhaps. Keep in mind while his face might be handsome, pretty is not his way. Though I should not have to tell you that."

"No." Niala knelt on a cushion before the hearth. "And yet...."

She stopped, unable to speak her thoughts. Ares was not one to inspire tenderness, yet her heart ached for the burdens he carried. Inexplicably, she found she cared for him.

"And yet?" The youth sat down.

"He does not imprison me in a tiny cell or force me to fend for myself against those who inhabit this fortress. He has been kind to me."

It did not escape Niala's attention that the youth bypassed the large chair favored by Ares and chose, instead, the one on the opposite side of the hearth.

She noticed he kept his gaze from wandering the bedchamber, instead, focused on her as he bent forward. Niala listened to the timbre of his voice when he spoke, trying to connect a name to this dark winsome man who seemed to know her well.

"Kind? Niala, you jest."

Something edged closer. A vague remembrance of another time, another place. Niala heard a rhythmic pounding in her head, singing or humming, but she could not make it out. She sensed it, though it was from a shadowed and smoky place.

Smoke that smelled of spices, of bodies pressed together, chanting, drumming. She did not realize her eyes were closed until they flew open again to meet his worried gaze. She remembered him, but from a distant story being told somewhere else.

"Niala? What is it? What is wrong with you?"

"I cannot remember your name."

"You cannot remember?" With abrupt and jarring motion, he stood, his forehead creased with a frown. "That is strange. What else do you not recall?"

Niala pressed her fingertips to her temples; her head had begun to ache again. "I do not know. So many things. Everything."

"Everything? How? How did this happen?" The young man pressed his lips together in a tight line. "Did he cause it?"

"Who?"

"Ares. Did he force this loss on you somehow? Some new treachery I am not aware of, some new torture he has devised to satisfy his hunger?"

With angry eyes flashing, the young man paced away from the hearth to the center of the chamber and back again.

"I can only tell you the little I recall. I was locked within darkness and it seemed I floated in the air. Golden ropes crisscrossed my body and tightened if I moved."

"Stasis." Deimos' jaw clenched. "It is a way of binding your spirit without placing real bonds upon your body. It causes you to sleep in peace, with no care as to what goes on around you. Even so, that should not have caused memory loss."

"Perhaps it was when I freed myself from those ropes." Niala could not help the slight smile. "I think Ares was greatly surprised because of it. And driven to anger, of course."

"Of that, I am certain. Anger is a perpetual thing with Ares. It is like saying the sun shines."

"Please, your name?"

He returned and sat beside her on another cushion. "I am Deimos."

"We know each other?"

"Yes."

There was an understated plea for Niala to remember him and when he could see she did not, a shadow of unexplained pain fell over him. There and gone again so fast she was not certain she saw it. She could not take her gaze from his face, seeing there some new piece of her past.

Reaching out, Niala was compelled to run her fingertip along his cheekbone and down to dip into the crease, and then stop at his jaw. His head turned ever so to the side, as if he would press his lips against her palm.

A shudder of longing passed through Deimos at her touch. He wanted nothing more than to take Niala in his arms and press her to his heart. To whisper that everything would be fine and he would take care of her. He knew in that instance he loved her, that he had loved her since first laying eyes upon her. But Niala Aaminah belonged to Ares and was forbidden territory.

Deimos took her hand in his, drawing her fingers away from his face. "Why did Ares put you into this sleep?"

"I am not certain." Niala's pulled her palm free from his, though she did not want to let go of his warmth. He, too, seemed reluctant to release her and yet, he did. She laced her fingers with her other hand, clenching them until her knuckles were pale.

"She threw herself over the railing and that is why she is not allowed outside." Eris appeared next to them, a curious gaze taking in their close proximity.

Deimos leaned away from Niala and scowled at his brother. "What are you doing here? Go away."

"I am to watch over her."

"If that is so, why was she outside when Ares demands that she stay within these walls?"

With a sly smile, Eris shrugged. "She asked, and why not? She has very little pleasure here."

"Why would you do that? Do you want to see her fall to her death?"

Eris bent and whispered in Deimos' ear, "Father says she will not die, she is of the immortal caste."

At Deimos' sudden intake of air, Eris stood straight and winked at Niala. "She seemed so sad, I could not bear it. I, too, dislike being locked within these dismal walls. You will not tell, will you?"

Deimos did not reply. He could not. He could only stare at Niala and wonder if there was truth to Eris' tale or if he made it up to keep from trouble.

"What is it? Why do you look at me with such strangeness?" Niala rose to her feet. "Ares will not say why I would do such a thing, but you know, do you not? You both know."

"To wake up here would be enough for most," Eris muttered.

Deimos, too, stood up while waving the boy away. "There were circumstances that most likely led to your actions."

"What? What is it no one wants to tell me? Was I so despicable that death should be my reward?"

"Death that you cannot have," Eris sang out, dodging an elbow aimed at his head. "But oh, so many others can."

"What does he mean?" Niala's eyes were wide and filled with indescribable torment as another hint of the past played out in her mind.

"Eris, leave us now."

"I am her servant, I must be within her call."

"Leave. Now."

The boy pouted, lingering for another moment then, with a huge sacrificing sigh that echoed a bit of relief, Eris disappeared.

"You believed that death was your only relief." Deimos hesitated, wanting to offer comfort. He wanted to tell Niala about Najahmara and her role within the tight knot of priestesses, but then he would have to tell of the horror that came after and that he could not do.

"Niala, you were mad with grief. There was an invasion and many people you loved were killed. I have no doubt you wanted only to join them."

"And now, I cannot even recall their names." Her voice swelled with bitterness. "Though I feel their presence all about me, begging me to help them, and I am incapable of offering comfort. And worse, I am held prisoner here, without relief, without company. You are the first I have seen, other than the green one who brings me food."

Niala moved closer to the heat, hugging herself. "Sometimes I wake during the night and Ares is lying beside me. Asleep? Contemplating his battles? I do not know.

Her voice caught and she thought herself more the fool for spilling her distress, nevertheless, she could not stop. "He does not touch me, though I know he desires me. I feel his lust, I see it in his eyes, the way he watches me, but he does not."

"Is that what you want? Him? Do you want him?"

Niala lifted her shoulders and avoided Deimos' gaze. There was an odd twist to his tone and Niala felt a tingling on the back of her neck. Niala shuddered as a wave of inexplicable fear washed over her.

It emanated from Deimos, flowing around her, then was gone almost as fast as it had appeared. Was it a threat? A warning? Or more nonsense, for it seemed that was the rule of order at Athos.

Niala hesitated, biting her lips. There was no way to explain the babble of sentiments that swarmed inside her, or the desires that haunted her dreams. How many times had she awakened, drenched in sweat, moaning with pleasures that were not real? How many times did she feel his hands as he caressed her, driving her mad with desire, only to open her eyes to find herself alone?

"Sometimes. I am lonely and he is my only consolation."

"You do not mean that. Or do you?" Deimos raised one hand as if to push away an image.

Niala took a deep breath. "You cannot comprehend my misery. I know not how long I have been here. I cannot even count the passing of time, for I sleep so much that day and night have become confused.

"And when I am awake, I stand out on the walkway and look at the hills, longing to set my feet upon them. Without knowing why, I am desperate to let the earth run through my fingers, to touch trees and grass. I do not know who I am, or from where I came, or why I am here. Is it any wonder that I might turn to him for comfort?"

"Forgive me, Niala." Deimos bowed his head, staring down at the floor. "It is none of my concern."

"I am tired of secrets. You ask because you want to know and for that there is a reason. You are not the only one who questions me, and why? No one will say. Every word is cloaked in mystery and I am left to wonder what it is all about."

As Deimos opened his mouth to reply, Niala held up one hand.

"No, do not say you are sorry. If you must speak, tell me something that will help. Who am I? Why am I here? Ares would have me believe I have been here most of my life, but I know it is not true. He presses me over and over to accept my role as an immortal, to become a deity to the human realm as I am destined to be.

"And if that is not enough, he talks of a time so far past that few even know of it. He talks of mortals named Ilya and Anyal, and how we once were them. How those lives led to this existence, but I cannot grasp his meaning. I do not know what it is he demands of me and then he grows angry. His punishment is to leave me here alone, and not allow me beyond these chambers.

"I find myself thinking of ways to appease him, to make him stay with me. I grow distraught when he is gone, though I swear I will not, and I am ever more happy to see him when he returns. I crave his attention, and more and more, I wish for his embrace. Perhaps for any embrace. Just to be touched, to have arms around me."

Niala's expression was filled with such loneliness, Deimos' very soul ached for her. "If I could help, I would."

"No. There is naught you can do." Niala slumped with resignation, too weary to defend her thoughts. Staring into the flames, she ignored the hand he placed on her shoulder.

"And he, he withholds affection to punish me because I cannot be what he wants. He will not even partake of a meal, but makes me eat alone while he watches. I can scarce bear another minute of it. Since Thaleia has gone, I am desolate."

"I would share a meal with you. I would share anything with you." Deimos could not help the words. Held within them was all the pain of his longing, all his love.

With lips parted, Niala drifted toward him as if in a trance. Eyes closed, she reached for him. She felt his desire vibrating, calling her into his arms. It was what she wanted - to be loved.

Deimos ran his fingers along her shoulders, to her back and around her body. Their lips touched in a gentle kiss before Deimos jerked away.

"No. No, we cannot."

"Why? Why can you not offer me the comfort Ares denies?"

"You belong to him." Jaw clenched, Deimos stared into her eyes, wishing he dared to go further but feared the punishment would not be his, but Niala's were Ares to find out.

"I belong to no one." Niala broke their gaze and moved in front of the fire, rubbing her palms up and down her arms to dispel the sudden chill that shook her body.

"You are right, and yet we are under his command. We dare not do something that would endanger either of us."

Deimos took her arm and led her from the bedchamber to the main room where the oblong table in the corner was now crowded with food. "Since there is little else I can do, we can, at least, take pleasure in a feast."

Niala offered Deimos a wan smile, grateful that he did not flee Athos. Instead, he chose to offer some small bit of cheer. She sat in the chair Deimos held out for her, staring at the festival of foods before her.

"I have never seen a finer banquet." Niala's eyes grew wide at the multitude of dishes. The fare Ares supplied was always simple hard bread, nuts, cheese, and grapes. The food spread before her was a delight of tantalizing scents and sights.

Juicy rich fruits in never before imagined colors. Tart roots and rice wrapped in green leaves, smoked fish, soft cheeses that melted in her mouth with the never-ending rounds of hot bread laden with fine honey.

Instead of the usual water, Deimos offered her dark red wine, first sharp to her tongue, then smooth as she grew accustomed to it. Deimos, too, drank the wine and indulged, just as he said he would.

"You do not mind the…umm…results?" Niala gestured at the still food-laden table.

"Not as much as some." Deimos could not help but laugh. "I have been trained to go with no sustenance because my father believes it to be a compulsion. The more you have of food and drink, the more you will seek it out."

"I am told you do not need it to survive."

"No, it is an indulgence. There are those among us in the immortal realm who spend all their time on this pleasure. They weaken and lose power."

"And then what?"

"And then, they forget who they are and what they are."

Deimos swallowed a sip of wine and wiped his mouth with the back of his hand. "They become servants."

"Servants to whom?"

"To their desires. They no longer control; they are controlled. And that allows for much evil in the world."

Niala frowned. "I do not understand."

"It is hard to explain." He pointed at himself. "We have a symbiotic relationship with the mortal realm. This relationship is in constant flux. As mortals gain insight, so do we. As we garner courage, so do they. What happens here." He held up one cupped palm. "Must balance there."

Deimos held up his other hand, also cupped. "If we fall prey to our weaknesses, mortals grow weak as well. My race was created to hold the patterns of the mortal world, to keep them from distortion, but we are, after all, living beings."

"And mortals?"

Unblinking, Deimos inspected the food before him as if the answer he sought was somewhere within the blend of textures and tastes. "Another story altogether."

He hesitated. "You spoke of Ilya and Anyal."

"Yes. Ilya and Anyal, and another. Elche." Niala could not keep the quiver from her voice. "I have tried to make sense of what Ares says, but always, I am confused. Not even Thaleia could explain."

"Thaleia? You did not talk of this to Thaleia."

"The green one said to ask her, that Thaleia would know."

"Eris told you to ask Thaleia?"

"He saw I was distressed. He was only making an effort to assist me." Niala's hands fluttered above the table. "I did not mean any harm."

"No, of course not." Capturing one of her hands, he squeezed her fingers. "What did Thaleia say?"

"Well, she seemed very surprised and, I think, upset by it. She said to pay no attention to Ares' tales for he made them up to suit himself."

"Did she say why he might do that?"

Niala shook her head. "Just that he did such things when the mood struck him and that I should not concern myself with it. I told her there was something about the story that rang true and since then, I have not seen Thaleia. I am afraid I offended her in some way."

"You did not offend her." Deimos released Niala's fingers. "She was called away, back to her home on Cos. She had to depart with no time to bid you farewell."

"Are you certain it was not this story of Ilya and Anyal that made her leave so swiftly?" Deimos knew the truth. Niala saw it written on his face and in the way he avoided her gaze.

"I feel there is much beneath the surface, much that must be revealed. Please, Deimos, tell me what you know."

"Niala, if you could bring back your memory, these past events would not be such a mystery. You would understand and I would not have to explain, but I owe you at least this much."

Niala watched his long fingers crumble bread between them in an absent gesture as she waited for him to continue.

With a heavy exhale, Deimos began the story. "I must first explain what happened before the mortal race was conceived, so you will better understand their roles. First, there was Chaos."

Deimos spread his hands wide. "A vast pool of elemental energy that desired form. From this mire sprang Earth and Sky, Night and Day, Sun and Moon, Wind and Water and Fire and many others."

He nodded, deep in thought. "Many others, but we are concerned with Earth. Gaea is the ground beneath our feet, the soil; she is Fertility, the egg from which life springs. Kulika is the sky above us."

Deimos glanced up at Niala and saw Niala's forehead crease at the mention of Kulika. Hoping to hear more, she did not stop him.

"Kulika is Proliferation, the seed of life. At creation, the Blue Serpent coiled around the Abundant Green Earth. Together they brought forth the seas, the mountains and the vast plains, and all the creatures that abound there.

"Kulika brought fecund growth to Earth, thus Gaea turned lush and green, and was pleased. They birthed Uranus, the Starry Sky, who was to surround Earth at night while Kulika and Gaea made love."

Deimos drained his mug of wine and poured out more, offering the flask to Niala.

Niala held out her mug to be refilled. "Where, in all of this, do Ilya and Anyal fit in?"

"Patience." Deimos smiled. "Now, Uranus watched over Kulika and Gaea, but instead of remaining their protector, he became jealous of his father and amorous of his mother.

"Ultimately, Uranus usurped Kulika's place and became Gaea's lover, and from them came the first race of immortals, giants called the Titans. Of the Titans, Chronos and Rhea gave birth to my grandparents."

He waved his hand in a dismissive gesture. "Those are stories for another time. Let us go back to Uranus and Gaea. Uranus was created to be truly magnificent and given great power, power that kept Kulika at bay. But this did not stop Gaea from longing for Kulika. Uranus, ever watchful, sought to block any attempt they made to be together."

"How very cruel, to keep two lovers apart in such a manner." Niala sipped the wine and coughed as the bold flavor hit her tongue and went down her throat.

Deimos gave a hearty laugh of good humor. "With each drink, you will grow accustomed to the taste."

Patting her lips with a piece of cloth, Niala returned his smile. "Perhaps. Please continue the story."

"Gaea saw the form the giants took. She watched as their bodies moved about on two legs and feet, with strong trunks, arms and shoulders, hands to touch and faces that shone with beauty.

"She desired form very much, for though she is the Spirit of Earth, she is without body. She is everywhere and she is nowhere. She could not walk or speak or touch or smile. She could not make love in the way she saw her children and this she yearned for."

Pausing, Deimos dipped baked dough filled with chopped dates and nuts into a pool of honey and bit into it. Mouth full, he mumbled, "This is my favorite of all things."

Niala could not take her gaze from a dribble of honey running down his chin. Her breath caught as Deimos swiped a finger across the droplet and sucked at the stickiness, enjoying even that tiny amount with sensuous delight before continuing his tale.

"Gaea approached her children to ask them to share their bodies with her, so that she could be like them. Not at all times, mind you, for she was what she was, but sometimes, when the desire struck. She wanted to enter one of them, to feel, to smell, to touch, to make love with one of their bodies. She also wanted Kulika to enter form to be with her. With such an arrangement,

Uranus would not suspect they were together."

Licking his fingers clean, Deimos drank more wine. He was enjoying the moment, all caution having fled.

"The Titans were appalled at the suggestion and whispered amongst themselves that Gaea and Kulika planned to overtake them. The Titans feared they would wind up banished back into the Netherland of spirit without form.

"As a whole, they refused. Gaea was furious but she could not force them to accept her request. Instead, she decided to create another race, one that would be made up of the elements and, in the end, would return to the elemental state.

"She formed a body from mud, taken from her very bosom - one solid body with two heads, four arms, and four legs, already joined together, a being that Uranus could not tear asunder. The wind gave it breath, water gave it blood, and fire fused it into flesh. She and Kulika eagerly inhabited this body, but at their first attempt to unite as a couple, it did not work as well as she had hoped."

Deimos paused his story to watch Niala take a delicate bite of a sugared date. Her tongue caught the flakes stuck to her upper lip as her eyes closed in delight. Next, she reached for a slice of bread and butter, consuming it with slow appreciation.

"You were saying?" Niala touched his hand.

"Do you want to hear more?"

"Yes."

That one word, spoken so sincerely, brought Deimos to an aroused state. He could scarce speak but pressed on.

"The body was awkward and inanimate. They could not make love to each other. Frustrated, she searched the Netherland for two spirits who would join together and descend into the body she had created. Gaea wanted them to bring life to the form, and once it breathed, accommodate herself and Kulika whenever they requested."

Deimos paused again as Niala brushed crumbs from her gown causing the fabric to mold to her breasts. One hand lingered as their gaze caught and held, until Niala looked away.

"These two, Gaea and Kulika, wanted each other very much, it would seem."

"Yes. Do their names sound familiar to you?"

"No." She took a spoonful of honey to spread on a second

piece of bread.

"And the honey?" Deimos watched for signs that Niala recalled the ritual within the cave but there was not a single flicker within her amber gaze.

"It is very good."

"Yes, it is." Deimos nodded and went back to finish his story.

"There were two who volunteered. Why would spirit do such a thing? There are many reasons offered, but I believe it was curiosity. These two joined and descended into this one body, giving it life, but it was still awkward and not at all what Gaea wanted. In a fit of pique, she split them in half and they became male and female. Gaea called them Anyal and Ilya, First Man and First Woman."

"He believes me to be Ilya, this First Woman?" Wiping her hands clean of her meal, Niala spoke in a tone of pure disbelief.

"Who you once were," Deimos corrected. "And there is more to this tale. Another task was given to Anyal and Ilya, and that was to birth the mortal race. As the tale goes, there were no children born to Ilya, though they tried for a very long time.

"In the end, a grief stricken Ilya fled into the wilderness leaving Anyal alone. Gaea refused defeat and brought forth another female from Anyal and called her Elche, Second Woman, and Elche became the mother that Ilya could not.

"And then Ilya returned, out of love, out of guilt or desire, no one can be certain, but when she discovered that Elche had replaced her and that Elche had borne the children meant for Ilya to have, Ilya became very angry. She felt had been betrayed, not only by her mate but by her creator." ⌐ she

Niala pressed fingers to her temples. "Even if I had been this Ilya, this ancient creature made of mud - and I do not accept this as truth - why does that concern Ares now?"

"You were all spirits drawn from the chaotic darkness and thrust into physical form to satisfy Gaea's desires. Even so, it was a temporary state as those bodies made from the elements could only exist a short time. Short from an immortal standpoint, that is.

"From a mortal view, it was hundreds of years before their bodies began to deteriorate, and when they did, death took each one. As a gift for servicing her needs, Gaea made it possible for these three spirits to incarnate once again, but this time, they could become one of the immortals and choose the role they would fulfill.

"Gaea thought this an appropriate reward and was pleased that Elche and Anyal accepted. Elche is now Aphrodite, to bring balance and harmony in her role as Immortal Love. Anyal chose to become Eternal War - Ares, the Destroyer, he who causes upheaval and pain."

Niala stared at the flames leaping within the boundary of the stone hearth. The scent of burning wood was pleasant and the warmth comforting and for a scant moment, Niala could fool herself into the belief all was well.

"It is a strange tale you tell, Deimos, and yet, still, I do not understand. Let us say that it is all true and that I am, indeed, this Ilya. Why, in the end, does it matter?" She waved toward the darkened recesses of the chamber, her vision caught between light and shadow. "Why am I a prisoner?"

"Less a prisoner and more one who is protected." Deimos spoke with great care. "There are things that occurred in recent memory and the root cause for your presence here at Athos. While it seems cruel, it is Ares way of safeguarding you against danger."

"What danger? What is so terrible I would be kept in this cold barren monstrosity without companionship, without...." Niala stopped and stared at Deimos, her breath catching in her throat. "Without love?"

In that moment, Deimos wanted to show Niala how much he cared. He wanted to stroke her smooth skin, to kiss every bit of her body, to make love, to show her how full his heart was with his desire. Instead, he looked away from her searching gaze.

"Ares does love you. In his own way which is most often mysterious and draining. He does not communicate his feelings - I dare to say he does not know how. His chosen lot in life is one of brutal punishment and is not conducive to large expressions of affections."

"Is it possible I am doomed to be here forever?" Rising from her spot before the hearth, Niala stood before a shuttered window. "Never to see beauty again? Never to know what lies beyond these stone walls? Never to know compassion, never to be surrounded by those whom I love and who love me? All I have to look forward to is isolation, silence, coldness?"

With the suddenness of a surprise winter storm overtaking unsuspecting travelers, freezing them in their tracks, Niala was overtaken by images of blood spilled, shrieks of agony and the roar of an annilating fire.

A sheen of sweat dampened her skin as she went glassy-eyed and stared off into a distant place only she could see. Her lips moved but what she said was lost to Deimos even though he rose to stand beside her. When he touched her shoulder, she shrieked and struck out at him.

"Niala, Niala, please."

With a little gasp, she sagged into his arms, her lids fluttering as the whites of her eyes rolled upward. Deimos held her against his chest, feeling her heart beat next to his own. Longing once again settled across his shoulders and he placed a kiss on her forehead. He could not help the wish that she would stay in his arms with a willingness brought on by ignited passion.

A tremor shook her body. Deimos found a fur to wrap around her, and led her back to the cushions before the hearth. When he felt the coldness of her flesh, he folded her icy fingers into his own warm hands and pressed her palms to his lips. When she moaned, he put his arms around her and held her until she could gain focus.

"What horror has befallen me that I would see so many lives lost?" Niala twisted her hands into the fur, drawing it to her chin. "I see so much pain and death, over and over. Fire burning flesh, charring bone. I hear shrieks of agony. What manner of a beast did this? And to whom? Did I know them? Are they my tribe?"

Tears ran down Niala's face and dripped from her chin to her heaving breast with no motion from her to blot them away. Deimos' heart ached when he saw her confused expression, yet there was nothing he could say that would ease the sorrow, except the truth.

"Yes, they were your tribe."

"Are they dead? All dead?"

Deimos ran fingers through his own tangled black locks and gave a sharp pull just as a reminder it was not his place to console her, nor was it his place to explain. He had done enough harm for one day.

"I only wished to give you comfort." His voice was filled with remorse. "And I have added to your misery."

Niala released the fur and took hold of his shirt front in an iron grip. "Do you know where they are? Do you know where my people are? Take me to them, please. I beg you. Take me home."

Deimos' gaze rose to the hooks above the mantel, to the resting place of Amason. The sword was not there, which meant Ares and Amason were on a bloody rampage and at the mercy of whatever vengeance the mortal world had created. That he, Deimos, had not been called to partake of this battle was curious.

And temporary.

Ares would soon return.

"I cannot." Deimos smoothed curls away from Niala's wet face, reveling in the touch to her cheek. "You must first heal the wounds, both seen and unseen, before you can right any wrongs that may have happened. You must rest and become whole again."

"And then? Then will you return me to my people?"

"Ahh, my love." This time Deimos did not hesitate. He kissed her sweet lips, tasting the salt of her tears mixed with a hint of the honey she had consumed.

As his mouth moved over hers, he realized he held his breath in fear that the moment would be stolen away, that Ares would appear and they would both suffer his fury. Or worse, Niala would reject him, push him away and say she did not love him. Yet Deimos could not stop.

Did not want to stop.

Would not stop.

His kisses became more demanding and Niala returned them with a hunger beyond physical sustenance. The confusion, the loneliness, the unexplained sorrow that tore at her heart all melted away within Deimos' embrace.

The feel of his mouth upon her flesh made her blood pound. The touch of his hands moving along her curves as he tenderly sought her most intimate places made her shudder with pent up desire.

Niala could scarce breath as Deimos lifted her and brought her to his lap, without their lips parting from each other. Her arms went about his neck, her fingers dug into his shoulders as her body strained forward. The clean scent of eucalyptus wafted from his skin as he pushed her gown up and loosened his trousers.

She bit at his lips and chin, sucked at his throat, tracing her tongue down to his chest until he brought her face up to greet his insistent mouth. His member found her wetness and entered without delay. Niala moaned and pressed harder against him until Deimos lay her down on the fur spread upon the floor. There, he could satisfy the depths of her passion. He could give her everything, his body, his heart, his soul.

And Niala accepted all of him.

They both knew it was wrong to join together, but neither could pause their lovemaking long enough for reason to surface. They knew Ares the Destroyer might well kill each of them for this transgression, but they did not care.

In that moment, nothing else mattered.

Whatever was to befall them could wait.

For the first time, Deimos was in love and freely rejoiced in the physical expression of his heart.

For the first time in the stark existence she had awakened, Niala felt alive.

Epilogue

There was little choice for those who survived the raging fires that destroyed Najahmara but to go forward. With hollow empty eyes, the people began to rally, to find loved ones buried beneath the charred wreckage, and return the dead to their beloved Gaea. The few healers left tended to the injured. Every view haunted the survivors as the smoke continued to waft from the ruins, reminding them of their loss. Yet they took up the task at hand with great fortitude.

Slowly but surely, the legion of men who had scattered in terror began to gather on the edge of the forest. The women who trailed the army caught up to the remaining legion and made camp. They existed for a short time within this limbo, lost and confused, until receiving word that their king had endured. By then the provisions were depleted and they had nowhere else to go except into Najahmara.

In the following months, soldiers worked side by side with the good folk of Najahmara to clear the rubble and rebuild the village. There was much distrust amongst both sides, for neither understood the truth of what had taken place, all the while life went on and a temporary peace was established.

Deimos did not return to Najahmara, nor did he speak of this mortal valley to Niala Aaminah. Upon Ares' return to Athos, Deimos was banished from Niala's company. Though he did not believe his father knew the truth of their liaison, he agreed for Niala's sake, and left his broken heart to mend on its own.

Aphrodite continued to press for a daughter, drawing Ares' attention further away from Athos. Niala was once again left alone in the gray fortress upon a cliff above a raging sea to contemplate the mystery of her life.

IMMORTAL FOLK

NAME:	ROLE:
Aglaia	Love's Brilliance/Dismay, Middle Grace,
Aglauros	Mother of Eris, Wood Nymph
Anteros	Love's Response/Manipulation, Deimos' twin
Aphrodite	Eternal Love/Hatred, Wife to Ares, and briefly, Hephaestos,
Ares	Endless War/Creator, Husband to Aphrodite, lover to Niala,
Cedalion	Mountain Dwarf, loyal servant to Hephaestos
Corvidae	Raven Spirit Guide
Chronos	Titan, father of Zeus
Deimos	War's Terror/Survival, Son of Ares & Aphrodite, Anteros' twin
Delphinus	Dolphin Spirit Guide
Enyo	War's Disgrace/Pride, Eater of souls (female)
Eris	War's Strife/Peace, Son of Ares & Aglauros
Erinnyes	War's Punishment/Reward, Ares' minions (androgynous)
Eros	Love's Passion/Fury, Son of Ares & Aphrodite, twin to Phobos
Euphrosyne	Love's Rejoice/Grief, Youngest Grace
Gaea	Immortal Earth/Abundance, Mother of All, mate to Kulika
Hephaestos	Alchemy/Separation, Second Husband to Aphrodite
Hera	Queen of the Immortals, Ares' mother
Hermes	Communication/Silence, Zeus' messenger
Keres	War's Penalty/Return, Ares' minions (androgynous)
Kulika	Immortal Sky/Proliferation, Blue serpent, mate to Gaea
Nemesis	Love's Revenge/Forgiveness
Odyne	Love's Pain/Balm
Oizus	Love's Misery/Joy
Phobos	War's Panic/Surrender, Son of Ares & Aphrodite, twin to Eros
Rhea	Titan, Mother of Zeus
Synod	Winged horse in service to the Immortals
Thaleia	Love's Bloom/Decay, Middle Grace, (female)
Zelos	Love's Jealousy/Truth (female)
Zelus	Love's Rivalry/Friend
Zeus	King of the Immortals, Ares' father.

MORTAL FOLK

NAME:	ROLE:
Ajah	Sixteen year old girl, Priestess in training
Anyal	First Man in ancient story of creation
Azhar	Hattusilis' first wife
Benor	Trader from the Steppelands
Connal	Zan's brother, soldier in arms
Deniz	Twelve year old girl, priestess in training
Edibe	Helped rescue Niala from Athos, founded Najahmara
Elche	Second Woman in ancient story of creation,
Hattusilis	King of the Steppeland invaders
Ilya	First Woman in ancient story of creation
Inni	Third Priestess of Gaea
Jahmed	Second Priestess of Gaea
Laida	Sixteen year old girl, Priestess in training
Layla	Rescued Niala from Athos/Niala's lover, founded Najahmara
Mahin	Rescued Niala from Athos, founded Najahmara
Niala Aaminah	First Priestess of Gaea – Ares' obsession
Pallin	Fourth Priestess of Gaea
Seire	Fifth Priestess of Gaea, Niala's daughter
Seyyal	Helped rescue Niala from Athos, founded Najahmara
Telio	Nephew of Hattusilis, invader from Steppelands
Tulane	Fourteen year old girl, priestess in training
Warsus	Slayer of Niala's original tribe
Zahava	Teacher/Healer, term of respect
Zan	Second in command, invader from Steppelands

LOCATIONS

ANKIRA: City in the Steppelands from which Hattusilis and legions began their journey. (Mortal Realm)

ATHOS: Mountain home of Ares the Destroyer, a gray fortress located in Thrace. (Mortal Realm)

COS: Island home of Aphrodite, a beautiful, sunny isle located in the South Aegean Sea. (Mortal Realm)

ELLOPIA: Homeland of Eris, the Sacred Forest of the Sylphs (Mortal Realm)

LEMNOS: Island home of Hephaestos, a green, verdant isle located in the North Aegean Sea. (Mortal Realm)

NAJAHMARA: A village nestled between the Bayuk and Maendre rivers located in south Cappadocia. Founded by Niala Aaminah and her four companions. (Mortal Realm)

NETHERLAND: Where evolved Spirit Beings reside. (Immortal Realm)

OLYMPUS: Home of the Council, a golden city with Zeus and Hera reigning as king and queen. (Immortal Realm)

SHADOWLAND: Where spirits of the dead reside. (Immortal Realm)

STEPPELANDS: Far northern reaches of Cappadocia. (Mortal Realm.)

MAP OF THE KNOWN WORLD

ABOUT THE AUTHOR

Ruth Souther has written three Mythic Fantasy novels *(Immortal Journey series*) and an intuitive instructional book on Tarot (*The Heart of Tarot*) all available through Amazon. She lives in Illinois and is happily married to a wonderful man. They have four amazing children, along with their spouses, grandchildren and great-grandchildren. Life is good.

Facebook: Immortal Journey Book Series

www.ruthsouther.com

www.astarsjourney.com

AND NOW FOR A
SNEAK PEEK AT

SURRENDER
OF EGO

VOLUME TWO
OF THE
IMMORTAL JOURNEY
SERIES

ONE

King Hattusilis watched dawn creep into the simple bedchamber by way of shadows on the ceiling. He managed little sleep during the night and as the patterns of murky gray crawled across the wooden beams, he was further reminded of the destruction outside the walls of his residence.

As if he needed prompting to recall how terribly wrong the invasion of Najahmara had gone. The once glorious campaign led in the name of Hattusilis' deceased wife, Azhar, ended in a bitter setback: in a blind panic, he went into the unlit caverns high upon the ridge and fell prey to an unseen enemy.

His legs were crushed beneath a stone urn, one foot nearly torn off, the bones broken in both ankles, one knee destroyed, and all the flesh bruised and swollen. The pain was maddening and still, after seven months, he could scarce walk on his own.

The incursion to Najahmara was supposed to bring wealth and position after he and his legions of soldiers conquered the fabled Najahmara. Hattusilis snorted in derision. Benor the Trader had said the streets were paved with gold and the lush valley was ruled by a beautiful queen just waiting for her king to come along.

Lies, all of it.

What waited for them was a monster that spit fire, one who killed everything in the path of its fierce flames without discretion. Soldiers and natives burned to death in tandem – those who were fortunate, for the others suffered a hideous demise – torn to bits by the same creature.

Hattusilis shifted in restless agitation as the guilt once again built inside his chest. The stories of the beast were just that, stories, for he had witnessed none of it. He had been caught up in what seemed to be a wondrous adventure, a ritual that brought him into the presence of the earth mother Gaea. He had been delirious with joy, unaware of that his nephew, Telio, thought he had been stolen away.

Telio began the brutal attack on Najahmara to find him. Which, of course, suited Telio's bloodlust. No one need deny that was the underlying reason Telio took command.

Hattusilis shifted again and gasped as the pain in his left leg shot from his toes all the way to his hip.

Much to his frustration, he needed a crutch to support his dragging leg when he attempted to walk. The simplest tasks took great concentration. When Hattusilis coughed, dull pain pressed inside his chest and he could not yet take a full breath. Though his injuries were healing, it was too slow.

Gripping the blankets between his clammy fingers, he eased onto his back, eyes closed, taking care that he did not disturb his wife, Pallin, who lay next to him.

Did he deserve such punishment for the carnage of a peaceful valley and her people? For the souls of his own men who trusted him?

Before he knew it, Hattusilis dozed and the vilifying thoughts receded. When next he awoke, the morning had brightened to a rosy glow. The winged creatures outside launched into glorious song, invoking a brief smile on his sallow features.

He wished to rise out of bed as any normal man would do and sit alone in the gardens behind what was left of the temple. However, he could no more climb to his feet without help than Pallin could with her burgeoning pregnancy. More often than not, his temper got the best of him and he would curse Najahmara's goddess.

Pallin chastised him for his impatience, repeating over and over how fortunate he was to have survived the accident in the caverns. She did not understand why he was in the recess where the harvested grains were stored. She said it was Gaea who kept him alive, not his god, who would rather deal death than life.

Each time Pallin mentioned the mishap, Hattusilis shuddered. He dreamed often of that night in vivid detail. He remembered the mystery of slithering sounds and sibilant echoes of a voice that had no owner. It was the siren call from an invisible beast that led him from the entrance into the depths of Gaea's sacred chamber.

The fear increased even in the daylight as he recalled the way he followed the voice deeper into the darkness as if entranced and without wits. He felt as if something followed him, something large and dangerous. He recalled when the torch blew out, even though there was no wind, leaving him in pitch black, frantically groping along the cave walls. He stumbled along bathed in sweat as he crept deeper into the tunnels rather than out.

The most terrifying of all was a hissed warning, then the lash of coils that knocked him into the urn that rolled on top of him. A strong man alone could not have pushed it over and yet it fell, trapping him under it. Every night he relived the excruciating pain and the fear he would die alone in the darkness. He prayed it would be swift, all the while knowing it would not, and felt the panic rise all over again.

At times he heard the hiss of the invisible serpent while awake – a maddening whisper that said '*let me in and I will heal your pain.*'

Was he mad? He simply did not know.

Hattusilis laid for a moment longer, listening to the bird's sing and the chatter of small animals as daylight erased the pink wash of early morning. In the distance, he heard the muffled sounds of his household and knew soon his own morning meal would arrive.

To be treated as an invalid was worse than death.

If he believed an apparition such as the giant serpent could truly heal him, would he say yes, join me?

Feeling foolish, Hattusilis shook away his nightmares. He should call for help to get up but could not tolerate one more day of this pandering to his injuries. With a deep and determined breath, Hattusilis struggled to a sitting position. He made it to the bedside, threw off the linen sheet and put feet to the floor, in spite of the stabbing pain.

Though wobbling, he pushed himself upright. One leg cooperated, the other remained stiff and unbending. As he reached for the cane leaning against the foot of the bedstead, he lost his balance. Twisting to catch himself, his chest exploded as if a firebrand ignited within his body. He gasped, clutched at his side and fell with a loud thump. The woven rug covering the solid-packed dirt floor did nothing to break his fall and the jarring of his wounds left him sobbing in pain.

Pallin woke with a start, one hand extended to feel for her mate. She heard a noise, but could not tell if it came from outside or inside. When she discovered the space beside her was empty, she called anxiously, "Hattu? Where are you?"

"I am here." Suppressing the agony, Hattusilis lifted one hand above the side of the bed. "Go back to sleep."

"What is wrong?" Pallin floundered to sit up within her nest of covers. "Are you ill?"

"It is nothing."

"Why are you on the floor?" Scooting to the edge like a lake crab, Pallin peered at him. Seeing all color drained from his face save for a sickly ashen cast, she said in a low voice, "Did you dream again?"

Hattusilis gave an abrupt shake of his head to ward off the question, all the while biting his lip to keep from crying out. He could not muster the strength to tell his story to Pallin, though he adored her.

"I attempted to go about my duties as a man should." A sour taste was in his mouth as he finished, "I could not manage even that without help."

"My husband, are you hurt?" Pallin climbed from the box-like platform they slept on, one hand held against her bulging middle. As she stood up, she, too, groaned and rubbed her back. "I do not like this thing, Hattu. It is too hard. It is not good on our bones."

"I will have Zan add more padding."

"Do not think about that now." She crouched beside him and touched his face with cool fingers. "You are warm with a fever, let me get you a powder."

As she went to rise, he grabbed her wrist. "No. I do not need it."

"But you do, I can see it in your eyes. I will send for Jahmed while Zan helps you back to bed."

"No." Hattusilis tightened his grip. "I do not want it. I do not want anyone to see me this way. Leave me alone for a moment."

"Hattu, do not fret so. You will heal from these wounds, it just takes time."

"How much time? The winter season is gone, planting is upon us and still I cannot move about on my own."

"You walk, just slowly, and far sooner than either Jahmed or I expected. Hattu, you suffered grave injuries. We did not think we could save you and yet, here you are with two legs, two feet."

Pallin smoothed his hair back and kissed his forehead. "Now that you have thrown yourself to the floor and had a tantrum, we must get you up. Since I cannot alone lift you, I must get Zan."

Raising one hand in protest, Hattusilis let it drop and nodded. He knew she was right though it still rankled to know he was as helpless as a new babe.

He was rewarded with a loving smile as Pallin pulled on a gown before going to fetch Zan. When Zan arrived a few moments later, he gave Hattusilis a glower that spoke far more than words.

"Were you hovering outside our doorway?"

"I brought your breakfast," Zan responded with an injured tone. With ease, he picked Hattusilis up and set him on the edge of the bed before handing him the crutch that had been out of reach.

"I will not take my meal in bed."

"As you wish, though I should raise the question with Queen Pallin."

"Do not ask her. I have given an order." Hattusilis plucked at the covering, his features squeezed into a peevish frown.

"You have?" Blinking, Zan bit back a grin. "Of course. Where do you want to take your meal?"

"I do not know. Anywhere but here." Disgusted with the ordeal, Hattusilis shrugged. "The gardens."

"Perhaps you should rest before we take a walk."

"I am your king, it is time I behaved as such and did more than lie down or sit in that god-forsaken chamber."

Zan nodded with all earnestness. He understood Hattu's frustration, for he, too, was a man who was accustomed to a life out of doors, a man who preferred a canopy of stars to a roof and walls. It was cruel to keep Hattusilis locked inside, particularly when he must hold court in the round room where his nephew Telio had died.

Though the women scrubbed and scrubbed, they could not wash away all the bloodstains, nor could they erase the presence of evil that had invaded their temple. For Zan, it was the giant serpent that killed his men, but he knew for Queen Pallin it was the rape and murder of her sisters.

The degradation could never be entirely cleansed and thus the priestesses gave up the chamber without argument. They set their altar to their goddess somewhere else, somewhere hidden, for the atmosphere in Najahmara had changed with the second wave of invading soldiers. Those men who had fled in terror had now returned, along with the wave of soldiers on foot and the women who followed behind.

Najahmara had evolved into a diverse community at extreme odds with each other. Not a day went by without some odious deed committed in the name of a god or goddess.

Did either of those deities revel in the pain?

Zan wondered but said nothing.

"Where is my wife?" Leaning on Zan's arm, Hattusilis glanced in both directions of the corridor. Dressing had worn him out though he would not admit it.

Zan flushed. "She had need to relieve herself and then she said she was getting a fever powder."

"I do not want a powder. I told her as much." Hattusilis' voice grew spiteful. "She does not listen to commands at all."

"She fears you knocked something loose and wants a cloth to bind your ribs. I beg you to be more careful, my King."

"Yes, careful. I grow weary of being careful." With a sigh, Hattusilis sank down in a chair shaded by an open-sided tent facing toward the lush growth of the gardens.

The path in front of him led to the sparkling pool in the center. It was a vision of blue and green, surrounded by a riot of blooming flowers and fully leafed trees that offered a perch to the melodious song of the many birds.

There was no such oasis in the Steppelands. Water was scarce, too precious to do more than serve the people and the herds roaming the hills. Water could not be wasted on beauty.

"Not that our homeland does not have its own attraction," Hattusilis mused to himself. "Though the plateaus of the Steppelands are stark and rocky, the valleys are covered in a fine green blanket of grass."

He smiled as he recalled the heady scent of the tiny blue flowers that sprouted on the hillsides and the beauty of the bushes that bloomed fiery red in the spring. Trees with needle-like leaves lined the higher slopes as sentinels watching over the land and stayed dark green throughout the coldest months.

In Najahmara there was no true changing of the seasons for it remained warm most of the time.

"What is that?" Zan emerged with the meal tray and set it beside Hattusilis. "What do you mumble to yourself?"

"I was thinking of the Steppelands."

"Do you miss our native soil?"

Chewing absently on a piece of bread, Hattusilis paused before speaking. "Sometimes. Life was simple there. A king was king. There was no discussion around it. A king took a wife and she became queen. We did not debate on what it meant."

"You speak now of your bride." A twinkle lit Zan's eyes.

"She resembles Azhar, but she is nothing like her. Pallin behaves not like a queen but as a servant. As now, where is she? She leaves a warrior playing nursemaid." Hattusilis clicked his tongue. "As my wife, she should attend to only my needs. It is not fitting for her to work in the kitchens or care for the sick. It is not right."

"Hattu, you judge too harshly. Azhar was raised to be a queen, albeit not intended for the enemy's king, but as wife to a man of her own royal lineage. Still, she knew her place within her tribe." Zan chuckled. "Pallin also knows her place. It is just not where you expect her to be."

"She is pregnant with my son, my heir. I do not approve of these activities."

"You fear you will lose her and the babe the way you lost Azhar."

Hattusilis spit on the ground to show his annoyance, but did not respond. There was truth to Zan's comment.

He stared at the towering plateau behind the gardens. From his seat, he could see the cave entrance off to the right. He was struck by an instant chill and shivered in his thin, ankle-length tunic despite the fact the heat of the day was already bearing down on the land.

"Pallin is in no danger of wasting away." Zan continued on as if Hattusilis had responded with favor. "These are a different people, Hattu, unlike any we have encountered."

"That much I see for myself." Hattusilis winced as a drumbeat began, slow at first, but growing into a steady cadence.

For the past few days, from dawn until dusk, the constant pounding of rhythms echoed across the broad landscape, bouncing from one side of the valley to the other. Hattusilis was reminded of the cave ritual, of the dazed state that took him before a goddess, and left him in a trance so profound he did not remember making his way back to the cave the next day.

He had awakened inside with torch in hand, gripped with fear, knowing he was not alone. He had heard a voice calling him, calling him to go further into the depths.

Eyes glassy, he heard the voice speaking into his ear, *'Let me in, king, and I will restore your health.'*

"Hattu, what is it?"

Wiping the sweat from his brow, Hattu sucked in a deep breath. "I hate the drums. Make them stop."

"Is that all? You look ill. Are you certain you did not hurt yourself when you fell?" Zan gave Hattusilis a lowered-brow, squinty-eyed gaze that penetrated beyond the visible. "It is not just the drums."

Licking dry lips, Hattusilis croaked, "Water, please." After drinking, he wiped his face with his sleeve. "Pallin tells me it signals another celebration."

"Yes, that is true. They prepare for their spring rites, though it is some weeks away. It is to be held up there." Zan pointed toward the rocky ridge.

"The cave?" Panic etched a shrill tone to Hattusilis' words. "I will not allow them to hold this ritual."

"Not the cave, but above it, on the plateau."

"Up, down, in, out, I do not care. I command they do not hold the rites." Rising on shaky legs, Hattusilis gripped his cane and held himself steady. He ignored the shooting pains from thigh to calf and the numbness of his foot. Limping, he moved along the path between the flowers and the herbal plants.

"I wish you would wait for Pallin to return with the medicine." Zan blocked his way.

"She has forgotten me, so eager is she to tend to others. Get out of my way."

Stepping aside, Zan followed Hattusilis' slow progress. "Hattu, we cannot take this away from the people."

"And why not? I am their king now. It is not our way."

"Our way is not always best."

"Do you speak treason?" Hattusilis paused in his hobble toward the shining pond of water.

"That is not what I meant, my king. I believe our way is not always best, that is all. I see nothing immoral with roasting meat and feasting though-out the night."

"And drinking barrels of beyaz until everyone falls down senseless only to wake the next morning, sick and puking with a head the size of a boulder."

"What is wrong with that?" Zan grimaced. "I have done my share of it, to be sure, as have you, and yet I tire of that game. These people offer us something new."

Hattusilis turned to stare at Zan, his lips puckered into a frown. "You have changed, Zan. I can scarce believe as much since you disdained any tradition brought from the sand dwellers. You called them barbaric, uncivilized."

"Yes, and you took offense because they were Azhar's people, though we slaughtered them like sheep."

"I did not want her to know of the killings for she suffered enough as it was." Regret was plain on Hattusilis' face.

"It was you or death. She chose you."

"In the end, she made it clear she would rather have died with her tribe. She never forgave herself. Or me."

"Neither have you. Still you do not learn your lesson."

"What lesson?" Sinking down on a backless bench near the water's edge, Hattusilis concealed a moan. "What gibberish are you spewing?"

Zan sat beside him, hands clasped between his knees as he stared at the reflection of the clear sky in the green water. "Have you ever seen the night sky reflected in this water?"

"No, nor do I wish to see it."

"It is as if their goddess rises from the earth in all her radiance and floats on the surface to bask in the silver light of the moon. The most peace I have had in my life has been beside this pool."

Zan bowed his head, staring at his interlaced fingers. "I grow weary of war, Hattu. I am no longer a young man and I have not the stamina to continue traveling. I have no wife, no children, no home. That disturbs me."

"Does that mean you have found a woman?"

At Hattusilis' sly glance, Zan turned red.

"No. But I search for one who could love me. These people have been grievously wounded and yet they hold no ill will. They do not smolder beneath the surface and plot their revenge."

"How do you know that? Perhaps they hide their planning well."

"I walk among them day by day. I witness their generosity. Over half of them were killed in the fires along with our men and, now after the foot soldiers arrived, along with the service women, we outnumber them."

"All the more reason they should accept our way."

Zan ignored the comment and went on. "Their homes were destroyed, but their will to survive is strong. They offer me whatever they have, food, water, shelter, a simple smile. I have wandered beyond the valley, to those who care for the orchards and fields of grain. It is the same there, they, too, hold no grudge."

"You have become soft," snorted Hattusilis. "It is best you do not engage in battle again for you would surely be killed."

"I always believed I would die in battle. I thought that was where I belonged and what I wanted." Zan shook his head. "I have found it is not."

"And what does that have to do with this lesson I have not learned?" Curiosity drove Hattusilis to ask, though there was no other whom he allowed to speak to him in such away.

"Control, Hattu. You seize power and then you wield it with unbending zeal."

"As any sovereign would do."

"You do not allow for change. Everyone must conform to our way."

"I do not see the problem."

"And so it is, my King, you suffer loss with no solace except to take more."

"What have they done to you? This does not sound like the Zan who set out on the journey to Najahmara."

"I am not the same man." Zan met Hattusilis' gaze and read the thought behind it. "Do not question my loyalty. I will forever stand beside you and serve your will. I am asking, though, that you reconsider your decision to stop the ritual."

"I do not understand this stubbornness," Hattusilis grated.

"It is important. They celebrate spring, when new life begins." Shifting uncomfortably, Zan added, "It is a mating ritual."

"A what?"

"A mating ritual." Zan coughed. "Many of our men are looking forward to it."

Hattusilis rubbed his naked chin, unaccustomed to his beardless state. "They need not wait for a ritual to take a mate."

"Do you hear yourself?" Zan rose, irritation strong in his voice. "Take. Always we take. It is time for us to give and this celebration is something they need. It will help heal the wounds and allow us to partner with them."

Hattusilis sat in silence for a long time, watching the face of the ridge. With a sigh, he held out one hand for Zan to help him up, while the other dug the cane into the soft earth.

Closing his eyes for a moment, he attempted to blot out the wretched cave. "Have your celebration. I hope you find a woman to lie with and it improves your disposition."

Smiling, Zan murmured, "Thank you, Sire."

"There is just one thing, though." Hattusilis paused on the return to the temple. "Do not hold it on the plateau."

"Where would it be, if not there?"

"Anywhere else." Cocking his head to one side, Hattusilis pursed his lips. "If it is to be a healing ritual, then let it be on the shores of the lake. It is suitable, is it not?"

"I do not know."

"That is where it is to be held. There, or nowhere."

"As you wish, my King." Zan gave a slight bow, grateful that he had won even a small skirmish with Hattusilis.

Made in the USA
Charleston, SC
16 March 2016